W9-DAJ-922

" . . . JANE ARCHER SHOWED US ALL HOW TO WRITE PASSION, ADVENTURE, SUSPENSE, AND—MORE THAN THOSE— LOVE."
—Deana James, author of *Acts of Love*

"SHE WANTS YOU. SHE'S HAD YOU. I KNOW IT." DEIDRE SEARCHED HUNTER'S FACE, TRYING TO READ THE TRUTH IN HIS DARK EYES.

"Damn it, Deidre, I don't want her!"

Not believing him, she turned from him, but Hunter grabbed her and crushed her against him. "I want you. Only you."

In a wild swing of emotion, he suddenly didn't care if he hurt her. He had to break through her cold exterior and prove their desire was real. He jerked the shawl from her body and dropped it to the floor, then he pressed his lips to hers in a forceful kiss. She remained unresponsive, but soon she opened her lips and melted into him.

On fire now to possess her, he deepened the kiss then jerked open her bodice and ran his hands over her curves. Next he lifted her in his arms, carried her to the bed and covered her body with his own.

Hunter had no thought but to melt his Ice Princess so it took him several moments before he realized something hard and cold pressed against his side. Then he noticed how still she lay beneath him and raised his head in shock as he realized what she held.

"Get off me, you stupid oaf, or I'll empty both barrels of my derringer into you."

JANE ARCHER

WILD WIND!

PINNACLE BOOKS
WINDSOR PUBLISHING CORP.

For Dean, again
And Speedy, too
With honors to R.C.

PINNACLE BOOKS

are published by

Windsor Publishing Corp.
475 Park Avenue South
New York, NY 10016

First Printing: February, 1993

Printed in the United States of America

Liberty is the mother of virtue, . . .

Mary Wollstonecraft
Vindication of the Rights of Woman, 1792

Table of Contents

Part One
Thunder on the Horizon

Chapter 1

Hunter leaned against the rough adobe of the Three Rivers stage depot in south Texas. Insects buzzed lazily in the late afternoon heat. People laughed and talked as they waited for the incoming coach. But he stood alone. Silent.

Not long after, the Corpus Christi stage pulled in and stopped. Passengers descended. They squinted into the bright sunlight and tried to knock the dust from their clothing, but gave up and moved on to the shade of the depot and their friends. Laughter again filled the air. But Hunter remained motionless, waiting.

A young woman leaned out of the stage and glanced around. She was dressed simply, almost severely, in a long black skirt and a white blouse buttoned to her throat. Closing the small book she had been reading, she tucked it in her reticule, a small drawstring bag, then looked again. And frowned.

Hunter straightened. She wasn't beautiful. Striking, yes. But not beautiful. She wouldn't worry a man's mind. He was glad.

But as she stepped down, showing an ankle, he changed his decision. Nothing she wore could hide the fact that her tall, slim body was made for a man's pleasure. He couldn't think of a red-blooded male alive who wouldn't itch to get his hands on her.

He stepped forward, cursing to himself. She'd not be easy to forget, for she looked sad and sultry and haughty at the same time. He wasn't given to a poetic turn of the phrase, but she'd suddenly become hauntingly beautiful. And it made him hate her with a swift, hot rush of emotion.

But he quelled that feeling. Nothing stopped him from doing his job. Efficient and thorough, he'd never let anybody down . . . not if the pay was right. And right now the pay was plenty all right.

He reached the stage and held out his hand to help her down from the coach's step. "Miss Clarke-Jarmon, I'm here to take you to the Bar J Ranch."

She looked into his eyes.

He'd have been blind not to notice her pale blond hair pulled back tight in a chignon, her moss green eyes, or her full lips. Unblemished, her ivory skin accented a heart-shaped face with prominent cheekbones. As far as he was concerned, she had too much of a good thing in all the right places.

"Where are my parents?"

She had an accent, but it was uniquely her own and somewhere between Yankee, Southern, and Texan. Low and melodic, he felt the vibration of

12

her voice up and down his spine before it settled heavily in his groin. She was going to be trouble. "They couldn't make it. Problems."

"But—"

"They send their regrets." He dropped his hand, realizing she wasn't going to take it. She thought she was too good to touch him. He felt anger flush his face and was glad his wide-brimmed hat shaded his reaction.

She stepped past him, looked around, then glanced back. "Please see my trunks are loaded onto the wagon. I'd like to be home tonight."

He moved in close, wanting to see her reaction. His height alone intimidated most people, as well as the black clothes he usually wore.

"Is there a problem?" She looked beyond him.

She didn't intimidate. At least, he couldn't do it strictly with size. Damn Clarke-Jarmon blood. "Stage ran late. Why don't you get a good night's rest and we'll leave at dawn. That way you'll be fresh to see your parents in the morning."

"Won't they worry?"

"No. The stage is late more often than not. They said to stay in town if it was getting on toward evening."

"And what is this mysterious problem that keeps both my parents from meeting me?"

"Some cattle took sick. Your parents were needed."

"And you weren't, Mr.—"

"Hunter. I was needed, but somebody had to come after you."

She exhaled sharply, glanced up at the sky to see the low position of the sun, then looked back at him.

13

"All right. Tomorrow morning then. I *am* tired. Do you suppose the hotel is clean?"

"I doubt if it's up to your standards, Miss Clarke-Jarmon, but it ought to do." She didn't seem to notice his barb, for she'd turned to watch the stage and he felt like a boy dismissed by somebody in authority.

"My trunks."

"Which one is yours?"

She smiled. "All those on top."

"That's seven or eight."

"Nine, to be exact. You're a big, strong man so surely you can get them to my room, then to the wagon and home for me, can't you?" She threw him a mocking glance.

"No way in hell am I, or anybody else, carrying all those to the hotel, upstairs, back downstairs, and to the wagon. You can have one for the night. That's all."

"In that case, would you remove my carpetbag from inside the coach, Mr. Hunter? That will be sufficient if you will make sure my trunks are safe for the night."

"Hunter. No mister." He jerked the carpetbag out of the stage. "Your trunks can stay in the stagecoach office for the night."

She inclined her head. "And the hotel?"

He pointed down the street, then motioned at a man unloading the coach. "Put Miss Clarke-Jarmon's trunks in the stage office. We'll want them at dawn." When he turned back to her, she'd started down the boardwalk without him. Cursing silently, he took long strides to catch up.

14

* * *

In a small room in the Three Rivers Hotel, Deidre Eleanor Clarke-Jarmon paced. She hadn't bothered to wash her face or knock the dust off her clothes yet. She was too tense. She'd wanted to be at the ranch by tonight. She felt frustrated at having to wait any longer. The trip from New York City had seemed to take forever. Now she was delayed in Three Rivers for the night and she'd have to endure dinner with an overbearing cowboy. The thought was insufferable.

Hunter. He wouldn't even admit to having a regular name. Well, perhaps it fitted a man like him. He would have no respect for a woman's rights or sensibilities or concerns. He might appeal to a different type of woman with his dangerous good looks. He had black hair, brown eyes, tanned skin, and a strong facial structure. But a man who wore black clothes on a lean, hard body and a shiny pistol on his hip did not inspire admiration, envy, or wild passion in her.

Of course, no man inspired wild passion in her. She was a liberated woman, or she was trying to be if only her parents would ease up on their tight control. After all, she was nineteen years old. She was grown. At twenty, her mother, the celebrated heiress Alexandra Clarke, had endured a harrowing journey from New York City to Texas in order to keep a promise to her dying friend, Olaf Thorssen. And along the way she had met Jake Jarmon. They'd fallen in love, married, and the result had been herself and her brother, Lamar

Thorssen Clarke-Jarmon, or Thor as she'd dubbed him at a young age.

But she was her mother's daughter. Her parents and brother might still occasionally call her Dee Dee, but she was Deidre, named after her maternal grandmother. And she was ready to prove her worth, to become a woman, and accept responsibility. If she could only get her parents to agree.

She walked over to the washstand and poured water from the pitcher into the basin. She was used to running water and more comforts than the room afforded, but it seemed clean and she was grateful for that. Besides, the room's simple pine furniture and brightly colored quilt on the bed had rustic charm.

As she splashed water on her face she thought of Simon Gainesville. And smiled. His bespectacled face and endearing grin would soothe her now, along with his liberated mind. But he was far away in New York City. As a young newspaperman on his way up, he'd been a friend and confidant for over a year. She knew he wanted their relationship to be more, but she wasn't ready to settle down. She had yet to make her mark in the world, to find her place.

Unlike her brother who was in college, she had been sent to a Southern finishing school and she was still angry about not getting a proper education. In defiance, she frequently slumped whenever she was out of her corset. Life was unfair to women and she was determined to change it.

But first she had to talk with her parents. And before that she had to endure dinner with a man who, unlike her supportive, intelligent Simon, probably couldn't even carry on a decent conversation. And, of course, he wouldn't know or care about woman suffrage like Simon did. Getting the vote for women was the most important thing in her life, other than becoming an independent young woman.

And she was prepared to endure all to obtain her parents' consent for her plan so she could convince them and anyone else who cared of her maturity and strength as an individual. After all, it was 1888 and women weren't little ladies anymore.

She dried her face, pushed stray hair back into her chignon, then knocked the dust from her skirt. Checking her appearance in the oval mirror over the washstand, she decided she looked tired and disheveled. But what did it matter? She would only be with the cowboy this evening and she didn't plan to spend long in his company. She could eat fast when the occasion warranted it.

Putting her room key in her reticule, she pulled out the book she was never without. *Vindication of the Rights of Woman* by Mary Wollstonecraft was a continual source of inspiration to her. She held it tightly a moment, tucked it back into her reticule, then left the room.

Hunter stood when Deidre Clarke-Jarmon entered the small cafe just off the lobby of the Three Rivers Hotel. He didn't figure she'd like the place, the food, or the company, but it was the best he could do. Anyway, it was easier than taking her back to the Bar J Ranch after dark and he wouldn't mind watching her eat in a common cafe.

When she reached him, he stood and pulled out a chair across the table from him. He seated her, then sat back down, figuring he'd surprised her at his ability to be a gentleman. But he could be a lot of things and not all of them good. It kept a man alive.

"Food'll be right out." He didn't smile. "I ordered for us."

"Even if that may be customary for a gentleman, you have no idea of my preferences."

"I ordered the best in the house."

"And what might that be?"

"Steak and potatoes."

"Of course." She unfolded the blue and white plaid napkin beside her silverware and placed it on her lap to delay further conversation. Glancing around, she noticed the cafe had the same rustic charm of her room, with simple pine furniture, blue and white plaid cotton tablecloths, blue curtains at the windows, and fresh flowers on the tables.

"You won't get any better meat anywhere. Bar J beef is served in Three Rivers."

"You don't have to sell me, Mr. Hunter. I spent much of my childhood on the Bar J. However, since I've been in New York City I've developed a fondness for seafood."

"No mister." He leaned toward her. "They've been pulling some big ones out of the Nueces River."

"I had in mind shrimp or lobster."

"Catfish not good enough for you, Miss Clarke-Jarmon?"

"I like it perfectly well. I like steak perfectly well. I was merely telling you my preference."

"Not everybody gets to eat their preference."

"Really." She glanced away from him, determined not to let him draw her into an argument although he seemed to be trying to do just that. A waitress was headed their way and she sighed in relief. Maybe food would stop his talk.

A woman wearing a simple blue dress and a white apron set rolls, butter, and water on their table, then left as silently as she had arrived.

"It looks good." Deidre picked up a roll, buttered it, then took a bite, glancing anywhere but at Hunter. This man with his dark, hooded eyes was too intense, too masculine, and way too big. She supposed he fit into the larger than life culture of Texas and the West, but in her current world he was simply out of place.

Hunter watched her eat, fascinated with her lips, her mouth, the tip of her pink tongue. And when she finally looked at him, he was caught with admiration lighting his eyes.

"You're not hungry?" She was surprised he didn't eat. She felt starved.

"You don't know how much." Not able to slake his hunger on Deidre, he picked up a roll and bit into it.

Not long after, the waitress returned and placed platters with sizzling steaks, potatoes, and corn in front of them.

"I haven't seen this much food on one plate in a long time." Deidre hesitated. "I almost feel guilty."

"Don't. I'll eat anything you can't." He cut into his steak and stopped talking.

Glad of the silence, she followed his example, wondering how she could possibly eat it all. But on the other hand, she disliked the idea of sharing her food with Hunter. Caught in a dilemma, she kept eating, even after she was much too full.

Hunter finished his steak, ate the last piece of potato, then leaned back in his chair. It creaked.

"I feel like that chair sounds."

"Good food." He glanced at what was left on her plate. "You going to finish that?"

"No." But she desperately wanted to say yes.

He speared the last of her steak with his fork and transferred it to his plate. The first slice he made was where she had been using her fork and knife to cut. It was the closest he could come to touching her lips. As he put the piece of steak into his mouth, he looked at her.

She blushed lightly and glanced away, hating the intimacy.

As he chewed, he continued to watch her, thinking about her blush. Maybe she wasn't as tough as she acted. "Thanks."

"I wouldn't want to see any food go to waste."

"With me around, you'll never have to worry about that."

"I won't be at the ranch long."

"No? Where're you going?"

She stroked the outside of her glass of water. "That's something I'm going to discuss with my parents."

Hunter's eyes narrowed as he finished her steak. "It must be important to you."

This time *her* eyes narrowed. "Yes."

He nodded once. "You want desert?"

"No thank you."

Standing, he threw down some bills. "Come on, let's walk off this food."

"I'm rather tired. I think—"

"You haven't seen Three Rivers in awhile, have you?" He pulled out her chair as she stood up.

"No, but—"

"We'll be leaving early so you'd better see it tonight."

She walked from the cafe and stopped in the lobby. Turning to face him, she frowned.

Smiling a crooked smile, he took her arm and steered her to the front door. "My job is to take care of you till I get you to the ranch and tonight that means taking you out for a constitutional."

She pulled her arm from his grasp.

He opened the door and gave her a slight bow.

"Oh, all right." She stepped outside, deciding not to force the issue. Soon she'd be at the ranch and she could forget about him. But she wished she wasn't spending so much time in his company, for there was a magnetism about him, something that seemed to draw her to him despite his attitude. And she didn't like the feeling. After all, he was nothing like Simon. Thinking of her friend, she smiled.

"You like the night?"

She realized Hunter had been watching her and had misinterpreted her smile. It was just as well. Glancing around at the small town, she inhaled deeply. "Yes, Texas has a scent all its own, wonderful land, warm people. I miss it all when I'm away, but I also miss the plantation in Louisiana and the

21

house in New York City. You see, I don't really have a home."

"You've got more homes than most people." He started down the boardwalk.

She kept up. "No. My mother has her family home and shipping firm in New York City. Father has his Uncle Lamar's ranch and his father's plantation. I am simply their daughter."

Hunter stopped and looked at her. "You're a funny girl."

"Young woman. I'm nineteen."

"I'm twenty-six."

"And you have no home of your own?"

"I'm a drifter. I go where the work takes me."

Deidre walked on. "And no family?"

"None to speak of." He watched the sway of her long skirt, then caught up.

"You're free then. You can do whatever you want. Whenever. However. I suppose you don't realize how lucky you are."

"A man's never free as long as he has to eat."

She looked at him as if seeing him for the first time. He seemed more than a drifting cowboy. "But you can work at any job you can get."

"But I *have* to work."

"I'm a woman. Do you know what type of jobs are available to me and what they pay?"

"But you don't need to work. You have that freedom."

She frowned. "Everyone works, just in different ways. Besides, I'm dependent on my parents and as a woman I have few work options. And I can't even *vote*."

"Why'd you want to vote?" He ran a hand

through his thick hair. "A woman who looks like you can get anything she wants any time she wants. Trust me, you *don't* have to work. And you've got rich parents, too. That's an easy life any way you look at it."

Insulted, she stepped back. "Fool. I'm not that kind of woman." She turned on her heel and headed for the hotel. Soon she heard his heavy, booted stride behind her, but she didn't hurry. She wouldn't give him that satisfaction.

He caught up and whirled her around, gripping both her shoulders with hard hands. "You're the damn fool, Miss High and Mighty."

"I'd never sell my body."

"Too bad. I'd be first in line to pay." He gazed at her lips, then back into her eyes.

Shocked, she realized he wanted to kiss her. For a moment she wondered what it would feel like to have his hot lips pressed against hers. Horrified at her thought, she jerked away. "I'll be going to my room now. I don't need any more insults from you."

"Too good for the hired help?" His dark eyes blazed. "You can turn a man's head and you know it. If you weren't so pigheaded, you'd have recognized a compliment when you heard one." He put his hands on his hips. "Vote! You've got better ways to spend your time."

"Fortunately, the way I spend my time is my choice." She clenched her fists. "If you refrain from touching me again, trying to use your superior physical strength to intimidate me, I won't mention your rude behavior to my parents."

"I'm real grateful." His voice rasped with sarcasm.

"You should be. You don't want the Clarke-Jarmon family as an enemy."

"And they wouldn't want me as their enemy either." He frowned. "If I was going to get in trouble for touching you, I'd have touched the hell out of you." He lifted a hand, then dropped it. "But I doubt if an Ice Princess like you knows what that means."

She tossed her head. "I have no intention of stooping to your level of thought. Good night and I won't thank you for a pleasant evening." She started toward the hotel.

In a few strides, he was by her side. Taking her hand, he pulled it through the crook of his arm and held it there. "Like it or not, you're my responsibility till I get you to the Bar J."

Chapter 2

"Your parents won't have any complaints." Hunter flicked the reins over the backs of the mules. "I got you home safe."

Deidre saw the red tile roof of the Bar J hacienda in the distance. Home or, at least, her parents' home. She glanced at Hunter's stern profile from the far side of the wagon seat. He'd been quiet on the way out from Three Rivers and she'd matched his mood. But she couldn't say how safely he'd gotten her home, for in their short time together he'd managed to get under her skin. And she didn't like it.

Hunter drove under the arched entry way, proclaiming *Bar J Ranch*. As the mules pulled the heavy wagon up the incline, he glanced at Deidre. "Next time you ought to think of the mules' backs, and mine, when you bring nine trunks for a visit."

She didn't look at him or respond, but she felt the barb. Truth to tell, most of what she'd brought were presents and items from New York City her parents couldn't easily get in Texas. But she didn't tell him that, preferring to let him dislike her for being an Ice Princess. Maybe that way he'd keep his distance.

Inhaling the dry, hot breeze that swept over the valley, Deidre smiled to herself. She loved Texas and basked in the wide open spaces. But she knew from experience that after she'd been here awhile, she'd miss New York City or Louisiana. Roots. She didn't know if she were missing them entirely or simply had too many. Either way, she was determined to make a place for herself in life.

She glanced around, noting the good condition of the barn, the bunkhouse, the corral, the henhouse, and the other outbuildings. A lot of work kept a ranch the size of the Bar J going, but this time of day most of the cowboys would be out on the range with the cattle.

Focusing on the hacienda, she thought of how much work and money her mother had put into expanding and furnishing the original adobe structure built by Lamar Jarmon. She felt a slight tug of sorrow. Uncle Lamar had been dead only a few years and she missed him. He'd lived to a ripe old age, her father always said, and had enjoyed his life. But Uncle Lamar wasn't the only one gone now. Ebba, who'd help raise her, had died and been buried in the family cemetery, too. Deidre always visited their graves when she returned to the ranch.

She forced her thoughts away from the sorrows

of the past and focused on the hacienda again. Her mother had kept the original arched entrance to the house, adding a red tile roof, black wrought iron trim, and several more rooms. She had also updated the kitchen and added bathrooms, all with running water. But they still burned candles and kerosene lamps for light. Other than that, the house was as comfortable as anything in New York City.

Hunter drove the wagon up to the front door. "Where do you want all these trunks?"

"In the house, of course."

"Where in the house?"

"In my . . . in the storeroom off the kitchen will be fine." Clenching her fists, she realized she'd almost told him to take the trunks into her bedroom. And the last place she wanted him was there.

Wrapping the reins around the brake handle, he jumped down and headed around the wagon.

She didn't want him to help her down, so she started to step from the wagon, but a voice stopped her.

"Dee Dee, darling, you're home." Alexandra Clarke-Jarmon hurried from the hacienda toward the wagon.

"Mother!" Deidre grinned and held out her arms.

But Alexandra didn't reach her first. Hunter put strong hands around Deidre's waist and lifted her from the wagon. His hot dark gaze met her icy green one before he stepped back and let her go. Then she was in her mother's arms, being hugged and kissed and made over.

"We've been worried." Alexandra finally stepped

27

back and looked at her daughter. "You grow more beautiful every time I see you. Surely you must be followed by beaus wherever you go."

Hunter cleared his throat as he walked to the back of the wagon and began unloading the trunks.

Deidre didn't spare him a glance, but took her mother's hand and led her toward the hacienda. "Where's Dad? I must talk with you both. There's been more trouble with the shipping firm."

"Oh, no. What now?"

"I'm sorry to bring bad news, but—"

"Just a moment." Alexandra turned to Hunter. "Jake's in the barn. Would you get him?"

Hunter nodded, then started across the yard.

"Our troubles have continued here, too. First, let's get you something cool to drink." Alexandra opened the front door. "Lemonade?"

"Wonderful." Deidre stepped into the hacienda, noting as always how cool it was inside due to the thickness of the adobe walls.

As her mother went to the kitchen, Deidre walked into the main room that Uncle Lamar had built. Her mother hadn't changed it and she was glad. The area was large and furnished sparsely with dark, massive furniture, elaborately carved in the Spanish style. There were brightly colored rugs and wall hangings on the floors and walls which were Mexican and Indian. It was very much a man's room, but she liked it all the same.

"Marta is bringing lemonade." Alexandra walked into the room and kissed Deidre on the cheek. "Have you been well?"

"Yes. And you?"

"I'm healthy as a horse, as you know. Jake's been

28

fine, too, although I think all the problems are beginning to wear us both down."

Concerned, Deidre looked at her mother for any sign of illness, but saw nothing worrisome. Although now in her mid-forties, Alexandra had hardly changed, simply adding a few strands of silver to her strawberry blond hair and laugh lines around the outer corners of her eyes. Deidre wished she were as beautiful and serene.

"Are you still seeing that newspaper man?" Alexandra hugged her daughter.

"Simon Gainesville. Yes. But he's strictly a friend."

"Sometimes that's best. When your father and I first met we were far from friends." Alexandra chuckled at her memories. "That came later."

"I'm not interested in finding a husband right now. I've told you that. In fact, that's part of why I came home."

"Dee Dee!" Jake Clarke-Jarmon strode into the room, his blond hair tossled, his blue eyes crinkled at the corners, and a wide grin transforming his face with pleasure.

"Dad." Deidre flung herself into his arms. "It's so good to see you."

"Now that you're out of school, you can stay here all the time."

"I know. Thanks. But there's business to—"

"You don't have to worry your pretty head about business. Your mother and I'll take care of that. And Thor when he graduates. You ought to be going to parties and flirting with beaus."

"Marriage." Deidre frowned, her euphoria with seeing her parents quickly dwindling. "I haven't been going to parties. I have better things to do with my time. I've been attending woman suffrage meetings."

"I thought you'd outgrow that." Jake frowned.

"I'm a woman. I want to vote when I come of age." Deidre's voice rose in volume.

"You can depend on your brother and me to take care of your rights, Dee Dee." Jake paced several steps, then turned back to her. "You'll never want for anything."

"That's not the point." Deidre started to say more, then noticed Marta standing in the open doorway holding a tray with glasses and a pitcher of lemonade.

"Please set that on the table, Marta." Alexandra watched Marta leave, then sat down and poured lemonade. As she handed glasses around, she smiled. "Now you two don't argue. Dee Dee is barely home and already—"

"I'm not arguing." Deidre took a sip of lemonade, but it tasted bitter.

Jake sat down beside Alexandra. "Your mother's right. You're still young and impressionable. These suffrage rights women have influenced you, but when you find the right man you'll settle down, have babies, and forget all about voting. It doesn't mean much anyway, not with the Yankees trying to control everything."

Alexandra squeezed Jake's hand. "I'm a Yankee, darling."

He grinned. "And you'll never let me forget it, will you?"

"Never. But as I've said before, Dee Dee has a point. My problems with the Clarke family began because I was a young woman with few rights and viewed as a pawn in a company that had been left to me by my parents. If I'd been a man, my life would have gone quite differently."

"You don't regret meeting me?" Jake put an arm around her shoulders.

"No. But the right to vote, property rights, all that our Deidre has decided to struggle for would have helped keep me from being so badly hurt when I was just a year older than her."

Jake hesitated. "I can't fight you both. I want you to be happy and safe. That's what I'm here for."

Alexandra smiled tenderly at him. "But Deidre's a young woman now and she must make her own way in life, just as we did. We can't always protect her, no matter how much we want to."

Encouraged, Deidre sat down and leaned toward them. "That's just what I'm here to discuss."

Her parents looked at her.

"Two more Clarke ships went down in the Bahamas. Nothing's left."

"No!" Jake set down his glass of lemonade.

Alexandra's face paled. "But that makes four in the last six months."

Jake stood up and paced. "And it's not all. We've been losing cattle to rustlers. Oh, not just a few here and there, but too damn many and our cowboys aren't catching the rustlers. I've hired more men, but we can't get it stopped."

"And that doesn't cover the cotton and sugar crops we've had stolen out of warehouses in Louisiana." Alexandra looked at Jake in alarm.

"I know." Deidre glanced from her father to her mother. "I think somebody's out to sabotage the

Clarke-Jarmon businesses and bring us to our knees so we'll have to sell cheap or we'll be run out of business so somebody else can take over."

Jake stopped. "Don't you think you're overreacting? We have problems, yes. But somebody trying to destroy us? That's too much."

"Dad, I've not forgotten what you told me about Stan Lewis and the Clarke cousins and how they tried to force mother to marry Lewis so they could take over Clarke Shipping. Do you suppose Clarke relatives are after it again?" Deidre kept her voice firm and in control. She had to impress them with her ability to be calm and businesslike.

"I don't think so." Alexandra shook her head. "Winchell, Wilton, William, and of course Stan Lewis, have been dead for years and their sons have seemed content to work within the company."

"Weak men." Jake resumed pacing. "I don't think they have enough brain or backbone among them to put together a plot to ruin us or try to take over."

"Then what's going on?" Alexandra focused on her husband.

"I don't know." Jake sat down beside Alexandra and pulled her close. "What Deidre is suggesting doesn't make sense. All our problems could simply be a series of unfortunate accidents."

"But we need to know and stop it if there's something sinister going on. Don't you agree?" Deidre pressed her advantage.

"Yes." Jake gave his daughter a thoughtful stare.

"Then I propose to go to the Bahamas undercover and investigate the ship wrecks. What I learn there will help us understand what to do next, if anything."

Stunned silence followed her words.

"I gathered all the information sent from the Bahamas to the New York office about the wrecks before I left. I've studied them. Of course, nothing suspicious is confirmed, but I didn't expect it to be. I've talked with Simon about how to conduct an investigation, how to go undercover, and I've learned from the suffragists how to behave as a strong, independent woman to get what I need. Actually, I'm ready to leave at any time. I just wanted your support, morally and financially, to carry off my plan." She smiled, hoping she looked confident.

"Are you out of your mind?" Jake stood up.

"Deidre, we can hire someone to look into this matter." Alexandra stood, too.

Not about to be intimidated, Deidre stood up, took a deep breath, and confronted them. "I didn't expect you to agree immediately. I know that as your daughter you want to keep me protected, isolated, uneducated, and married. But I want to prove myself, not only to both of you but to myself and anybody else that as a woman I can carry my own weight and live my own life and take care of myself."

Alexandra reached out to her daughter, then dropped her hand. "I understand, darling. Really I do. At twenty I undertook a long, harrowing journey to avoid a marriage and keep a promise to a dead friend. But you have choices I didn't. Your father and I have worked hard to keep you from experiencing the tragedies I did. Please, don't throw away all we've worked so hard for."

"This is about going to college, isn't it?" Jake exhaled sharply. "All right. Pick a college that accepts women, pick a subject, and you can start classes. But don't come crying to us when men don't want you because you're educated."

"I'd like to stay a few days, then get right on this case. The colder it gets the harder it'll be to pick up clues." Deidre's chin jutted out. "I really think we have a problem. Thor can't leave college. You two must be here to run all the businesses, especially if anything else goes wrong. I'm the only family member available to go, the only person we can really trust in this situation. And I want to go. I'll prove myself worthy. You'll see."

"You're beautiful, you're smart, you can have whatever you want." Jake took his daughter's hands. "We love you. We want you to be happy. Do you want a trip to Europe before starting school? I'm sure one of your girlfriends would go with you."

"Dad, I don't want a trip or even college right now. I want to help my family, our business. I want to prove myself. Can't you understand?"

Suddenly a loud clunk sounded in the hall. They whirled around. Hunter stood in the open doorway, a trunk at his feet.

Furious, Deidre took several steps toward him, then stopped. "How long have *you* been eavesdropping?"

"You told me you wanted your *nine* trunks in the—"

"What did you hear?" Deidre hated the idea of him hearing her begging her parents for permission to do something.

"Come on in." Jake motioned toward Hunter.

Hunter walked cautiously into the room.

"Hunter's been with us about six months now. He came to us well recommended, not only as a cowboy but as a gunman, too. We wanted protection for the ranch and the other cowboys." Jake clapped a hand on Hunter's shoulder.

"Fine." Deidre shrugged. "I don't have any complaints about him getting me home."

"I didn't think you would." Jake watched Hunter. "He's proven to be a reliable man of his word."

"And good with a gun." Alexandra looked at the pistol riding low on Hunter's right hip.

"So?" Deidre felt impatient. "He's got nothing to do with me going to the Bahamas. And I'll tell you straight out, I'm going with or without your permission or help."

Jake glanced at his daughter. "I'm not surprised. You've got too much of your mother and me in you to take no easily, not when you're set on proving yourself. Maybe we've been too protective. I don't know. I do know we can't keep you locked up the rest of your life for your own good."

Deidre smiled. "Then you'll help me?"

"For your information, we hired somebody to check out the first wrecks. He never reported back." Jake frowned. "But accidents happen."

"I can go?" Deidre could hardly contain her rising excitement.

"I don't think these ship wrecks are personal, Deidre. But four ships in six months and a lost investigator indicate a serious problem." Jake appeared stern. "If your mother and Hunter agree, you can investigate with our help if Hunter accompanies you as a bodyguard and partner."

Deidre simply stared at him in stunned silence.

Alexandra hugged Deidre. "I don't want you to go, darling, but I understand your viewpoint. If Hunter will take the job, I'll agree. But don't put yourselves into unnecessary danger. Find out about the wrecks, then come right back here with the information."

"And we'll take it from there." Jake nodded.

"Hunter!" Deidre gasped, whirling to look at him before turning to confront her parents. "You'd saddle me with a babysitter? I can't believe it. I don't need him."

"Dee Dee, you can shoot a pistol, a rifle, handle a knife, but only reasonably well. Hunter is a professional." Jake looked grim. "Hunter, will you take the job? Double pay."

"If you're sure that's what you want, I'll say yes to keep her out of trouble." Hunter's dark eyes narrowed. "But I don't think she should go either."

Deidre threw up her hands. "I can't believe this. I'm a grown woman. And you'd send me off without a chaperone and with a strange man? What about my reputation?"

"I'm not going to endanger another innocent." Jake took Deidre's hands and squeezed. "Besides, what girlfriend do you know who'd go with you into this kind of danger?"

"It won't be dangerous." Deidre held onto her father. "I'll be clever. Nobody will ever know I'm there."

"We trust Hunter to take care of you." Alexandra smiled at her daughter. "He'll make sure you have separate rooms and whatever is necessary to protect your reputation. He's a bodyguard. Now, do you accept his help?"

Deidre dropped her father's hands and paced away from the group. She hated the idea of being in Hunter's company, but she also wanted her parents' financial and moral support. She supposed the best thing to do was agree and then get rid of Hunter at the first opportunity. He didn't seem that smart or dangerous so she shouldn't have much trouble losing him.

Turning back, she smiled. "Thank you. Yes, I agree." She hugged her father, then her mother, giving Hunter a dark glare over Alexandra's shoulder.

Hunter returned her gaze, his look steady, calculating, then he smiled a crooked smile. "I'll finish unloading the trunks." As he walked away from them, he decided he'd just earned himself a bonus, for Deidre and her parents had played right into his hands with as much gusto as a catfish after a worm on a hook.

From now on, they'd play his game.

Chapter 3

Hunter stood in the shadows of an unsavory part of the small Texas port of Corpus Christi. But he wasn't bothered. He'd developed an instinct for spotting trouble and never relaxed his guard. Feeling the weight of his pistol on his hip, he knew he could handle most anything that came along. But he didn't want problems. He wanted to slide in and out of this town easy.

At the moment he didn't think that was going to happen. Miss Deidre Clarke-Jarmon was making her first bid for freedom. Alone. At night. On the waterfront. He ran a hand through his thick dark hair. Did she really think she was invulnerable? Did she honestly think she could come down here with a handful of money to rent a boat and not be stripped of everything valuable?

He watched as she approached a lone seaman.

They talked. He couldn't hear their words, but there was no doubt she was so green she was dangerous. Her parents had been right to protect her. But they were wrong to trust him. He was no protection at all when it came to Miss Clarke-Jarmon.

As he continued to watch, two more men joined Deidre. None of the seamen wore guns, but they might have knives tucked somewhere. Deidre was hemmed in, but didn't seem to realize her danger. When she opened her reticule, he tensed.

He'd have to rescue her. She was worth more to him alive than dead, but he wanted her to get a good scare first. After that, she'd be more dependent on him and maybe even grateful. His eyes narrowed, thinking of what form her gratitude might take. He had a sudden, sharp image of her standing before him, slipping her clothes slowly, sensuously from her body until she stood exposed before him. And he knew exactly how she'd look naked. He'd known that from the first moment he saw her step from the stage in Three Rivers.

Suddenly the group began walking. He shook his head to clear it of the distracting image of Deidre. Money hadn't changed hands yet. What was the seamen's game? But he wasn't born yesterday. He figured they wanted to get her alone in some secure spot to take advantage of her.

Closing his hand over the butt of his pistol, he snapped off the thought of just what they wanted to do to her. And followed.

They took her to the Gulfwind Tavern. Music, laughter, and voices drifted outside the open door, along with yellow light. For a moment four shapes were silhouetted in the doorway, then they disappeared inside.

Like a shadow, Hunter slipped in behind them. Smoke hung heavy in the air and the smell of cheap liquor and sour breath was strong. Tinny piano music came from one corner of the crowded room. Seamen grouped around tables, talking, arguing, drinking, and gambling. At the bar, more men leaned into their liquor.

That's where he spotted Deidre. She looked like a diamond in a bin of coal. One of the sailors talked into the ear of a bartender while the other two watched their prize. Accepting money, the bartender motioned toward the stairs. The seaman nodded, then grabbed a full bottle of whiskey with one hand and Deidre with the other.

She jerked back, looking surprised. But the other two wrapped arms around her and pulled her away from the bar. At the stairs, she struggled, glanced back and cried out. Her voice was lost in the din of the tavern.

Hunter walked quickly across the floor, his senses alert, then hesitated at the bottom of the staircase. As Deidre was pulled from sight at the top, he glanced around, made sure no one was watching him, and walked up the stairs.

He turned left at the top of the staircase and moved with a stealth honed from years of tracking prey. It was easy enough to find their room. He stopped outside a door that only slightly muffled the sound of male voices pitched against Deidre's rising protests. When he heard the rip of cloth, he figured she'd learned her lesson.

For a moment he wished he hadn't waited so

40

long, but he had a score to settle with rich, pampered ladies and Deidre had helped even it.

He drew his pistol and kicked in the flimsy door, catching them by surprise as he stepped into the room. Light from a single lamp on a table by the bed lit the area, throwing shadows on the frozen scene. The sailor still held Deidre and the bottle of whiskey. The other two men stood silent, watching Hunter.

"You have something of mine." Hunter moved further into the room.

The man holding Deidre cursed and smashed his bottle of whiskey against a wooden chair. Glass and liquor cascaded to the floor.

Deidre tried to get away, but the sailor pushed the sharp, jagged edge of the bottle against her neck. Blood trickled toward her bare shoulder where her blouse had been ripped. She froze, focusing on Hunter.

"Get out if you want the woman alive." The seaman leered. "We're only gonna use her for the night. You can have what's left."

Hunter didn't like the situation. But he was a professional at this game and they weren't. "I think you've mistaken this lady for something she's not." He felt the weight of his gun in his hand, but he didn't want to use it. Too much noise and attention. Damn her. "Take her money and buy what you want, but give her to me. I'll call it even."

The seaman laughed. "I've got both now."

"But you'd be dead before you use them."

"I'll kill her." The sailor blustered, glanced at his companions, then back at Hunter. "If you don't leave right now, I'll slit her throat and when we're done I'll dump her body in the Gulf. Nobody'll be the wiser."

Hunter's eyes narrowed. "Go ahead. Then I'll shoot you. And your friends."

"You wouldn't dare." But the seaman had paled and his hand shook slightly as it held the bottle to Deidre's neck. "The law'd be down on you so fast—"

Hunter cocked the hammer of his pistol. "Make your choice."

The sailor's eyes dropped to Hunter's gun, then back to his opponent's face.

Hunter's gaze never wavered.

"Okay. Take her." The seaman pushed Deidre from him. "No woman's worth this much trouble."

"Deidre, get the hell out of here." Hunter waited while she hurried past him out the door.

Watching him, the sailor dropped the broken bottle to the floor. "It's over. You got what you wanted."

"What I want is for you to look over your shoulder every time you even think of treating a woman like you did this one." Hunter stepped backward and left the room.

He headed toward the stairs, listening for any sound from the room. Cowards were dangerous because they had no honor. With them, you had to watch your back. At the top of the staircase, he glanced back but saw no one following. He uncocked his pistol, dropped it in his holster, then started down the stairs.

As he walked back through the tavern, he was glad the sailors had wanted easy prey and not put up too much fight when it'd turned hard. But until he got Deidre out of Corpus Christi, he was going to keep her in the hotel.

Stepping outside, he took a deep breath of the warm, muggy air and glanced around. He saw her fleeing figure. She hadn't waited, hadn't felt a need to thank him. He cursed, suddenly angry. What had happened to gratitude?

In a few long strides he caught up with her. Grabbing her arm, he whirled her around. She screamed, but he cut off the sound with his hand. He could feel her heat this close, smell her fear. But most of all he felt his response to her. He moved his hand from her mouth to the back of her head, tilting it so he could check her wound by lamplight.

"A scratch. You'll be okay." He dropped his hand although he didn't want to stop touching her.

"Hunter, you scared me." She took quick, shallow breaths, glanced anxiously around, then focused on him. "I was going for help. Are you all right?"

Surprised at her words, he didn't know whether to believe her. If he hadn't made it out of the tavern alive, she'd have been rid of him. And maybe never blinked an eye in regret. Taking her elbow, he led her down the street. "We've had enough trouble. Let's get out of here."

As they walked, she placed a small, warm hand over his fingers. "Thanks. I don't know what I'd have done if you hadn't found me."

"The next time you get ideas about ditching me, remember tonight." His voice was harsher than he'd meant it to be, but he was having trouble breathing. The warmth of her hand against his conjured up images best left in the dark.

She jerked away from him and stopped. Pale street light illuminated her face, showing her fury. "How *did* you find me at just the right time?"

He didn't say anything.

"You followed me, didn't you?" She inhaled sharply. "You saw me talk to those men, go into that tavern, then followed me upstairs." She stepped back. "You could have stopped them any time."

"I got you out of there. You aren't hurt."

"You wanted to teach me a lesson, didn't you?" She put her hands on her hips. "You could've gotten us all killed. It was that close. My throat's bleeding. I went through all that so you could show me how weak I am and how strong you are. That's horrible." Her green eyes glinted. "Well, your nasty little plan didn't work. But I learned a lesson all right. I learned not to trust any man and to pack a pistol." She whirled around and started down the street, holding the ripped shoulder of her gown in place.

Hunter kept pace. He'd planned to comfort her, take care of her wound. Now he'd be lucky to keep her with him at all. But he'd come too far and too much was at stake for her to ruin his plans. He'd take her to the Bahamas one way or another.

When they reached the Bluebonnet Hotel, Deidre marched inside, ignoring him, the few people in the lobby, and hurried up the stairs. At her room, she inserted the key, opened the door, then turned around to face Hunter.

"I believe we have nothing more to discuss. You may return to the ranch and if my parents' insist I'll hire a bodyguard of my own choice." She stepped backward and started to close the door.

Hunter pushed in past her. He glanced around the room for any possible danger, then shut and locked the door. Leaning against it, he crossed his arms over his chest. "We've got plenty to talk about."

Clenching her fists, Deidre faced him. "I've had enough of brutal men trying to dominate me tonight. I did *not* invite you into my room. I do *not* want you here." She paused, pulling the torn fabric back up on her shoulder. "This entire incident is a perfect example of why women need the right to vote."

"Believe me, being able to vote wouldn't have helped you a damn sight tonight."

"It's the principle! Until men stop regarding women as personal or public property, we will be caught in situations like this. Now, once more, please leave."

Hunter walked into the room, glancing around, noticing how the sight of her personal belongings made his gut run hot. "Life's not a bunch of words out of a book. Life is *not* fair. I'm bigger, stronger, and in situations like tonight smarter. You need me to get what you want. Why don't you admit it and use me?"

"Use you?" She frowned.

"That's real life. And it's got nothing to do with who votes in some damn fool election. Everybody uses everybody else to get what they want. And, sometimes, it comes out even."

"Oh, so you're a philosopher, too." Her voice was

thick with scarcasm. "I can't tell you how impressed I am with your manly strength and power and smarts *and* philosophy."

He grinned. "You've got a wicked tongue, Deidre Clarke-Jarmon. You make me wonder just what all it can do."

She walked to the door. "I'm not going to listen to you anymore. If you won't leave my room, I will." She turned the lock. "I can scream. I can cause a scene. I can send a telegram to my parents. You may be all that you say, but I have options. But I prefer no trouble so I'll leave for the night."

Hunter shook his head. "Don't leave. I want to talk to you." He held his hands out away from his sides. "If I promise to be a gentleman will you listen?"

"But you *aren't* a gentleman."

"Do you want to go to the Bahamas and catch your prey or not?"

"Yes, but—"

"Then sit down and let's talk."

Deidre hesitated, searched his face, then walked across the room and sat down in the rocking chair beside the bed. She hoped she wasn't making another dangerous mistake, but she'd left the door unlocked.

Sitting down on the bed across from her, Hunter stretched out his long legs so that his boots almost touched her hightop shoes. He had to set some things straight here if he didn't want to fight with her all the way to the Bahamas.

"First off, I admit it. When I realized you were trying to lose me I got mad. I wanted you scared. I wanted you to know how much danger is out there. But I didn't mean it to go so far." He looked her up and down. "Dressing like a lady and going down to the docks at night is about as stupid as you can get. It's asking to get robbed, raped, or killed."

She watched him, thinking that so far his words sounded true. She'd been terrified on the waterfront and she wouldn't be here now if not for him. Maybe she needed more help than she'd originally thought. "You should have helped me sooner."

"I wish I had. It got out of hand fast." He felt the intimacy of the room getting to him. He touched the tip of his cowboy boot to her shoe. She glanced up, but didn't pull back. "I'm still your best bet for getting what you want. Your parents are paying me extra and that's what I want. Will you work with me?"

Hesitating, she looked him over, anger fighting with fear fighting with determination. She wished he didn't affect her so strongly, making her enjoy the cozy setting, the quiet conversation. Then she reminded herself he was a cowboy, a gunslinger, a man who knew nothing about the importance of woman suffrage. But he was right about one thing. She should use him if she could. "Yes, I'll work with you. But no more lessons like tonight."

"Good." He leaned forward, running the tip of his boot lightly against the arch of her shoe.

She pulled back her foot. "If that's all, I think you should leave."

He looked at her throat. Against pale skin, her blood was dark, but the bleeding had stopped. "I'll tend your wound first."

Self-consciously, she put a hand to the cut. "I

brought medicinal tinctures with me. I'll take care of it myself."

Hunter took her hand in his, then stood, pulling her up with him. "I can do a quicker job of it. Get what you want and I'll put it on."

She hesitated, mesmerized by the kindness in his dark eyes. For a moment it was hard to believe this was the same man who'd made her so angry before. "Just a moment."

Walking over to her carpetbag, she pulled out a leather bound container that was lined with dark blue velvet. In separated areas were nine dark bottles of tinctures. She choose the correct one and a clean cloth, then handed them to Hunter.

He took them from her and walked over to the lamp on the table beside the bed.

Following him, she sat on the edge of the bed, feeling nervous at his closeness and her vulnerability. Arching her long neck, she let the torn fabric lay against her arm, baring one shouder. When he'd applied tincture to the cloth, he turned back to her, hesitated, then reached out and slowly slid his left hand up her bare shoulder to her neck to her head. She shivered and caught her breath. He held her head steady as he gently cleaned the wound.

When he'd finished, he straightened and showed her the cloth with pink stains. "The cut's already closed up. You'll be fine. You might want to wear a scarf around your neck till it's completely healed, but that's about all you'll need to do."

"Thank you." She stood up abruptly, feeling desperate to get away from him. Instead, she made the situation worse for he didn't step back. Standing so close to him, she felt the heat of his body and caught his scent. More disturbed than ever, she sat back down.

"Are you okay?"

"Yes. I'm fine."

He set the tincture and the cloth on the table beside the lamp, then sat down beside her. "I've been thinking."

She took a deep breath to still her racing pulse. They shouldn't be alone in the room and certainly not sitting side by side on the bed. But her limbs felt heavy and she didn't want to move. Instead, she looked at him and was once more lost in the velvety darkness of his eyes.

"When we get to New Orleans I think we ought to shop for you."

"Why?" She felt surprised at the sudden change of topic, especially since it was such a personal one.

"It's a simple fact that your dressing and acting like a lady won't make it easy for you to go where we'll probably have to ask questions."

Deidre frowned. "What's wrong with my clothes?"

"As my woman, I'd dress you a hell of a lot different and take you everywhere I went."

She looked scandalized. "As *your* woman?"

"Right." He warmed to his idea. "We'll get you some flashy clothes and we'll stay in the same room once we get to the Bahamas."

Deidre stood up, furious, as all thoughts of gentle brown eyes receded from her mind. "Forget it. I have no intention of sharing a room with you. Besides, my parents would be horrified. You're supposed to be protecting my reputation as well as my life."

He got to his feet. "I'd sleep in the chair." He walked to the door. "If you think you'll find your prey at church or a social or a tea, think again." He opened the door and stepped into the hall, shutting the door behind him. When he heard her turn the lock, he walked across the hall to his room.

Inside, he lit the lamp. He took off his gunbelt and hung it over the back of a chair. He wasn't sleepy or tired. Miss Deidre Clarke-Jarmon had fired his blood. Would she accept his offer? It'd make his life easier in one way, but if he had to share a bedroom with her and keep his hands off of her all at the same time he didn't know if he'd have the strength.

He paced, then poured himself a whiskey. He'd stay awake till they boarded the boat for New Orleans. He wasn't going to let her slip away again. But as he listened, alert to the sound of her door opening, he imagined instead he could hear her slipping off her white blouse, then her black skirt, then her petticoats. When he imagined lace and silk against her pale skin, he groaned.

Jerking back the sheer curtain over the window in his room, he glanced out over darkened Corpus Christi. Deidre might be an Ice Princess on the outside, but he'd bet his life that she was hot as a prairie fire inside. And she had claws she wasn't afraid to use. He liked that in a woman.

He knew another woman with claws. Lady Caroline of New Providence Island, Bahamas. She was a wildcat. A user. And she had bought and paid for his loyalty. In this double game, he'd gone to the highest bidder.

Lady Caroline. As lush and hot and sensuous as

the tropical islands she called home. She didn't just heat up a man's bed. She burned it to the floor. And she wasn't some virginal intellectual who hadn't yet figured out what was good for her. Lady Caroline was in the prime of her forties, a woman who knew exactly what she wanted and how to get it. She lusted after power and wealth and excitement. But most of all she wanted revenge.

Hunter could understand that. He'd like a taste of it himself. He poured another whiskey, wondering how much of Lady Caroline's story was true. Maybe all of it. Maybe none of it. Maybe parts of it. He didn't care. He was being paid and well. Deidre was a surprise bonus that should bring him Lady Caroline's gratitude. She'd reward him in bed, but there'd be extra gold, too. And money was what counted. Nothing else. Except revenge.

As he drank the whiskey, he thought of Lady Caroline's story. Born in the Bahamas, she skipped over her childhood on a fading cotton plantation to the excitement of the blockade-running days of the War Between the States.

The islands boasted the nearest safe ports to the South and privateers plied the Bahamas with gold and excitement. One Rebel Captain in particular caught Lady Caroline's interest and she had a sizzling affair with Captain Jake of the Flying J. But with the end of the War came an end to the gold and the privateers. Once more the Bahamas languished and the gold flowed outward. Along with the gold went the privateers, and Captain Jake Jarmon.

But he returned to Lady Caroline one last time, asking for her help. She gladly gave it until she discovered it was for another woman, a rival named Alexandra. Then she flew into a fury and drove them from New Providence Island. But the anger never abated. She nurtured it even as she went on to marry an elderly minor British nobleman, Lucas St. John. She moved to England, leaving her brother Hayward in charge of the family's plantation.

With the death of St. John and with no children from the union, the estate and title returned to a male member of the St. John family. Furious at once more being abandoned by a man but left with a small inheritance, Lady Caroline returned to the Bahamas, to Hayward and the plantation. And plots of revenge.

Although her husband was now beyond Lady Caroline's anger, Jake Jarmon and his family were not. She wanted the Clarke-Jarmons hurt. If she could find a way to take everything they had, she would. After all, if not for Alexandra Clarke, it would all be hers anyway as the wife of Jake Jarmon.

So she had hired Hunter, a man she had learned had few scruples and a hard hand. She had sent him to the Bar J Ranch to cause trouble and get information. Now he was returning with a hell of a lot more.

Tossing back the last of his whiskey, Hunter felt savage elation tempered by a growing concern for Deidre. But he forced the feeling of unease aside, concentrating on gold, passion, and revenge.

Chapter 4

"I'm not sure this is a good idea." Deidre balked outside the front doors of Mimi's Couture in New Orleans. She turned around to face Hunter. "I think it'd be a better idea to drive out to Jarmon Plantation."

"No. We've got an agreement. I want to see you in some color and silk, satin, lace."

She looked him up and down. "Then you wouldn't mind if we bought you a few colorful brocade vests and maybe—"

"We're not talking about me." He scowled. "I'm not dressing like a dandy."

Tilting her head to one side, she put a finger against her chin as if seriously considering his attire. "Black. Leather. Trousers. Shirt. Vest. Cowboy boots. Hat. Do you even own a coat?"

He grabbed her arm and turned her back toward the doors. "Some women like the way I dress."

"Those involved with funerals, no doubt."

"We agreed to buy you new clothes, not me. Are you trying to renege on the deal or what?"

Before she could respond, the front doors of Mimi's opened and several ladies strolled out. Glancing at Hunter, they smiled, then whispered to each other, casting admiring glances backward as they entered a carriage and were driven from sight.

Hunter watched them leave, a smile on his lips.

"They're gone now." Deidre felt surprisingly irritated at his open admiration for Southern women in silks and satins. "If you like simpering ladies perhaps you'd better run after those. I'll be happy to return to the hotel."

Glancing back at her, Hunter noticed a dark-haired woman holding open the doors to Mimi's. Her black eyes sparkled in amusement, giving testimony to the fact that she'd overheard Deidre's words.

"Would you care to come in now? I'm Mimi."

Deidre whirled around, her face turning pink with embarrassment. Before she could speak, Hunter put a warm hand on her back and ushered her inside.

"You have a Clarke-Jarmon account, don't you?" Hunter was only too happy to spend his employers' money.

"Yes, monsieur."

"This is Deidre Clarke-Jarmon. I'm selecting her some new clothes. We're in a hurry so we'd like to see first anything you already have made."

Mimi glanced at Deidre and smiled. "You look very much like your mother. You haven't been in here for a long time, but I'm pleased to help you."

Deidre nodded, then glanced around at the luxurious decor of the store. "I usually shop in New York City."

Mimi raised a brow as she looked closely at Deidre's simple black skirt and white blouse. "That must be an English design. It is certainly not French." She shrugged at Hunter.

"She's been at school, but she's taking a trip to the Bahamas and her parents want her to have some new clothes." Hunter glanced around, knowing what he wanted Deidre to wear from her skin outward.

"I can speak for myself." Deidre felt embarrassed again. She'd forgotten all about coming here as a child. Since she'd become a suffragist, she'd had all her clothes, kept simple of course, made by a seamstress in New York. To someone like Mimi, she must look hopelessly out of fashion. And worse than that, how did she explain Hunter's presence or his determination to select her clothes?

Hunter walked around the room, touching intimate silk apparel, bolts of cloth, a pattern book, then turned back. He smiled at Mimi. "You're probably wondering what I'm doing here with Deidre. My name's Hunter. I'm a friend of the family. They're tied up at the ranch and since I was coming this way on business they asked me to help out." He let his gaze wander over Deidre's attire. "They thought a gentleman's opinion might persuade her to select a different style of dress."

At the insult to her clothes, Deidre wanted to

drop through the floor or throw a lamp at his face. But she had to admit he was good at telling a lie. His fabrication would go a long way toward saving her reputation if news of her shopping trip with him ever got out. Not that she really cared about anyone's opinion, but her parents would.

"I understand perfectly, monsieur." Mimi smiled at Deidre. "And you want to please the gentleman, don't you?"

Deidre nodded, keeping her eyes downcast so her anger wouldn't show. She'd find a way later to repay Hunter for this indignity.

Mimi clapped her hands. "Then let us begin. You will want something for the evening, no? For sultry afternoons, too? And mornings for relaxation?"

"And underwear." Hunter grinned.

Deidre stifled a groan and walked away. She wanted to hide and yet couldn't quite ignore the bubble of excitement at the prospect of showing Hunter just how good she could look in high fashion. On the other hand, she wasn't used to calling attention to herself and she suddenly shivered. She had relied on her intelligence all her life. This was a new game and she wasn't sure how to play it, or even how safe it would be.

But she reminded herself that she was an independent young woman and if adopting a new persona to achieve her goal was necessary then the price would be worth it. Straightening her shoulders, she turned back to see Mimi settle Hunter behind a screen. Walking into the dressing room near him, she began to undress as Mimi brought in clothes.

As time passed, Hunter realized he'd have been

a lot less bored if he'd been in there helping Deidre change. As it stood, he wasn't seeing any more of her flesh than he ever had. As she came out, modeling one gown after another, he quickly realized she was still swathed head to toe, only now in expensive fabrics and complicated designs. He'd brought her to the wrong place. She was being dressed as a lady and that's not what he wanted.

He took a drink of brandy. It was the closest thing they had to whiskey, but in his mood it wasn't close enough. Damn. He should have taken her to that special shop he knew about that catered to ladies of the evening. He was damn sure the Clarke-Jarmons wouldn't have an account there. It looked like if he wanted to turn the ice princess into a sultry woman he was going to have to pay for it himself.

And it might be worth the price.

Troublemaker. He smiled, a grim movement of his lips. That's what Deidre would call him if she knew his plans. But he'd been called that before. Since birth.

He poured himself another drink as his mind roamed. His mother was Apache-Irish, a half-breed scorned by all, but his father, Alberto Cazador Raimundo de Gustavo, led an exalted life as a Spanish grandee in southern Arizona. His parents weren't married so Hunter was called a bastard. Troublemaker. Breed.

Even after his birth and the complications it brought, his father couldn't stop wanting his mother and she couldn't stop loving him so she lived the life of a fallen woman on Raimundo Rancho. It wasn't much of a life, but maybe it was better than anything else she could have excepted. But that didn't stop his bitterness for her outcast, lonely state.

He'd had it better, sometimes. He had been alternately given a place with his father's family, education, presents, fine clothes, horses, servants, until his father's wife complained loudly enough, then he would be sent back to the arms of his mother. Her life was eased by her grandee's love, but she and her son were dependent on his charity. Back and forth he went, for his mother wanted what was best for him and his father tried to give it but never succeeded for long.

Finally his mother died giving birth to a dead child. His father offered to send him to college, but he rejected the offer. He'd had enough of name-calling and rejection. And he'd had enough of his father's *real* family hating him. He took off on his own with nothing but his pistol, horse, and the clothes on his back to help him create a new life away from the memories.

But the memories followed him. He tossed back another swallow of brandy as he looked out over the exclusive dress salon. He felt a fraud in both worlds, rich and poor, knowing enough to pass in either but uncomfortable in both.

His childhood had left him with a hatred born of the insults, taunts, and pain inflicted on him by his father's relatives and *real* children. And that hate centered on the wealthy and the aristocratic. He wouldn't vent his hate on blood kin, for he had vowed to his mother he would never hurt her beloved grandee. But he was free to hate others of their ilk and through their loss build his own power and freedom.

So he knew well women like Lady Caroline and the woman Deidre would become. As a young man, he was initiated into lust by beautiful, lonely noblewomen. They wanted his body, his youth, but not him. He never forgot or forgave.

He watched Deidre step out of the dressing room in yet another gown, and he thought how much pleasure it would give him to despoil her innocence, how sweet the revenge would be when he buried himself deep in her body. But he wanted her to want him, to give herself to him so that her debasement would be complete.

Yet a part of him warred with this desire, reminding him that Deidre was innocent. But he felt a need to punish her for invading his senses, his mind, making him want her like he'd never wanted another woman.

What he had, body, mind, and soul, he kept for himself. He never gave anything away. He also never put himself in a position so anyone could take anything from him. That fact was true till he'd gazed into the green eyes of Deidre Clarke-Jarmon and knew he'd have to fight himself to keep from giving his all to her.

But none of his thoughts stopped him from hating the dress she now wore. He nodded and she returned to the dressing room. He finished the brandy and stood up. There was no point in thinking about the past or his lust for Deidre. Both made him mad and he didn't need emotion clouding his reason.

Glancing around, he decided that up till now he hadn't known shopping could be so hard. He'd about had enough. He walked outside, paced up and down for awhile, noticed the sun lowering in the west, then stepped back inside.

And froze.

Deidre moved slowly toward him, smoothing the front of an evening gown. He felt his gut churn. It'd been worth the wait. This is what he wanted for her. Only now that she was wearing the right gown, he wanted to tear it off her body and see more of the creamy flesh exposed by the low neckline. Then he wanted to imprint his body on hers so she was branded by him for all time. He tried to replace the lust with anger, but it didn't work. All he could imagine was Deidre nude in bed, beckoning to him.

Mimi followed Deidre. "Monsieur, you must persuade her to take this gown. It is perfect for her."

Hunter hardly heard her words.

"Notice the dark green satin bodice accentuates her eyes. The cream ruffle around the neckline sets off her skin beautifully and in color repeats the skirt of cream brocade striped with green sprays." She turned Deidre around. "And the detail. Please note the small bustle since large ones are no longer so popular. Instead, I have added a full flounce edged with a pleated ruffle. The sweepers to keep it clean are of cream silk. Delectable, no?"

"We'll take that one." Hunter didn't want to know what the damn frills on the gown were called. He didn't even care about the dress anymore. He wanted Deidre out of it and in bed.

"But I'll need more than an evening gown, Hunter." Deidre wanted to tug up the bodice for she'd never worn anything so low before. But she'd seen herself in the mirror and she'd seen Hunter's reaction and she wanted the gown, too.

"A few tucks here and there and this gown is ready to go." Mimi smiled. "Mademoiselle Deidre has also selected a fawn tweed suit of jacket, waistcoat, and skirt. And, very sensibly, a riding habit of dark green cloth with black velvet collar and cuffs, and a cream silk waistcoat."

Hunter grew impatient. The main thing he knew was that he didn't want Deidre trussed up from neck to toe again. "Those sound hot. What about a cooler afternoon dress?"

"The violet and green sprig muslin?" Mimi deftly placed several pins in Deidre's gown to correct the fit.

"Yes." Hunter wanted to be gone.

"That's lovely, too."

"Okay." He decided to put a quick end to the matter. "Send the muslin and this evening gown, with silk underwear and whatever hats, gloves, and shoes she needs to wear with them, to the Orleans Hotel."

"But I want the others as well." Deidre threw him a dark glance. "They won't be too warm for New York City. Mimi, please send the riding habit and the afternoon suit to me there." Her green eyes sparkled. "And will you make me a bicycling dress and send it, too?"

"Bicyle!" Hunter stepped toward the door. Deidre had gone too far.

"And won't you send that little billed cap along for me to wear with it."

Mimi smiled. "You want the bicycling dress of cloth jacket and skirt to be worn with gaiters, boots, and gloves?"

"Yes. Dark green, I think."

"Good choice."

Hunter jerked open the front door, then glanced backward. "Madame Mimi, remember she's going first to the Bahamas. She'll need some cool clothes. If you can have them ready in three days, send them on to the hotel. After that—"

"Send everything else to my New York address." Deidre followed him to the door. "Going somewhere already?" Her tone was Southern Belle sweet, but her green eyes glinted mischievously.

"You finish. I'll send a carriage for you in an hour." He shut the door and strode away.

Mimi chuckled. "Men. I'm surprised he made it as long as he did."

Deidre turned back. "So am I. He's right about something cool. Perhaps you could make me a simple cotton skirt and a silk blouse."

"I can have those made up in three days. Several. Interchangeable. What we lose in simplicity of style we can make up in color and accessories. Please come and look at these glorious new colors of silk."

Dutifully, Deidre followed her into the back of the store. Much to her surprise, she realized she was enjoying herself and she wouldn't have taken anything for the look in Hunter's eyes when he'd seen her in the evening gown. If you wanted to impress a man, clothes would do it. Perhaps if Hunter became distracted enough, she might be able to lose him or at least control him better.

She felt satisfied with her choice of clothing so far. By the time she reached the Bahamas she'd be able to maneuver in any part of society necessary to uncover the truth about the lost Clarke ships.

And that, she reminded herself, was what this was all about.

When Deidre returned to the Orleans Hotel, she was smiling smugly to herself. She hadn't returned in an hour in the carriage Hunter had sent for her. Instead, she had spent the rest of the day at Mimi's selecting clothes, then stopped by the Cafe du Monde for coffee and *beignets* till evening had settled over the city.

Feeling quite independent, she walked through the lobby of the luxurious hotel, then up the stairs to her room. She didn't need Hunter to take care of her. She'd done very well for herself. And she was equally proud of the new clothes she had selected. They wouldn't arrive for several days, but when they did she'd be ready to take on whatever awaited her in the Bahamas.

Until then she planned to enjoy the delicious food served in the city, purchase a derringer to carry in her reticule, and visit one of her favorite bookstores.

Relaxed, she turned the key in the lock and stepped into her room. The area was lit by soft light from the gas lamp on the wall and she glanced around to once more appreciate the luxurious French decor. But she paused, her gaze caught by the pile of boxes and bags tossed onto the center of her fourposter bed.

Then she shrugged, dismissing her surprise. Mimi had worked more quickly than she had anticipated. Setting her reticule on a table, she crossed the room and picked up a hat box. The label on it was not Mimi's design. She read aloud, "Fancy's Fittings." She repeated the name printed in red and black on the box. Frowning in confusion, she checked the other boxes. They all were from Fancy's Fittings.

There must have been a mistake. Someone else's clothing had been delivered to her. But that seemed odd. How many Deidre Clarke-Jarmons could there be staying at the Orleans? Only one. She moved the packages around, searching until she came to a piece of white paper tucked under the band around a hatbox. Again she read aloud, "Deidre Clarke-Jarmon, Orleans Hotel. Hunter."

Dropping the piece of paper as if she'd been burned, she backed away. Hunter had bought her clothes. He hadn't liked what he'd seen at Mimi's, except for the evening gown. He'd gone somewhere else. But she'd never heard of Fancy's Fittings. He must have paid for the clothes himself. She felt her face heat with embarrassment. A man did not buy a lady clothing, not unless . . . unless . . .

She turned away to avoid looking at the incriminating evidence on the bed. What did Hunter think of her? What would her parents think? But most of all, what did she think? She felt a tendril of excitement uncurl in her stomach. She looked back at the packages. What had he bought her? What had he wanted to see her wearing? And why had he been willing to spend so much of his money on her?

Thinking of his brown eyes, gentle, impatient, heated, she shivered. What had been the expression in his eyes when he'd picked out these clothes for her?

Without making a conscious decision, she reached out and slid one of the dress boxes toward her. She had to look. She had to know. She untied the string, then opened the box. Red satin shimmered in pink paper. She caught her breath. Red! Bright, shocking crimson trimmed with moss green to match her eyes.

Reaching forward, she pulled the fabric outward, feeling the cool softness crush in her hands. Luxurious. Sensuous. Naughty. She shook her head to dispel the thoughts, then shook out the gown. She wasn't surprised to see the low neckline or the slender sheath of a skirt pulled back into small bustle that rippled down into a train. It would conform absolutely to her body. If it fit. And she had little doubt that it would hug her body like a second skin.

Looking down at her simple white blouse and black skirt, she realized there couldn't have been more of a contrast. But she also knew without a doubt that Hunter hadn't selected clothes for a lady. She shivered. He wanted her dressed as a woman of the night.

His woman. That's what he had said in Corpus Christi and that's what he had meant. Somehow his words hadn't been real then. Now they were. She caressed the fabric, then set the gown back in its box. Walking over to the window, she looked out over the French Quarter. What did she do now? Should she be angry? Insulted? Should she toss it all back in his face?

Suddenly she realized she should be wondering how she felt and not how she ought to respond.

She thought of Hunter, of his hard, lean body, his strength, his voice, his intense brown eyes. A deep warmth invaded her and she realized that he made her feel sensual, made her want to touch him, to feel his hands on her body. She was shocked at her thoughts. Simon Gainesville had never made her feel this way.

She also realized that these new feelings made her feel powerful and excited. She wanted to explore them. She wanted to follow her feelings. She wanted to feel free to be a woman, not a lady. If men were free to explore their sensuality, why not women? That right might be as important as the right to vote.

Her excitement built. Why shouldn't she dress in the shocking clothes? Nobody she knew would see her. Except Hunter. And he was hired help. If she wanted to explore this new side to herself, he would be the perfect man to show her. After all, she would only flirt with him and in a few weeks they'd part company and no one would be the wiser. But she would have gained valuable knowledge about herself which she could later share with someone appropriate for her, perhaps even Simon.

Now that she thought about it, she simply hadn't been looking at the situation in the right way. Of course, she hadn't had much interest in it before. Yes, Hunter was definitely the man with whom to explore the freedom and power of this new aspect of herself. But only so far.

Humming a popular tune, she decided to see what he had selected for her underwear. When she pulled out a red taffeta petticoat, she laughed outloud.

Part Two
Descent into
Darkness

Chapter 5

Deidre opened the last floor to ceiling window in her room at the Royal Victoria Hotel in Nassau and stepped out onto the balcony. She looked in delight at the lush botanical garden and inhaled the sweet scent of exotic flowers. Tall palm trees towered over the three-story hotel, the largest and most luxurious in the Bahamas. Vines, shrubs, and flowers nestled around the stone walkway that meandered through the garden.

For the moment she was alone, but Hunter was not far from her thoughts. Upon arrival earlier, she had learned of the two bedroom suite on the third floor of the hotel and persuaded him it was the right choice. He had agreed, she realized, to impress anyone who might be watching them rather than because it suited her.

Still, she had the freedom of her own room. The

longer she was with Hunter the more she needed distance from his overpowering presence. Since she'd met him he'd filled her nights as well as days, for she dreamed of him, of strong arms around her, of lips teasing her into responses she'd never thought of before. Yes, she needed freedom and space, but a single door between them at night would not be enough to stop the thoughts.

She forced her mind from him to her surroundings. Beautiful. Languid. Seductive. The Bahamas were islands flung like jewels across the Caribbean Sea.

It was hard to believe they could also be so deadly and dangerous. Sailors had long feared them. And with good reason. The tricky Bahamian waters, legendary for their vicious winds and currents, inadequate lighthouses, ill-charted waters, and rocky coasts, had destroyed thousands of ships and boats over the years.

Now Clarke ships had gone down in them, too. Only it was odd to lose four ships in the same area in just six months. Especially since recently the danger in Bahamian waters had lessened with improvements in sailing and ships. So why *four* Clarke ships now?

She pushed back a strand of stray hair as a moist breeze cooled her. Stepping forward, she placed her hands on the white wooden railing that enclosed the balcony. From the third floor she could easily see clear, turquoise water lapping against the bright white sands along the northern coast of New Providence Island.

Hunter had been right about cool clothing, but she had learned he was frequently right. That fact did not impress her unless it helped her find out who was trying to destroy her family. She shivered, despite the warmness of the day, and reminded herself that she must not be seduced by the beauty of her surroundings nor the warmth in Hunter's brown eyes. She had a job to do and one she must do well, for her future depended on it.

She pushed the glory of the islands from her mind and turned back toward the hotel, thinking of the cool shade of her bedroom. White lacy drapes at the windows moved in the afternoon breeze. In the distance she could hear the sound of voices on the quay, sailors and merchants and higglers.

But she wasn't ready to step into their world yet. She wanted the afternoon to prepare herself, get her balance after the voyage from New Orleans, and take a long bath. She might even read a chapter in *Vindication of the Rights of Woman*, although she realized that right now she was more interested in practice than philosophy.

Tonight would be soon enough to start her search, soon enough to play her role as Hunter's woman, soon enough to find out what he'd learned this afternoon. And in the days ahead she would look into woman suffrage on the island and seek out the women who were working for their voting rights under British law. She had time for it all.

Smiling in satisfaction, she stepped into the cool whiteness of her bedroom.

From the shadows of an ancient casuarina tree, Hunter watched Deidre walk back into her bedroom. He hit the bark of the tree with his fist, using pain to dispel her lingering affect. She'd been wearing the green silk bedgown he'd bought her. And little else. Suddenly he was mad at himself for making her even more sensual than before. With her new self-awareness due to the clothes he'd bought with his own hard-earned money, she was harder than ever to control.

Impatience gnawed at him. He wanted to be gone, but he'd had to make sure she was settled first. With Deidre he never knew what to expect and although he had persuaded her to spend the afternoon getting used to the island heat, he hadn't known if she would stay in her room or not. From her clothes and relaxed demeanor, he decided his ploy had worked.

The Royal Victoria Hotel was a good place to keep her. Lady Caroline and her brother Hayward had connections with the hotel and Deidre would be watched. He would also receive special and prompt service because, although it was not general knowledge, those who worked at the Royal Victoria knew he was a friend of the Graves' family. And nobody wanted to displease Lady Caroline.

But he waited awhile longer to make sure Deidre stayed put, trying not to think of the way the gown had revealed her body. He'd been trying not to think of her body for days and it had only made the situation worse. He wanted her and despite his oath not to touch pampered ladies, he knew he was going to break it. But he figured he could justify the oath-breaking by calling his actions revenge. He didn't often delude himself, but revenge took some of the sting out of his defeat to desire.

When she didn't come out again, he pushed away

from the tree and made his way through the garden to West Hill Street on the south edge of town. Undercover in the lush island growth, he mounted the horse he'd left tied there and headed down the street. He rode up to the Strand, the road that ran along the harbour, and headed west toward New Graves Plantation. And Lady Caroline.

As he rode along the coast, he looked out over the turquoise waters and inhaled the fragrance of the sea and the island. Although he appreciated the lush beauty, it couldn't compare to the stark purple mountains and arid land of southern Arizona. He missed the dry, stinging heat of the summer and the coolness of a mountain oasis in winter. But he had no home, no place to call his own. He preferred his nomadic life to the problems of family and commitment.

Past Delaport Point, the coast became rocky and he looked inward for the palm-lined road that led to New Graves Plantation.

Not that it had probably ever been much of a plantation. The earth on New Providence was spread thin on coral reefs. But that hadn't been known by the Loyalists who after the American Revolution moved their slaves and plantation ideas to the Bahamas to try to grow cotton and sugar. The British government had given the men land, then later freed their slaves. None of it had worked out quite like the Loyalists had planned, but several colonial mansions still dotted the coastline to give testimony to their dreams.

He saw the entrance to the plantation and turned his horse southward, still thinking about the economy of the Bahamas.

Now what he mostly saw produced were pineapple, sisal plants for rope, and the most natural of all, sponges. But planters still grew some cotton and sugar. Primarily the Bahamas had done well on the misfortune of others. Wars had always brought gold, especially the War Between the States. The island had been an early pirate refuge, then later home to privateers and wreckers.

But the days of riches from shipwrecks were fading due to a growing number of lighthouses, improved mapping of the waters, and more steamships with iron and steel hulls. That's why he was surprised at the loss of four Clarke ships in such a short period of time. It smelled. He wondered what had happened to the people aboard those ships. And if the wrecks had anything to do with Lady Caroline's revenge. He intended to find out.

Following the smooth road, he quickly arrived at Palmetto, the mansion on New Graves Plantation. Lady Caroline had told him all about it. The colonial Georgian style house was a duplicate of the family mansion that had been left behind in Maryland close to a hundred years before. At least it was the same except for the wide verandah and white columns that had been added in concession to island weather and changing style.

He'd have been impressed except for thoughts of the slaves who must have built and maintained the house for the Graves' family.

As he rode up to the wide staircase that led to the verandah, a small man with a single, dark plait of hair down his back hurried from around the side of the house. Before Hunter could dismount, the servant held his horse and bowed slightly from the waist.

Hunter got down, and nodded his thanks. As his horse was led away, he climbed the stairs, thinking about the fact that Lady Caroline hired only Chinese laborers, contracted for periods of five years, to tend the mansion, the gardens, and see to her personal needs. None of them were women. He supposed she must have lady friends, but he'd never met one.

As for the Chinese, they were popular in the West Indies to replace slaves who had replaced indentured servants. He'd learned the British government paid most of the laborers' fare from China and back. There was no way around the fact that planters usually avoided hiring local men or women for wages. He supposed the closer they could get to slave labor the happier they were. But it didn't make much sense to import workers since the freed slaves on the islands had quickly proved they worked harder, better, and made more money as free people.

But it wasn't his concern. He believed in freedom and equality and he had it. Beyond that, why should he care?

Before he got to the massive front doors, they opened. Lady Caroline stood silhouetted in the doorway, poised with a hand on one hip, a challenging look in her eyes, and her ample breasts more than half exposed. It was just about the homecoming he'd expected, but now that he saw it he wasn't so sure he wanted it.

Lady Caroline's auburn hair had been styled in curls on her head and she was elegantly gowned in a shade of turquoise that made him think of the sea. Powder and rouge and kohl had been artfully applied to her face. Whatever age she was didn't matter. She was sensual, seductive, and beautiful. And for the first time since meeting her, he wasn't sure he wanted her.

Shocked at himself, he slowed his step. He was thinking of blond hair and green eyes. He was thinking of Deidre. And he silently cursed. This woman had everything the Ice Princess had and more besides. He wanted an experienced woman, a woman with her own tastes and desires, a woman who appreciated him for all the right reasons. And he liked her all the better as part of a business deal.

Shrugging aside his distraction, he put a hand under Lady Caroline's chin and tilted up her head. She was petite where Deidre was tall. He cursed to himself again as he crushed out traitorous thoughts and lowered his face to kiss the crimson lips of Lady Caroline. He felt her arms go around him, pulling him closer, deepening the kiss as she thrust her tongue into his mouth.

He went cold inside. As quick as he could, he ended the kiss and stepped back. For the first time in a long while he felt used by a woman. And he didn't like the feeling.

But this was business. It was okay, or should be.

Lady Caroline smiled, a provocative movement of her sensual lips. "You missed me, didn't you?"

Hunter glanced up to see Hayward enter the foyer and walk toward them. Lady Caroline's brother was of medium height, slight of build, and his unruly brown hair had slightly receded and grayed. He took off spring pince-nez to reveal soft brown eyes, then tucked his eyeglasses into the pocket of the jacket of his white suit.

An intellectual, Hayward had many lady friends in Nassau and he was considered the primary patron of the local library and music association. For a moment Hunter feared Deidre would like this man when she met him, for she would appreciate his education, his scholorly pursuits, and his gentle good looks. Maybe Hayward was the kind of man to melt her icy reserve.

Suddenly Hunter wished he hadn't come back or brought Deidre. He didn't want her around the Graves, not subject to Hayward's possible lust or Lady Caroline's revenge. But he reminded himself that Miss Deidre Clarke-Jarmon was business, not pleasure. She was worth money to him and that was all that mattered.

"Hunter, glad to see you, old man." Hayward shook Hunter's hand, clasped him on the shoulder, and led him inside. "How have you been?"

"He looks fine." Lady Caroline's husky voice purred and she put a small, pale hand on Hunter's arm as she steered him into the drawing room to the right. "But he'll be better now that he's back in our care."

Hayward chuckled as he poured three whiskeys into crystal glasses, then handed them around. "My sister was born knowing how to please men. It's the best thing she does."

"More important is how they please me." Lady Caroline pulled Hunter down beside her on a settee. She moved her leg so that their thighs touched, then she tipped her glass to his. "Here's to our wayward boy come home." Her large brown eyes were doe soft, but a tightness about her lips revealed her inner tension.

They all drank, but Hunter found the liquor burned his throat and he couldn't help thinking of Deidre watching the scene with her knowing eyes and pious judgment. He decided she wouldn't understand, but then it'd be the least of all he was doing for her to understand. If she ever found out the truth, it'd be hell to pay.

"So, what brings you back to New Providence?" Hayward lounged back in a wing chair and crossed his legs.

"I've got some information for Lady Caroline." Hunter finished the whiskey and set aside the glass.

Hayward rolled his eyes upward, then shook his head at his sister. "I suppose I should be grateful to Caroline. Since she got back from England she's set things right with the house, the gardens, even got some sugar cane growing out somewhere. And these Chinese are quiet, efficient workers. But I'm afraid she disturbs my rustic, intellectual life."

"Hayward, you know you like the improvements I've made to Palmetto."

He glanced around at the richly decorated room. "Yes, but I was about to sell the plantation and move into Nassau. I'd have been close to the library and—"

"We're not that far away and New Graves Plantation is our family's heritage. I'd never have agreed to selling it and you know it."

He sighed and sipped his whiskey. "As long as I'm left to my books and music and ladies."

Lady Caroline turned to Hunter. "He always complains like this, as if I'm disturbing great thoughts. But he's glad to be free of his former shabby gentility."

Hayward nodded. "She's right about that. Still, I like my life ordered."

"And predictable." Lady Caroline rubbed a hand down Hunter's thigh and smiled seductively at him. "I've always been the wild one of the family, but Hayward supports me in all I do."

"I'm glad my daughter is safely out of harm's way." Hayward cast a dark glance at his sister.

"There's a lot I could teach her, Hayward."

"School will teach Arabella all she needs to know."

"I didn't know you had a daughter." Hunter leaned forward,

Hayward nodded. "I was married for a few years to a Spanish lady from Cuba. She didn't care much for our island nor me after awhile. But she did give birth to Arabella before she died."

"Oh, Hayward, you make it sound so dry and boring. It was tragic. She was so beautiful and to die so young. And not even for love." Lady Caroline smiled at Hunter. "I would never be so foolish."

Hunter raised a brow, not doubting her words for a moment. "Does your daughter live here?"

"Oh, no. She lives with her grandparents in Cuba. What would I know about raising a daughter? But she's always come for visits."

"Enough of Arabella." Lady Caroline set her crystal glass on a rosewood table. "I want to talk with you, Hunter. I need to hear your news and it will bore Hayward, I'm sure. We'll walk in the gardens. I have some new plants to show you."

Hayward stood up. "I'll be in the library if you need me."

"As if we couldn't have guessed." Lady Caroline stood, held out a hand to Hunter. When he stood up, she pretended to lose her balance and fell against his chest, laughing and caressing him.

Shaking his head at her antics, Hayward set his empty glass aside and left the room.

Lady Caroline kept Hunter's hand in hers and led him outside. On the verandah, she pointed out several new flower gardens, then walked around the side of the house to lead him deeper into a secluded garden. In its center a sundial had been set, with a stone bench nearby. Without saying a word, she turned and twined her arms around his neck, drawing his head down to receive her kiss.

He tried to force passion by returning her kiss, by stroking her body, by reminding himself that it had been a long time since he'd had a woman. But his emotions wouldn't listen to reason and he could think only of Deidre even as he tried to convince both Lady Caroline and himself that he still wanted her.

Finally she stepped back, looked him over, and smiled. "I'm surprised at how much I missed you. You'll stay tonight?"

"No. I must get back." Now was the time to tell her about Deidre, but he didn't want to do it. He didn't want to betray Deidre. Furious with himself, he thought of gold and revenge to make himself do the job. "I'm staying at the Royal Victoria."

"You can't get there what you can here." She

smiled playfully and ran her hand up and down his chest. When she started to go lower, he stepped away. Pouting, she followed him. "Have I suddenly lost my allure?"

"I brought somebody with me."

"What!"

Hunter chuckled. "I think you'll be pleased. But I want you to promise me a bonus before I tell you who it is."

She smoothed down the front of her gown. "A bonus?" Cupping her breasts, she smiled seductively at him. "I'll be happy to give you a bonus."

"Gold, too."

"If it's worth it, yes. But you'll get me no matter what." She took one of his hands and placed it over her breast. "Tell me quickly your news because I need you in my bed now."

He squeezed her breast, watched her breath catch, then dropped his hand and turned his back on her. He was reminded of his youth in Arizona, of the ladies there, and of their soft beds and softer bodies. He wouldn't be used again. "I've brought Deidre Clarke-Jarmon, daughter of Jake and Alexandra."

Lady Caroline inhaled sharply and caught his arm, tugging at him. "How? Why? What's happened at the ranch?"

He turned around to face her. "I caused them trouble like you wanted, but they didn't know I was doing it. They came to trust me."

She nodded, her fingernails biting into his arm. "Deidre came home from New York City with news about four Clarke ships going down off New

81

Providence Island. She persuaded them to let her investigate the problem and they agreed only if I came as her bodyguard."

"How clever! Yes, you get extra gold." Her dark eyes shimmered with excitement. "Bring her here at once. I want to see her. Does she look like her mother?" Suddenly she stopped and looked closely at Hunter's face. "Is she very beautiful? Do you want her?" Fury tranformed her features. "Have you already had her in your bed? Is that why you're now so cool? If you want her, I'll destroy both of you. Do you hear me?"

Hunter was surprised at her anger. "No. She's a lady. And don't talk about destroying me. You can't."

"I'm a *lady*." She tossed her head and some of the curls came free to lie against her shoulders. "I won't stand it. You hear? I won't stand for you to want her."

Pulling her against his chest, Hunter ran his hands up and down her back, trying to soothe her. "I'm here, aren't I? I brought her to you, didn't I? Do you think a young, green girl could compare to you?"

Caroline leaned back to look up at his face. "No. But men are strange creatures and illogical." She turned her back and paced. "I want you to bring her to me immediately. I'll hold her hostage. Then her parents will be completely at my mercy." She turned toward him and smiled. "You've done well, Hunter. Very well indeed."

"I think you should wait to show your hand. Give yourself time to make plans about Deidre and her parents. She's safe with me. I'll keep her busy on the island following leads on the Clarke ships. That way I can continue my deception and be of more help to you."

Lady Caroline raised an eyebrow, considering him. "You have separate bedrooms at the Royal Victoria?"

"Yes."

"Good. You may be right. At any rate, we'll do as you suggest while I consider my plans. But I want you to bring her out here to meet me. I want to see for myself if she has the beauty and charm of Alexandra." She cast him a suspicious glance. "And she can meet Hayward as well. We can all become friends, then I'll see what I see."

He nodded, realizing he hadn't thought about Lady Caroline being jealous of Deidre. What if she saw something he didn't want her to see, like his passion? Would Deidre become Lady Caroline's rival as well as victim? And then what would Lady Caroline do? Could she be as vicious as she hinted she could be? Not for the first time he wished he'd taken Deidre far away. But this was his job and it paid well. He had no time in his life for young ladies who were so green they were dangerous.

"Hunter, something else. How did Alexandra and Jake look after all these years?"

"They looked fine, I guess."

"I mean. Were they like me? I've changed little in my life."

"I never saw them before, but they look about like you. Agewise."

She frowned, obviously not pleased at the news. "Come upstairs and show me how much you missed me."

"Deidre's expecting me back. She didn't know I'd left town and I can't stay gone long."

Lady Caroline slapped him.

Furious, he stood absolutely still.

"I never want to hear again that you can't do something for me because of Deidre Clarke-Jarmon."

Hunter turned ice cold inside. "And if you ever slap me again, I'll break your arm."

She smiled. "I love it when a man talks tough." She pulled down the bodice of her gown to reveal her breasts. "I can't wait for the bedroom. I want you now." She reached for him.

"You'll have to wait." He turned on his heel and walked away.

At the front of Palmetto, he called for his horse, expecting Lady Caroline to come after him. But only silence followed him from the gardens. As soon as his horse was brought around, he was on his way back to Nassau, knowing he'd probably made a dangerous enemy.

Yet as he rode east, he couldn't think of anything but green eyes warming with pleasure at the sight of him.

Chapter 6

As evening enveloped Nassau in darkness, the sweet scent of night-blooming flowers permeated the air. Noises of the day gradually ceased and fog crept in from the sea. Wrapped in the splendor of the evening, Deidre wandered along the path through the garden of the Royal Victoria Hotel. She felt transported back to an era of pirates, Spanish galleons, gold, and bold men with few scruples and much lust.

She laughed at her idea, knowing she was thinking of Hunter, then stopped for the sound of her own voice had seemed too loud. Suddenly she thought of danger. And shivered. The Bahamas might be likened to a beautiful but deadly flower which lured you in then caught you unaware.

She was being fanciful, no doubt brought on by the magical quality of the night and the island. She should go back to the lobby of the hotel and await Hunter. But she was tired of that. And where was he anyway? If he didn't return soon, she would go out on her own. She had a derringer now which she carried in her reticule at all times. She'd never be caught off guard again, with or without him.

Sighing, she wished she were here strictly for pleasure. Maybe she could return for that some day, but in the meantime she had better go back inside the hotel and get on with the business at hand.

As she walked along the path, she continued to enjoy the fragrance and sight of exotic plants by the light of an almost full moon. Hesitating on the verandah outside the hotel, she looked inside at people talking, moving about, perhaps on business or pleasure. They seemed as exotic as the garden in their brightly colored clothes.

Pushing open the door, she walked into the lobby. She noticed people turning to watch her. Perhaps she appeared as foreign to them as they did to her, or maybe she was simply sensitive to the contrast in the peacefulness of the night and the noise inside the hotel.

"Deidre!"

Surprised to hear her name called, she turned. And saw Hunter. He seemed swarthier, more piratelike than ever, with his dark hair worn unfashionably long, his face shaved smooth, and a dangerous, challenging quality to him that set him apart from others. Although at present he didn't wear a pistol on his hip, he still wore all black clothes with black boots that reached almost to his knees.

She thought he might have a knife, if not a gun hidden on him.

She waited for him to come to her, concerned that he had been gone so long. But she wouldn't give him the satisfaction of knowing she had waited on him, worried about him. She didn't even want to admit that fact to herself.

When he strode to her side, he lifted her hand and pressed a soft kiss to its back. Raising his head, he smiled, his brown eyes warm, and tucked her hand into the crook of his arm. "Are you ready for an evening on the Strand?"

"I almost left without you."

"Do you want an apology?" As he led her forward, people parted for them.

"No. I assume you have news for me. But don't expect me to wait around for you in the future."

He pressed her hand. "I was reestablishing some old acquaintances. It took longer than I'd expected, then I bathed and changed."

As they stepped outside, she was no longer aware of the sweet night smell, but rather of Hunter's spicy scent and his strong presence.

He called for a carriage and soon they were riding up East Street. But she kept her distance from him, sitting as far away as she could and concentrating on the buildings along the street.

"Are you mad?" His voice was soft and low.

She looked at him, surprised at his words. "No."

"Why didn't you wear something I bought you?"

Glancing down at the yellow sprig print on white of her skirt, she put a hand to the high neck of the simple white silk blouse. "I didn't know where we were going or what we would be doing so I thought I'd wear something of my own."

Hunter raised a brow. "You look clean and sweet."

"Sweet! I'm not that."

Taking her hand, he looked at her long, slim fingers. He ran a calloused thumb back and forth across her knuckles. "You look like you could be going to the library or to a music gathering. That's not where I'm taking you."

When she could stand no more of the tension he was creating inside her, she pulled her hand away. "I can change."

"No. Not now. We'll think of something." He watched her for a moment, then leaned over and began unbuttoning the top buttons of her blouse.

Shocked, she pushed his hand away. "What do you think you're doing?"

"I'm getting you ready for street life."

"I hardly think that—"

"You do it or I'll do it."

Green eyes locked with brown.

Deciding to do whatever it took to get information, she unbuttoned the top three buttons. But it seemed silly, insulting, and embarrassing.

"Good." He leaned toward her, unbuttoned a fourth one, then spread the neckline into a V-shape to reveal the cleft of her breasts.

She knocked his hand away, rebuttoned the fourth button, but left her skin above that exposed. Looking away, she ignored him in favor of watching the harbor up ahead. More lights and more people were there, as well as noise.

"Driver, stop here."

Looking around in surprise, she watched in amazement as Hunter hailed several young women walking along the street. They laughed as they hurried up to the side of the carriage.

Hunter put a hand on Deidre's shoulder. "My companion needs a shawl. I'd like to buy that pretty green and red one you're wearing."

The young women laughed, and the one wearing the shawl stepped forward. She smiled. "How much are you offering?"

Deidre heard him name an outrageous sum, but soon he had the shawl in his hands. The driver clicked to the horse and they moved on toward the Strand.

Hunter shook out the shawl, then handed it to her. "This'll fix you up. You can even put it over your head."

"It belongs to a stranger."

"Belonged."

"Do you honestly expect me to wear this?"

Hunter scowled. "Are you too good for it?"

She wanted to throw the shawl away, but instead she crumpled it in her hands, noticing for the first time that it was silk. When they drove under a street lamp, she saw the shawl's colors were a brilliant green that blended perfectly with her skirt, with white and red and yellow patterned in exotic floral designs. It was a gorgeous shawl. Suddenly she felt ashamed. Not everyone could afford custom clothing whenever they wanted. The shawl had probably meant a lot to the young lady who had obviously needed the money more.

Looking at Hunter, she bit her lower lip. He was staring away from her. Angry? Hurt? She reached out and touched his arm. He glanced back. No emotion crossed his face, but his eyes had a closed, shuttered look.

"It's a lovely shawl." She put it around her shoulders. "Does it do what you wanted?"

"Yes. But that attitude'll get you nothing you can't pay for." He paused. "But that's never been a problem for you, has it?"

"No, I guess not." She fingered the long, green fringe on the shawl. "But I'm not insensitive to others either."

He didn't respond.

The carriage stopped. Hunter got down, then extended his hand and helped her from the coach. It drove on.

"This is the Strand. It's the main street of town and runs along the harbor." Hunter tucked her hand into the crook of his arm.

Deidre allowed him to lead her, aware of the people in carriages, surreys, and on foot. She also noticed the restaurants and taverns. She was surprised at how British it all looked, but she knew she shouldn't be because the Bahamas had long been a Crown Colony.

"I'm not taking you on a walking tour tonight, but there's a few things you might want to know about." Hunter pointed toward three large building. "Those are the Public Buildings. I've heard Loyalists had them built based on the design of Governor Tyron's Palace in New Bern, a capital of North Carolina."

Deidre noted the impressive architecture, muted with shadows and lamp light. She would return during the day to see it all better.

"The library's behind them." He looked down at her. "I figured that's a place you'd want to go." The library reminded him of Hayward Graves. And Lady Caroline. But he didn't want to think about them. That was trouble. He pushed them from his mind and walked faster.

They continued down the Strand, then turned up Charlotte Street. Walking right up to the edge of the harbor, Hunter stopped. He pointed.

"This is the Market Range. Nassau has one of the greatest natural harbors anywhere. The boats and ships dock right here."

Deidre was amazed they stood so close to the water. She could hear gentle lapping against the white sands.

"Mail boats and sponge boats dock here. And its the main market where women, and some men, sell their straw work and wood carvings."

"I'd like to shop here tomorrow."

"Okay, but right now we're going to ask some questions. There'll still be people around. Sailors working on their boats. Higglers getting their wares ready to sell. Revelers, maybe. Let's see what we find."

"Fine. You're leading tonight." She was content to be with him no matter where they went. She felt surprise at the realization.

"You don't let anybody lead you much, do you?"

"Do you?"

He smiled, a crooked movement of his lips, then walked on, keeping her hand at his elbow.

They came upon a sponge diver, sorting through sponges. When Hunter called to him, the mulatto stood up, and nodded.

"How's the crop?" Hunter picked up a sponge, weighed it in his hand, then handed the diver some money. He gave Deidre the sponge.

She placed the small sponge in her reticule, the green bag that matched her skirt.

"Good, but less every year." The diver watched them warily.

"Did you hear about four big ships going down near New Providence in the last six months?"

The man grew still. "Many boats die here."

"Big ships. Maybe steam."

"Another man came and asked questions about those ships. He went away. Perhaps he learned a wise man will not talk about wreckers in the Bahamas."

Deidre squeezed Hunter's hand, realizing the diver was talking about Bill Brown who'd been sent to Nassau to investigate the wrecks.

"But two more have gone down since that man asked questions."

The diver turned his back on them. "Many things happen in the Out Islands that we don't know about here in Nassau."

"Please, would—" Deidre stopped speaking when Hunter squeezed her hand.

"I'd pay for information."

The diver turned back, looked in all directions, then focused on them. "Danger makes a man smart. Gold makes him stupid." He shrugged and held out a hand.

Hunter paid him, then waited while he counted the money and nodded that it was enough. "Were those four Clarke shipwrecks accidents?"

Hesitating, the diver looked around again.

"Maybe. But rumor says no. Not so many big ships go down now. Clarke Shipping." Shrewd dark eyes looked from Hunter to Deidre then back again. "Rumor has it that any Clarke ship comes through here goes down." He shrugged.

Deidre inhaled sharply. "What happened to the people on those ships?"

"Some lived. Some died."

"I mean, what did they say?"

The diver shook his head. "Those people don't talk to me. But you might ask Old Nate at Smuggler's Den." He turned from them and climbed aboard his boat.

"Thanks." Hunter walked on, holding Deidre's hand now.

"Smuggler's Den? Real smugglers?"

"Maybe, but I doubt it. Some of those places have been around a long time."

They kept walking till they came to a lonely spot. Hunter stopped and looked out over the sea. "I don't know if we can get anybody to talk with us. These people and their ancestors have been wreckers for generations. They're not going to tell outsiders much."

"But they've got to." She gripped his hand. "We must find out if somebody is luring our ships to destruction. And who's doing it."

"I don't think we'll get much more information around here. Do you want to try Smuggler's Den?"

"Of course I do."

"Okay, but you've got to promise to stay close to me and follow my lead."

"Really, Hunter, I can take care of myself." She dropped his hand and stepped away from him.

"If you want to find out anything, you need to do as I say."

"All right, but one of these days the tables will be turned and I'll be telling you."

"Fine with me." They walked back to the Strand and kept on going, past people, lights, and buildings.

"Maybe we should have hired a surrey." Deidre realized she hadn't worn the proper shoes for walking so far.

"We're almost there."

They arrived at a dilapidated building, grayed and weathered with age. It was so close to the water Deidre decided one strong wind and the tide would sweep it out to sea. No sign announced it as Smuggler's Den. Instead, horses and a few buggies surrounded the lee side while boats of many shapes and sizes were moored on the ocean side.

They walked across a rickety porch, through an open doorway, and into a room filled with men and a few gaudily dressed women. Barmaids served liquor and food as fast as they could move it through the area. A smooth, weathered bar took up one wall and Deidre decided the theme could only be described as nautical. Fish nets, lines, sinkers, stuffed fish, and parts of ships adorned the walls. Wooden barrels set on one end served as tables. She realized that smugglers could just as easily have been wreckers and wondered if she might find pieces of Clarke ships here or there.

Hunter pushed their way through to a keg with two stools near a window. She set down while he pulled the other stool close to her so their backs were to the window. She was glad of the fresh sea air to cut the whiskey and smoke and body smell of the room.

"What do you think?" Hunter glanced around.

She didn't reply, for she was thinking about the warmth of him, of his sensual lips, of his hard body.

"Deidre?"

She jerked her mind away from her thoughts, disgusted with herself, and noticed the puzzled frown on his face. She clasped her hands together on top of the table, leaving her reticule in her lap. "What did you say?"

He leaned closer and covered her hands with his own. "I won't let anybody hurt you. Don't worry."

Her heart beat fast. She should move her hands but she needed his touch. She wasn't worried about anyone else harming her. She was worried about what Hunter might do to her heart, to her life, to her plans. Shaking her head, she tried to dispel the lethargy that was stealing over her, for in this place so far from her normal world she felt as if she could be anyone she chose . . . even Hunter's woman. And would that be so bad?

"Deidre?"

"I've got a derringer in my reticule."

He threw back his head and laughed, squeezing her hands at the same time.

She didn't join his laughter. It wasn't funny. She was an independent young woman and she could take care of herself. Frowning, she focused on him.

When he finally stopped laughing, he shook his head. "Is it a one shot or two?"

"Two."

"Did you buy it in New Orleans?"

"Yes."

He patted her hands, chuckled again, and caught the attention of a barmaid. "It might help, but in a place like this I don't know how much."

Deidre frowned harder and jerked her hands away. She craddled her reticule in her lap, feeling the comforting weight of the derringer. He was wrong. She could shoot her way out of this place if necessary.

"Two whiskeys." Hunter watched the barmaid walk away. "If you dressed more like that, you'd fit in here."

Narrowing her eyes, Deidre unbuttoned the fourth button of her blouse and leaned toward Hunter, knowing she was showing more of her flesh than she'd ever shown to any man before. But she didn't want him watching another woman and she was mad at his laughter.

The humor immediately left his eyes.

She smiled in grim satisfaction.

"Button your blouse."

"But you wanted me to fit in. As far as I can see this is what will do it."

"I don't want any other man to see you."

"Oh, really?" She turned away from him, straightened her back, knowing it would thrust out her breasts.

"Damn!" He jerked her toward him, buttoned her up to her throat, then sat back in silence.

She simply stared at him. He'd reacted a lot more than she'd expected. She felt avenged. "I thought—"

"Don't think!"

The barmaid set two whiskeys on the keg and as Hunter paid for them, she moved up close to him.

Deidre could smell the cheap perfume and focused her anger on the other woman. "You've got other customers. I suggest you see to them."

Surprised, the barmaid turned to look at Deidre. "Okay, honey. I don't step on another woman's turf, but if you ever get done with this one, throw him my way." She gave Hunter a sultry smile.

"Do you know somebody named Old Nate?" Hunter pressed a tip in the barmaid's palm.

"Sure. Runs this place. You can't miss Old Nate. Look for the sailor with one arm and close to a hundred years old. Smartest old salt I ever met."

"Is Old Nate around?"

"Sure. But don't go looking. Nate'll be around." She glanced at Deidre. "Remember what I said about your man." She walked off, swinging her hips a little more than was necessary.

"Bold as brass." Deidre looked at Hunter. "She sure never set foot in a finishing school. Do you suppose she's a suffragist?"

Hunter laughed again.

"I'm tired of you laughing at me. I'm serious."

"I know. That's what makes it so funny."

"I'd be glad to have a woman like her attend a meeting with me." Deidre's voice held admiration.

"You're supposed to be jealous of her. Remember, she's trying to get your man."

"Oh, yes. That's the game we're playing, isn't it?" Hunter lifted his whiskey and saluted her.

She clinked her glass to his.

"Here's to success."

She drank to that, but the whiskey burned down her throat to her stomach. She choked, caught her breath, and coughed.

Patting her back, Hunter turned her face against his shoulder so the sound was muffled.

Nestled against him, she noticed he was warm and strong. She felt chilled, then too hot. Leaning back, she looked up into his eyes. Melted chocolate. And she was melting into him. He lowered his face and even though she knew he was going to kiss her she didn't move, didn't try to stop him. Instead, she held her breath, anxious for him to touch her, to ease the tension, to justify her dreams or fears.

But she wasn't prepared for the heat or the tenderness or the flood of emotions that filled her when his lips pressed against hers. She heard him groan so softly that she wasn't sure he had and realized she had moaned ever so softly, too. When his hands tightened on her shoulders and the kiss hardened, fire built deep within her.

"Hey, you youngsters never can wait, can you?"

Deidre jerked back, embarrassment flooding her face crimson as she looked into the sharp eyes of an older woman. The lady was one armed, dressed in sailor garb, with white hair pulled back in a tight chignon. She was tall, slim, straight-backed, with wrinkles etched into her tanned face.

"The name's Nate. Old Nate. Or Natalie to my parents, bless their long gone souls. How's the whiskey?"

"Bad." Hunter grinned.

"What the hell'd you expect in a place like this?"

"You're a woman!" Deidre couldn't keep the amazement from her voice.

"Hell yes, last time I looked. The most feared

pirates ever to sail the Caribbean Sea were women. Myself, I went to sea at ten, stayed there even after I lost my arm in the rigging, but I finally had to give it up at eighty. Not that I couldn't keep up. It wasn't dangerous enough to keep me interested anymore."

"Eighty." Deidre's eyes shown with admiration. "You'd call yourself an independent woman, wouldn't you?"

"Hell yes. I'm the best navigator these parts ever saw. Ships'd take me on just to get through the Bahamas in one piece. I never lost a ship."

"That's wonderful." Deidre decided Old Nate wouldn't need a derringer. Nobody'd bother her.

"What do you know about the four Clarke ships that went down in the last six months?" Hunter turned the conversation to help them.

"Who's asking?"

"We're looking into the matter." Hunter pushed some money toward Old Nate.

She shook her head. "Another man asked and disappeared. I'm gonna do you a favor and warn you off this one. Let it go." She stepped back from the table. "But come by any time." She fixed them both with a sharp stare, then walked away.

"Do you suppose she's a suffragist?"

"I doubt if she has time. But I'd bet my life she's hiding something."

"Do you think we can get her to tell us?"

He watched Old Nate as she greeted other customers, pounding some on the back, hugging a few, and laughing and talking as she made her rounds. "I don't know, but we can try again later."

"Let's do. I want to discuss woman suffrage with her, too."

This time Hunter didn't laugh. He finished his whiskey and stood up. He held out a hand, looking at Deidre with warm brown eyes. "We've got some unfinished business."

Chapter 7

"What unfinished business?" Deidre thought she knew the answer and her heart beat fast with anticipation.

Hunter drew her hand through the crook of his arm and led her away from Smuggler's Den. But not back toward Nassau. Instead, he walked along the beach. Moonlight turned the surf silver as it rolled into shore. The sound of the sea and the darkness of the night entwined them in a cocoon of intimacy.

He stopped, watched the ocean for a moment, then turned toward her. His eyes were dark with desire.

Caught by the power of the night, by the strength of new emotions, Deidre gripped his arm. She must be practical. She must remember her reason for being with him in the Bahamas. "We're working

101

together. The kiss earlier was a part of our act, wasn't it?"

He watched her, noticing how her green eyes were as luminous and unfathomable as the sea. But her lips trembled. He touched her lower lip with the tip of his finger, then gently outlined its delicate curve. "If it was an act, then this is a part I must play." He lowered his head.

Knowing she should resist, stop the entanglement before it went farther, she still raised her face to meet him.

They kissed. Gently. As if wary to venture farther for fear of the flames that might engulf them. Moments passed.

Suddenly he groaned and pushed fingers into her hair, dislodging the pins, setting the long tresses free. He grasped her soft hair in one hand and with the other drew her against him. But never broke the kiss.

She shivered and clutched his shoulders for support as her body responded to him.

Raising his head, he looked into her eyes. "I won't hurt you."

"Remember, we—"

He took her lips again, but this time delved deep into her mouth with his tongue, tasting her sweetness, making her his in a way he had thought of for so long. But the kiss quickly tormented him, made him want more. Much more. He moved his hands to her shoulders, her back, then started lower. He stopped, remembering she must be a virgin. Regretfully he raised his hands to her face, cupped the soft skin, felt the delicate bone structure, and stopped the kiss.

Turning away, he focused on the sea, trying to still his racing heart, slow his breathing, and ease the pain in his body. He didn't think he'd ever wanted a woman so badly. He shouldn't touch her. She was all he had avoided for so long. But he burned with need.

Deidre felt cold and lost with him turned from her. Had she done something wrong? She knew nothing about this type of passion. She tried to slow her breath, tried to control the devastating emotions that had made her heart race and her body ache deep inside. She hadn't wanted him to stop. Ever. Wherever he had been leading her she had desperately wanted to follow.

"Hunter?"

He placed an arm around her shoulders as if to shield her from pain or cold or loss. Or himself.

She leaned against him, relishing his closeness, and watched the sea. The rhythm of the waves as they broke against the shore echoed the beat of his heart.

"I shouldn't have done that. I apologize."

"No, don't." She touched his lips with a fingertip to still his words. "I wanted you to kiss me."

He saw the truth of her words in her eyes, but it didn't change the situation. "This can't come to anything. I'm the hired help. You're the princess. Besides, I'm not used to holding back with a woman."

"We still have a job to do. We still have roles to play." She hesitated, feeling his warm body against her. "I want you to kiss me again."

He set her away from him. "This isn't a game. Don't tease."

"I'm not." Emboldened by her need, she reached up to him, stood on tiptoe, and pressed her lips to his while at the same time pushing her breasts against his hard chest.

He groaned, then dug fingers into her hair and held her head as he returned the kiss, thrusting into her mouth, savoring her taste, her softness, imagining he was thrusting into her body at the same time. He dropped one hand to clasp her hips as he pushed against her in a desperate need to release himself deep inside her.

But when she moaned, her fingers digging into his shoulders, her body heating in response to him, he drew back, slowly ending the kiss, slowing moving his hands until they hung limply at his side.

"You don't know what you're doing." He watched her eyes darken with wonder and desire and knew he should have been pleased. He was close to revenge for all the rich women who had used him. Deidre wanted him. But suddenly it was not enough. He knew how easy it was to lust for another's body. Women had played that game with him when he was too young to understand. No, it was not enough.

Now he wanted Deidre to want him for himself, not what he could teach her that she'd never learn in a fancy finishing school. He forced anger to replace passion.

She'd have to love him first. He was shocked at his decision. What difference would it make? He could take the Clarke-Jarmon daughter, then throw her away when he was done. What better revenge?

Lady Caroline couldn't do so well. But thoughts

of his employer made him go cold. He no longer wanted to do Lady Caroline's dirty work and the thought of touching her after having kissed Deidre made him feel disgusted.

Turning his back on Deidre again, he fought his emotions, fought to get back in control. But once more he had the terrible feeling Deidre would be his downfall. Yet he couldn't stop his decision to make her love him, to make her hurt for all the rich women who had used him.

"Hunter?"

"Have you decided to be a tease with the hired help?"

"I don't think I know how to do that." She took his hand in hers. "Is there someone else?"

He thought of Lady Caroline. Was Deidre a mind reader? "There've been a lot of women."

"Do you love someone? Are you engaged? Married?" When she realized she was holding her breath, she let it out slowly and reminded herself that he was an experiment, an experience, and nothing more.

"No. I'm a drifter. I don't stay in any place long enough for that." He kissed her lightly on the lips. "Let's go back to the hotel. Maybe tomorrow we'll get some answers."

"But Hunter—"

"Don't tempt me any more."

As they walked back toward Nassau, Deidre forced herself to push thoughts of his kisses, the feel of his hands on her flesh, of his hard body against hers from her mind. But it wasn't easy.

Not long after they reached the Strand, Hunter

hired a carriage to carry them back to the hotel. Silent, they sat on either side of the seat, emotions running high but controlled for the moment.

Although grateful not to have to walk, Deidre also realized that this way they would return to the hotel faster and she would soon be alone. Even with Hunter quiet and withdrawn, she still relished his company. She marveled at her reaction to him since it was so unlike anything she had ever experienced before.

She thought of Simon and their long walks and conversations in New York City. How could she suddenly be so intent on another man, someone so far removed from what she liked and understood? But she had no answer to her question.

Relaxing against the seat, she looked out over the town and fingered the long fringe of the shawl Hunter had bought her. It had been a thoughtful act, but she didn't want to think about his kindness, or concern, or desire. She must simply concentrate on getting information. Old Nate was at the top of her list to question and she'd start there tomorrow.

At the Royal Victoria, Hunter handed her down from the carriage, then escorted her inside. Few people were in the lobby and the area was quiet. They started toward the staircase.

"Mr. Hunter, wait!" A man from the registration desk hailed them, then hurried over with a large basket of fresh fruit and flowers. "This was left for you, sir."

Confused, Hunter accepted the basket.

"And a note." The man glanced at Deidre, then winked at Hunter. "You might want to read it alone."

106

"Alone?" Deidre snatched the cream colored envelope from Hunter, pulled the single sheet from inside, then froze as she read it. *A token of my esteem and affection. Our quarrel is forgotten. Please bring your friend to visit soon. Love, Lady C.*

"Deidre—"

"Reestablishing old acquaintances. A drifter." She raised her chin. "I'm not that green." She thrust the note and envelope into the baskèt, then turned abruptly on her heel. But not before frowning at the hotel employee who quickly hurried back to his desk.

As she headed for the staircase, she heard Hunter catch up with her. But she ignored him.

"Deidre, I can explain this, but not in the lobby. We'll talk about it in the suite."

He grasped her elbow, but she jerked away and walked faster.

Neither said another word until they reached the door to their suite. She stopped and turned to face him. "I suggest you get another room for the night. And I'll get another bodyguard, if I need one, tomorrow."

He unlocked the door and pushed her inside. Locking the door behind him, he set the basket on the first table he came to, then faced her.

"Your smooth words aren't going to work this time, Hunter." She tossed her reticule on the bed, then crossed the room to look out over the darkened garden.

"Will you listen?"

She kept her back to him.

"Lady Caroline and her brother Hayward are friends of mine. I went to visit them today, hoping to learn something about the wrecks. I told them about you and now you're invited to visit New Graves Plantation." He hesitated at her lack of response. "Some people would consider it an honor."

She shrugged. "And the quarrel?"

He thought fast, hating the lies but knowing he couldn't tell the truth. "Like all natives of this island, they protect their own. They wouldn't discuss wreckers."

Turning around, she watched him for a moment, then walked back across the room. "That's not all, is it?"

"What do you mean?"

"That note. The fruit, flowers." She looked him over. "You made love to her when you where there this afternoon, didn't you? Then you kissed me, claiming you had no ties."

"Wrong." He grasped her shoulders, knowing he should be pleased at her pain but he wasn't. Her pain had suddenly become his pain.

She shrugged out of his grasp, but held her ground. "You think I can't tell. That note said it all."

"It said nothing of the sort. She invited you to visit them. Is that so bad?"

"You kissed her, then me." Deidre searched his face, determined to read the truth in his brown eyes. But they were dark, revealing nothing.

"I don't want her."

"She wants you. She's had you. I know it." Deidre turned to stomp across the room, amazed at the pain that gripped her heart. What was wrong with her? She'd never acted this way before. Could it be jealousy?

"Damn it, Deidre!" He followed her, grabbed her again, and crushed her against his chest. "I want you. Only you." And to prove his words true, he forced his mouth to hers and pressed his body to hers. But she remained unresponsive.

In a wild swing of emotion, he suddenly didn't care if he hurt her. He had to break through her cold exterior, had to prove their desire was real, had to make her forget Lady Caroline. Finally he felt her relent and open her lips to him, or had he forced her? He wasn't sure. He simply pushed into the warm, sweet depths of her mouth and felt his hunger ignite.

He jerked the shawl from her body and dropped it on the floor. He ran his hands through her long hair, turning it into a wild tangle. Desperate now, he stroked lower to her breasts, felt their soft mounds and jerked open her bodice. On fire to possess her, he ran his hands over her chemise-covered breasts, felt the tips harden, and trembled as his own response to her blazed out of control.

Lifting her, he maintained the kiss as he carried her to the bed. As he lowered her, he covered her with his body and pressed against her in a wild need to spill his seed deep inside her. Finally he placed hard kisses over her face, down her throat to the tops of her breasts. Then he moved back to her mouth.

When she touched him with her hands, across his back, along his shoulders, down his arms, he shuddered, knowing he had finally reached her, made her realize the power, the importance of the passion between them. He groaned and pushed a knee between her legs, spreading her thighs so he could get closer to the heart of his desire.

He had no thought but to melt his Ice Princess so it took him several moments before he realized something hard and cold and metallic pressed against his side. And then he noticed how still she lay beneath him. He raised his head and looked at her in wonder.

"Get off me, you stupid oaf, or I'll empty both barrels of my derringer into you."

Now he knew what she had been doing when her hands left him. She had used them to reach her reticule and take out her gun rather than caress him. He was shocked. And with the blood still pounding in his head he had trouble thinking, much less reasoning with her. And with himself.

What had come over him? She was an innocent young lady. He knew that. He'd never forced a woman in his life. He was surprised at his own violence. Here she was threatening to kill him. And she had the right. He rolled over to one side, then stood up. The pain in his body from lack of release mirrored the pain in her face.

Had he lost his mind? He wanted her to love him, not hate him. He wanted her to give herself to him, not be taken in a moment of lust. Pushing a hand through his hair, he backed away. He didn't know what to say.

She sat up, holding the derringer on him with a shaky hand as she stood to face him. "I think you proved your point. You want me. All right." She took a deep breath to control her ragged breathing. "But I think any woman would do. Perhaps you didn't touch Lady Caroline this afternoon after all and perhaps you should have."

"I have no excuse." He balled his hands into fists. "But your gun wouldn't have stopped me."

"No?" Her cool green eyes held disbelief.

"You'd have hesitated to shoot and I'd have over-powered you."

"So big, so brave, so smart, so powerful." She walked toward him, her hair a wild golden mane around her shoulders, her breasts pushed high by her corset and covered only by her silk chemise. Her blouse hung crumpled from her shoulders, only partially tucked into her wrinkled skirt.

"Not where you're concerned." He turned his back. Derringer or not, he wanted her even more than before. He was damned now for sure. Maybe he should have taken her anyway. But that was wrong and he knew it. Yet no rational thought touched his lust for her. She'd driven him out of control and he didn't like the feeling.

"Don't try to get my sympathy." She clasped the derringer with two hands, trying to stop the shaking in her body. She was wracked with so many con-flicting emotions that she could hardly think straight. But she knew one thing for sure and that was that she would never let Hunter touch her in anger. Desire. Passion. Lust. Maybe.

He walked out onto the balcony and took a deep breath. The peaceful quiet of the garden and the island were in sharp contrast to what was happening inside their suite. A sweet-smelling breeze cooled his body and he turned back. She still held the gun on him. He hated that. And had to change it.

Moving back into her bedroom, he held up his hands, as if in surrender. "You can put down the derringer. I won't touch you." He sat down.

"I'd like you to leave now." She held on to the gun, her voice unsteady.

He abruptly got up, went into his bedroom, and came back with two glasses of whiskey. "Here, drink this." He held out a glass to her.

"Set it down."

Tossing back his drink, he set hers on a nearby table, then he sat back in the chair. "I admit I was out of line, but you'd given every indication that you—"

"Kiss. That's all we'd done." She picked up the whiskey, but kept the derringer in her other hand. She took a quick sip and was grateful for the warmth.

"Deidre, I'm not going to hurt you. I was trying to prove to you that I didn't want Lady Caroline. It got out of hand." He didn't want to explain. If she hadn't been so young and innocent, she'd have understood. He got up and paced. He had no experience with young ladies fresh out of finishing school.

"I want you to go." She finished the whiskey, felt steadier, and set the glass aside. For the first time she realized her dishevelment and pulled her blouse together.

"Not till we settle this."

"It's settled. I can't trust you. You must hate me or something."

Anger overtook him. He whirled around and stalked back to her. Surprised, she glanced up but reacted too slowly to stop him from twisting the derringer out of her hand. He set it aside and put his arms around her.

She stood stiffly in the circle of his arms, refusing to look at him or struggle. How could she have let him take the gun so easily from her? Now nothing separated them.

"Please, Deidre, stop this. I've apologized. That's all I can do."

Suddenly all her emotions coalesced into anger and she hit his chest with one fist then the other and over and over until she abruptly stopped, breathing hard. She stepped back, realizing fully his physical power for her blows had had little effect on him. But they had released the tension in her. "It's not fair to use your strength against me." She met his eyes, then tossed her head and her golden mane flew about her face.

Reaching out, ever so slowly, he pushed her hair back, then traced the contours of her face with the tip of his finger. "How could you think I'd want anyone but you?"

She trembled under his touch, but didn't back away.

"To be fair, you can touch me. Anywhere and as much as you want. Practice your womanly wiles on me if you want." He smiled. "I don't think you'll get a better offer from a man." He tickled her under her chin. "Come on, I won't bite."

"I bet you do." Her green eyes had gone from hurt to angry to mischievous.

"Why don't you bite me?"

"Why should I?"

"You could think of me as a teacher. I'm a man who's offered you his body with no strings attached. You're bound to be curious."

"What makes you think I'm not experienced?" She pouted, pursing her lips as if to tease him, and realized he'd just offered her what she'd been considering all along.

He laughed. "I told you I've known some ladies and I'd bet everything I have that you're an innocent."

She hesitated, wondering how he had talked her around to no longer being angry or frightened. Instead he had her comtemplating using his body any way she wanted. Well, it would be a sort of revenge for the way he'd tried to use her. If she hadn't thrown her reticule on the bed and if her derringer hadn't been in it, she wondered how far he'd have gone and how long before she'd have succumbed to the heat of her own desire.

"Let's eat a piece of fruit."

"What! That's from Lady Caroline."

He walked away, then glanced over his shoulder as he selected an orange. "And who better than her to help end our argument?" He came back to her, chuckling.

She returned his smile, suddenly enjoying the irony of it all. Obviously she had overracted to Lady Caroline. Hunter probably was closer to the brother than the sister. "All right." She reached out to take the orange.

Holding it out of her reach, he gestured toward the bed. "Why don't you lie down and let me feed you?"

She backed away suspiciously. "Now Hunter—"

114

"You have my promise to stop at once anything you don't like." He tossed the orange in the air, then caught it.

Walking over to the bed, she sat down, then laid down. She didn't move.

He joined her. "Scoot over."

Grudgingly, she made room for him.

Sitting on the edge of the bed, he pulled a dagger out of his boot. He cut a small round hole in one end of the orange, wiped off the blade, then replaced the knife in his boot. He leaned over her. "Open your mouth."

She did, but watched him warily.

"Shut you eyes."

Frowning, she did.

When she felt the first trickle of sweet orange juice touch her lips, she realized he was squeezing the orange with his hand. Strong. Determined. Willful. She could hardly think of enough words to describe him. But she opened her eyes to warn him not to go too far.

"Close your eyes."

Again she did as he told her. More juice dribbled into her mouth, tickling her lips, tasting sweet and tangy, making her want more. But she raised her head, afraid of choking, and orange juice cascaded down her throat to her chest.

"Bad. I'll have to clean up your mess." He bent over and licked her lips, teasing them before he moved lower, following the line of juice to her breasts.

She caught her breath, aflame with the sensations he was causing within her. She could hardly believe this gentle, teasing, sensual man was the same one who had so roughly pushed her onto the bed before. She felt chilled as his warm lips and moist tongue toyed with the cleft of her breasts in his search for more orange juice.

He licked ever closer to the peak of each soft mound. With one hand, he enclosed a breast, then through the sheer silk gently stroked the nipple till it was taut. When he put his mouth to the tip of her breast, she moaned and shivered. Suddenly, unable to stand the tension he was building in her, she pushed him away and sat up.

He stayed close and watched her regain her composure. And, in truth, he needed the time, too. Keeping a rein on himself was proving hard to do, much harder than he'd imagined. But if it would get him what he wanted in the end, he could control himself no matter what.

"I—I think that's enough for tonight." She turned dark green eyes on him, searched his face, then fell back against the pillow. "I believe there may be much for you to teach me so that I can be a completely independent young woman."

"Is that so?" He grinned. "Then we ought to go on a maroon tomorrow."

"A what?"

"Maroon. It's a local custom. We won't actually be marooned. Instead of going on a picnic, native islanders go on a maroon. I'll rent a boat and we'll sail over to Hog Island. It's abandoned and not far away."

She sat up, excitement making her eyes shine. "What a lovely idea." She glanced around the room. "We'll be safe, won't we? I mean, no pirates or wreckers or—"

"We'll be safe."

She frowned. "We'll have to work first. At this rate I'll never find out about the shipwrecks."

"This is only your first day on the island. You've done plenty." He kissed the tip of her nose, tossed her the orange, then crossed to the door leading to his bedroom. "I'd wish you sweet dreams, but I'd rather you tossed and turned thinking of me."

She watched him walk into his bedroom, then close the door behind him. She pressed the orange to her lips, then walked over and picked up her derringer.

He wasn't a man to trust.

Chapter 8

Deidre wore a simple gray, professional suit with a white silk blouse as she walked up the steps to Nassau Public Library. She had gotten up early, dressed, and eaten breakfast in a restaurant on the Strand, managing to avoid Hunter. She'd wanted time alone to ponder the previous evening, but she'd already found she couldn't think straight about what she'd felt in his arms.

So instead of thinking about him, she'd decided to do some investigating on her own. She was more determined than ever to earn respect in her new role as investigator for Clarke Shipping. The weight of the derringer in her reticule matched the weight of responsibility on her shoulders.

She noted the unusual architecture of the library as she opened the front door. She'd learned it had originally been built and used as a prison around the turn of the century. She wondered if notorious pirates and privateers had once been chained inside. Laughing a little at her fancy, she stepped into the library. Not a pirate or chain in sight. Instead, books lined the walls.

She walked up the main desk. And smiled.

A slim woman with iron-gray hair pulled back in a tight chignon looked up at her over gold rimmed pince-nez. "May I help you?"

"I'm doing research on wrecking as a . . . social, political, and economic factor in the Bahamas. My name is Deidre . . . Jarmon." She hoped she sounded convincing and wished she'd considered her cover story in more depth beforehand.

The librarian smiled and stood up. "I'm Imogene Hatfield. It's delightful to meet you. You're obviously American and you must be from one of their women's colleges. What a wonderful opportunity for you. How exciting." She walked around the desk and shook Deidre's hand. "I would have loved that opportunity at your age, but my family was opposed to education for women. It's so difficult for a woman to extend her influence outside the home."

"But you've done well." Deidre glanced around at the library, hoping this woman could and would help her.

"I've done as well as I could. But come and sit down. This is a slow time for me and I have the chance to chat." She led Deidre to a group of chairs in a corner by large, open windows that overlooked a lush garden.

Deidre sat down in a horsehair wing chair.

Taking the chair next to her, Imogene smoothed

the skirt of her navy blue dress. "Would you care for tea?"

"No thank you. I've just had breakfast."

"Please forgive my impatience, but I have so little opportunity to talk with educated young ladies from America that I can hardly contain myself." She adjusted her pince-nez. "I know you've come here for information, after all this is a library, but first let me ask you about something vital to me."

Deidre nodded.

"What is the latest news on woman suffrage in America?"

"Are you a suffragist?"

"Yes, indeed."

Delighted, Deidre knew she'd met a kindred spirit. "So am I! And I'd like to know about the British suffrage movement. I'd planned to ask about it while I was in Nassau."

"What a happy coincidence we've met. I so seldom get firsthand news."

"I wish I could give you good news." Deidre hesitated, deciding where to begin. "American women have worked long and hard for suffrage."

"I know. So have we."

"They thought they'd finally be granted equality under the law in 1870 when the franchise was given to newly emancipated Negro men." Deidre shook her head. "Imagine, after working for years and years to help free the slaves and gain rights for everyone, women were denied suffrage although freed *male* slaves were given all rights."

"A terrible blow for women."

"You've probably heard this, but leaders of the movement have limited their struggle to getting the right to vote for women. Equality under the law has become a distant dream. For now."

"Do they anticipate achieving voting rights soon?"

Deidre shook her head. "No one knows. Ten years ago Senator Sargent of California introduced the Anthony Amendment, a woman suffrage measure named after Susan B. Anthony who wrote it."

"What happened?"

"As you can imagine, it didn't pass, but supporters continue to introduce it to each session of congress." She sighed, then quoted the amendment. "The right of citizens of the United States to vote shall not be denied or abridged by the United States or by any state on account of sex."

"So simple, so necessary for women, and yet so difficult to be made part of the law." Imogene grew quiet.

"But we must keep trying. For some of the women it may not happen in their lifetime, but that doesn't stop them from struggling for their daughters and granddaughters."

Imogene nodded. "I understand. I work for all women, too. Woman suffrage goes slowly in Britain as well. Did you know that when Jacob Bright presented a bill for woman suffrage in the House of Commons in 1870 we thought we were close?"

"And now?"

"Eighteen years have passed and we seem farther away from our goal than ever."

"I'm sorry." Deidre clasped Imogene's hand, squeezed, then leaned back in her chair. "But we mustn't ever give up hope."

"We won't." She took off her pince-nez and

rubbed the bridge of her nose. "The trouble now is the adverse reaction. You must be experiencing it in America, too. It follows every time women make the tiniest gain or call attention to their inequality under the law. You haven't lived long enough to see it repeat itself yet, but you will if we don't get suffrage soon."

"Is there anything we can do? I mean, more than we are now?"

Imogene leaned forward, her eyes intense. "Young women like you are our future, our inspiration. If we do not achieve our goals in our lifetime, at least we know the struggle will continue."

"Never fear. Women won't stop until they have equality by law. Anything less is wrong."

Imogene sighed. "And we will continue to pass the torch."

"To sisterhood." Dedire felt tears sting her eyes.

Imogene raised an imaginary glass and they saluted each other. "But I should ask you about why you sought out our library. I know you've come here for more than conversation. How may I help you?"

Dedire hesitated, wanting to continue their discussion but knowing her time was limited. Above all, she wished she were the college student Imogene Hatfield thought her to be. She wished as well that she could be completely truthful. But that wasn't possible, not with so much at stake.

Clearing her throat, she adjusted her thoughts. "If you could recommend any books about wreckers, they would be most useful. But what I'd really like to learn about are recent incidents." She took a deep breath to steady her voice. "In fact, I've heard that several large ships have gone down in this area in the last six months."

Imogene glanced around, then focused on Deidre. She nodded. "True. And you aren't the only one who's asked. A man who questioned locals about those ships disappeared. I'm going to warn you to be careful. You might be better off to confine your research to the past."

"But it would be so much more relevant to show the connection of the Bahamas with the United States from past to present."

Imogene nodded, thought a moment, then leaned forward. "I can understand your quest for knowledge. I have a similar desire. Wreckers have always been a part of the Bahamas. They have done good by saving people and goods, but there is a darker side to them, too, such as former pirates and privateers. Now not so many ships are lost here and that's why it was a surprise when four ships of Clarke Shipping from New York suddenly perished."

"Do you know any more about those?"

"Accidents happen." Imogene glanced around again. "But lights can be placed in dangerous areas or extinguished during a storm. The results could be a shipwreck."

"But the investigations?"

She shook her head negatively. "You're talking about the Bahamas. And you're talking about wreckers who protect their own. Of course, the shipwrecks were investigated, but during a storm who knows what might happen?"

Deidre nodded, feeling the information she desperately needed slipping away. "But if this did happen, and perhaps it didn't, wouldn't it require a great deal of planning, a number of people to rescue the merchandise and the crew and the passengers on the ships?"

"I've heard most of the crew and passengers survived, but during a storm how can they be sure what happened either?"

"Is there someone I could talk to about this? I wouldn't use their name in my research, but it's a fascinating study on the misfortune of one being the fortune of another. I'd like to talk with an actual wrecker."

Imogene smiled sadly. "Fortune and misfortune. That is very much the story of the Bahamas from the native islanders worked to death as slaves by the early Spanish up until the present day."

"But do you know the name of a wrecker?"

The front door opened and a slim man of medium height dressed in a white suit walked inside the library. He had receding grayish-blond hair and a gentle expression on his handsome face. He glanced around, saw Imogene, and started toward her.

Imogene stood up, then leaned toward Deidre. "I warn you again to be careful. If you persist in your search, you might try Captain Sully." She straightened and smiled. "I'll set out some books for you if you care to study them later."

Deidre stood, watching the librarian hurry over to the man.

"Good morning, Mr. Graves. How are you?"

"I'm fine, Miss Imogene. I wanted to know if that new shipment of books we ordered had arrived."

"No, I'm afraid not." Imogene frowned. "But surely it will be here soon. In the meantime, I have another list of books to order I would like you to check."

Deidre watched Mr. Graves, wondering if he could be the brother of Lady Caroline. How many of the Graves' family still lived on New Providence Island? She wished she could ask this man, but knew it wasn't the right thing to do. As she walked by them, she nodded, taking the opportunity to study Mr. Graves just as he studied her. His face held a puzzled expression as if he'd seen her some place before but couldn't remember when or where.

As she reached the door Imogene called to her. "If you're interested, a few of the local ladies have a suffrage meeting on Sunday afternoons at two o'clock here in the library. You're welcome to join us."

Deidre whirled around. "I'd love to attend. Thanks for inviting me. If I'm still on the island, expect me then."

"We'll look for you." Imogene smiled, then turned back to her list.

As Deidre stepped into the late morning sunlight, she felt pleased with herself. Not only had she gotten information, but she'd met a suffragist as well. Her day was going well. Encouraged, she hailed a carriage and asked to be taken to Smuggler's Den. After giving her a surprised look, the driver headed down the Strand.

She enjoyed the ride, watching the ocean, the buildings, the people. The slow pace of Nassau reminded her more of New Orleans than of New York City. But nothing she'd ever seen before could compare to the turquoise waters and white sands of the Caribbean Sea.

By daylight Smuggler's Den looked even more disreputable than the night before. But it was open. She paid the driver, got out of the carriage, and walked over to the building. The scent of sea, sand, and wood filled the air. Wooden planks creaked beneath her feet as she crossed the front porch. And stopped.

Now or never. She took a deep breath, pulled open the front door, and stepped inside. A few men sat slumped over barrels, holding onto glasses of whiskey or beer. They looked as if they had been there all night and might be there all day.

Another barmaid had replaced the one from the night before. When she saw Deidre she hurried over. "Miss, are you in the right place?"

"Yes, thank you. I'd like a table by a window and I'd like to speak with Old Nate, if she's here."

"Sure she's here. She's always here. At her age she don't sleep much and she's got a cot in back for when she does."

As the barmaid led Deidre across the room, she glanced back. "What'd you want to drink?"

"Brandy."

"Whiskey close enough?"

"Yes."

Deidre sat down at a barrel and looked out the window at the shimmering ocean as it lapped against the beach. She hated to admit it, but she'd been more comfortable with Hunter at her side the night before. She didn't like the way the male customers were watching her, but she simply raised her chin and patted the derringer in her reticule.

She didn't have to wait long. Soon Old Nate came out of the back room. She picked up a tray with two whiskeys and carried it over. Setting down the drinks, she fixed Deidre with a hard stare.

"Where's your man?" Old Nate's voice was low and husky but firm.

"I came alone. And he's not my man." She hesitated, trying to think of some excuse for being with Hunter. "We're simply working together."

Old Nate nodded, picking up her whiskey. "Why'd you want to see me?"

"I'm researching wrecking in the Bahamas. For a college project."

Old Nate frowned. "Do you value your life?"

"Yes, of course."

"Then you'd better stop asking questions right now. Wrecking has been the business of the Bahamas for as long as anybody remembers. It's not now what it was, but you don't want to go stirring up those waters."

"If it's because I'm a woman, you needn't fear for me. I can take care of myself."

Old Nate laughed loud and long. "You and how many like you? College? And are you a suffragist, too?"

"Yes. I thought you might be one, but—"

"I don't have time for education or voting or answering silly questions. I've been working since I could walk. I can read a little and write my name. My Momma, bless her soul, made me learn before she died. But I can tell you straight out book-learning and voting won't help a woman survive on the seas. Experience. And toughness. That's what everybody, man or woman, respects. And it'll keep you from going hungry."

Deidre couldn't think of a good reply, so she remained silent, digesting what she'd heard.

Old Nate tossed back her whiskey. "But you wouldn't know nothing about working hard, would you?" She snorted. "Go ahead with your fancy education and fancy suffrage rights, but remember it takes something else for most women to make it."

"I didn't mean to offend you. I admire what you've done with your life."

Old Nate put her hand on the barrel and leaned toward Deidre. "Let me give you another warning. You're not tough enough to stand alone. Go back to where you came from and leave the islanders to their lives."

Suddenly angry, Deidre swallowed her drink, choked, restrained the cough, and felt the liquor burn all the way to her stomach. It gave her courage. She stood and glared down at Old Nate. "I'm trying to help my family and I'll do whatever it takes to get some answers around here. As far as women go, I know getting the vote won't solve all our problems but it's the least we ought to have when it comes to the law."

Old Nate chuckled. "Maybe you've got more spunk that I thought. What's this about your family?" She sat down and motioned for the barmaid to bring two more drinks.

When Deidre was settled before another whiskey, she gave Old Nate a hard stare. "My mother inherited Clarke Shipping and I had to promise to bring

Hunter as a babysitter to get to come down here and investigate those shipwrecks at all."

"Babysitter? I'd have pegged him as a hell of a man. And, believe me, at my age I know the difference. Get what you can from him while you can."

"He's not my main concern right now."

"You smell of money, so why'd you put yourself in danger?"

"My parents didn't want me to, but I'm determined to prove myself a responsible and independent young woman."

Old Nate nodded.

"Four Clarke ships went down around here in the last six months. I don't believe it's a coincidence. I want to find out who's behind these wrecks, if anyone is."

"A man disappeared asking too many questions." Old Nate looked toward the back door.

"I know." Deidre sipped her whiskey, disliking the taste but needing the warmth. "But that's not going to stop me."

"You'd better be careful where you ask your questions. Sailors start coming in here around noon and nothing says which one's a wrecker. In the Bahamas nobody talks about wrecking with strangers if they want to stay healthy."

"If you'll help me, I won't ask anyone else."

"You've got courage. I like that. But you don't know what you're getting into." Old Nate sipped her drink. "First off, nobody knows for sure if those wrecks were accidents or not. Somebody made money off them and we're all better off not knowing that person's name."

"Captain Sully?"

Old Nate's mouth set in a grim line. "Where'd you hear of him?"

"It doesn't matter. But I thought I'd look him up."

"Stay clear of Sully. You find him and it'll probably be the last thing you do."

"I can take care of myself."

"You're a fool if you go after Sully. You don't know enough to be afraid."

"But I must prove myself."

"And you must get the right to vote." Old Nate drummed her fingertips on top of the barrel. "A person has a right to their own mistakes. It's the best way to learn. And if women get the right to vote in my lifetime, I'll be first in line to cast my ballot. But I've got to live to do it. And so do you."

"If you're interested, there's a woman suffrage meeting at the library at two o'clock on Sunday. I'm sure Imogene Hatfield and her friends would be glad to have you there."

"Me with those fancy ladies?" Old Nate snorted.

"That's what suffrage is about. It's for all women of all ages, of all colors, of all religions."

"This dog's too old to learn new tricks."

"I'm planning on attending the meeting, would you go with me?"

Looking her up and down, Old Nate grinned, revealing a full set of teeth. "I just might take you up on the offer. It'd sure set those ladies on their ears."

"Please come with me. I know they'd be glad to see you."

"Hell. Come to think of it, why shouldn't I vote? I've done about everything else in my life."

"You *should* vote. All women should." Deidre hesitated, excited about getting another woman to join the movement. "It's settled then. I'll come by for you Sunday afternoon."

"You may just have enough smarts and spunk to make it."

"And I always carry a derringer."

Laughing, Old Nate sobered. "You come by on Sunday and maybe I'll go, maybe I won't. But right now I'll give you some more advice for free. Stay away from Captain Sully. Don't go trying to find him around here, not now, not later. Don't tell anybody else in the Bahamas who you are. And get your man in bed and keep him there." She stood up. "Life's a lot shorter than you think at your age and when you get to the end you'll want to look back on the pleasure you've had."

Deidre stood again. "And the success."

Old Nate gave her a sloppy salute. "You're my kind of woman. I hope you live long enough to enjoy your life and your success."

Deidre watched her walk into the back room and shut the door. She had expected more help, not more warnings. Tossing some money down on the barrel, she walked outside. The day no longer seemed as bright and shiny.

But maybe she'd get Old Nate to attend the suffrage meeting on Sunday. That was something.

Chapter 9

Restless, not knowing where to turn next, Deidre walked around to the back of Smuggler's Den. Turquoise water lapped against white sand. A few small boats were moored there. She watched the ocean, thinking. In the Bahamas nobody knew anything, or so they wanted her to believe. She was an outsider and even confessing the truth of her mission to Old Nate hadn't helped get information.

Still she had one name. Captain Sully. But how did she go about finding a sea captain?

On second thought, maybe Old Nate had told her without meaning to do it. She'd said sailors started arriving around noon, but not to question them. Did she mean Captain Sully was a regular customer? And if he were, that might mean he'd be getting here soon. No wonder Old Nate had wanted her gone.

Excited, she looked out to sea, scanning the horizon. She could see several boats heading inland. Anticipation made her heart beat faster.

From the left near the shoreline came the sound of men's voices calling to each other, joking and laughing. Soon a small dinghy sailed up. Three men got out, pulled their boat to shore, and noticed Deidre. Silence descended as they strutted up to the back porch, watching her all the while.

Absorbed in her own thoughts and concerns, she didn't realize how out of place she looked. But she wasn't paying much attention to those men anyway. They didn't interest her since they'd come from the island. She was waiting for people to sail in from the sea. That's where she expected Captain Sully to be.

One of the men stopped beside her, pushed his cap back from his tanned face, revealing a bald head, and leaned close. "Looking for a man to buy you a drink, sugar?"

The stench of whiskey-soaked breath reached her at the same time as the words. He was about her height but there the resemblance ended for he was stocky, muscular, with sleeves rolled back to reveal brawny, scarred, tattooed forearms. Although she wanted to step back, even run away, she held her ground and tried to ignore him.

"What's a fancy girl like you doing here? Your man up and leave you?" He grinned, revealing two gold front teeth. "If that's true, I'll take his place." He put his hands on his hips and glanced at his friends to confirm his cleverness. They joined his laughter.

She realized they weren't going to go away without getting some type of response from her. "I've been visiting with Old Nate."

The men laughed all the harder.

"Old Nate!" The man in front of her leaned even closer. "And I've never sailed the sea."

"It's none of your business anyway." She was tired of their laughter, tired of everyone discounting her.

"Listen, little lady, everything on this island is my business. And now you are, too." He took her arm. "Come on inside and I'll buy you a drink. All this talking's made me thirsty."

Deidre pulled back and tried to jerk her arm away.

He grasped harder, digging his fingers into her soft flesh. "Around here, people do what I want or wish they had. Understand?"

"Let me go!" She raised her reticule to get her derringer. But he jerked her against him, causing her to lose her grip on the drawstrings. She barely held onto the bag. That scared her. She pushed against him, hating the feel of his hard body.

"Does the little lady want to play?" He laughed, and his friends joined his mirth.

"No!" Although she continued to struggle, he held her against the length of him. The heat and stench of him were almost unbearable and she'd never seen such cold, lifeless eyes. She'd use the derringer if she could get to it, but if she wounded or killed this man, what might his friends do?

"That's right, sugar, heat up for me."

"Leave me alone or I'll kick and scream." She wasn't nearly as helpless as he seemed to think.

"Nobody tells Captain Sully what to do! Right, men?"

Deidre vaguely heard the others agree, for she was focused on the amazing fact that she had found Captain Sully. Or, rather, he had found her. Sometimes life was easy. But she also suddenly understood Old Nate's warning. This man was dangerous. But so was she. And, no matter what, she had to get information from him.

She forced her body to relax and tried to look sultry. "It seems we have something in common. Neither of us likes to be told what to do."

He immediately recognized the change in her body and the tone of her voice. Grinning, he flashed his gold teeth. "I like a fiery woman. And quality, too. You ready for that drink now?"

Glancing at the other men, she looked back at him. And pouted. "I'd rather drink with you alone."

He seemed mesmerized by her lips for a moment, then shook his head. Slipping an arm around her waist, he held her to him possessively. "You don't waste any time, do you?"

Trying not to gag on his stench or his touch, she forced her body to remain pliant. "Life's too short. Don't you agree, Captain Sully?"

"So you've heard of me."

She tried to look impressed, maybe a little in awe, and glanced up at him coyly through her eyelashes. Amazingly, it had the desired effect for he hugged her tighter.

"Men, get me a bottle of whiskey from Old Nate. I'm taking this one with me. I know a cove not far from here. That sound good to you, sugar?"

Deidre couldn't keep from shivering with alarm. She didn't dare go that far alone with this man, but how did she keep his interest and get her answers safely on dry land? She glanced at his boat, then back at him. "You're going to think this is really silly of me, but I'm terrified of small boats."

"You don't have to be afraid of nothing with me around." He rubbed a hand up and down her arm.

She heard the fabric of her jacket catch against his callused skin and stifled a sigh. After this, she'd probably have to throw out the new suit and blouse. But how could she bear to wear it again after his touch? She knew her mind was wandering to avoid dealing with her dangerous situation and it wasn't smart. But she didn't have an answer for him.

"Ain't that right, sugar?"

"Brave. You are *so* brave to go out on that great big wide ocean in a tiny little boat. But I just can't do it. Please don't ask. The thought almost makes me cry with fear."

He cleared his throat in confusion. "Don't cry." He patted her arm.

"You don't think less of me, do you? It's my only fear, I promise." She looked at the back door of Smuggler's Den, then back at him. "Perhaps it would be best to go inside and talk awhile. We could make plans. Alone."

He grinned, stopped patting her arm, and pressed his mouth to her ear. "Don't worry no more. I can take care of you any which way you want. Everybody in the islands knows Captain Sully treats a woman right."

"Oh, you are such a man." As she muttered the words she heard boots strike the back porch. But whoever had arrived had come from the Strand, not the sea. Not knowing if she were in for some new danger she glanced up, and gasped.

136

"Deidre, what the hell are you doing here?" Hunter jerked her away from the sailor, his eyes black with fury.

She felt her face flush with embarrassment and anger. Pulling away from Hunter, she stood between him and Captain Sully. Hunter *would* show up just when she'd found the man who might tell her all she needed to know. She tried to ignore him, hoping she could recapture the moment.

But Hunter had no intention of being ignored and it was a moment he'd like to forget forever. He glared. "You'd better stay away from my woman or I'll—"

Captain Sully drew a knife from his boot in one smooth motion. "Who's woman, stranger?"

"Mine. She came to this island with me and she's leaving with me."

Sully flipped the knife back and forth between his hands. "She came looking for a man." He spit. "And she found one."

"Deidre, go back to the hotel." Hunter stepped toward Captain Sully.

Furious and afraid, she clenched her fists. "Go ahead and fight, but it won't do you any good. Right now I don't want any man and when I do I'll decide which one."

When they ignored her, concentrating on each other, her fear overcame her anger. Was Hunter unarmed? Captain Sully had a wicked-looking knife. She couldn't take any chances with Hunter's life, or Captain Sully's either until she got her information from him. She didn't want the kind of attention a fight would bring to them all. And what if Sully's two friends decided to join the fray? Men!

She felt the weight of her derringer in her reticule, but knew it would do little good in a group. She'd tried to make them listen to reason, but they'd not responded to her. At this point she needed help, and she knew where to get it. Opening the back door of Smuggler's Den, she hurried inside.

"Old Nate!" She rushed across the uneven plank floor to the long bar in back. "Captain Sully and Hunter are about to fight."

Old Nate dropped the cloth she'd been using to wipe down the bar and gave Deidre a hard stare. "You couldn't let well enough alone, could you?"

"I thought Hunter was at the hotel."

"You should've stayed away from Sully. But that don't matter now. Nobody's busting up my place." She picked up a shotgun from behind the bar and strode quickly to the back door.

Deidre followed, amazed at how well the older woman was handling the shotgun with one hand. How rough would she get? "Please don't hurt them."

Old Nate didn't reply. Instead, she pushed open the door and leveled her shotgun at the four men standing on her back porch. "Sully, you know better than to cause trouble around here."

Captain Sully frowned. "He started it."

"Where's Deidre?" Hunter glared suspiciously at Old Nate.

"She's inside." Old Nate stepped onto the porch, but held the gun steady. "You men want to fight over a woman, okay. But not around here. My place's been torn up one time too many."

"Those old barrels? I'll buy you new ones." Captain Sully pulled his cap down tight.

"I said nobody was fighting on my property." Old Nate backed up the gun with her voice.

It looked like the older woman had the situation under control so Deidre stepped out. "Now will you pigheaded men listen to reason? Old Nate won't have her place torn up and I won't be fought over like a scrap of meat."

Captain Sully chuckled, flicked his knife back and forth once more, but never took his eyes from Hunter. "You're more'an a scrap of meat, sugar. You're the whole damn hog."

"Thank you so much. I feel better now." Deidre's voice dripped with scarasm as she moved cautiously along the porch, keeping her back to the wall. "Now, Captain Sully, if you'll tell me where you receive messages I may contact you later."

He grinned. "Right here, sugar."

"I've never taken your messages and I'm not starting now." Old Nate threw him a furious glance.

"Don't pay her no nevermind." Captain Sully revealed his gold teeth again. "You want to see me, tell Lottie. She works here most evenings." He scowled at Hunter. "And you, mister, better stay out of my way or you'll end up feeding the fishes."

"The lady's mine." Hunter grasped Deidre's arm. "You better remember that."

Captain Sully stepped forward, ready to get Deidre away from his rival.

"Hold it right there, Sully, or you'll be feeding the fishes yourself." Old Nate cocked the hammer on her shotgun.

"Don't make me mad, old woman." But Sully stopped.

"I told you. I will not be fought over." Deidre

jerked away from Hunter, threw an apologetic glance at Old Nate, then hurried around the side of Smuggler's Den. She'd finally realized that if she were gone there would be no reason for the men to fight. And she didn't want anybody hurt. Besides, she was so furious she couldn't stand the sight of them anyway.

When she reached the Strand, she was lucky to find a carriage for hire. She quickly stepped up to it. As the coach pulled away, she settled back against the soft seat, feeling her emotions seethe in frustration.

Suddenly Hunter jumped into the moving carriage and sat down beside her. "What the hell do you think you've been doing?"

Shocked to see him, she quickly covered her dismay by returning his attack. "What I've been doing is none of your concern." She tossed her head, trying to slow the racing of her heart. She was glad to see him safe, despite her anger. Still, if he hadn't interfered, she might have all her answers by now. All in all, she was mad, worried, upset, and disappointed. At this rate, she'd never get any information.

"How can you say that after last night? Or after your parents hired me?"

"Easy! I can say it easy."

"You almost got us killed again." He held a tight grip on his emotions. He was so mad he wanted to shake some sense into her just like he'd wanted to draw his knife and finish Sully. But he'd restrained himself. It wouldn't have been smart to call that kind of attention down on them. But he'd have felt a whole lot better now if he'd at least busted Sully with his fists.

"I did not." She refused to look at him. "For your information, I was following an important lead. You ruined my plans."

"If your plans were to get that man's hands all over you, then you damn well succeeded."

Jerking her head around, she frowned at him. "You don't have the slightest idea what you're talking about."

"No?" He grasped her shoulders and shook her. "When I find you at a waterfront dive, a dirty stranger's hands on you, with two more sailors looking on, just what the hell do you think is going on?"

"Obviously not what you thought."

He pushed her back from him in disgust. "Deidre, I've said it before and I'll say it again, you're so green you're dangerous."

"And I'm sick of hearing that. I was taking care of myself. And when you interrupted, I got Old Nate. *I* did that." She punched her chest with a finger. "Me. Stupid, green, little me stopped that fight without anyone getting hurt. I doubt if you could have done so well." She inhaled sharply, some of the tension, some of the anger melting out of her. She was right. She *had* done well.

Hunter clamped his lips shut, watched the people on the streets, then turned toward her. "You scared about ten years off my life. A man like Sully has got no respect for a woman, *any woman*. What if I hadn't gotten there in time?"

"I told you. I had it all under control. You worried and interfered for nothing."

He pushed long fingers through his hair. "You won't listen to reason, will you?"

"I will listen to how to get information to stop Clarke ships from going down. That is all I'm interested in and you know it."

"After last night, I thought—"

"I don't want to talk about that either." She moved as far away as she could get from him.

"We had plans to go out to Hog Island. That's how you slipped away from me. I was getting everything ordered and organized. You made me feel like a real fool."

"Well, that makes two of us. Can you imagine how I felt when you came busting into a delicate situation that I had carefully set up?"

"Deidre, I don't want to hear about you and Captain Sully. You are never to talk to that man again. Do you understand?" He stopped, shook his head, and glared at her. "What the hell did you want him for anyway?"

"Oh no, you said you never wanted to hear about him again. My lips are sealed."

Suddenly he chuckled, a husky sound deep in his throat. "But I know how to unlock them." He leaned toward her.

She held out her hands to push him back, suddenly breathless as feelings from the night before cascaded through her. "Forget it. I have more important matters on my mind today."

Chuckling again, he lifted her hand to his lips and kissed each fingertip.

Shivering, she jerked her hand away. "Don't think you can get around me with this type of behavior."

"What about our maroon?"

"I don't have time now." But she couldn't keep traitorous thoughts from lingering on the image of the two of them on a tiny island. Alone.

"Everything's ready. All we have to do is change at the hotel." He leaned close, his breath warm against her cheek. "You wouldn't want to waste the picnic lunch, would you?"

"I don't know how you can expect me to go with you after all the trouble you've caused me today."

He leaned back, grinning because he'd seen the desire in her eyes. He'd take her on the picnic, but he wasn't done with Captain Sully. Not by a long shot. "I was trying to keep you from harm, Deidre. That's my job."

She hesitated, wanting to go with him but not wanting to appear weak. "You're right. That's what my parents are paying you for, isn't it?"

"Yes. And I thought we were in this together. Why did you leave without me?"

"I wanted to prove I could learn something on my own."

He clasped her hand, pushing his fingers between hers and holding on tight. "That's why I went to Old Nate's first. I knew you'd want to question her some more. Did she put you on to Sully?"

"She warned me away from him."

"I'm glad to hear that." He squeezed her hand. "Let me deal with him."

"But—"

He put a fingertip to her lips. "I've got some information, too. Why don't we go on the maroon. We can picnic and share what we've learned at the same time. Okay?"

Exhaling sharply, she looked down at their hands entwined and felt a deep, hot yearning inside her. She found it hard to resist this man and right now she didn't want to any longer. "All right."

He smiled, pleased he'd won the battle. But the war was far from over. He'd never lost one yet, but he'd never come up against a woman like Deidre either. Suddenly he wondered if she'd turned the tables on him from the start. Had she already won the war and now simply tossed battles to him as sops to his ego? He didn't like the thought, but once he hadn't liked spoiled little rich girls either.

Yet Deidre refused to fit that mold or any other. She didn't know it, but she was already as much her own woman as the image she struggled to become. That scared him. Could an independent young woman, a suffragist, ever share her heart, her life with a man? Or was she simply a wild wind blowing through his life on its way somewhere else?

If she was, he determined to be the flame that ignited them both into the fiery heat of passion.

Chapter 10

Hunter guided a small sloop out of Nassau harbor. Deidre sat near the picnic basket, watching as they glided between New Providence Island and Hog Island. He headed toward the lighthouse on the western finger of Hog Island, for he knew the perfect secluded beach where he wanted to take her.

Although he was more at ease on horseback, he relished controlling the sailboat through the beautiful Bahamian waters. He cut in between Long Cay and the western tip of Hog Island, giving Deidre a close view of the lighthouse.

He pointed toward the impressive structure. "Its cornerstone was laid in 1816 when it was built from limestone quarried nearby."

Deidre nodded, wondering if this were the lighthouse that had failed to warn Clarke ships. "The water's so calm I can't imagine the area ever being dangerous."

Hunter chuckled. "The islanders will tell you different. They still talk about the hurricane of 1866 when sixty-foot waves surged across Nassau Harbor. They crested level with the lighthouse's gallery."

"No matter what they say it's still hard to believe." But she could now understand better how any ship caught in a storm of that magnitude would be in trouble. Is that what had happened to Clarke ships?

But with no answer to the question, she turned her mind back to the beauty of the day. A brilliant blue sky was broken only by a few wispy clouds here and there. Sunlight sparkled over the sea. Now and again a fish broke the surface of the water before disappearing into the depths again. Seagulls called as they circled overhead.

Paradise. The island should be called Paradise Island, not Hog Island. Here she could easily imagine all her troubles gone. Only happiness and pleasure could exist in such a rarified atmosphere as this.

Her thoughts turned to Hunter. She watched him handle the boat, his muscles straining against the black shirt he wore, the hard curve of his thighs outlined by his trousers. Once more she felt a deep stirring within her. Hunter. He made her want him without doing anything. His presence alone sparked her desire and when he turned his attention to her she knew she would find it difficult to resist anything he suggested.

But did she want to resist? No. Should she resist? Yes. She had no business getting involved with a man while she was on such an important undertaking and especially with a man so unsuited to her. But passion continued to override reason. She could rationalize her desire by wanting to experience all an independent young woman should know in order to succeed in the world. Yet she knew her attraction to Hunter went well beyond that.

Taking off her new straw hat, bought from a native higgler before they sailed, she fanned her face, knowing the heat she felt came from within rather than from the warmth of the day. *Hunter.* Perhaps she wouldn't wait for him to turn to her. He had promised to teach her anything she wanted to know, to let her touch him without returning the gesture. But she knew, had known for too long, that she wanted him to touch her, to further spark the desire within her.

Shivering, knowing her thoughts would only bring trouble akin to a hurricane, she forced her mind back to the beauty of the day. Yet she knew the peace of the moment allowed her too much time to think of pleasure.

As he navigated the western tip of Hog Island, Hunter pointed toward a strip of white sand bordered by tall, feathery casuarina trees on the northwestern edge of the island. "We're heading toward that beach up ahead."

"It's lovely." Deidre felt excitement build inside her as she watched the island and thought of the isolation and seclusion of the beach. As they sailed, she looked over the island, realizing it was long, narrow, and flat. Trees and other native growth obscured the interior, but she imagined it was much the same.

Finally, he headed the boat inward, letting the wind catch the sails to glide them to shore. He took off his shoes, rolled up his trouser legs, and slipped over the side. Standing in clear, turquoise water to midcalf, he pulled the sloop onto shore. When it was steady, he turned to her, a gleam in his dark eyes. He held out his arms.

She knew he meant to lift her to the soft sands, but a perversity filled her. She handed him the picnic basket, then stepped down by herself. Once on firm ground, she glanced up at him.

"You can't let anybody do anything for you, can you?" He frowned.

Suddenly she felt childish and slightly ashamed. She'd intentionally ruined the mood, the moment, and wasn't sure why. "When I need help, I'll ask for it."

Shaking his head, he turned away and walked up the beach toward the base of the trees. When he was in the shade, he looked back.

Shimmering in sunlight, Deidre stood still on the white beach and looked out to sea. She took off her hat, pulled the pins from her hair, and shook out the long tresses. Sunlight struck her hair, turning it gold.

His breath caught in his throat and he clenched his fists to stop himself from going to her and burying his face in her hair. If he did, would she reject him again? Sudden anger coursed through him. He'd had enough of tiptoeing around her, trying to please her. She'd become more than a job, more than a punishment to other women. She was trouble, but he'd known she would be from the first moment he'd seen her.

He cursed silently. With nowhere to vent his anger, he dropped the picnic basket. He quickly unbuttoned his shirt, pulled it off, and tossed it to the ground. Barefoot, wearing nothing but black trousers, he walked away from Deidre and all he'd planned. At the water's edge, he unbuttoned his trousers, dropped them to his ankles, then kicked them aside. Naked, he splashed into the cool depths, glad of a way to wash her from his mind.

Shocked, she watched him swim out to sea. Not knowing what to do or think, she looked at his trousers, at his shirt, at the picnic basket, then shook her head. Was this a game? A dare? A gamble?

He had shown her his body. Nude. Or at least the back of it. But that was enough, more than enough, to spark an even deeper desire in her than she had felt before. Why had he gone swimming? What about their maroon, the picnic? Was he so angry he didn't want to talk with her? Was he even coming back? She glanced uneasily at the sloop. She had no idea how to sail it. She hesitated. Or did he want her to join him?

She knew how to swim, but she didn't have the proper clothes. Today she'd dressed simply, coolly in a green print blouse and a dark green skirt. Suddenly she felt much too warm. And brazen. She began unbuttoning her blouse. She hoped she wouldn't live to regret her decision, but she wasn't letting Hunter get away, whatever his plan. And she wanted to swim, too. Her fingers shook as she realized the enormity of what she was doing. But if she couldn't have the right to vote, she could at least have the right to swim nude in the ocean.

Fortunately she hadn't worn a corset. She quickly

took off her blouse, chemise, skirt, and petticoat. As she undressed, she noticed Hunter stop swimming and turn to watch her. She hesitated, then thought of Old Nate. The one-armed sailor would never be too shy to do or take what she wanted. And neither was Deidre Clarke-Jarmon. She slipped off her drawers and shoes.

Naked, she felt a cool breeze caress her skin as she walked rapidly, boldly across the beach into the water. It lapped invitingly against her ankles, her knees, her thighs, her waist, then she leaned into the water and swam toward Hunter. She felt afraid yet anxious to see the expression on his face.

She didn't have to swim far, for he came to her.

"Deidre." His brown eyes were molten chocolate as they searched her face. "You're beautiful."

Smiling, glad to know he was pleased, she nodded and swam right on past him. And laughed at his dismay. Suddenly mischievous, she felt freer than she ever had before in her life. No restrictions of family or society or of right and wrong, or of tight corsets and hot clothing were allowed in the Caribbean Sea. But most of all she felt free with Hunter. She turned to see him following her, his eyes worshipping her, making her feel capable of doing anything.

Laughing again, she threw back her head and looked at the azure blue sky. Was this what it was like to be an independent young woman? If it were, she never wanted to let it go. Turning, she splashed water at Hunter's face.

He roared with mock anger, then laughingly splashed water back at her as he swam closer.

She shook water from her face and moved away,

letting him chase her back toward land. But she was no match for his strength and soon he caught up with her. Yet he didn't touch her and suddenly she ached for his warmth, for his arms around her, for his lips on hers.

"Oh, Hunter." She knew the expression on her face, the desire in her eyes, spoke much more than words could ever reveal.

"Let's go back." He spoke in a husky, almost pain-filled voice, then struck out for shore, glancing back to make sure she followed.

She paced him, but when she saw him stop and stand in water reaching to his waist, she felt embarrassed to join him. Confused, she treaded water, keeping her body covered, although in the clear turquoise depths most of her was exposed.

Noticing her anxiety, he moved toward her and took her hand. He led her back with him until she dropped her feet to stand beside him, water cascading down her breasts to fall in sparkles to the sea. He looked at her, making no attempt to hide his fascination and appreciation of her nudity.

"You're beautiful, Deidre." He cleared his throat.

"So are you." For as he had looked at her, she had taken the opportunity to examine his chest, the sculptured muscles, the dark hair, the bronze skin. And in the depths of the water she could see the hazy outline of his erection.

He chuckled, reaching out to her. "I think that's supposed to be handsome." He held her face between his palms and leaned forward to brush his lips across her mouth. "I want you."

Tingles of pleasure and excitement raced through her body. She leaned toward him, touching his shoulders, then his chest, feeling the damp skin stretched over hard muscles. He followed her example and cupped her breasts, then ran thumbs over her nipples to feel the taut peaks.

They groaned together.

He pulled her against him and she felt the point of his desire slid between her legs, nestling there. He stroked her hair, pressed kisses to her face, then grasped her hips to pull her against him. His breath was hot on her sensitized flesh when he spoke. "Deidre, I can't take much more of this."

"Kiss me." She turned her face and captured his lips, driving her tongue deep into his mouth, tasting the saltiness of the sea and feeling the heat of his desire.

He groaned and returned the kiss with fevered movements of his tongue as he stroked her back, holding her steady to withstand the push of his body as he desperately tried to merge them without actually burying himself deep inside her. Feeling her hands caress him, her mouth on his, her body rubbing against him, made him wild with desire. He had to take her, release himself deep within her fevered body.

But, no. He'd promised her to restrain himself. He'd promised himself not to get involved. She'd teased him too many times before. And revenge seemed less important by the moment. It was now or never. He could stand no more. Breaking away, he dove into the water and swam out to sea.

Left alone, Deidre felt tears prick her eyes. How could he have had the strength to stop? She didn't know exactly what she wanted but she knew she'd not reached her fulfillment yet. She needed him, wanted him, but he'd left her. Still she'd pulled a gun on him the last time. And he'd promised to do only what she wanted. But she hadn't told him to stop. She hadn't wanted to stop.

Frustrated, more angry with herself than with him, she splashed water on her face to cool her fevered flesh. He was right. They had no business doing this, especially not here, not now. After all, anyone could sail by. She looked anxiously out to sea, but no boat was in sight. What was wrong with her? Had she no morality, no control? Again she felt like crying. She had always been so much in charge, the Ice Princess as he had named her. But no more. He had turned her into the Fiery Queen of Passion.

She walked toward shore, trying to still her emotions, trying to regain control, trying to forget the feel of his body against hers. But the image of him naked, of their bodies pressed together in the warm waters of the Bahamas was printed forever on her mind.

When she walked out of the sea she felt exposed, vulnerable, and quickly picked up her clothes and sought the shadows of the trees. Redressing, she watched Hunter swim back to shore. When he stepped from the water, she saw him completely nude and exposed to her. She gloried in his beauty, wanting to stop him as he pulled on his trousers, to ask him to come to her, to teach her all there was to know of love.

Love? How odd she should think that word. No, not love. Passion. Desire. What they felt wasn't love. It couldn't be love. They were too unsuited, too different. Simon was the man to love, despite the lack of physical passion. She must be mental, not emotional when she chose a man to love. Anything less was unsuitable to her goal in life.

Yet as Hunter walked toward her, she had to resist the urge to run to him and fling herself into his arms.

When he reached her, he smiled. "Clothes can't improve on the natural, Deidre."

She blushed, then returned his smile. "I agree."

Laughing, he picked up his shirt and put it on. "Let's get on with our maroon. Want some food?"

"Yes." She was glad to see him in good humor again and it affected her, making her happy, too. "I'm starved."

His eyes darkened. "So am I, but food'll have to do, I suppose."

Blushing again, she held out her hand. "Hunter, I—"

"Come on." He took her hand, then picked up the picnic basket. "Let's find a place under the trees."

Relieved not to have to explain what she wanted, she happily followed him. He selected a spot in the shade, spread a blanket, then sat down, holding out his arms to her. She sat down beside him and leaned into his strength. He hugged her close a moment, then sat back.

Growling with mock ferocity, he shook his head. "Better get out the food. I'm hungry enough to nibble on you."

She wished he would, then wished she hadn't thought that, then wished the day would never end.

He opened the basket, tossed a large napkin into

154

each of their laps, spread a cloth on the blanket, then set out the food. "Okay, let's see what they packed for our feast. It looks like salmon, corned beef, pickled oysters, cider, and Madeira."

"What! No fruit?"

He laughed. "You *are* a tease, aren't you?"

"Only with you."

"Good." He looked into the basket again. "As a matter of fact, we do have some fruit. But no oranges."

"Oh no. I'm devastated."

He chuckled. "There are some small sweet bananas in here I'll be happy to feed you."

"After the other night, it's the only way I'll eat now. Unless you're around at all my meals, I'll simply waste away to nothing." She turned teasing green eyes on him.

"I won't ever let either of us go hungry." Suddenly his dark eyes held no teasing light but rather a solemn intensity. He pressed his lips to hers in a quick but tender kiss, more promise than passion.

A little breathless, she looked at him in confusion, then turned away. "Is there any bread?"

He pulled out a crusty French loaf. "We have everything the lady could desire."

"You certainly do." And she laughed, amazed at her newfound audacity.

Joining her laughter, he nuzzled her ear. "At this rate, I don't know if we'll ever get any food in us."

She pouted. "Remember, you promised a picnic."

"So I did. Then let's get on with our feast so we can get on to more important matters."

"And what might those be?" She batted her eyelashes in mimicry of a Southern Belle.

"I hate to bring it up, but there's the matter of our job, our information to share."

"Oh, Hunter! How can we joke when so much is riding on what we learn?"

"We'll take care of that, too. Give us time. Okay?"

Nodding, she absentmindedly tore off a hunk of bread. She *must* remember to take care of business. She simply *must*. But it wasn't easy with Hunter around. Especially not when he took the piece of bread from her and held it to her lips. She took a small bite, then a larger one until she felt her teeth touch his finger. Teasingly, she nibbled his finger, then leaned against him, laughing at the sheer joy of being with him, of feeling free and beautiful and loved.

She stopped and sat back, chewing intently to cover her sudden change of mood. Why had she started relating everything they did to love? It was a ridiculous thing to do. Wasn't it enough for two people to enjoy each other's company without being in love? She and Simon had enjoyed many outings together and she'd never thought of love.

"Deidre?" Hunter's voice held concern.

She put a brave smile on her face, swallowed the bread, and reached for the salmon. "Now it's your turn."

He opened his mouth.

As she fed him, she realized it was a bad idea. She'd had no idea how sensual it could be or how trusting the other person had to be to allow you that closeness. She realized now how it must have affected him when he'd fed her the orange juice. She shivered, knowing they were rushing along a path that led them toward one conclusion. It wasn't love, of course, but passion. And she wasn't sure if it was the right thing to do.

But when he bit the tip of her finger, she realized she no longer cared about right or wrong. "You're bad." She shook a finger at him in mock sternness. "You won't get any more food if you don't—"

But she never finished her sentence for he pulled her against him and covered her mouth with his. When his tongue thrust deep inside, she moaned with pleasure, with relief, with rightness, and clung to him as she returned the kiss, wanting nothing more than him.

Finally, he lifted his head, looked deep into her eyes, and smiled a crooked movement of his sensual lips. "If we're going to do anything more than this, you'll have to move across the blanket from me. Even then, I don't know if it'll help."

"I'm not sure I want that kind of help."

Touching her wild mane of hair, he thought a moment. "I want you to be sure, Deidre. No questions, no doubts." He shook his head. "Move over there, will you?"

Pressing a hot, hard kiss to his lips, she sat back, frowned, then moved away from him. "You know you're fast losing control of this situation, don't you?"

He nodded.

"I don't think I'm going to be put off much longer."

"Spoken like a true independent young woman."

"Pass the pickled oysters." As their fingers met around the jar, she smiled. "Independent young women get what they want, eventually."

"Like the vote?"

"Exactly." Then she began eating, suddenly ravenous, for she realized how susceptible he was to her and it was a heady feeling indeed.

As they ate, they watched each other, the ocean, the swaying casuarina trees, the birds flitting around, darting in and out of the surf. And when they spoke, it was of inconsequential matters. They enjoyed the silence and peacefulness of the island, as well as the pleasure of being together.

Finally, Hunter stretched out, folded his arms behind his head, and shut his eyes.

Deidre watched him, thinking how they had suddenly come to trust each other. The realization surprised her, for it had happened so quickly and in the midst of so much else that she hadn't thought of it until just this moment. She hadn't considered them as friends before. Lovers, yes. Partners, yes. But friends? Somehow that involvement was scarier than the others because it spoke of a commitment that she was not at all sure she was ready or willing to give.

She sighed and laid down, too, craddling her head on the crook of her arm. She yawned, thinking that he was right. It was the perfect moment for a nap.

Awakening to something tickling her nose, she sat upright, pushing it away. Hunter held out a banana. She took it from him.

"Must I feed myself?"

"It may be the only safe thing to do." He grinned.

She unpeeled the banana, then slowly, sensually ate it, her eyes never leaving his face as she watched the expression of his frustrated desire. Mischievously, she reached for another.

"No. One's all I can stand."

Laughing, she dropped the banana. "All right. You get your way this once." She shook out her hair, then noticed the sun had lowered in the west and felt disappointed. Their day would come to an end after all.

He followed the direction of her gaze. "We'll have to start back soon. I wish we didn't have to, but we've both got a job to do."

"And we'd better get on with it. Right?"

"I've learned something about the Clarke ships I don't like."

"What?" She leaned toward him in anticipation.

"Wrecking is an old business in the Bahamas, but it's one that's slowly lost importance here due to iron and steel-hulled steamships and better navigation."

"I know."

He held up a hand. "I'm not accusing anybody out right, but I'm beginning to think those four Clarke ships went down to wreckers who set up lights in the wrong place during storms."

She exhaled sharply. "Just like I thought."

"It's one thing cleaning up after a storm and making money on wreckage, but it's another to cause a wreck and make money on it. People died!"

"It's horrible."

"You came up with the same name I did. Captain Sully."

"Do you think he's behind a gang of wreckers?"

"Maybe. But I've got no proof."

"Neither do I. And I've learned nothing more than you." She crumpled her napkin in frustration. "What can we do?"

"We'll keep asking questions. Somebody, some-where will talk. But Bill Brown, that investigator your parents sent, is dead if I don't miss my guess. I bet somebody shut him up and fast."

"We've got to be careful."

"That's why I don't want you going off on your own, or talking to Sully without me." He frowned. "I'll tell you true, if we find out somebody's wreck-ing ships I'll be the first one to stop them. And it won't be for pay."

She leaned over and squeezed his hand. "I'm glad to know you feel this strongly."

Holding her hand, he looked out to sea. "I'm learning there's more to life than money or re-venge."

"Is that what's driven you so far?"

Without responding, he started repacking the picnic basket.

"Hunter?"

He gave her a wary look.

"Thanks for the maroon."

"We can maroon anywhere we're together." He stood and pulled her to her feet. "Let's get back to Nassau."

Chapter 11

Sunset on the western horizon blazed red, orange, and magenta as Deidre and Hunter walked up to the Royal Victoria Hotel. A wind gusted around them, blowing dead leaves and dust in small spirals here and there. The scent of tropical flowers sweetened the air.

Hunter glanced up at the sky. "Looks like we might get a storm later. I'm glad we got in when we did."

Deidre followed his gaze, but didn't know enough about island weather to predict anything. She tucked her arm through his. "With you, I'm not worried."

"Neither of us is hurricane proof."

"I bet it'll just be a little rain to cool off the island. That'll be nice." She felt relaxed, happy, and content. Rain or not, she looked forward to dinner

161

with him at some exotic Nassau restaurant. But first she'd bathe and rest. Tomorrow would be soon enough to pick up the trail again.

Inside the hotel, Hunter left the picnic basket at the desk and turned to leave. But the clerk stopped him, thrusting out a cream-colored envelope.

Deidre felt suddenly apprehensive. The note looked similar to the one Lady Caroline had sent before.

Opening it, Hunter scanned the message, then looked at the clerk. "Is the Graves' carriage still here?"

"Yes, sir. The driver's been waiting all afternoon."

"I'll take care of it." Hunter grasped Deidre's elbow and led her to a private corner of the room. "Lady Caroline and her brother invited us to dinner tonight. She sent their carriage. She wants us to spend the night since we'll be staying late."

Deidre felt disappointed and excited at the same time. "Should we go?"

He hesitated, tapping the envelope against his palm. "You wanted to question them. I suppose there's no point in waiting." He looked at her in concern. "Are you too tired? I can send the driver back with a note explaining we returned late."

"I'm not that tired, but I'd looked forward to us spending the evening together."

"So had I." And his warm brown eyes let her know how much.

"But we're here on business and we shouldn't pass up the opportunity, should we?"

"It's up to you. But if you agree to go, you must

be careful. Whatever questions you ask mustn't be obvious. You know the danger we're in here."

"But not with people like these, surely."

"You never know who's listening."

She nodded. "Let's go tonight. But I expect your full attention while we're there."

"You always have my attention, but tonight you'll have to share it. Lady Caroline likes to be the center of any social event and we don't want to anger her."

"As hostess, too?"

"Yes. Wait till you meet her and you'll understand."

"All right, but I'm not going to like it."

"You can stand it for the sake of our investigation, can't you?"

"I suppose so. But I must have time to bathe and dress before we go."

"They'll wait. It'll do Lady Caroline good." He tucked the invitation inside his jacket. "As far as the weather, maybe the rain won't get here till tomorrow."

"I'm not worried about a little rain."

"A little rain's one thing. An island storm is another." He smiled. "Why don't you go on up to your room and I'll talk with the driver."

She nodded, then pursed her lips in a silent kiss before turning to walk up the stairs.

As Deidre and Hunter rode down the Strand toward Palmetto on New Graves Plantation, the moon glowed full in a darkened sky. The wind had died down, but the air held a heavy quality and the surf was high. A few wispy clouds scudded in front of the moon, partially obscuring its brightness with long fingers of darkness.

Hunter was little aware of the beauty of the night. His thoughts revolved around Deidre and Lady Caroline. Dinner at Palmetto wouldn't be a casual affair, despite the wording of the invitation. Deidre didn't know it, but he was leading her into a trap. Once there, could he stop it from snapping shut on her? More, should he try? His jobs had always come first in his life. He was known to be a man with few scruples and a hard hand. That's how he got work.

He'd vowed to stay away from rich, pampered ladies. He'd never let a lightskirt interfere with his life. Yet the more he was with Deidre the more he wanted to protect her and keep her safe. For himself.

He cursed silently, noticing the unrelenting pace of the carriage. He was acting the fool about Deidre and knew it. He'd better stop right now. He worked for Lady Caroline. Delivering Deidre Clarke-Jarmon into her hands would bring him gold and a woman who knew how to please a man. A smart man would take those and let the innocent young lady go.

So far he'd rustled Bar J cattle, cut fences, and caused problems around Jarmon's ranch. All at Lady Caroline's command. But he'd never hurt a woman, even if she was rich and spoiled. He didn't plan to do that now. He'd do his best to keep Deidre safe, but in the end he was Lady Caroline's hired help and that's where his loyalty had to rest.

He cursed silently again. Even reminding himself

of gold and revenge didn't make him feel better. He was worried about Deidre and nothing in his life had prepared him for the feelings she aroused in him. Now all he could do was remember the past and act like she meant nothing to him. She was a job, no more.

He looked at her. She'd dressed for him. He hadn't known it would touch him so much. And it made him angry. Why had she picked tonight to please him? He'd never wanted her more. But above all he had to keep Lady Caroline from realizing that fact. For tonight Deidre had to be the Ice Princess despite the way she looked. If he kept that in mind, he might make it through the night in one piece.

Deidre didn't notice him watching her. She felt consumed with disappointment and excitement. A moonlit drive with Hunter was wonderful, but it would soon end with a situation she wasn't sure how well she could handle. On the other hand, perhaps it was best not to spend so much time alone with him for he played havoc with her thoughts and emotions. And soon she must leave him.

But that wasn't a thought she liked. She glanced at him, vividly aware of his strong profile, his set lips. Suddenly she realized he was tense and that intensified her own worry. Yet she wouldn't let unnamed fears control her. She had a job to do and the Graves were part of solving the puzzle, she hoped.

Glancing from Hunter down at her hands, she stroked the soft silk shawl he had bought her on their first night in Nassau. The beauty of the design and the brightness of the color cheered her. She played with the fringe, running it through her fingers.

She'd dressed for him this night, no doubt about it. She wore only clothes he had bought for her.

Feeling sensual and decadent, she had on crimson silk underwear, black silk stockings, and a gown of crimson satin trimmed with black braid. It was in the latest style. The low-cut bodice set off the curve of her breasts and she wore a black satin ribbon around her neck with a simple ruby pin in its center. The skirt was pulled into an apron effect that became a small bustle in back, emphasizing her small waist.

If she had some trouble breathing in the tight corset, for once it seemed a small price to pay so she could compete with the legendary Lady Caroline.

She smiled to herself with chagrin. Her suffragist friends in New York City would hardly recognize her. In fact, with her styled blond hair and crimson clothes, she'd barely recognized herself in the mirror before she'd left to join Hunter. But his instant and obvious appreciation of her appearance had told her she'd made the right choice.

As the carriage turned down the road on New Graves Plantation, Hunter clasped her hand and squeezed. "You'll enjoy seeing the mansion. Lady Caroline brought china, silver, crystal, furniture, art, whatever back from England to add to her family's collection."

"I didn't think the plantations on New Providence did that well financially."

"As far as I know, they don't."

"Then—"

"Don't ask me where they get the money. Maybe from her late husband or investments."

"Wreckers?" She scarcely breathed the word as the thought suddenly struck her. She glanced at the driver to see if he'd heard, but he remained impassive.

Hunter stroked her fingers. "Don't let your imagination run wild. Soon you'll be seeing wreckers everywhere."

She didn't reply, for a chill had invaded her. Pulling the shawl more closely around her with one hand, she clung to Hunter with the other. And all the while her mind told her to be reasonable. A family like the Graves couldn't possibly be involved in wrecking.

When the carriage rolled to a stop in front of Palmetto, she had regained her composure. But she was determined to be more cautious, more aware than ever. If there were answers to be found here, she would get them.

Hunter helped her down, letting his hands linger around her waist longer than necessary. Leaning toward her, he smiled. "You're more beautiful than ever tonight."

"You selected my clothes so you have no choice but to say that."

"Clothes are nothing without the woman." He leaned closer still. "But I'd rather see you without them."

She blushed. "You're making me regret coming here when we could have been alone."

He tucked her hand into the crook of his arm. "I already regret it."

As he led her toward the mansion, Hunter noticed the driver move the carriage around the side of the house. Servants would carry their carpetbags inside and put them in bedrooms. He didn't like the idea of being separated from Deidre so at the least he'd have to watch her room. And he'd have to be careful to make no more suggestive comments. But seeing her in the red gown was like playing with fire and he wasn't sure how he was going to control his body.

Walking toward the mansion, Deidre couldn't help but be impressed by the beauty of the Colonial Georgian structure and the luxuriant grounds around it. Light glowed in the downstairs windows, a warm and cozy invitation. As they mounted the stairs, the massive front doors opened.

A petite woman stood silhouetted in the doorway. "Hunter, at last. Where have you been all day, you naughty boy? Hayward and I have been beside ourselves with worry and anger." Lady Caroline's husky voice teased, part charm, part challenge.

"Anger?" Hunter kept Deidre close to him as he moved up the stairs.

"Of course. If I thought you had anything more important in your life than me, you know I would be furious and devastated."

"I took Deidre on a maroon at Hog Island." He knew she teased, but he also knew there was truth in her words.

"Really? If I'd known, I'd have waited to send the invitation. After all, how could dinner at Palmetto compare with lunch on Hog Island?" Her voice dripped sarcasm.

"I'm a lucky man today." Hunter chuckled, a forced sound. "I get to do both." He reached the verandah. "Lady Caroline, I'd like you to meet Deidre Clarke-Jarmon."

"Delighted, I'm sure." Lady Caroline ignored Deidre to hold out her hand to Hunter.

As he took it, she leaned close, pressed herself against him, then stepped back. She smiled in satisfaction.

Hunter cleared his throat. "Deidre, this is Lady Caroline Graves St. John."

Enveloped in the scent of Lady Caroline's expensive French perfume, one she recognized but had never worn herself, Deidre felt fury run through her. Lady Caroline's boldness and arrogance with Hunter made her momentarily speechless. She clenched her fists to keep her anger and jealousy under control. And wondered, spitefully, what services the other woman had performed for the perfume.

"Please call me Lady Caroline. All my friends do. But do come inside. I'd like a better look at Hunter's young friend."

Put in that category, Deidre's fury rose higher, but she followed Lady Caroline into the foyer. She only hoped what she learned here was worth having to endure time with this woman. Hunter followed them inside, but she wished he were at least holding her hand again. In fact, she wished they were back on their maroon. If Lady Caroline pushed her too far, she just might tell her all about their swimming nude. That would put her in her place.

"How did you like the maroon, my dear?" Lady Caroline stopped for a close inspection of Deidre.

Uncomfortable, Deidre returned the scrutiny. She quickly decided Lady Caroline could probably turn almost any man's head. She only hoped Hunter hadn't been affected.

The older woman was darkly exotic in coloring, but her eyes showed her age rather than her body. Their expression said she'd seen all there was to see, experienced all there was to experience, and no longer made concessions. But her body spoke of the eagerness and ripeness of youth.

She emphasized her lush body. Her auburn hair had been artfully styled on her head, letting a few curls dangle to a bare shoulder. She wore a gold satin gown. Its bodice had narrow straps across her shoulders and a plunging neckline. The skirt was caught in pleats at a tiny waist to fall in soft folds to the floor. The gown was not fashionable, but rather a perfect compliment to Lady Caroline's body. Only a woman of supreme confidence in mind and body could have worn it.

Deidre envied that confidence and knowledge of life. She wanted it for herself. And she was getting it. She thought of the hot sands of Hog Island, of Hunter's hard, bronzed body. She blushed, remembering Lady Caroline's question about the maroon. "It was nice. I'd never done that before."

"Done what?" Lady Caroline raised an eyebrow at Hunter.

"Maroon." He rocked back on his heels, wishing he was any place else. "Where's Haywood?"

"He'll be here in a moment. Something suddenly came up. You know how it is." Lady Caroline watched Deidre. "You *are* young, aren't you?"

"I'm grown."

"Oh, yes." Lady Caroline cast another sharp

glance at Hunter. As she led them toward the parlor, she looked back. "With your face and body you must be married or at least engaged."

"No." Deidre followed Lady Caroline into the room, noticed the expensive furnishings, then concentrated on the other woman. "I'm a suffragist. I plan to work outside the home, to earn my own way in life."

"Brandy?" Lady Caroline poured three drinks in heavy crystal glasses and handed them around. As she sat down on a settee, she patted the seat beside her and looked at Hunter.

He sat down in a chair. Deidre quickly sat near him.

Lady Caroline pretended to ignore the slight, but her eyebrows met for a moment before she focused on Deidre again. "Why on earth would you want to work? There must be a dozen men anxious to drop to their knees in worship of you."

"I believe women should have the right to vote, to have well-paying jobs available to them, and to have control over their own lives. I don't want a man to worship or control me. I want him to be my partner in life."

Lady Caroline smiled, an indulgent expression on her face. As she took a sip of brandy, a strap on her gown slid down her shoulder to her arm. Leaning toward Hunter, she exposed a daring amount of cleavage. "Now I know what you were doing on the maroon, Hunter. Do you have the suffragist rhetoric memorized by now?"

Further incensed, Deidre stiffened. "I take it you aren't a suffragist?" She suddenly hated the cloying scent of Lady Caroline's perfume.

"No. The right to vote will not get me what I want. And why should I have equality when I've always been superior?" Lady Caroline cast a sultry look at Hunter. "Wouldn't you agree that I'm superior?"

Hunter didn't comment. He glanced around the room as if looking for a way to escape, then took a swig of brandy. It was going to be a long evening.

"But what of other women who haven't had the luxurious life you've lived?" Insulted by Lady Caroline for her age and beliefs, Deidre felt more impassioned than ever. "What of women who've been put in insane asylums so their husbands could have free rein over their homes and children? What of women beaten to death by brutal husbands and fathers? What of—"

"My dear, I invited you to dinner, not a suffrage meeting." Lady Caroline raised an eyebrow. "For your information I have lived enough years to know a few things about men. One. They are not to be trusted with your money, your love, your emotions, or your body. Two. They will take everything they can get and give as little in return as possible. Three. They can give women sublime happiness or abject sorrow. And most often both from the same man."

"But—"

"In short, I will not spend one more moment of my life asking or waiting for a man to give me something. No matter how much I may want it. I spent too many years that way and ended up almost destitute because of it. No, I am not a suffragist because I will not ask *men* for the right to vote or for equality. There is no point. At my age and experience, I take what I want and I keep what's mine."

Hunter lifted his brandy glass in a salute, then drained it. "A pretty speech, Lady Caroline."

"I thought you'd appreciate it, even if your naive young friend cannot."

Deidre felt a dull roar in her ears. Lady Caroline had twisted the meaning of suffragists into something stupid. "I understand your meaning, too, but I prefer to work within the law. We *will* one day have suffrage for women in the United States and England as well."

"Perhaps. Perhaps not." Lady Caroline finished her brandy. "In either case, I doubt if I will live long enough to see the day."

"Live long enough to see what?" Hayward Graves stepped into the room. He wore his usual white suit, but gone was his perfect grooming. A dark smudge marred one knee and his hair was windblown. When he saw Deidre, he stopped abruptly, looking as if he'd seen a ghost.

Chapter 12

"She resembles her mother a great deal, doesn't she?" Lady Caroline rose, poured a brandy and handed it to Hayward. "This is Deidre Clarke-Jarmon."

Hayward set down in a wing chair, his gaze never wavering from Deidre.

"I saw you at the library." Deidre smiled.

"She's Alexandra's daughter?" Hayward gulped down his brandy. "I didn't recognize her earlier. It's the setting. Alexandra spent time in this very room."

Deidre glanced around with a puzzled frown. "You know my mother?"

"And your father." Lady Caroline poured more brandy for everyone. "Captain Jake of the Flying J. Now there was the man to linger in the dreams of a woman."

"Alexandra's daughter." Hayward shook his head. "You're her equal in beauty. I should have realized the relationship when I saw you at the library, but you looked different then." He examined her red satin gown and nodded to himself in understanding. "How is Alexandra?"

"Mother's fine." Deidre felt a change in the atmosphere of the room, as if it had suddenly become dangerous. Her parents had never mentioned either of these two people. "How do you know my father?"

"Ask Caroline. He was her find." Hayward continued to stare.

"I knew him during that nasty but financially rewarding War of Northern Aggression, as Southerners like to call it. Captain Jake was a blockade runner who used Nassau as his base."

Hayward chuckled. "And you were his port, right?"

Lady Caroline raised an eyebrow. "When he was in the Bahamas he was mine."

Deidre couldn't imagine her father with anyone but her mother. She tried to keep the shock from her face. Could they be telling the truth? She sipped brandy to calm herself.

"I'll never forget the Blockade Runners Ball." Lady Caroline's eyes grew bright. "It was held at the Royal Victoria Hotel. Three hundred people attended and consumed three hundred fifty magnums of champagne. Jake and I were the most handsome couple there. And the center of attention. I'll never forget that night."

"I was there, too." Hayward sloshed the brandy in his glass. "But of course I couldn't compare to the mighty Captain Jake or the other blockade runners. But I'll never forget it either. Money flowed like champagne. There were cotton buyers, munition dealers, Confederate officers, Yankee spies, and newspaper correspondents. Some of them were the most beautiful and crafty women in the world."

"My mother couldn't have been there. She's from New York City. Her family supported the North." Deidre felt as if she'd stepped into another world, one she didn't like. And if Lady Caroline didn't stop giving Hunter sly, suggestive little glances, she'd be tempted to take him back to the hotel.

"We met her after the War." Hayward leaned forward. "Jake brought her here with some wild story about finding her at sea, clinging to an oar. I wanted to marry her, but she ran away with Jake."

"She *took* Jake away." Lady Caroline glared at Deidre.

"But you both found other loves and married, didn't you?" Deidre tried to make peace, for the tension in the room was building. She felt worried. Had Hunter known about the Graves family connection to her own and, if so, why hadn't he told her? How had Lady Caroline known she was a Clarke-Jarmon if Hunter hadn't told her? And why were the Graves still so interested in her parents? Could they have followed the Clarke-Jarmon family through newspapers over the years?

"We both married, yes." Lady Caroline smiled, a predatory movement of her lips, and let her gaze rest on Hunter. "And we both found other loves."

Deidre knew she should feel relief at this news, but she didn't. In fact, she felt more concerned than ever. Lady Caroline looked at Hunter as she would a lover and Hayward watched her as if he wanted her for desert.

Suddenly she had an eerie feeling that what had happened to her mother in the Bahamas was now happening to her. Could events so long past be resurrected? She immediately pushed the thought away. She was letting her imagination get the best of her and that wouldn't help her get the information she needed. She must concentrate on getting facts.

Hunter cleared his throat and looked anywhere but at Lady Caroline.

"I'm sure my parents have fond memories of the Graves family." Deidre smiled, attempting to relieve the tension in the room.

"Do you, indeed?" Lady Caroline bared her teeth, but the movement had little in common with a smile. "Perhaps you should ask them how they remember their last night in the Bahamas twenty years ago."

"I will." Feeling more confused than ever, Deidre decided to turn the conversation to something that might help her search. "In the meantime, I'm enjoying the beauty of the islands. It's so peaceful here, so unusual, so—"

"Sultry. Sensual." Lady Caroline looked at Hunter.

"Deidre's interested in local legends of pirates, privateers, and wreckers." Hunter decided he'd better try to get the conversation onto neutral ground and pretend to help Deidre's investigation.

"Really." Hayward sipped his brandy. "I'd be

happy to share my personal books with you. I have my own library here at Palmetto if you'd like me to show you what I have."

Lady Caroline laughed. "I doubt if she wants to see what you value most any more than her mother did."

Hayward turned a dull red.

"I'm sure it'd be most interesting." Again Deidre felt lost, as if a secondary conversation she didn't understand were going on around her. Still, she had no intention of missing out on her chance of learning something to help the investigation.

"Probably not. Musty old books." Lady Caroline threw a disgusted look at her brother. "But how I'd like to have lived in the seventeenth century. Most of the Caribbean was like a pirate nation, with the black Jolly Roger flying over countless ships."

"Were pirates similar to wreckers?" Deidre tried again to move the conversation back in a direction that would help her.

Lady Caroline nodded. "And privateers. The British were at war with the Spanish then, so anything that hurt Spain was condoned by Britain. Spain felt the same about England. And the Caribbean was no man's land right in the middle of the trade route. Oh, what glory days."

"It sounds deadly and dangerous." Deidre was surprised and uncomfortable with Lady Caroline's obvious relish of such bloodthirsty times.

"It was!" Lady Caroline leaned forward, once more revealing her deep cleavage. "I bet you've heard of Blackbeard, really Edward Teach. But Anne Bonny and Mary Read were known to be the most cruel pirates of all. They were responsible for executions, murders, slaughter of captured crews, and overrunning entire towns. Gold and glory were their reward."

"Maybe one day Caroline Graves will be listed in history books along with Mary Read and Anne Bonny." Hayward taunted his sister. "You'd like that, wouldn't you?"

"I'd like to be remembered, yes. And if it is as a strong woman who took what she wanted, then I'll be happy."

Deidre hardly knew what to say, for she suddenly realized the Graves could very well be wreckers. Or perhaps they lived in their dream world of past glories of the Caribbean. Maybe that was why Lady Caroline had once wanted a blockade runner named Captain Jake.

"Too bloodthirsty for you?" Lady Caroline stood and poured herself another brandy. "I suppose nothing like salvaging from dead and dying bodies bloated by sea water has ever entered your safe little world."

"Lady Caroline." Hunter got up and went to her. He poured himself a drink. "Deidre doesn't need to hear that type of thing."

"Protecting her, are you?" Lady Caroline leaned against him, but he drew away. With narrowed eyes, she watched him return to his chair near Deidre. "What did you two do on your maroon?" Her dark eyes glinted dangerously.

"Hunter brought a picnic lunch." Deidre didn't know how they would ever get through dinner, much less the night. And she wasn't learning much of anything except that the Graves were dangerous people she would avoid in the future. No wonder her parents had never mentioned them.

"I bet he did." Lady Caroline sat down on the settee. "And did he show you how to eat it, too?"

"Caroline! You're treating her the same way you treated Alexandra." Hayward frowned at his sister. "She's young and innocent."

"Men! You always think a pretty, young face is innocent. But I know better." Lady Caroline crossed her legs, then uncrossed them restlessly.

"Please." Deidre interrupted the growing argument, desperate to smooth over the situation. "I'd like to hear more about the pirates and wreckers."

"Wreckers." Lady Caroline rolled her brandy glass between her palms. "Is that what you think happened to the Clarke ships? Is that what your parents think? Is that why you're here?"

Deidre bit her lower lip.

"Well, let me tell you something about wreckers." Lady Caroline's eyes held an expression of crafty knowledge. "New Providence Island has always made its fortune on the misfortune of others and—"

"Caroline!" Hayward stood up. "I'm sure dinner is ready to be served. Any more talk like this will ruin our appetites."

"What does it matter now, Hayward? Deidre is our guest the same as her mother was twenty years ago. But I can guarantee you the ending will not be the same."

Hayward held out his arm. "It's time for dinner. Join me." His voice held absolute command and his dark eyes were hard.

"Oh all right, if you're going to be silly about Alexandra's daughter, but you're simply putting off the inevitable." She set down her glass and stood up. Looking over her shoulder, she slipped her hand around Hayward's arm and smiled. "You two will join us, won't you?"

As she watched them walk from the room, Deidre stood. She didn't know how she could get a bite of food past her lips. Hunter took her arm and drew her toward a window. She wanted to lean into his strength, but she no longer knew if she could trust him. What had he been doing in the Bahamas before he went to work for the Bar J Ranch? How much did he know that he'd never told her? Was he leading her investigation on a wild goose chase?

Then again, maybe Lady Caroline had been teasing her about the wreckers. But Hayward had stopped his sister quickly enough when she'd begun to talk about wreckers. Deidre sighed. She didn't think she would get much information from them. Not now. She wished she could leave and return to the hotel. But what about Hunter?

"Lady Caroline's outspoken." Hunter put a warm hand on her shoulder. "I suppose it was a surprise to learn they'd known your parents."

"Yes." She started to turn toward him, but out of the corner of her eye she saw movement outside the window. She looked back and could have sworn she'd seen Captain Sully, followed by several men, walk around the side of the house toward the back. Maybe it had been her imagination or a trick of the full moon light. She shivered, started to tell Hunter, then stopped. What if she couldn't trust him? And what if Captain Sully worked for the Graves? She felt chilled to the bone. Suddenly she wanted only to get out of this house alive.

"A lot of the families around here have a history of wrecking, but it doesn't mean they lure ships to their death."

"No, of course not."

"How cozy." Lady Caroline's satin skirt swished behind them. "Is the night more exciting than my dining room?"

Deidre flinched and stepped away from Hunter. If she couldn't trust him, what would she do?

"Sorry if we kept you waiting." Hunter tucked Deidre's hand into the crook of his arm.

"You seem to be making a habit of that today." Lady Caroline cocked her head to one side. "Pirates the like of Anne Bonny no longer sail the Caribbean Sea, but I'm as much her descendent as if she were my mother. Remember that if either of you decides to trespass on what is mine." She turned. "Dinner is served. *Now.*"

Deidre and Hunter followed Lady Caroline without saying another word.

The dining room was lovely in the soft candle-light of a magnificent chandelier that hung from the ceiling. In the center of the table set a beautiful floral arrangement of gorgeous tropical flowers. The table was set with an array of linen, china, silver, and crystal that would have made a pirate proud to steal. Even Anne Bonny herself. The thought didn't comfort Deidre.

Hayward sat at one end of a long table. Lady Caroline indicated for Deidre to sit beside him. She led Hunter to the other end where she sat down, pointing for him to sit beside her. Deidre thought it a most unusual seating arrangement. She wished she were closer to Hunter because Hayward's intense stare made her uneasy.

She wanted to run straight out of the house and never stop until she reached the safety of her room at the Royal Victoria. But without being rude or making herself look suspicious, she realized she should endure at least the dinner at Palmetto. But she would leave as early as possible. When she was back in Nassau, she would have a lot of questions to ask about the Graves family.

Lady Caroline rang a silver bell and Chinese men silently served food. They were efficient and the meal delicious, but Deidre had little appetite, especially as course followed course. After a few aborted attempts at conversation, they all grew silent and concentrated on the food and wine.

After awhile, Lady Caroline looked up and smiled at Hayward. "This reminds me of that last night when Jake and Alexandra sat at this same table eating dinner with us. Jake sat beside me and Alexandra sat beside you. Do you remember, Hayward?"

He set down his fork. "How could I ever forget? Your lust for inappropriate men is legendary."

"You have no room to talk." Lady Caroline drained another glass of wine. "But we weren't alone that night, were we? Doctor Elder was with us. He's long dead and gone now or perhaps I would have invited him to join us tonight. And you remember the sixth person, don't you, Hayward?"

He stopped eating and glared at her. "If this is a cruel game, I'm not interested."

"But what if I'd invited that sixth person to dinner?"

"You didn't!"

She smiled in satisfaction, cast a sultry glance at Hunter, then shook her head negatively. "But I can always change my mind."

"Bitch!" Hayward tossed back his wine.

Leaning toward Hunter, Lady Caroline once more exposed the cleft of her breasts. She picked up his wine glass. As she sipped from it, she watched him. "Should I invite—"

Suddenly voices erupted in the kitchen, angry oriental arguing with brutal American and British.

"What a night!" Hayward threw down his napkin and left the table.

As he headed through a door, Lady Caroline followed him, a bit unsteady on her feet.

Deidre sat frozen in her seat. She hadn't imagined Captain Sully at the window earlier. She'd heard his voice long enough at Smuggler's Den to recognize it anywhere and now she heard it in the Graves' kitchen. She trembled, then took a long drink of wine to warm herself. Something possibly dangerous and deadly was going on here. The Graves were obviously involved with Sully, but what about Hunter? She turned inquiring eyes on him. He watched the door, as if expecting a fight at any moment.

Hunter tried to remain calm. He'd recognized one of the voices in the kitchen and it wasn't one he'd ever forget. Captain Sully had made a mistake tangling with him over Deidre and he was ready to bust the man's head. But he hadn't expected a connection between Sully and Lady Caroline and

Hayward. He'd heard the rumors about Sully wrecking for profit. He'd even heard Sully was probably involved in the Clarke ships going down. But there'd been no proof and he'd never suspected the man might have a boss or partner.

Now he had a pretty damn good idea where the Graves were getting the money to finance their fancy house and rich lives. From dead men's hands. He might have a hard hand and he might be tough, but he'd never been involved in the killing of innocent people. And he wasn't about to start now. He wanted the Graves put out of business.

If he stopped working for Lady Caroline, it'd mean a big loss of gold to him, but he'd make it up somewhere else. The main thing was to keep Deidre safe and the Clarke ships safe as well. It looked like he was going to end up working for the Clarke-Jarmons after all.

But he had to have proof before he did anything and he wasn't going to get it eating dinner at Palmetto. He wanted to get the hell out and take Deidre with him, but he didn't want the Graves to be suspicious. He needed their trust if he was going to get the information he needed.

He took a deep breath and glanced at Deidre. She stared at him with a mixture of fear and worry and wonder. Damn! She had to be questioning everything he'd ever told her. But she could trust him. It was laughable, but she could. He supposed he'd known from the first moment he saw her step down from the stage in Three Rivers, Texas that she'd get her hooks in him.

But that wasn't his worry now. He had to make sure she didn't do something stupid like give away her suspicions and fears to Lady Caroline and Hayward. She had to keep pretending to be the honored guest no matter who or what came through that kitchen door.

He tried to smile, but realized it wasn't going to work. The situation was too grim. "You can trust me, Deidre."

Stiffening, she squeezed her glass of wine. "I'd like to go home."

"You'll be safe till tomorrow."

"No." She knocked over her glass of wine. Red stained the white tablecloth like blood. She abruptly stood up, dabbed at the spreading stain with her napkin, realized it wouldn't help much, and turned to flee the room.

Hunter caught her, whirling her around to hold her against his body. She struggled, then abruptly leaned against him.

"Listen, we don't have much time. I'll explain everything if you meet me on the beach about midnight. Go along the coast away from Nassau until you can't see the house anymore. There's a secluded cove. All right?" He held her away to look into her eyes. "Deidre?"

She stepped back. "How can I trust you? I don't know what's going on around here. I think Captain Sully is working here or something."

"Yes, I agree. But you can't leave now. It'd be too suspicious and dangerous. I'll keep you safe tonight. Say you'll meet me." His brown eyes glowed dark and intense.

She thought of all they'd shared, of her parents' belief in him, and of her present danger. Captain

Sully! Did she have any choice but to trust Hunter, at least for the moment? She nodded in agreement.

"Good. Now, no matter who shows up at this dinner table, act pleasant. You're the guest and you're happy to be here. Got it?"

She nodded again, but felt unable to speak.

Hunter heard the kitchen door open. He didn't whirl around, as was his instinct. Instead he pretended not to have noticed and raised his voice. "Deidre, accidents happen. You were startled by the noise in the kitchen and spilled your wine. I'm sure Lady Caroline will see that new places are set down at our end of the table."

"An excellent suggestion, Hunter." Lady Caroline walked over to them, with Hayward following. "I'm sorry our meal was disturbed. Good help is so hard to find." She gave Hunter a sharp look, then turned to the table and rang the silver bell. "We'll continue our meal."

"And we won't have any more guests." Hayward took Deidre's arm and led her to the chair across from Hunter's seat. "Sit down and relax. I'll pour you some more wine. And don't worry about the tablecloth."

"I'm sorry." Deidre tried to remember her manners, but more than that she tried to remain calm.

Hunter and Lady Caroline joined them.

When their wine glasses were refilled, Lady Caroline raised hers. "To old friends and new ones. To the past and the present. May all come full circle."

Deidre drank to the toast, but she didn't understand or like it. Only Hunter's steadfast gaze kept her from bolting away from the table.

Chapter 13

After midnight, Deidre descended the center staircase that led down to the foyer of Palmetto. She paused every few steps to listen, but the house remained quiet. She supposed there must be side doors or back doors, but she'd only used the front door and she wasn't going to explore now.

When she started across the marble floor of the foyer, she felt the coolness through her soft leather slippers. She hesitated, glanced back up the stairs, and wondered if she'd made the right decision about clothes. But she couldn't change her mind now.

She had decided that if she were caught, the best excuse would be a story about her inability to sleep that led to a late night stroll along the beach. To make this believable she had worn nightclothes. But now the green silk nightgown and robe made her feel much too vulnerable.

Yet she had no intention of turning back. She twisted the handle on the front door and pulled. The door didn't move. Her breath sounded loud in her ears. She fumbled around a few moments, found the lock, twisted it, then opened the door. It squeeked. She stopped, glanced back over her shoulder, then slid through the narrow opening. She made sure the door wouldn't lock behind her, then firmly shut it.

She tiptoed to a broad white pillar and hesitated while she scanned the area. When she didn't see anyone, she ran down the stairs, across the thick grass of the lawn to the beach beyond. She hurried to a palm tree and leaned against it as she stopped to catch her breath. She looked and listened again, then decided she was still safe.

She ran on, staying in the shadows of the trees as much as she could while remaining on the soft sands of the beach. She had no desire to venture into the dark, possibly dangerous vegetation of the plantation. She kept looking back until she could no longer see the mansion. Slowing to a walk, she looked around for the cove.

Perhaps it was so secluded she couldn't find it. That would almost be a relief. She didn't really want to confront Hunter. She wanted to return to the hotel, not having heard anything she had at Palmetto. But she couldn't turn back time, no matter how much she might like to do that. And she wouldn't stop the investigation no matter what she learned. There had already been too much death and destruction.

She walked on, hardly caring that the night was as beautiful as it had been on the drive from Nassau.

Moonlight still turned the ocean silver as the waves rolled into shore. But now she wondered about what was lurking in the dark depths of the sea. She shivered. If she didn't find Hunter soon, she *would* turn back.

"Deidre."

She jerked around, scanning the undergrowth along the beach, and tried to slow her racing heart.

"Over here."

Fortunately she recognized Hunter's voice. She moved toward the sound. When a hand snaked outward, grabbed her arm, and pulled through the dense growth, she didn't have time to hesitate or pull back. Before she realized what had happened, she was against Hunter's warm, bare chest, his arms wrapped tightly around her.

"Are you okay?" His strong hands rubbed up and down her arms.

"Yes." She shivered at his touch.

"They didn't see or hear you?"

"No. I don't think so. You either?"

"I hope to hell they didn't. Lady Caroline is as possessive as they come."

"And does she have reason to be possessive of you?"

He cleared his throat and set her away from him. "We've got to talk."

She was afraid she wouldn't like what he had to say. She glanced around. Private, secluded, waves lapped gently against the white sands of the cove. Moonlight softened the hard planes of Hunter's face, but it couldn't dispel the turmoil in his eyes.

"I'm listening." She tried to keep the edge from

her voice because she needed to get information, not make him defensive.

"I didn't know they were involved with Sully."

"Or that they may be responsible for wrecking Clarke ships?"

"No. Believe me, I hate that as much as you do. But we don't have proof. We don't know for sure. And everybody on the island knows Sully."

"And invites him to dinner?"

"He wasn't at dinner."

"He might as well have been."

"You can trust me, if you've started to worry about that. I'm not a close friend of the Graves. I'll keep you safe just like I promised your parents."

"How did Lady Caroline know about my parents?"

Hunter clenched his fists. "I told her. She'd explained to me about her early love for Captain Jake. You look like your mother. She was bound to meet you. I thought it best to tell her." He couldn't stand the lies and half-truths. He turned his back on her.

"Hunter?" Her voice was soft, not angry.

Did she believe him? He'd have to tell her the truth some time, but not now, not when they might be in so much danger. He wanted her safely away from New Providence Island before he quit working for Lady Caroline and proved if she and her brother were wreckers. To accomplish that, he had to tell Deidre even more lies. No matter. Her safety came first.

She touched his bare shoulder with a soft, tentative hand. "I want to believe you."

He covered her hand with his own. "You can."

He squeezed her hand. "If the Graves are working with Sully and they're wrecking ships, then I want to catch and stop them as much as you do. But if they think for one moment we suspect them, then we're in great danger."

She clung to him, wanting more than ever to believe him. "Yes. But we have to get information and I'm not sure we can get it here, danger or not. We could leave now and walk back to Nassau. From there we could investigate them, couldn't we?"

"I wish it was that easy. Believe me, nobody on New Providence is going to talk about the Graves, especially if they're wrecking ships. We've got to get the proof around here and to do that we must keep them from suspecting our real intentions."

"That means spending the night as if all is normal."

"We'll go back to Nassau first thing in the morning. I don't want you in any more danger."

"I want you safe, too." She leaned against him, needing his warmth, needing his strength. "Oh, Hunter. I thought this investigation would be so simple."

"Life isn't simple." He stroked her head, digging his fingers into the thick plait until her long hair hung free.

"We shouldn't be here in the cove, should we?" Her breath was warm against his chest. "I mean, what if they found us?"

"They won't. You're right, we should be snug in our beds under Lady Caroline's roof." What he didn't say was that if he was back at Palmetto, it'd be hard as hell to sleep alone whether it was Lady Caroline's bed or his. And at dinner he'd realized he could never touch her again. Deidre had gotten under his skin and he wanted no other woman but her.

"I'm glad you came with me from the Bar J. My parents were right about that. But I realize more than ever how important it is to experience life. I just didn't think it would be so complicated."

"You're doing fine." A tremor ran through his body as he tried to resist responding to her touch, the feel of her body against him. It wasn't easy and grew more difficult by the moment. "You trust me, don't you?"

She raised her head and looked into his eyes. Nodding, she put her hands behind his head, thrusting her fingers into hair as she pulled his head downward. She pressed her lips to his, then stroked his mouth with the tip of her tongue before placing soft kisses over his face. "I trust you. I need you. Let's don't go back to the house or Nassau. I want to stay here forever."

"I wish we could." He was fast losing control. He stroked down her back to her hips, feeling the tantalizing shape of her body through the silk.

"We can stay here at least till dawn. After all, I'm taking a midnight stroll because I can't sleep. You're fast asleep in your room."

He gathered her hair with his fist, then pulled back her head so he could watch her expression. "You should go back now."

"Why?" She searched his face for truth.

Passion simmered in the depths of his dark eyes. "I want you and I'm not as strong as I thought I was, at least not where you're concerned."

"Teach me how to be a woman, Hunter."

"Damn!" He dropped his hands, strode away from her, kicked at the sandy surf as he pushed his hands deep into his pockets. He was in pain. "Go now."

She stroked his back, finding the indentation of each muscle, then kissed the ridge of each scar. "You don't want me to go back."

He wheeled around and crushed her against him, pushing into her mouth to taste her sweetness before he lost all reason. As he kissed her, he pushed the robe off her shoulders until it fell from her arms to the sand. He explored her body with his hands, pressing her against his hardness until he could stand no more. He stepped back, breathing hard.

"I've fought this since Three Rivers." His eyes were darker than the night.

"It was meant to be. Here. Now."

Through the sheer silk of her nightgown he could see the taut tips of her breasts. There was no need to wait. He could have the revenge he had planned. He could take her virginity, use her body, then thrust her away from him, just as rich women had used him when he was young. Revenge was supposed to be sweet, but it made him feel sick inside. He couldn't do it to Deidre, but he couldn't leave her alone either.

Swearing, he turned off his mind and reached for her. As he kissed her, savoring her taste and feel, he slipped the nightgown down her shoulders until her breasts were bare. He cupped them, feeling the hard nipples against his palms, and stroked until she moaned and clung to him, pressing herself against him, returning his kiss, igniting with fire until the Ice Princess was burned away. The Fire Queen ruled here and she had him completely in her control.

And still he didn't care. He could think of nothing but being deep inside of Deidre. He pushed her gown to her hips, then to the sand. She stood naked before him, her hair a long, golden mass turned silvery in the moonlight. Not Queen but Goddess. And he was the worshiper.

She reached for his trousers and began to slowly unbutton them, a mischievous smile on her lips, dark passion in her eyes. She glowed, she aroused, she taunted until she reached her goal. She took him out, touched him, stroked his long, hard length, then looked back into his eyes. "Make me a woman, Hunter."

He shuddered. Jerking off his trousers, he tossed them away. And reached for her. She came into his arms, pressing her body against him, murmuring his name, her breath caressing his throat, his face as she pressed kisses against his heated flesh.

Restraining himself, he lowered her to the soft sand and knelt beside her. When he kissed her breasts, she moaned and ran her fingers deep into his hair. When he suckled each hard tip, she tugged at his hair, moaning louder, her feet restlessly digging tunnels in the sand. And when he moved lower still to the triangle of golden hair between her legs, she grasped his shoulders and shivered.

He touched her heat, felt her body respond, then slipped a finger inside. Yes, she was still a virgin. But he'd never doubted that fact. What amazed him was that she wanted him to release her, to make her a woman, to fulfill her desires. He was hired help.

That's all he'd ever been. And he couldn't under-stand her passion for him when she could have any man, handsome, rich, titled. A man who loved her.

But he wasn't going to question his luck. And he couldn't stop his desire. He raised her hips, posi-tioned himself at her core, then hesitated. "Dei-dre?"

She writhed against him, dug her nails into his arms, and tossed her head. "Please. I've been on fire for you since our swim. Don't torment me."

He kissed her hard. "Tender torment. That's what I'll give you." Then he eased inside her, con-trolling himself with more and more difficulty. When he reached the obstruction to both their pas-sion, he hesitated, pulled back, then plunged deep inside her. She cried out with pain, but he covered her lips, thrusting into her mouth as he thrust into her body.

She felt him inside her, hot, hard, wild, while outside she felt the cool water of the Caribbean lap over her legs, then flow around them as the waves moved in and out just as Hunter moved inside her. She knew they were being outlined in the sand as one, but she knew it wouldn't last. When they left, the sea would erase any sign of their desire. Would it be that way in their lives?

Tears stung her eyes as she moaned deep in her throat when she felt her passion build higher and higher, drawing them farther and father from real-ity. Ecstasy but sorrow, too. For who knew if the future would ever bring this type of happiness again. Yes, he had been right. Tender torment.

Suddenly her cries mixed with his as they rode

the wave of ecstasy to a searing climax. She hung there a moment, wanting it to last forever, then followed the wave in its unrelenting fall back to shore. Tears stung her eyes, but she smiled with pleasure. Now she was complete, an experienced young woman. And she would never be the same again. Thanks to a man named Hunter.

Reluctant to end the moment, he raised up on an elbow to watch her face.

She smiled.

He pressed a soft kiss to her lips. "Happy?"

Nodding, she stroked his face, as if memorizing each detail for the future. "I didn't know it would be so good."

He chuckled and laid on his side to pull her close. "It'll get even better."

"Really?"

Nodding, he traced down from her chin with the tip of his finger to her golden triangle of curls. "Yes. I'll prove it to you soon."

"Now." She reached for him.

Laughing again, he kissed her hard. "At this rate, it'll be real soon." As he stroked the smooth skin of her stomach, he thought he heard something move in the bushes. He stopped, listened, but heard nothing else. Still, he'd been brought back to the reality of their situation. "Maybe we'd better head back."

"But Hunter, you said—"

He put a fingertip to her lips. "I know, but should we push our fortune?"

"Yes." She put her arms around him and pulled him down so she could kiss him again. Teasing his lips with her tongue, she felt him harden against her leg. She raised her head, a mischievous glint in her eyes. "You can't say you don't want to right now."

He shook his head. "I can't say that, but I can say I know what's best for us." He began to get up.

"No. I know what's best for us."

She tried to pull him back down, but he gathered her in his arms and walked out into the sea. When the water was around his waist, he gently let her down into the ocean. She felt the coolness caress her almost to her breasts. She hugged him, never wanting to let him go.

But he was looking out to sea, suddenly realizing the wind had risen again. The full moon was almost hidden by clouds. He'd been right about the storm. He hoped it would hold off till they got back to Nassau.

"Deidre, we'd better get back. That storm may break sooner than I thought."

"I don't care. I'd like to be lost at sea with you."

He smiled, enjoying the playfulness so unlike her usual determined competence. As much as he hated to end their time together, he knew it was but the first of many nights with her. She was in his blood and until he got her out of it she was a part of him. To protect her was to protect himself. And to that end, he'd be Lady Caroline's good boy till he got Deidre safely off the island.

"You're right, I suppose." She watched the gathering storm.

"There'll be other nights for us, Deidre. And it'll be better."

She smiled and nodded. "I'll hold you to that, mister." She splashed water over her breasts, feeling cool and happy. Thinking, she walked back toward shore. Tender torment. She could stand the separation from him only because he had promised to be with her again. And she trusted him to keep his word.

As she let the wind dry her skin, she shook the sand out of her nightgown and robe. She slipped them on, then pulled on her slippers as she watched Hunter tug on his trousers. She hated to see him cover his magnificient body, but she promised herself she'd see it again the next day in her room at the hotel. Although that seemed a terribly long time, she'd simply have to wait.

Hunter took her hand in his and led her from the cove. As they stepped into the open onto the sandy beach, he stopped short at the sight of three people.

Captain Sully pointed a rifle at them.

Lady Caroline carried a long, black whip.

Hayward had a pistol tucked into his trousers.

Deidre felt chilled and clung to Hunter's hand. She thought the reception party was a bit overdone. After all she and Hunter could have simply taken a walk on the beach. No one could know what they had actually done. And why should they care anyway?

Unrolling the whip, Lady Caroline snapped it through the air. "I used this on Alexandra." Her voice raged with fury.

Deidre felt the whip snap perilously close to her face. "Is this your idea of after dinner entertainment?" She could hardly believe her voice was so calm, but at the thought of this woman hurting her mother she had grown furiously cold.

"No." Lady Caroline snapped the whip again. "You took my after dinner entertainment, lured him out here, and took what was mine just as your mother did twenty years ago."

"Lady Caroline, we went for a walk." Hunter wanted to thrust Deidre behind him, but he didn't dare appear afraid of Lady Caroline's temper.

"I'm not stupid. I saw what I saw. And it was the same as twenty years ago on this same shore. Jake and Alexandra. Deidre and Hunter." She spit on the sand. "I've loved two men in my life. I'd have given them anything. I did. But they both abandoned me. My husband promised to always to take care of me, but he died. And abandoned me."

"You have your brother." Deidre wanted to stop the other woman's pain, wanted to stop her own fear, wanted to be far away. When she had set out to seek her independence, she could never have imagined a scene like this or a woman like this. If Lady Caroline had had suffrage, would she have found it necessary to live through men?

"Yes, Hayward is loyal." Lady Caroline smiled, a grim twist of her lips. "But Jake and Hunter were both taken by Clarke women."

"You're upset." Hunter stepped forward. "There's no need to think this way."

Lady Caroline sent the whip flying and slashed it across Deidre's face.

Deidre moaned and covered her face with her hands, crouching down to get away from the whip as it came back again, cutting across her shoulders. She tried to push the pain to a far corner of her mind.

Hunter sprang at Lady Caroline, but Captain Sully stepped between them.

"Don't touch the lady or I'll blow you in two." Captain Sully cocked the hammer of the rifle. "I'd be happy to do it. You and Jake both took women I wanted. And I don't forget."

Hunter inhaled deeply, scowled at them, then turned back to Deidre. He pushed her behind him, then faced their opponents. "You're not hurting her again."

Lady Caroline snapped the whip and caught Hunter across the chest. Blood welled up in a long cut.

"If there's one thing in life I should have learned by now it's that I can't trust a man I love." Lady Caroline snapped the whip in the air over Hunter's head. "But I've also learned that revenge is sweet."

"We'll leave New Providence and won't come back." Hunter felt Deidre rise behind him, put her arm around him, and stand tall beside him.

"You'll leave our island and you won't be back." Lady Caroline no longer looked the lady, for her hair had come loose and blew about wildly in the wind. Her gown was stained around the bottom and one shoulder strap had ripped away from wielding the whip. "I waited for you." Her voice ended on a wail. "I came here, hoping to find you. And I did. With her."

"I didn't mean to hurt you." Hunter's voice was deep, calm, reassuring as he held Deidre close to him. He had to protect her. "But I won't let you hurt Deidre. You misjudged what you saw."

"Fool! Wrapped in each other's arms, naked in

the surf. Misjudged?" Lady Caroline snapped the whip across Hunter's chest again, then paced, sending her whip outward to make snake indentations in the sand. "I must change my plans. Revenge." She looked up and smiled. "I'm afraid, dear little Deidre, that you'll never get the chance to vote should the great white fathers in all their wisdom grant it."

"Let me keep her." Hayward straightened his shirt. "I'll punish her for you and you could watch."

"No!" Deidre clung to Hunter. "I'd kill myself first."

"That'll be *my* pleasure." Lady Caroline snapped the whip close to Hunter's chest. "That's the only kind of caress you'll ever get from me again. And you'll be begging for those when you see your fate."

"We aren't the only ones who know you're wreckers." Hunter played his last card, hoping to scare them. "If we don't come back to the hotel, you'll be investigated."

"Do you think we're fools?" Lady Caroline caressed the black leather of her whip. "I've had you both watched since you came back and told me your news, Hunter. You've got no help. It will simply be a terrible shame when your bloated, ruined bodies wash up on the shore."

"It seems a waste." Hayward's eyes glittered as he watched Deidre. "Leave her to me, Caroline."

"No! They're both mine. Revenge is mine." Lady Caroline slowly rolled up her whip. "And think on this while you await your death. Jake and Alexandra have unpleasant accidents awaiting them in their future."

"You can't do that." Deidre lunged toward Lady

Caroline, but Hunter pulled her back and held her against his chest.

"I can do whatever I want, little suffragist." Lady Caroline glared at Captain Sully. "Get some help. I want these two hidden till the time is right."

"It's a shame." Hayward took out his pistol.

Lady Caroline snapped the coiled whip against her thigh. "Come on, Hayward, we've got business to attend. The storm is moving in fast."

Chapter 14

Deidre felt like a heroine in a novel. And it wasn't pleasant. Bound, gagged, blindfolded, she'd been dumped into the bottom of a boat that now tossed about in the wind and waves of a building storm. She tried to find a more comfortable position, but couldn't. Her only comfort was the warmth and solidity of Hunter, who was doing his best to protect her even while sharing her predicament.

It was just as well she couldn't see her captors because the sight would surely have made her all the more furious. And fear. She'd never known terror such as this before. Lady Caroline, Hayward, and Captain Sully couldn't be real, couldn't be planning to kill. But there was no point in trying to think away the situation. She and Hunter *were* captives. They had to get free, or be rescued, or whatever saved heroines in novels.

But Clarke ships hadn't been saved. She shivered at the thought. Wet, cold, anger, fear drove out all feelings except one. Passion. What she had shared with Hunter on the beach warmed her inner core and helped sustain her. Thoughts of her parents and wrecked Clarke ships drove her anger. Somehow she had to use these feelings to drive out the ones that made her feel helpless.

Suddenly the bottom of the boat scraped against rock, sailors shouted, and Deidre wondered if they were all going to drown with no hope of rescue. But the boat steadied, the voices quieted, and she was jerked to her feet. She heard Hunter's mumbled protest behind her, heard a scuffle, then she was lifted in strong arms.

Soon she felt the steadiness of land as she was carried she knew not where. She only hoped Hunter was behind her. And she hoped wherever they were being taken would offer a chance of escape.

Finally, she was set down and her bonds loosened. As circulation tingled through her arms, she tried to get away, but she was quickly shoved against something rough and hard. Pushed down, she sat uneasily. As she was retied she clenched her muscles in a trick Simon Gainesville had once explained to her could be used to escape from bonds since the ropes would be looser when the muscles were relaxed.

But when she was retied, she couldn't tell if the ropes were looser or tighter. All she knew was that her arms had been pulled painfully back and extended around something hard and sharp, like a large rock. If she ever escaped, she had visions of trying to explain to Simon that all his careful instructions about how to get information undercover hadn't worked for her. And if she didn't return at all, he'd know for sure they hadn't. She hated to leave behind that kind of legacy.

Miserable, more uncomfortable than ever, she sat still and listened, hoping to tell by sounds where they were. She could still hear the ocean, but it seemed more muted now. Almost more than anything, she wanted to be dry, no longer chilled, and wearing enough clothes to protect her dignity as well as health. But it was a distant dream that made her more unhappily aware of her circumstances.

When she heard Hunter's muffled cursing and struggles, she was cheered only in that she wasn't alone. Happiness would have been to have him free and helping her escape. But at least she knew he was still alive and that gave her hope that they could yet escape together.

When her blindfold and gag were removed, Deidre blinked as she adjusted to her surroundings. Torches burned on what appeared to be the walls of some sort of cavern. She sat on sand and in front of her she could see the sea splashing against rock as it rolled inward. The cave opened onto the Caribbean, but the ocean had grown much more violent since she had last seen it. Could they survive a hurricane here or even a storm?

Lady Caroline walked in front of Deidre. "I admit this doesn't have the same comfort as Palmetto, but naughty behavior deserves punishment. Don't you agree, my dear?"

"Where are we?" Deidre's mouth was so dry she could hardly speak.

Lady Caroline chuckled. "A private, secluded, family-owned islet off New Providence. I can assure you and Hunter that you won't be disturbed here. Ever."

"Let Deidre go. She's done nothing. She knows nothing." Hunter's voice was low and raspy.

Deidre twisted her head around to see him. He was bound to a craggy rock that thrust out of the sand. He was a little behind and higher than her, for the floor of the cavern sloped into the sea.

"I'm touched by your concern." Lady Caroline pointed toward Deidre. "I'm so touched that I've made it possible for her to die first so she won't have to do it alone. Now isn't that thoughtful of me?"

"What do you mean?" Hunter pulled at his bonds.

"You're not going to get free so you might as well stop struggling." Lady Caroline raised an eyebrow. "The cave will fill with water to a certain point and that point is over the top of your head, Hunter dear. But as I said, it will reach Deidre first and you may watch her drown."

Hunter growled and jerked against his ropes. "You can't do this."

Deidre sat still, watching the sea as the current pulled it back and forth. How long did they have? The whip cuts on her chest and face suddenly burned. Salt water would sting the wounds, but perhaps she'd enjoy the feeling for it would mean she was still alive. As one of the last sensations she'd feel, she might actually treasure the feeling.

"I can do whatever I want." Lady Caroline paced the area. "This is my land, my island, my people.

You and Deidre are trespassers. But I have no time for small talk. The storm grows and work must be done."

Hayward walked over to look at Deidre. He shook his head, his dark eyes sad. "It is such a shame to lose you, but I will donate a section of the library in your honor. You name will not be forgotten."

Deidre frowned. "What a comfort!" Then she thought better of her words. "Hayward, you can save us. I'd be grateful, very grateful."

Hayward stepped toward her.

"Stop!" Lady Caroline glared at her brother. "Leave her alone. She'd be about as grateful as her mother for the help we gave her. Once Deidre was free, she'd be laughing at you all the way back to her family."

Frowning, Hayward walked away.

Lady Caroline moved close to Hunter. She touched a fingertip to his lips. "It's a shame to lose such a fine specimen of manhood, but you know too much and you've developed morals. A bad combination."

"Let her go." Hunter's voice held pain. "I'd stay with you."

"I'm afraid that will no longer do." Lady Caroline touched the whip cuts across his chest. "But you're right about one thing, Hunter dear. We're wreckers. In an age when that skill is almost gone, we've revived it. Not my Chinese workers, of course. They're for the plantation. But Bahamians, descendents of our proud ancesters."

"You can't keep it up." Hunter tried to use reason on her. "Somebody else will come to investigate."

"Perhaps they will meet with accidents, too. But

that is not my concern. Not now. The storm builds. And a Clarke ship sails to its doom. You wouldn't want me to be late for the party, would you?"

"No!" Deidre struggled to get free. "You can't kill more people. It's not right."

"Might is right." Lady Caroline smiled. "And the might is mine, all mine." She looked upward. "Hayward, it's time. You might as well tell Sully to get the men in position. I don't want any witnesses to this night's work."

"You should be proud." Deidre's voice was bitter. "Anne Bonney and Mary Read have nothing on you."

Lady Caroline gave a slight bow. "Thank you, my dear, for the compliment. Perhaps I will remember it and let your parents die an easy death."

"No! They'll come for me. And get you." Deidre strained against the ropes.

Walking away, Lady Caroline stopped and looked back. "Your family loyalty is touching, but ill-placed. These islands hide secrets that will never be discovered. And your deaths will simply be terrible accidents, for your bodies will wash in with all the others from the Clarke ship. A fitting tribute to your mother, I think."

"Lady Caroline, you can't win." Hunter tried one last time.

She smiled. "I always win when not betrayed. You should have thought of that before you changed sides." She gave him long look, then left the cavern.

Silence, broken only by the sound of the rising storm and cascading surf, filled the cave.

"Hunter?" Deidre twisted to look at him. "What are we going to do?"

"Keep pulling on the rope. Maybe it'll stretch or break."

"The water's getting higher, really fast now."

"Damn that woman to hell! I know it."

Deidre's ankles were bound together and she tried to loosen the rope, but she seemed only to scrape her skin raw. Her nightclothes had ridden up to her thighs and the sand felt increasingly rough as she moved her legs back and forth. At the same time she twisted her hands, trying to free her wrists, and she thought perhaps Simon's trick had worked a little. But not enough to set her free. Gritting her teeth, she felt tears sting her eyes.

"Deidre, if we don't get out of this alive, I want you to know—" He stopped abruptly.

"Yes?"

"Nevermind. I'll tell you when we're far away and free."

"That's right. We'll go to the Bar J or maybe New York City."

"We could buy you more clothes in New Orleans."

She smiled and almost felt like laughing, but instead tears crept down her cheeks. He was trying to cheer her and keep her mind off the rising water. How tender. In the midst of torment. She hadn't known how true his words would be. But at least she wouldn't die without being well on her way to becoming an independent young woman and a woman who'd known ecstasy in the arms of a man.

"Deidre?"

"I'm all right. The water's touching my feet, but I'm not frightened. I want to thank you for all your help and for what we shared in the cove."

"Stop it!" His voice was ragged. "Don't be a martyr. Fight! We've got to get free."

But she didn't really feel like fighting anymore. She could almost imagine voices of shipwrecked people calling to her to join them. Perhaps it was right that she go to help the people who had drowned on Clarke ships. She felt light-headed as the water rose higher, swirling around her thighs. Outside the storm grew stronger, the wind howled, the surf crashed against the rocks of the islet.

She wondered vaguely how long it took to drown. If she didn't hold her breath, it would be faster. That might be best. At least Hunter wouldn't have to watch her in pain very long, she hoped.

Suddenly the salty water of the sea stung the cuts across her breasts. The intense pain abruptly cleared her mind. She shook her head. What had she been thinking? She couldn't give up without a fight. She glanced back at Hunter. He was struggling desperately to get free. She could do no less. She twisted her arms, feeling the rock scrap against her until her skin was raw and stinging from sea water. She twisted her wrists back and forth, back and forth.

She caught her breath. For a moment she thought the rope had given, but perhaps it was only wishful thinking. She pulled again. The rope was looser, no doubt about it. She glanced back at Hunter. The ocean swirled around his thighs and was rising fast. Jerking hard on the rope, it gave enough for her to tug one hand free.

"Hunter! I've got one hand loose."

"Hurry."

Soon she had the other hand free, then she drug

herself over to him, not taking time to unbind her ankles. She set to work on his bonds, ripped a nail, then another, but finally freed one of his hands, then the other. He jerked loose, hugged her hard against him, then looked back at the rising water.

"Let's get to higher ground. This cave may fill completely. I don't believe anything that bitch said."

Deidre crawled forward until she was out of the water. Panting, hardly able to believe they were free, she again felt tears sting her eyes. But this time they were for happiness.

When Hunter joined her, he quickly untied her ankles, threw away the bonds, then gently massaged her stinging, lacerated skin. The increased circulation made it hurt all the worse, but she was thrilled to be feeling anything. He looked her over, examined her wrists and hands, then nodded in satisfaction. Finally, he untied his own ankles, rubbed circulation back into them, then stood up.

"Let's get the hell out of here." His voice was rough with emotion.

"We've got to be careful. Would they have left a guard?"

He shook his head in denial. "No. Between the storm, the ship, and us just short of dead, all hands will be down on the rocks and beach waiting for the wreck."

"Do you think we can save the ship?"

He looked down at her, his brown eyes suddenly soft. "You would think of others first, wouldn't you?"

"You don't want anybody else to die either."

"No. We'll do what we can." He glanced around. Debris from wrecked ships lay here and there.

Open trunks with spilled contents, dresses, hats, household goods in rotten, weathered states.

Deidre saw the direction of his gaze. "Our clothes could have been left like this, too. And our bodies—"

"Don't think about it! We're getting out of this alive." He walked over to the debris and started looking through it, tossing clothes here and there.

"Hunter! That's ghoulish."

"Help me. See if you can find any kind of weapon. A knife, pistol, cane, whatever will help us stop the wreckers."

He was right. Now was no time for delicate sensibilities. She joined his search. But at first she could hardly make herself touch the damp, smelly contents of the trunks. She couldn't stop thinking that it had all once been the prized possessions of people who had died tragic, brutal deaths at the hands of wreckers. When she came across children's clothes, tears filled her eyes, and she held them to her breast. Had someone's child died?

"Deidre!" Hunter jerked the clothes from her hands and threw them down. Grabbing her shoulders, he shook her. "Don't think about these people. Don't think about what almost happened to us."

She nodded.

"Think about our future. Think about your parents. Think about those people on the Clarke ship. You can do something to help all of us. It's too late for the dead. But you can avenge them and stop similar deaths."

Nodding, she felt slightly warmer. "I'm sorry. It's just that—"

"I know. I feel the same. But we can't have feel-

213

ings now. We can't hurt now. We're not free yet. And that ship out there is getting closer to these rocks by the minute. We're got to hurry."

"Yes. You're right." She shook her head to clear it. "We've got to fight our way free."

"Right." He massaged her shoulders a moment, then went back to his search.

Suddenly she felt exhausted, as well as wet and cold. But Hunter had said she couldn't feel those things and he was right. She glanced down at her sodden nightclothes. She couldn't fight the wreckers like this and if she had to run her clothes would slow them. She looked back at the trunks and felt a deep reluctance grip her. But she pushed the feeling aside. There were plenty of clothes in the trunks. Clothes they needed. Gritting her teeth, she began looking for more than weapons.

"Hunter, put this on." She tossed him a black leather vest about his size. She thought the leather would protect him more than cloth. Fortunately he already wore trousers, but his feet were bare.

He caught the vest, looked surprised, then as understanding dawned on him he looked a little sick. But he slipped it on anyway. "Thanks."

Continuing to search, she ignored the moldy smell and the clothes that tore apart in her hands. When she found a pair of black trousers that looked about her size, she slipped them on. She jerked off her torn nightgown and robe and tossed them down with the other debris. When she found a suitable black shirt, she pulled it on and tucked it inside. Finally, she buckled a belt around her waist. She had on slippers to partially protect her feet from the rocks. She was as good as she could get.

Hunter glanced up at her and nodded in approval. "That'll help, and so will these." He held out a silver dagger, an ebony cane, and a ceremonial short sword. He tested the blades. They didn't fall out, although both were rusted.

She felt relief surge through her.

He handed her the dagger. "This'll have to do."

"It's wonderful. Now we have a much better chance. And we have the element of surprise."

"We sure as hell have that." He stopped and looked sternly into her eyes. "If you have to use that dagger, use it hard and fast. Don't hesitate. Remember, these people are killers. If you go for the chest, pick the left side and thrust hard, upward between the ribs."

She nodded, but felt a little sick at her stomach. She might have to kill someone. She shivered. She'd never imagined having to do that, not ever. How could she? But how could she not? One life of a wrecker against many aboard a ship. Good against evil. She had to be strong and do the right thing, even if it meant killing another person. "I'll do my best."

He walked over to her and held out his arms.

Knowing she smelled like rotten seaweed, knowing she was bloodstained and cut across her face, knowing she couldn't possibly look worse if she'd tried, she smiled and went into his arms.

He held her tight, then placed a soft kiss on her lips. "If you're wondering, you've never looked more beautiful. And I've never been prouder of you."

"A dose of fancy French perfume would be welcome about now."

"Believe me, freedom will smell sweeter." He hesitated. "Are you ready?"

She gripped his hand. "I'll do my best."

"Then let's save a ship."

Chapter 15

Hunter stepped outside the cave. A wild wind whipped across the islet, tearing at him, biting him with cold and rain. Layers of fog swirled through the wind, obscuring then revealing the landscape. He gripped the sword and cane harder, wishing he could send Deidre to safety while he took on the wreckers alone. But there was no place safe on the islet and she'd be better off attacking than waiting for them to find her. Besides, he figured it'd take both of them, and more, to defeat the wreckers.

They wore dead men's clothes. Back in Arizona, the Apache would think it a suicidal action. Death follows death. But maybe here it would prove the edge they needed, maybe the dead would fight at their side to defeat the wreckers and save other ships.

Gripping the sword and ebony cane, he reached

for the animal in himself, the primal being who would carry him through fire and water, earth and air without him feeling anything except the red passion of battle lust. Inhaling sharply, he sniffed the wind, looked out to sea, and as the clouds and fog parted he glimpsed a ship. On the summit of the islet, a yellow light beckoned, promising the ship safety from the storm.

Anger ripped through him, then coldness and the urge to kill. He looked back at the entrance to the cave. Deidre waited there, just out of the wind's fury. She stood with her feet apart, her clothes making her appear to be a man except for the wild golden mane framing her face and shoulders. Her face no longer appeared male or female, but rather carried the look of a righteous avenger. He nodded in satisfaction. She would be all right, for at this moment her civilization had been stripped away.

He beckoned and she joined him. With little time to save the ship, he knew they still couldn't be careless for too much depended on their actions.

Bending low, he edged away from the relative safety of the cave. Deidre followed him. As he moved, sometimes crouching down on his hands and knees, he used the cane to find a safe path when the fog and rain obscured his vision. Although the rocks were sharp against his bare feet, he had grown up running barefoot across hot Arizona desert. A little pain wouldn't stop him.

He continued, dodging from rock to rock, glad their movement was covered by the sound and density of the storm. He had to get into a position where he could see the location and count the number of the wreckers. Until then he couldn't plan any type of action. He glanced back, made sure Deidre still kept up with him, then went on.

Finally he found a place that satisfied him. He stopped behind a ragged outcropping of rock and Deidre knelt beside him. He pulled her close to share their warmth. It couldn't stop the rain and wind, but he felt better for the shared closeness.

On his stomach, he crawled around the rocks until he could see the beach down below. As the fog cleared, he saw a ragged line of rocks jutting outward from the islet. He had little doubt the rocks would rip out the bottom of a ship, iron-hulled or not. Fury rose in him again, but it was cold and controlled.

Fog swirled around him and he waited. When it lifted, he found the wreckers. About a dozen men, maybe women too, were clustered together on the warm side of a rocky windbreak. As far as he could tell, they all wore pistols and knives. He wondered if Lady Caroline and Hayward were there, or if they had already returned to the warmth and safety of Palmetto. Captain Sully would be down there, or somewhere else on the island.

Baring his teeth, Hunter turned his attention to the light. Fog swirled and he couldn't tell if wreckers were up there or not. If he and Deidre were lucky, the beacon wouldn't be guarded and they could slip up and destroy it quickly and easily. But when the fog lifted, he saw two men tending the light. He hoped another man wasn't hidden in the shadows.

Cursing to himself, he crawled back to Deidre and took her in his arms.

"There're two men at the ship beacon, maybe more. We'll take them out, then run."

She nodded, her green eyes dark with determination.

"That'll alert the wreckers on the beach, a dozen or more." He hesitated. "I don't know if we can get away. The island's small."

She put a fingertip against his lips to stop him. "We'll give the ship a chance, then take our own chances. Okay?"

He nodded, then kissed her quick, hard, and maybe for the last time. "Whatever happens we'll do it together."

Getting to his feet, he headed for the rocky summit. She came right behind him. Now he was grateful for the storm since it should cover them long enough to give them a better than even chance.

Fighting the wind, the rain, and the rocky terrain, they moved upward, concealing themselves as they went. There might not have been much need—the men on the summit weren't expecting trouble. They were obviously concentrated on keeping the light blazing out its promise of safety.

When they got close enough to attack, Hunter searched the area again, but didn't find a third wrecker. Relieved, he gripped Deidre's hand and whispered in her ear. "Let me take them. If I run into trouble, help me. But, remember, be brutal. It's your only chance."

She squeezed his hand and nodded, hating to see him go but knowing there was no choice. Clenching her dagger, she watched him hurry away. He caught the first wrecker by surprise, but the second was on him before he'd finished with the first. As they struggled, she saw a wrecker fall. While Hunter handled the other, she moved quickly to the summit to put out the light. But just as she reached the lamp, she heard someone behind her.

"What the hell!" A wrecker jerked her around, surprise and confusion on his face as he realized she was a woman and about to extinguish the light. He hesitated.

Remembering Hunter's words, she bit her lower lip and putting all her strength behind the movement, thrust her dagger where she hoped his heart beat. She was surprised at how much strength it took, but she saw the sudden red on his shirt, heard his grunt of pain, saw him grip the hilt of the dagger between his hands, then stumble to his knees and fall to the ground.

Forcing herself not to think, not to feel, she whirled back to the light and felt hands join hers. She glanced up, fear tightening her chest. Hunter. She nodded in relief and together they put out the light.

He checked the man she'd stabbed, jerked out the knife, wiped it clean on the wrecker's clothes, and handed it back to her.

She hated to touch the dagger again, but she took it anyway since she knew she'd most likely need it again.

"They're all dead." Hunter hugged her. "Let's get the hell out of here."

"Look!" She pointed at the beach.

The wreckers below were looking up in confusion. When they saw Deidre and Hunter, they shook their fists and started climbing upward.

Hunter pulled at Deidre, but she resisted, looking out to sea. The fog lifted and revealed the ship. "Hunter, is it safe?"

He hesitated, knowing the wreckers would be on them soon. But he wanted to know if the ship was safe, too. The fog swirled around them, then parted again. The ship had begun its turn away from the rocky islet. He grabbed Deidre, hugged her hard, then set her back. "*Now*, let's get the hell out of here."

They ran, slid, stumbled, fell, picked themselves up, then hurried toward the shore away from the wreckers. They could hear the men cursing and calling as they reached the summit. But the weather protected Deidre and Hunter as they hurried onward. When they reached the other side, only the raging sea greeted them. They looked back. The wreckers had seen them and were gaining fast.

Hunter took her hand. They rushed along the shore, wondering how they could escape. Outnumbered, outgunned, they stood little chance.

Suddenly, Deidre stopped. She pointed at a rocky inlet with several small boats moored there to ride out the storm. "Can we survive in one of those?"

"I don't know. It's our only chance. Come on." He led her down to the water's edge.

Waves splashed up high against the rocks, tossing the boats about. Deidre felt a new fear rush through her, for to brave the storm in one of these boats seemed not much better than facing the wreckers. But perhaps this would give them a chance. She glanced back. The wreckers had found them again. There wasn't much time.

Hunter leaped into the water and cut the rope

on the first boat and tossed the end inside. Picking up Deidre, he waded into the water, then set her inside the boat. He pushed the boat outward, away from the inlet and toward the storm. Soon water lashed around his face and he clung to the side.

"Get in the boat." She reached out a hand to haul him in beside her.

He shook her head. "I've got to cut loose the other boats so the wreckers can't follow."

"How can they in this storm?"

"We can't take a chance. Lay down in the bottom, protect yourself. I'll catch up."

Horrified, she saw him swim back, waves crashing against him until the fog obscured him and the wreckers. He was saving her. He didn't think they both could make it. Sudden tears burned her eyes. No! She couldn't go without him. It wasn't fair. They'd both worked to save the ship.

As the boat moved toward the open water beyond the islet, she picked up an oar and attempted to steer it to the side. The boat caught against the rocks. She didn't know how long it could stand the punishment of the wind and rock, but she had to give Hunter a chance to reach her.

She looked backward and when the fog lifted, she saw the other boats loose and bobbing outward in the storm. Some were smashed back against the rocks, some continued to move outward. Then she saw the wreckers on the rocks. They were trying to get at the boats, wading into the water. But where was Hunter? Had they killed him? Had the storm drowned him? A terrible ache in her heart threatened to overwhelm her. Tears ran down her cheeks to mix with the salty water of the sea.

Her only chance was to go on, brave the storm, maybe somehow survive. But without Hunter?

The fog moved in, concealing everything, then just as suddenly rose. She looked again for Hunter. She didn't see him, but realized the wreckers had seen her. Some were running around the inlet to catch her before she made it out to sea. Now she had no choice. She had to live to tell the authorities about Lady Caroline and Hayward.

But how could she go alone?

"Hunter!" She cried out as loud as she could, hoping she would be heard over the sound of the storm. "Hunter! Over here." As she edged the boat toward the open sea she called to him over and over again. But she had little hope of him hearing her.

As she gained the opening to the inlet, she felt one end of the boat tilt. Whirling around, she held her dagger ready. The wreckers wouldn't take her easy. But it was no wrecker who drug his weary body across the bow to land in a heap at her feet.

"Hunter!" She pulled him to her.

He shook the water from his face, grabbed an oar, and made sure they cleared the rocks to enter the open sea. As the storm swallowed them, he let go of the oar and took her in his arms. "You shouldn't have waited." He took deep breaths. "They almost got us both."

"But they didn't. We're free!" She threw back her head and felt the rain pelt her face. It stung but she didn't care. They were alive and that's all that counted.

"Don't celebrate yet." He pulled her down into

the bottom of the boat and encircled her with his arms.

She snuggled against his warmth. They'd saved the Clarke ship. Now they were in the hands of fate, and the storm.

"I heard you call. I'd never have found you otherwise. Why'd you wait, Deidre?"

His breath was warm against her face and she snuggled closer. "We're partners. Remember?" It wasn't what she wanted to say, but she didn't know how to explain her feelings.

"Thanks." He held her, trying to ease the brunt of the storm with his body. But the boat was tossed about in the waves and rain poured down on them.

"Do you think we'll make it?"

"Depends on how soon the storm blows out. We've come this far, we'll damn well swim if it comes to that."

Smiling, she held on to him. With Hunter by her side, how could she fail?

As the storm continued to rage around them, they clung to the boat and each other. But finally they could feel a drop in the wind, in the waves, and the rain slackened until only cloudy skies remained. Sitting up, they looked around, but all was a mass of gray. They tried to bail water, but they only had their hands and it didn't help much.

Suddenly the clouds parted and the sun came out, shinning down, making the water sparkle. The wind died. A calm settled over the area as the clouds moved out to sea. It was hard to believe such fury had tossed the small boat about such a short time ago.

"Where do you think we are?" Deidre sat up and rung water out of her hair.

"Let's hope we haven't been driven out to sea." Hunter scanned the horizon.

"Do you think they'll come after us?"

"I don't know if they can." He hesitated, gripped her arm, and pointed. "Is that land?"

"Look! Birds."

He hugged her close. "Give me those oars."

As he started rowing, Deidre looked behind them, still afraid the wreckers might somehow catch up with them. "What island do you suppose it is?"

"Hell, I don't care. The Bahamas are full of islets, islands, and outcroppings of rock. Land is all I care about."

"I'll spell you when you get tired."

"Ever rowed a boat?"

"No."

He shook his head. "I think I can row forever."

Watching him, the water, the land, she felt the sun warm on her head. Safe. Or almost safe. "We know who's behind the wreckers now."

He nodded, looking more like a pirate than the wreckers with his stubble of beard, wild black hair, and hard dark eyes. "And we'll get them stopped."

Wishing she could help, she kept glancing back, trying to keep her mind on the future, not the past. But she wore a dead man's clothes. And she had killed. She'd never forget the feeling as she'd plunged the knife into the wrecker. She shivered, despite the warmth of the sun.

"What's wrong?"

"I was thinking of the wrecker I killed."

"I'm sorry you had to do it. I've killed before and

226

I was trying to get there and do it for you." He hesitated, watching the land get closer. "It's worst the first time. Don't blame yourself. You had to do it. Remember, you saved the lives on that ship."

"I know, but—"

"Don't think about it."

She nodded, then swallowed hard. Had her mother been forced to kill when she'd had the harrowing experience of fleeing New York City? Maybe they could share their experiences some day.

"We're almost there, Deidre."

She forced the past from her mind and smiled. Nothing would suit her better than solid, dry land.

When he was close enough, Hunter jumped out of the boat and drug it onto land. Turning back, he picked up the dagger and put the blade between his teeth. Finally, he lifted her into his arms and carried her to the beach.

Pirate. Oh yes. She didn't struggle this time or play games.

He set her down, took the dagger from his mouth, and led the way.

She followed him away from the white sands of the beach to the shade of trees and shrubs. She realized he was tense. "What's wrong? The wreckers?"

"No. I don't see how they could have followed us in that storm. I want to make sure there's some fruit and water here before celebrating."

"Is this a real maroon?"

"Maybe." He squeezed her hand and smiled a crooked smile. "It's not the maroon with you I mind. It's not having food and water."

As they searched the island, he was glad to see it was bigger than he'd expected, with plenty of shade. Finally, he found what he wanted. Water. A small underground stream bubbled to the surface amid an outcropping of rock. And nearby a few trees bore native fruit.

He turned, grinned, and pressed a hard, hot kiss to her lips. He'd never felt so possessive of a woman before. He felt like he'd won her. He'd fought for her, brought her through the storm, found them food. And he still had one weapon to defend them.

"We're safe now?"

"Yes." He cupped his hands around her face. "I'm sorry she cut your face." He kissed the lash mark tenderly. "Does it hurt much?"

"Not now." She touched the whip marks on his chest. "Do they hurt?"

"Scratches. It'd take a lot more than Lady Caroline's whip to hurt me."

She nodded, suddenly feeling shy. They'd been through so much together so fast that intimacy had been thrust on them. Now she wasn't quite sure how to act.

"Are you hungry?"

"Yes. I'm starved."

He picked fruit for them, then sat down beside her by the bubbling water. He started to cut the fruit in slices with the knife, but remembered how Deidre had used it. He set the dagger aside. He handed her fruit and watched as she greedily bit into it. He drank deeply of the water, then joined her. The fruit was delicious, but it sure as hell wasn't a thick, rare steak.

Eating and drinking relieved her tension and

Deidre felt more relaxed than she had in a long time. It was going to be all right. They were alive and safe. She leaned back, suddenly overcome with a wild desire to experience everything as intensely as possible. Death had been so close. She'd almost lost Hunter. She glanced at him and felt passion surge through her. She wanted him as never before. Embarrassed at her sudden lust, she looked away.

He watched her with hooded eyes. "Why don't we get cleaned up."

"Wash our clothes?"

"And our bodies." He leaned forward and began unbuttoning her shirt.

She stilled, her breath caught in her throat at his touch. He didn't realize how difficult he was making this. She didn't know how to respond after what they'd been through, but the touch of his hands was sending heat throughout her.

Stripping her shirt from her body, he paused to look at her breasts. He frowned, then gently touched the whip marks across her chest. "Do they hurt?"

"They don't matter. Not now."

He stood up. "Come on. Salt water will help clean and heal them." He raised her to her feet and unbuttoned her trousers, pushing them down. After a long moment, he looked up at her face. He was breathing hard. "Quick. Go take your bath."

She understood. She was relieved he wanted her, too. But she needed to wash away the recent horror first. She kicked off her slippers and grabbed the clothes. She walked away from him to the sea, then stood in the gentle surf. She looked out over the

Caribbean Sea. The water that had been their enemy just a short time ago was now their friend. Life continued to twist and turn and surprise her.

She felt Hunter watching her. She glanced back. He hadn't moved. Her heart beat fast when she recognized the desire in his gaze.

Forcing herself to look away, she walked deeper into the turquoise water. After the storm, it wasn't as clear as before, but it was still beautiful. Using sand, she scrubbed the clothes as clean as she could get them, then stretched them on the beach to dry. As she rubbed her body with sand, she heard him enter the water.

He didn't come to her. Instead, he washed his trousers and the leather vest, then stretched them out beside her clothes. While he washed himself he watched her. Finally, he came to her, the expression in his eyes urgent.

She eagerly went into his arms. "Make me forget about death, Hunter. I want to think only of life, of us, of happiness."

Covering her lips, he thrust into her mouth, tasting her sweetness, the juice of the fruit, and her own specialness. He trembled with need so great he could hardly restrain himself from throwing her to the sand and burying himself inside her to release the need she aroused. Instead, he gently caressed her neck, her back, her hips, then pulled her against his hardness.

Abruptly, he stepped back and shook his head. "I'm not sure I can be gentle or slow."

She took his hand and led him across the beach to the shade of the trees. Sitting down, she held out her arms to him. He came to her quickly. She pulled his head down so she could kiss him, long and slow and sweet while her hands roamed his chest, his back, then lower, feeling the ridged muscles across his stomach. When she wound her fingers around his hard shaft, he groaned and pushed her back against the sand.

Massaging her breast, he followed with his mouth, teasing, tasting, nibbling as his hand moved to the soft, hot core at the triangle between her legs. When he felt how ready she was, he looked into her eyes.

"I can't wait either. Please, Hunter, make me feel alive again."

He spread her legs and entered in one swift drive, needing to feel alive as much as she. As he stroked inside her, feeling her tighten around him, feeling her hands on his back, feeling her legs hold him closer, he forgot death and destruction and terror. He thought only of life, of the future, of Deidre as he moved harder and faster inside her, driving their passion to new heights.

She moaned, clutching his shoulders as she cried out his name before he kissed her, plunging his tongue deep into her mouth to fill her completely.

When he felt the sharp release of ectasy take him, he felt her climax with him. They soared upward together. He held them there as long as he could, then they slowly descended back to reality.

He held her tightly a moment, then he rolled to one side to take his weight off her. Keeping his arms around her, he pressed gentle kisses to her face. "I'll get us back safely."

With her eyes closed, she sleepily shook her head. "I don't care if we ever go back."

Smiling, he kissed the tip of her nose. "We have to report the wreckers."

"Maybe they didn't survive the storm." She turned to toy with his scratchy beard. She rather liked the feel of it against her hand.

"Don't count on it."

"You need to rest first."

He nodded. "I'll try to get our bearings and we can start out at dawn."

"And in the meantime . . ." She traced a path down his stomach.

"We'll sleep, then I'll show you how much I want you." Pressing his lips to hers, he kissed her as if there was no yesterday, no tomorrow, only today forever.

When he finally raised his head, her green eyes were dark with the power of his kiss. "I'll sleep some other day. Now all I want is you."

Chapter 16

Sunday afternoon, Deidre walked down the steps of Nassau library with Old Nate at her side. Sunlight warmed the day. No storm was in sight. But she knew that could change in a moment, just as friends could become enemies and innocent people could become victims to someone else's greed. In her search to become an independent young woman, she had learned one vital lesson. Life was change, sometimes steady but just as often abrupt.

Now she wore a dead man's dagger in a sheath strapped to her thigh as well as carried a derringer in her reticule. She was prepared for anything. But she would never feel completely safe again. Even at a library.

The suffrage meeting had gone well. Old Nate had been a surprise for Imogene and the other ladies, but they'd accepted her after she'd told some of her life story and her view of the world. Deidre was glad. The woman suffrage movement could use Old Nate.

As they walked down the Strand, Deidre glanced around uneasily. Although everything looked as it had before she was kidnapped and almost killed, she now knew there was a dark side to everything. Even this slow paced, friendly strip of the Strand. She realized that until her trip to the Bahamas, she had lived in a carefully contained world. It was one her parents had created for her and never wanted her to leave. Now she understood why.

She shook her head negatively at a higgler who was selling straw hats, then went back to her thoughts. Life continued to surprise her. Once she and Hunter had returned, nothing had gone as they had planned. Fortunately, they'd marooned on a small island that turned out not to be too far from New Providence. He had gotten them back safely the next day and they'd celebrated their victory.

But it was short-lived. They soon discovered that law enforcement wasn't the same in the Bahamas as in the United States. They were the foreigners. Lady Caroline, Hayward, Captain Sully, and the wreckers were local citizens. Yes, the authorities agreed there had been wreckers working the local waters but that was not unusual. When pressed, officials had been sent to New Graves Plantation and the islets around it to inquire about the charges brought against the Graves.

Deidre and Hunter had wanted to go along, but they'd been ordered to stay behind. They had waited impatiently to hear the report. When they insisted, they had been told by the authorities that nothing suspicious or incriminating had been found so nothing could be proved. Besides, they had also been told, the Graves were members of a fine, old New Providence family and were not likely to be involved in luring ships onto rocky islets.

The only sop Deidre and Hunter got was an agreement from the authorities that in the future they would examine shipwrecks to see if any had been intentionally caused. But it was obvious the official stance was one of disbelief.

Deidre was not reassured. She thought her family was still in danger. And Clarke ships might still be targets. New Providence had no telegraph system. She wanted to get off the island as quickly as possible and warn the New York office and her parents. Until things changed on New Providence, she thought Clarke ships should take a different route.

Now she knew for sure the Graves were the wreckers who'd destroyed Clarke ships, murdered who knew how many people, and almost killed her as well as Hunter. She wanted Lady Caroline and Hayward stopped and punished. But without taking the law into her own hands, she didn't know how to make it happen.

She glanced at Old Nate. Maybe she should enlist the older woman's help. At least she felt Old Nate should know what had happened and what might happen again. Anyone could be in danger with the Graves and Sully still in business.

"I thought they'd be snobs at the library." Old Nate waved at several friends as she walked.

"They liked you."

"And why wouldn't they?" Old Nate chuckled.

"Are you going to attend the meetings?"

"If they changed from tea to whiskey, I'd be a damn sight more likely to go."

"I can see you're going to keep shocking them."

"It's good for them."

"I don't doubt it." Deidre wondered if Old Nate might be getting tired of walking. "Why don't we hire a carriage?"

Old Nate looked at her in shock. "Just to Smuggler's Den? What've we got legs for?" She increased her pace.

Deidre hurried to keep up, then decided it was time to tell about the wreckers. As she talked she realized how farfetched the tale sounded. If she hadn't actually experienced it herself, maybe she would find it hard to believe, too. She didn't mention Lady Caroline's jealousy because it was embarrassing and didn't seem relevant.

Old Nate listened without saying a word, but her pace increased until they were almost running down the Strand.

When Deidre finished they were near Smuggler's Den. Suddenly she realized how much she wanted Old Nate's opinion and support about what had happened. But what could one older woman do?

Old Nate gave her a hard stare, then walked over to the beach and stopped. "So that's how you got the mark across your face."

Deidre touched the tender, healing wound. "Yes. And the law won't do anything about the wreckers. They found no proof. I've got to leave right away to warn my family and Clarke Shipping. I wish the

236

Graves could be stopped, but at least I've warned you."

Old Nate squinted up at her. "You want me to do something?"

"Can you?" Deidre hoped she didn't sound insulting or skeptical. "I mean, if you hear anything you could let me know. Perhaps we could still get proof."

Looking out to sea, Old Nate pointed at the wide expanse of water. "A lot can happen out there with nobody the wiser. It'd be hard to prove."

"I understand that now."

"I've sailed these seas all my life. And that's a long time. I know every sailor, every family." Old Nate looked at her hand. "I gave an arm to that ocean. And I'm not the only one. We honor what's ours. The sea. The ships. Our skill." She clenched her fist. "It's one thing to salvage. It's another to kill ships and people."

The intensity of Old Nate's words sent a chill up Deidre's spine. "Lady Caroline has a vendetta against my parents. Perhaps it's clouded her reason. I'm afraid she won't stop now."

"I suspect you're right. But she's an islander. I wonder how far she'll want to carry this war from New Providence?" Old Nate turned back, anger in the lines of her weathered face. "We're not all like that. Most Bahamians are honest, hard-working folks. And we take care of our own."

Deidre opened her mouth to respond, but Old Nate held up her hand.

"Leave it to me. I'll talk to your man and—"

"But I know as much as him."

Old Nate shook her head. "Around here, there's

237

a right way to do something and a wrong. Leave it to me." She started toward Smuggler's Den. "All this talk's made me thirsty. Let's get a whiskey."

Deidre followed Old Nate onto the gray porch of Smuggler's Den, thinking that she needed to find a way to prove she could handle the situation equally as well as Hunter. But when they walked inside, he was waiting for them. He waved them over to a barrel by a window. While she joined him, Old Nate went after drinks.

As she sat down, she forgot about trying to prove anything. Simply being near Hunter excited her senses, made her want to be back at the Royal Victoria in their suite. In bed. She felt as if she could drown in the warmth of his chocolate brown eyes.

"How'd the meeting go?" He leaned toward her, searching her face as if to make sure she was all right.

"Better than you thought it would. It took a little while, but they saw the value of Old Nate and want her to come back."

"Good. She's a hell of a woman."

"I told her about the smugglers. She may be able to help." Deidre resisted touching him, but she felt so close to him after all they'd been through that sometimes it was hard to think of them as separate people.

Old Nate set a tray on the table. As she sat down, she picked up a glass of whiskey and saluted them. "I think I taught those suffragist ladies a thing or two."

Deidre and Hunter clinked glasses with her.

"I bet you did." Hunter drank.

"That Imogene isn't half bad." Old Nate looked thoughtful. "Fact is, she's talking about writing a book on my life at sea." She frowned. "Can you see anybody wanting to read that?"

"I'd like to." Deidre nodded vigorously. "I'll buy copies for myself and everybody I know."

Old Nate smiled, almost shyly. "I told Imogene if we were going to do it, we'd better get started. I'm planning to make a hundred, but who knows after that."

"We'll rent the Royal Victoria to celebrate your hundredth birthday and your book publication." Hunter grinned. "I guarantee it'll rival the Blackade Runner's Ball."

Old Nate laughed. "Let's drink to that."

They did.

Hunter shook his head. "You know, it'll never be the same around here if you and Imogene get together."

"Best thing to happen. It's been too dull lately." Old Nate held her glass up and examined its contents. "And this wrecking is bad business. I told Deidre I'd talk to you, then we'd visit some friends of mine. Caroline, Hayward, and Sully can't do much if they've got no wreckers working for them."

"You can do that?" Deidre looked at the older woman in awe.

"Not saying I can or can't. I'll look into the matter and your man'll let you know what happens."

"But I can help."

"Thought you had to get home." Old Nate took a sip of whiskey. "You got to get on with your life, but I'll expect you back for the birthday party."

"Of course I'll come back, but—"

"I'll work with Old Nate." Hunter interrupted as he nodded at the older woman.

"Leave it to us then." Old Nate tossed down the last of her whiskey and got up. "Remember. Watch your backs." She walked behind the bar and began polishing its shiny surface.

"What do you supposed she can do?" Deidre stopped her words when she looked up to see Lady Caroline, Hayward, and Captain Sully enter through the back door. She realized Old Nate must have seen them first. Her respect for the older woman grew even more.

Lady Caroline walked right up to them. And smiled.

Deidre couldn't decide between the dagger or the derringer, then realized that both shooting and stabbing were too good for the woman. A watery grave seemed best.

"What a surprise to see you here. I thought you preferred the open sea." Lady Caroline played the lady of the manor to the hilt. Hayward and Sully stopped just behind her.

Hunter gripped the glass he held, then casually took a drink.

"You left in such a hurry the other night, you forget your bags. We delivered them to the Royal Victoria for you." Lady Caroline sat down. "You don't mind if I join you, do you?" Hayward and Sully moved in close.

Deidre pulled the derringer out of her recticule, but kept it in her lap. She felt cornered and didn't like it. Yet they would never make her a victim again.

240

"We had some visitors out at Palmetto. Seems you had sent them. We were happy to take them on a little tour of the place, of some caves nearby, but they didn't seem to find what they were looking for." Lady Caroline raised an eyebrow. "Did you really think they would?"

"You're not as smart as you think." Hunter's voice was low and rough.

Lady Caroline smirked. "But I'm smarter than you seem to think, Hunter dear." She gazed at Deidre. "I should warn you that he can be quite ungrateful and not dependable, if you've hired him now."

"Hired him?" Deidre looked confused.

"Yes. Didn't you know?" Lady Caroline pressed her lips together, then smiled. "I hired him to sabotage the Bar J Ranch. He brought you here to sell to me. I planned to use you to get what I wanted from your parents."

Deidre sat stunned, trying not to believe her ears.

"I see you didn't know. I paid Hunter a lot of gold and not a little of my body for his services."

Hunter threw back the last of his drink, but said nothing.

"I don't believe you." Deidre felt frozen inside.

"As one woman to another, I'm simply trying to be helpful." Lady Caroline patted her hair. "You should know he likes his women easy. And he likes his gold that way as well."

"He helped *me*." Deidre gripped her derringer.

"Of course." Lady Caroline stood up. "He must have decided your parents would pay a higher price to save their precious dynasty. But it won't do them any good. Their days are numbered. Tell them that for me. It won't be long before I have all that belongs to them and their bones are bleaching in the sun."

Deidre drew the derringer and aimed it at Lady Caroline. "You dare to even think of hurting my family and anything that belongs to them ever again and you'll answer to me." She took a deep breath. "I can work just as well outside the law as within it. Now get the hell out of here and don't let the Clarke-Jarmon name pass your lips again."

"Big words from a baby. You've got your work cut out for you, Hunter." Lady Caroline raised a perfectly arched eyebrow. "And may the best *woman* win." She turned her back and walked out the way she'd come, with Hayward and Sully guarding her all the way.

When the back door shut, Deidre let out a sigh and dropped the gun in her reticule. She finished the whiskey in one swallow, felt it burn to her stomach, then turned to Hunter. "Can you believe her nerve?"

"I think we'd better talk."

"Yes. I want to talk with Old Nate about her friends and how we're going to put a stop to those wreckers. After that, I could use another whiskey."

Hunter stood up. "No. Not here. I'll get with Old Nate later." He threw some money on the barrel.

Confused, Deidre watched him walk over to the bar, say a few words to Old Nate, then come back. He took her arm and led her outside. She couldn't help looking around for Lady Caroline, but their boat had left.

Hunter flagged a carriage and soon they were on

their way down the Strand. He ran a hand through his hair and turned to her.

She smiled and patted the derringer in her reticule. "I took care of her, didn't I?"

Hunter reached for her hand and squeezed. "She told you the truth."

Deidre froze. "What?"

"She hired me to cause problems on the Bar J. I brought you to Nassau to turn you over to her."

She jerked her hand away. "You're kidding."

"No. I worked for her, but I swear it never involved killing anybody. I'd never have hurt your parents. Or you."

Feeling as if she couldn't breath, Deidre shook her head. But the stunned feeling was quickly being overcome with anger. "You've been working for her all along? You've been her lover even while you were with me?"

"No. I didn't touch her again after I met you. I couldn't. And I couldn't let you be harmed once I saw what she intended to do."

"But you worked for *my* parents. They trusted you. I trusted you."

"I told you from the first you were so green you were dangerous. To yourself. To others." He tried to take her hand again, but she jerked away. "The world doesn't run on faith or trust or kindness. Everybody's out for themselves and even the honest go to the highest bidder."

"No! Not everybody's bad."

"I'm working for your parents now, Deidre. I'll get with Old Nate and we'll find a way to stop the wreckers."

"No! You're fired! I'm going to New York and stop Clarke ships from sailing here. I'm going to warn my family. I'll deal with Old Nate and the wreckers as soon as I can."

"I'll take care of it. You go on. I'll let you know—"

She slapped him. "You're fired! Do you hear me? Fired! Stay away from my family." She stood up and tapped the driver on the back. "Stop this carriage." She leaped down and looked up at Hunter. "I'm leaving on the first ship out and you'd do well to stay out of my way."

"Deidre, no!" He paid the driver, tipped him heavily to keep his mouth shut, then followed her.

She headed up the walk toward the Royal Victoria.

Grabbing her arm, he jerked her around. "How can you act this way after what we've meant to each other? What about the storm? The maroon? Our kisses?"

"Nothing! It all means nothing because you've been lying through your teeth every minute. Liar!" She turned around and started walking away.

He caught up with her. "Deidre, I'm sorry. But how the hell was I to know I'd meet you on this job? I promise I didn't know about the wreckers or I'd never have worked for her. I admit I understood her need for revenge, but I never thought it'd go so far."

Stopping, she turned stormy green eyes on him. "I don't want to hear any more excuses. Go away." She hurried up the final few yards to the hotel and disappeared inside.

He followed her, trying to think of some way to

reach her, some way to make her understand. He felt as if she had taken hold of his heart and wrenched it out of his chest and taken it with her. Stupid. He'd known better all along than to get involved with a rich, pampered lady. He'd been doing his job, yes, but he'd saved her, saved them both, and the ship. What more could she ask?

Inside the hotel he saw her talking with a clerk at the desk. She nodded, then turned around. When she saw him, she glared.

He needed to get her alone and talk it out. Better yet, if he could take her in his arms he'd make her understand how right they were together. Once she felt passion for him again, she'd forget about the anger.

She walked over to him, her green eyes wintry. "I have a place reserved on a ship that's leaving today. The hotel staff will pack my trunks and send them down to the wharf. I'm leaving now. Thank you for your help in escaping the wreckers and saving the Clarke ship. I'll see you're suitably re-warded. It'll be sent here to the hotel." She hesitated, then raised her chin. "Goodbye."

He couldn't believe her. But she had turned and was walking away from him. "Deidre!" He hurried after her.

Outside, she stepped into a carriage and was driven away. He started to follow. He could have caught up with her. But he stopped.

What the hell did he think he was doing? He couldn't compete with the power of money. He'd been up against that and a closed family as a child. He'd lost then just like he'd lost now. Whatever she wanted, she got. Even him. When she got tired of something or it caused a problem, she threw it away. Even him. He couldn't compete, couldn't get close. And why would he want to? He'd had enough of women like her to last him a lifetime. He was a fool to think it'd ever been more than a job. For either of them.

He walked back into the hotel. He'd finish his work on New Providence. Old Nate would help him. Then he'd go back to the States. He'd had a gut full of the Bahamas. He never wanted to see a turquoise sea or white sands again. Suddenly maroon had become a dirty word to him.

Starting up the stairs, he looked back. When he realized he was watching for her, hoping she'd come to her senses and run back to him, he shut down that part of his mind. He had a job to do. Stop the wreckers. And when it was done, he'd move on like he always did.

For a man like him, a man with few scruples and a hard hand, there was always plenty of work.

And that was all he needed.

Part Three
Rainbow Within the Clouds

Chapter 17

"You haven't acted the same since you got back." Simon Gainesville took off his spectacles and wiped them with his hankerchief. "From your clothes to your attitude."

"I'm not the same." Deidre Clarke-Jarmon gazed at her friend with warmth. He was tall, thin, intense, with dark blond hair, gray eyes, and a narrow face. His clothes were always slightly rumpled, as if he'd fallen asleep in them. But his mind was sharp.

"You haven't settled back in yet, that's all."

Shrugging, she glanced around the popular French restaurant. At one time she had been impressed with the elegant decor. It had been her choice to meet here. Simon didn't care where he ate and couldn't afford a place like this without her signing the bill.

"Deidre, you're not eating. Do you want me to finish your lunch for you?"

She pushed her plate toward him. "You look thinner. Have you been skipping meals? You know you must eat to keep up your strength." He was always short of money and always hungry. As a newspaper reporter he didn't make much, not yet anyway, and what he did make he gave away to causes and people more needy than himself.

He picked up his fork and pointed it at her. "Now that you're back I'll probably gain weight. You always take good care of me."

She smiled. Somebody had to do it. When he was on the trail of an article or helping someone, he frequently forgot about himself. Sighing, she realized too often she felt like his nursemaid.

"So. Are you going to let me do that article about Clarke Shipping, or not? Bahamian wreckers are bloodthirsty enough to make good copy."

"I don't think so, Simon. I'm not sure it's all settled yet. I may have to go back."

He set down his fork. "Not without me, you're not."

She raised an eyebrow, realizing she had affected Lady Caroline's superior attitude. "Are you saying I can't take care of myself?"

"No. I'm saying the place is dangerous. And I'd like to write the story." He drank half a glass of water. "Now that I think of it, it's a great idea. When are you going back?"

"I don't know." For some reason she'd never noticed how pushy Simon was with her before. He was the son of a Quaker minister, his family hadn't had much money, but through connections they'd

250

gotten him an excellent education. He had graduated near the top of his class at Harvard. He'd learned a lot there, but he'd learned his respect for women and a determination to right all wrongs from his Quaker church and his own personal view of life.

Although he continued to talk about wreckers and the Bahamas, Deidre's mind wandered. Would Simon be willing to sacrifice himself, and anyone else, to his dreams and ambition? Suddenly she felt chilled. She had always respected his intelligence, his education, his determination, his goals. But now she feared he might be willing to sacrifice them both for his ideals, just as Lady Caroline had been ready to do. Of course, it wasn't the same.

She picked up her tea cup and sipped. She watched Simon without hearing his words. When she'd first met Hunter, she'd compared him to Simon. Now she was comparing Simon to Hunter. She couldn't help remembering Hunter's physical strength, his sensuality, his skill with life. Startled, she realized she had learned as much from Hunter's education in life experience as Simon's education at Harvard.

But Hunter had betrayed her. And Simon was still her friend. She glanced out the window at the busy street, her eyes narrowed in thought. She realized she'd picked up that mannerism from Hunter. Sighing, she looked back at Simon. Had she no life of her own, no personality? Did she have to depend on men to teach her, to show her, to make her a whole person?

No. She'd set out on this journey to become an independent young woman. She had learned a lot, but now she realized there was still much more to explore. She hadn't yet become her own person and she wasn't quite sure how to go about it. But she did know that being Simon Gainesville's handmaiden was not the way. And succumbing to the lure of untrustworthy men like Hunter wasn't either.

She raised an eyebrow and narrowed her eyes, suddenly feeling a new strength flow through her. "You are not to print an article about Clarke Shipping's problems in the Bahamas. We don't want customers and passengers worried."

Simon stopped in mid-sentence, obviously surprised at the interruption. He frowned. "You *are* changed. Did you tell me everything that happened to you?"

She smiled, a secretive, seductive movement of her lips.

Simon leaned forward, as if he were seeing her for the first time. He seemed mesmerized by her mouth.

"Remember, you wanted me to be an independent young lady. Well, I'm learning." She pressed her lips together. "Until I've talked with my parents, I don't want you mentioning Clarke Shipping in the *Tribune*."

He watched her lips a moment longer. "All right. If you promise you'll take me with you back to the Bahamas."

"No. I can't." Amazed at her ability to withhold her approval, she suddenly felt good about herself. "I don't know what will happen and I simply can't make a commitment like that right now."

Simon pushed his plate away from him. "Independence is one thing, Deidre. This is something else."

She started to say she was sorry, but bit her lip instead. "I have my family to think about and the employees of Clarke Shipping."

Still frowning, he nodded. "I guess you've got a point. The fact is, there's plenty to report right here in New York City. I'm writing a story about the terrible conditions of child labor."

As he went on to describe the horror he'd seen, she nodded, thinking about what she and Hunter had been through, of the people who had died on Clarke ships. She had plenty of her own rights to wrong. She'd help Simon all she could, but she had business of her own now, too.

"Deidre!"

"What did you say?"

"That is a good example of what I'm talking about. You had a rough time. I know it. Everybody knows it. But you survived, found out what you needed to know, and now you can go on with your life. There's too much to do for you to rest on your laurels. And I think you've done enough toward becoming an independent young lady."

For the first time since meeting him, she didn't want to hear what he had to say. Maybe she was still tired or maybe nothing here seemed real anymore. How could this restaurant compare to the gritty reality of Smuggler's Den? Right now she'd really like to be talking with Old Nate, the tough, one-armed sailor. They would be drinking bad whiskey and Hunter would be leaning close to her. Hunter. She could almost feel him near her. Now that was reality. *Her* reality.

"There you go again. What do I have to do to get your attention?"

She shook her head. Simon was right. She had changed, but that was what she'd set out to do. She glanced down at the empty plates. She'd lost her appetite since returning to New York and no amount of fancy food seemed to change that fact. Was she really the same person who had told Hunter all about her food preference in the hotel dining room at Three Rivers? Had she actually been that arrogant? Right now, if Hunter offered her a Bar J steak she'd probably be hungry. But she didn't want to think about him anymore.

"The *Tribune* is sending me to cover Lucy Stone's speech sponsored by the American Woman Suffrage Association this afternoon. Do you want to go with me?"

"Lucy Stone?" Deidre felt her mind pulled back to the present. "She's a wonderful speaker, isn't she?"

"Golden throat, no doubt about it."

"I just wish she hadn't separated, along with Howe, Blackwell, and Livermore, to start the American."

"That happened twenty years ago. Will you let it go? I know you prefer the National Woman Suffrage Association, but the American publishes *Woman's Journal* and has a large following, too. They're doing good work."

"You're right." Deidre leaned forward, glad to be back on firm ground. "But Susan Anthony and Elizabeth Cady Stanton are trying to get *federal* legislation for woman suffrage, including equal pay for equal work. The American thinks working to achieve that end through the states is best."

"It's going to take both, if I don't miss my guess. They ought to team up again."

"Maybe they will some day, but right now the American thinks the National is too radical."

Simon finished his water. "Anthony and Stanton as a team can't be beat. Stanton's the philosopher and Anthony's the organizer. Of course, it was Lucretia Mott, beloved Quaker teacher, minister, and abolitionist, who inspired Stanton and helped her organize the Seneca Falls convention. When you think of what they've done for women's rights since that first convention, it's amazing."

"Forty years ago. I've missed a lot." Deidre stroked the side of her fragile crystal glass.

"You ought to be glad. A woman had so few rights in those days she wasn't considered a real person."

Deidre nodded, feeling a spark of emotion. "I mean, women couldn't even *speak* in public, except in Quaker churches, control their own earnings, or have guardianship of their children if divorced. And that's not talking about the right to vote or own their own property."

"At least they're now earning a little more than a fourth of male wages for similar work." Simon's voice grew intense. "And they've got some other rights, depending on the state or territory, too."

"It's not like women didn't ask before. In 1776 when the United States Constitution was being written, Abigail Adams wrote to her husband and asked him to 'remember the ladies and be more generous and favorable to them than our ancestors.' He didn't listen to her, did he?"

"No."

"We have more rights than Abigail Adams, but we still have a long way to go." She smiled, realizing why she'd liked Simon in the first place. She reached across the table to squeeze his hand. "It's good to be back and talk about all this with you." She knew Hunter couldn't have carried on this type of conversation with her. But then, with Hunter she'd hadn't wanted to talk so much or think so much or intellectualize life so much.

Simon stroked her hand. "We can share a lot, Deidre. You know I want to marry you. We make a good team. Woman suffrage isn't the only wrong to right. Slavery is ended, but Negroes still don't have equal rights. Men and women and children are trapped in sweatshops and jobs that endanger their health and don't pay enough to live on. Housing for too many people is bad or nonexistent."

Nodding in agreement, she realized she knew just as much as he did about the situation. The Civil War had turned many women and children out in the streets to find work when their husbands and fathers didn't return or were crippled. Work women had once done at home had been industrialized. Many women with children were abandoned by their husbands. And a third of grown women simply never married. They all needed work outside the home, but there was little to recommend it except necessity.

Deidre sipped her tea as she thought of the report she had read before going to Texas. Four million women were already employed outside the home and the demand for them was growing. But they were wanted for the lowest paying jobs, usually so-called service industries such as clothing manufacture, laundries and cleaning, cotton textiles, shoes. They also worked as housekeepers, stewards, and family servants of all kinds. In short, they were still being offered the work they had done at home before industrialization.

On a happier note, she also knew women were creating an educational system all across America as they started schools and colleges, graduating women teachers. Although it was an uphill battle, they were making education available not only to boys but to girls as well and not only for the rich but for the poor, too.

Women had also created the nursing profession, seeing the need during the Civil War and encouraged by Florence Nightingale in England. After Elizabeth Blackwell's long struggle to receive a doctor's degree, she had opened the Woman's Infirmary Medical School in New York City. She and her all female staff trained women who wanted to become nurses and doctors. The school was such a success that her system of teaching medicine from practical work in hospitals and clinics instead of from theory became the norm in all colleges.

Negro women were also working hard to help their race and sex. Harriet Tubman and Sojourner Truth had worked as abolitionists as well as suffragists, along with others who were equally as committed. Both were powerful speakers who continued to struggle for equality.

Sighing, Deidre understood the cost individual women had had to pay for the progress that now benefited many. But women no longer struggled alone. Help had come in the form of the American and National Suffrage Associations, labor unions, the Grange for farmers, the Women's Christian Temperance Union, Quaker churches, and halfway houses for the needy. Newspapermen like Simon were doing a lot of good, too.

She finished her tea and smiled. She felt good to be part of the growing movement.

"Millionaires who live like kings while their workers live in squalor have got to be forced to change." Simon hit the table with his fist.

Defensive, Deidre squared her shoulders. "My family provides jobs and pays its employees livable wages, but sometimes I worry about my privileged life."

"Don't feel guilty." Simon shook his head. "Use your position to make changes as other women who inherited wealth have done. Just think, Sophia Smith of Massachusetts founded and funded Smith College to provide and promote equal education for women." He took a deep breath. "That's what I like about you, Deidre. You want change, you're working for change, and your family has the money and jobs to make it possible."

She nodded, but shivered inside. What about sharing passion, love, life, family? Suddenly she realized that Simon could never desire her in the same way that Hunter had. Simon's passion was focused on righting wrongs for groups of people. She wasn't sure how real individuals were to him. Maybe she shouldn't have gone to the Bahamas. Then she'd never have known the difference and been happy with the dreams Simon offered. He was a good man. He was right in his dedication to helping others. But was he right for her?

"Deidre?"

She looked at him.

"I've never seen you so distracted."

"I have a lot on my mind."

"You've got to get focused again and I know the way to do it. Let's go hear Lucy Stone speak."

She set aside her napkin and stood up. "Good idea."

Early that evening Deidre walked up the steps to the entrance of the Clarke mansion. Simon was right on her heels, talking about Lucy Stone's speech. The front door opened from the inside to reveal Maud McGill. Deidre smiled at the housekeeper as she walked across the threshold. Maud and her husband Sam were the caretakers of the house and grounds. They'd been with the family as long as Deidre could remember. She knew her mother had total confidence in them and Deidre had always adored them.

Maud, a petite woman with iron gray hair and hazel eyes, closed the front door, made sure it locked, then turned to Deidre. "Will you be wanting dinner?"

Deidre noticed Maud's lips were pursed which meant the housekeeper was displeased. She wasn't surprised. Maud had never approved of Simon as a marriage partner for Deidre, although she thought highly of his determination to help people. Deidre had never understood Maud's disapproval of the possible marriage before, but today she began to understand. Deidre wanted to be first in a man's life and she didn't much think that would ever happen with Simon. She supposed Maud had always known it.

"Hello, Mrs. Maud." Simon smiled. "You'd have liked the Lucy Stone speech we heard today."

Maud inclined her head, but her lips remained pursed.

"It was wonderful." Deidre realized she didn't want to spend the evening with Simon, as they had so many times, working through dinner and wine, then moving to the parlor, all the while discussing problems, strategy, goals. He had kissed her after one of those sessions, but now she realized it hadn't sparked her nearly as much as the idea of getting the right to vote. And it had not compared to Hunter's kisses at all. But she didn't want to think about the man she had left in the Bahamas.

"Dinner?" Maud pushed.

"I'm tired." Deidre threw Simon an apologetic glance. "I think I'll go to bed early. Maud, why don't you bring tea to the parlor?"

Maud nodded in approval, her lips relaxing. "I made some fresh gingerbread. I'll bring that, too."

"Wonderful." Deidre watched her walk away, almost wishing she wasn't being left alone with Simon.

He took her arm and led her toward the parlor. "Are you feeling well? You haven't seemed yourself all day."

"I'm all right. Just tired."

In the parlor, she edged toward a chair, but he steered her to a couch and sat down close to her. Taking her hand, he twined their fingers together.

All she could think of was how Hunter had done the same thing but with such different results. She reminded herself that relationships weren't built on passion alone. Still, she wanted to pull away from Simon. He reminded her to much of her loss of Hunter. But she didn't move because she didn't want to hurt his feelings.

"I don't mean to rush you." Simon took a deep breath and turned to face her. "But after your dangerous trip to the Bahamas, I'm worried about you. I think we—"

"Here we are!" Maud bustled into the room, set the silver tea service down on a table near them, then set about placing china cups on saucers, pouring tea, serving up hot, steaming gingerbread, then handing it all to them. She gave Deidre a hard stare. "Remember, you want to get your rest after that trip." She turned to Simon. "Don't keep her up late." After a last backward stare, she left the room.

"What was that all about?" Simon got up and shut the door behind Maud. "I guess she's worried about you, too." He sat down, picked up his plate, ate the piece of gingerbread, then went through two more pieces before he picked up his tea cup and leaned back near Deidre.

She knew exactly what Maud had been doing, although it was most unusual for the housekeeper to interfere in her life. Maud must really be worried. It made Deidre more concerned, but she reminded herself that Simon was a very good man, deserving of respect and loyalty.

Simon finished his tea, set the cup aside, started to take Deidre's hand, noticed she held a teacup, then settled for an intense look on his face. "Where

261

was I? Oh yes, I don't mean to rush you, but we've known each other for over a year. You know how much you mean to me. I want to take care of you, protect you, see you get all the rights a woman deserves. And I don't want you to be in danger like you were in the Bahamas without me there to help you."

Sipping her tea, Deidre stalled to get her emotions under control. Had Simon changed, too? "I don't understand. You were so helpful before I went to see my parents. You encouraged me to use the experience as a young woman coming of age, gaining strength from struggling to deal with the reality of life. Why now do you think I need protection?"

"Deidre! You were almost killed. You were degraded. You were alone with only strangers to help you."

"But I came out alive. I found out about the wreckers. No Clarke ships are going through that area now. I learned. I grew. And I'm not done yet."

Simon shook his head. "If I'd had any idea it would come to all that I'd never have encouraged you. You're a gently bred woman. Wreckers! Pirates! Sailors!"

"Suffragists are traveling all over the country, from farm house to ranch to town spreading the word, collecting signatures on petitions, giving speeches to total strangers. You approve of all that. How is what I did different?"

He sighed and poured himself another cup of tea. "Well, for one thing it was more dangerous. The other is that I don't want to lose you. Not to death or to a cause or to another man."

"Man?" Her green eyes widened in alarm. She'd not told him the depth of her relationship with Hunter. Had he guessed something?

"I love you, Deidre. I want to marry you right away. Then we will be a team. We can fight battles, right wrongs together. We can be like Lucy Stone and Henry Blackwell. You can even keep your last name like she did when we marry. But let's not wait."

She set down her teacup and stood up to pace the room. She hardly noticed the softness and the faded hues of the Aubusson rug under her feet or the patina of the rosewood furniture. The soft rose and blue patterned upholstery and drapery were completely lost to her. Her mind raced in one direction then another. Stone and Blackwell. Clarke-Jarmon and Gainesville. She shivered. No, not yet.

Walking over to the door, she opened it. "Simon, I'm more tired than I realized."

He got up and hurried over to her. He shut the door and took her in his arms. "I can make you happy." Lowering his face, he touched his lips to hers. Gently, then harder, trying to force entrance to her mouth.

She pulled away. "Simon, no. Not now. I—I'll think about what you said, but I must have time."

Dropping his hands, he looked at her with sad gray eyes. "I'm beginning to understand why men marry women and try to keep them at home."

She stepped back. "What do you mean?"

"You've been so sensual, so beautiful since you returned. I can hardly stand the idea of another man watching you, wanting you." He took a deep breath. "It's that man your parents hired to help you, isn't it? What did you two do all alone on those islands?"

She slapped him. The sound rang out loudly in the room. "How dare you question me."

Grabbing her shoulders, he shook her. "You were mine before you went away and you will be again." He pulled her to him and forced his mouth to hers, demanding entrance, forcing himself on her as his hands roamed her back to her hips. He pulled her hard against him, letting his passion flow over her.

Once more she wrenched away, wiped her mouth with the back of her hand, panting slightly. "What's wrong with you?"

"I can be as passionate as the next man if that's what you want. I've been gentle with you, patient, and it's been difficult waiting, courting." He touched his face where she had slapped him and took a deep breath. "Your coldness is making me crazy. I want you. I need you. Don't do this to us."

"I told you I'd think about what you said."

"Deidre, I don't want to lose you." He held up empty hands. "I love you. You're a beautiful, desirable woman. I'm a man. I have needs. I'm sorry if I offended you, but you mean so much to me."

"Give me time." She jerked open the door.

Maud stood in the hall.

"Will you show Simon out?" She looked at the man she had once thought she loved, then turned and walked away.

Chapter 18

Deidre looked out the window of her bedroom on the second floor of the Clarke mansion. Night had fallen. The street below was lit by lamplight and moonlight. Shadows suggested hidden secrets and hungry animals. She dropped the heavy drape and turned back.

She had always liked this room. It had been her mother's before marriage. The colors were green, blue, lavender, black. Wedgewood. Stripes of the colors in embroidered silk made up the draperies over the windows and the upholstery on the wing chairs by the fireplace. The high post of the bed had a straight canopy. The matching silk canopy and bedcover were of an oriental floral design in Wedgewood colors. With age, all the colors had muted into softness. Normally she could relax within these four walls.

But not tonight.

Thoughts swirled through her mind, refusing to be reasonable or to go away. Instead, she felt tormented by her own mind. And her past. Had she been unforgivably cruel to Simon? Should she have given Hunter a second chance? Was she afraid of making a commitment to a man? And if so, was it because she feared giving up her independence? Did she fear giving up rights under the law once she married? Could she depend on a man to look out for her best interests, especially when she stood to inherit a fortune?

Her parents were a good example of a strong, happy, supportive marriage. But she knew many marriages that were good for the husbands only. The women stayed in them because they had no way to earn enough money to take care of themselves and their children. It didn't seem right. Why should women and children be penalized so men could be free to pursue any action, be it business or pleasure?

Straightening her shoulders, she paced, wishing her mind would be still. But she'd studied too much, learned too much, and now experienced too much to ever be completely trusting and innocent again. She had proved her ability to stand on her own during her quest of the wreckers. True, she'd had help, but also true she'd found that help. Now she knew that having done it once, she could do it again.

She sat down at her dressing table and looked at herself in the mirror. On the outside she didn't look so different, except for the fading pink slash across her cheek. Also different was the turquoise satin nightgown Hunter had bought for her in New Orleans. She enjoyed the feel of its soft fabric against her skin, the way it clung to her breasts, outlining their fullness. She could imagine Hunter walking up behind her and leaning down to nuzzle her neck and stroke her breasts. She felt her nipples harden.

Looking aside, she tried to stop the thoughts. Hunter was far away. She'd sent Simon away. For the first time she felt she was truly on her own. As an independent young woman, she had dreams and goals of her own.

Yes, dreams and goals.

She picked up the notes she had been making over the past several days. With time to think and plan, she had decided that in order to help herself, the family businesses, and woman suffrage, she needed higher education.

Before the Civil War, no women's colleges had existed and women were not allowed to attend men's colleges. But fortunately for her that had now changed. She had choices. If she wanted to stay in New York state, she could attend Vassar, or Cornell which had become coeducational. If she went to Massachusetts, she could attend Wellesley, Smith, or Radcliffe near Harvard.

The thought of attending a real college with subjects and requirements the same as at the men's colleges made her feel excited. She could become a teacher, a doctor, a lawyer, an astronomer, but it would be difficult as a woman to find work outside teaching. She might be smarter to concentrate on taking business classes so she could help with Clarke Shipping or the Jarmon Plantation or the Bar J Ranch.

But her brother Thor was studying business at

college. Her father would be active in the businesses for a long time to come. What about her mother?

She set aside the notes on women's colleges and picked up the telegrams she'd been steadily receiving since she'd returned. As she read through them again, she realized something was changing. First the telegrams had been from her father, but after securing the Bar J, he had left for Louisiana to take care of problems there and dismiss anyone who worked for Lady Caroline. He didn't plan to be gone long.

Left alone, with plenty of time to think, Alexandra had asked Deidre to come back to the Bar J. But Deidre had sent a telegram telling her mother that she wanted to stay near the Clarke Shipping office in case any new problems turned up regarding Lady Caroline. Her mother had agreed, then cabled later that she felt guilty for not having been more involved with the business her parents had left her. Deidre had done her best to reassure her mother that there could have been no way to anticipate Lady Caroline's twisted mind.

She set aside the telegrams. Her mother was worried about her, about the family, about the business entrusted to her so long ago. Now that her children were grown, the ranch and plantation secured, would Alexandra turn her attention to Clarke Shipping?

Deidre hoped she would and hoped she would be allowed to help even while she attended college. Let Thor manage Jarmon Plantation since he loved it so much, let her father continue to expand the Bar J Ranch, but leave Clarke Shipping to mother and daughter. She smiled. Study business, yes indeed, then find a way to provide more good jobs for women.

That decision made, she decided to visit her mother as soon as the wrecker situation was completely under control. Together, they could discuss the future of Clarke Shipping and Deidre's plans to attend college.

Feeling more settled, she thought she might be able to sleep. She laid down on the soft, comfortable bed, but immediately felt wide awake. She picked up *Vindication of the Rights of Woman* from the bedside table, opened it to a chapter, but couldn't get her mind to focus on the words.

Hunter. Beds reminded her of the man who had so excited her senses. Images of brown eyes, thick black hair, and tanned skin flitted enticingly across her mind. She could almost smell his scent, feel his fingers caressing her skin. Oh, Hunter.

She set the book aside as tears filled her eyes. She wouldn't allow herself to cry. Independent young women did not cry over ruthless men who had betrayed them.

The thought of Hunter touching Lady Caroline made her furious, but it was a fury that had begun to cool as time and distance worked their healing magic.

Lady Caroline hadn't been brought to justice. Could Deidre depend on Hunter and Old Nate to stop the wreckers? Should she depend on them? Now that Clarke Shipping had changed its route, now that her parents had been notified and were taking action on their own, should she let it all go and focus on her own life?

She'd heard nothing from Old Nate or Hunter

in two weeks, although she had sent them both money in payment for their services. She'd also sent Imogene donations for the Nassau Library and the New Providence Woman Suffrage Association.

All seemed in order, or as much as she could make it now. But she longed to know if the wreckers had been permanently stopped. And more, she longed to feel Hunter's arms around her.

Could she have been so wrong about him? Had she been more hurt than anything? After all, they had saved each other's lives. He'd said that once he'd met her, he hadn't gone back to Lady Caroline. Could she blame him for what he'd done before they met? Could he blame her?

She thought of Simon. Was their intellectual closeness any less intense than Hunter's physical liaison with Lady Caroline? How would Hunter feel about Simon if he knew? She smiled, thinking of Hunter jealous and hurt and angry. She liked the idea. But he was far away, maybe no longer in the Bahamas. Perhaps she would never see him again.

Sitting up in bed, she felt her heart beat fast. Maybe she should return to Nassau, confront Hunter, get it settled between them, and find out about the wreckers.

She lay back down. She had no intention of going crawling back to him. He'd probably moved on, anyway. In a week or so, she'd send telegrams to Imogene and Old Nate to learn what had happened there.

Tears filled her eyes again and her heart felt heavy. Hunter and all they'd shared seemed far, far away. Another time. Another life.

And what of Simon Gainesville? He said he loved

her, but was it love for something he'd created? If he had molded her into the image of his perfect woman, could he now not help but want to possess her forever?

She shivered and pulled the covers up around her chin. Her relationship with Simon was more complicated than she'd realized. She didn't want to think it, but Simon could make good use of her family's connections, power, and money in his campaigns and career. She didn't blame him for wanting that because she wanted to use it to help, too. But she wanted desperately to be loved for herself. She wanted a man to burn for her, to lose himself inside her as if there were no tomorrow. As Hunter had done on Hog Island.

Had he loved her then? Or had it been simple passion for him?

And, more important yet, had she loved him?

She sat up in bed again, then swung her feet over the side. Love! Had she fallen in love with Hunter? Had it been more than excitement, education, desire?

She had thought she loved Simon. But now she realized she loved him as a friend. For Hunter she'd thought her feelings were strictly passion. But what if her love for Hunter encompassed passion and friendship and ideals?

Dangerous. What could be more dangerous than that combination? And yet it had worked for her parents. Jake Jarmon and Alexandra Clarke had fought and loved and gone through agony and loss to finally reach each other. Their love had endured, had seeded itself in two children, and grown stronger through the years.

She sat down on the edge of a wing chair. Love. Hunter. She felt excited, trapped, exhilarated, afraid. What did he feel? She had no way to know. Perhaps he had already forgotten her.

And what did she want?

She still wanted to vote.

She wanted love but she wanted freedom, too. Could a woman have both?

Sighing, she returned to bed. It wasn't something to settle in a single night. She had too many questions, too many doubts, but she understood herself a little better and maybe that would help. Shutting her eyes, she willed herself to sleep, not knowing if it would be better to dream or not to dream of Hunter.

Bright and early the next morning, Deidre walked into the kitchen. Surrounded by warmth, wonderful scents, and a cheery room, she felt some of her confusion and doubt lift. Here she felt at home, loved, in control. But even here she had a nagging feeling of something left undone. Hunter came to mind but she stopped that thought.

Seeing her, Maud hurried over. "You'll be wanting breakfast now, won't you?"

"Yes. Thanks. I thought I'd go down to Clarke Shipping and see how much trouble I can cause."

Maud chuckled and began gathering food.

Deidre set two places at the table, then motioned for the housekeeper to join her.

Maud set food on the table, then sat near Deidre to warm her hands over a mug of tea laced with cream and sugar.

As Deidre poured cream and honey over a steaming bowl of oatmeal, she felt better. Soft, sweet food comforted her as it did when she was a child.

Maud pursed her lips. "That Simon coming back?"

"Simon?" Deidre took a bite of food, then smiled in contentment.

"Don't play games, missy." Maud tapped her finger on the table. "Did he hurt you?"

"No." She hesitated, feeling her appetite wan. "But I realize now he thought he had more rights where I'm concerned than he ever had."

Maud looked pleased. "What about that man who's been haunting your eyes since you got back?"

Deidre completely lost her appetite. "What makes you think there's another man?"

Chuckling, Maud glanced around the cozy kitchen. "I know you. And I've lived a few more years than you. I figure the man I'm talking about is the one who helped you. What's his name?"

"Hunter."

"When's he arriving? I'd better get a room ready."

"He's not coming here. Ever." Tears stung Deidre's eyes and she dropped her spoon in the oatmeal. She stood up, blinking hard. "My eyes aren't haunted. I'm simply busy. I've been making plans for my future. Right now I'm going down to Clarke. Maybe they've heard something from the Bahamas."

"Is this Hunter still there?"

"How would I know?" Deidre walked to the doorway, then turned back. "Simon is supposed to go with me to a piano concert this evening."

"Simon?"

"I already asked him. The Woman's Piano Trio is performing original compositions by Clara Schumann and Fanny Mendelssohn. I do so love women's music and it's disgraceful the way their work is normally overlooked. Maybe overlooked is too mild a word. Suppressed would be more accurate. Anyway, I'd like to wear that green silk gown I got in New Orleans."

"I'll see if it's ready, but it's not Simon's kind of dress."

"So. I don't know if I'll even go with him. I'm going to ask Charlotte, too."

"Good. Better not be alone with Simon. It'll do you good to spend some time with your women friends. You've been alone too much since you got back."

Feeling irritated at being told what was best for her, Deidre frowned and walked from the room. Then she hesitated, realizing Maud was looking out for her best interests since her parents weren't there. Relenting, she turned back and walked into the kitchen.

Maud stood still, her lips pursed.

Deidre hugged her. "I'm sorry if I was snappish. Thanks for caring."

Maud returned the hug, then set her back. She blinked away tears. "You'd better hurry along or you'll be late."

"Thanks."

As she walked away, Maud called after her. "There's something for you in the foyer. Messenger brought it early."

"Really?" Deidre felt excitement race through her. Had she finally heard from Hunter?

She hurried to the foyer. A small package had been placed on the table. It wasn't addressed which seemed odd, but she opened it anyway. She discovered a jeweler's box, opened it, and saw a small gold heart etched with an arrow through it. She felt a sinking sensation in the pit of her stomach. This wasn't like Hunter. She opened the small white card and read it outloud. "Forgive me? See you tonight. Simon."

She dropped the box and card on the floor, then stalked from the mansion. A carriage awaited her. She stepped into it, then sat down on the leather cushion. Anger rushed through her, although she tried to control it. Why the pin? Simon had rarely given her anything and certainly not jewelry. The heart with an arrow through it felt like a slap in the face. Was he trying to make her feel guilty for shooting an arrow into his heart? Was he trying to show ownership by getting her to wear it?

Well, she wouldn't do it. He'd expect to see the pin on her gown that evening. Hunter's green gown. She clinched her fists. Not likely!

She took a deep breath. Hunter had bought her all those clothes and she'd not reacted this way. Simon had bought her a simple gold pin. But the reasons for the gifts were miles apart. Hunter wanted her sensual for him. Simon wanted to possess her. But, wait, Simon supported woman suffrage. Hunter took women for his own pleasure.

Possession. Pleasure. Had both men had the same

motivations? Or did she simply not understand men at all?

She pressed her palms against her forehead. All this was giving her a headache. Whatever reason they'd had for buying her gifts, she didn't care. She loved the clothes Hunter had bought for her and encouraged her to buy for herself. She hated Simon's pin because it would make her feel guilty every time she wore it. And she had *nothing* to feel guilty about. She'd never promised him marriage. They'd been friends. He'd pushed for more.

And she wouldn't be pushed, not anymore. She wasn't right for Simon and she'd tell him so that night. But she'd still ask Charlotte to come along. She wanted a buffer for as long as possible. If she hadn't asked Simon a week ago, she'd cancel her invitation. But she wanted them to stay friends, to work for woman suffrage together. She only hoped he would listen to reason.

As the carriage pulled up in front of the Clarke building, she pushed thoughts of Hunter and Simon from her mind. She was thinking of men too much lately. She should be thinking of the family business or her own future. She needed to write a letter to each of the colleges she was considering and find out about enrollment. Once she started taking classes, she wouldn't have time to think of Simon or Hunter. And that was the way she wanted it.

The driver opened the carriage door, helped her down, then opened the front door of the Clarke building for her. She smiled her thanks, then stepped inside, knowing she hadn't really needed his help. Once more she was struck by the dimness inside the place. Heavy, dark furniture simply added to the problem. In short, it didn't look modern. And it wasn't.

Perhaps, if money were available, they could transform the offices into something more cheery, more updated. Of course, it would still have to look respectable, solid, comfortable. What would her mother say? She hoped she wasn't going to have to forget all her dreams for Clarke Shipping.

One change had already been made at the front desk, thanks to her own insistence. Charlotte Aikens, a woman in a man's world, sat at the front desk, typing.

Deidre paused to watch her, amazed at how fast she could use the typewriter. Charlotte was one of many women moving into business offices. Deidre had worked hard to get her a job at Clarke Shipping. As the first woman to invade the male domain, Charlotte hadn't had an easy time of it but she loved the work. Deidre planned to encourage the company to hire other woman typists.

In fact, she wanted to learn to type herself. She'd found out recently that there were already more than sixty thousand typewriters in use. She definitely thought it was the wave of the future and she wanted to be part of it. And she especially wanted to see more typewriters in use at Clarke.

"Good morning." She walked toward Charlotte's desk.

Charlotte finished typing, then looked up. She grinned. "If you've come to work, you're already late. The Clarke cousins have been at it for an hour or so."

"But are they getting anything done?"

277

Deidre walked up to Charlotte's desk, thinking that she'd never quite straightened out her relationship with the Clarke second and third cousins. Perhaps that was because she'd never spent a lot of time around them. She did know that jobs at Clarke always went first to relatives and she thought it was due to policy and tradition rather than to her mother's preference.

But she also knew her mother had stayed out of dealing with the cousins as much as possible in the past. She wasn't surprised. It all went back to a time before her birth. By right, Alexandra had inherited Clarke Shipping as the only child of her parents. But the male Clarkes thought they should inherit and be in charge. They had tried to take the company away from her by marrying her off to one of the cousins. But her mother had foiled all their plans by running away, meeting Jake Jarmon, and marrying him.

Deidre glanced around. Maybe now her mother would come back and really take charge of her inheritance. Alexandra could stand the cousins on their ear and make Clarke Shipping a force to be reckoned with. And her daughter would be right in there to help and support her.

"What are you plotting?" Charlotte set aside the page she'd just finished. Petite, with wild red hair pulled back snugly in a chignon, she wore a simple gray skirt and a white blouse. Not traditionally beautiful, she had charm and wit and energy. She was also an ardent suffragist whom Deidre had met at a National meeting.

"Ideas for the business. I think I'll go back to mother's office and plot some more."

Chuckling, Charlotte put a fingertip to her lips. "Please don't tell the cousins. You know how they hate change."

"But Clarke Shipping needs it. After looking over the information on our fleet of ships, I realized some of them aren't even iron or steel hulled. We may be sending clipper ships out there for all I know."

Charlotte shook her head again, her blue eyes twinkling. "If you have your way, you're going to have this company going overland."

"That's not a bad idea. I've been thinking of it myself. I'll be sure to mention it to mother. I'm going home to talk with her about the business soon. In fact, I believe she's thinking of taking a more active part in management."

Charlotte lowered her voice. "Please don't tell anyone here that. They're disturbed enough by your presence and losing those ships in the Bahamas. If your mother decides to do it, she'd better tell them herself."

Deidre sighed. "It's because we're women, isn't it? I don't suppose getting the right to vote will change male opinion about women in business and politics."

"Why should it? Do you really think they want the competition?"

"You've got a point, a real good point. But at least we've got more of an opportunity for equal education now." She leaned closer. "Did I tell you I'm thinking of going to one of the women's colleges. Maybe Vassar, Smith, or Radcliffe."

"Deidre! That's wonderful. I wish I could do it, too." Charlotte hesitated. "But I've got to work. You know I'm helping to support my parents since Dad got hurt."

"I know. But did you think about attending Cornell here in town? It's coeducational now."

"I've got to work."

"You wouldn't have to attend full time. Maybe you could get off work early or come in late or something. I'd be happy to pay for it."

"No." Charlotte shook her head hard. "I won't take charity."

"What about a small loan from Clarke to pay tuition that would make you a more valuable employee?"

Charlotte grinned. "Is that possible? I mean, the loan, adjusted work hours?"

"I don't know. Don't say anything to anybody. Let me talk with mother about it. I'll look at Cornell's class schedule and find out about tuition." She narrowed her eyes. "Of course, we should offer the option to men, too, if they need or want it."

"Thanks. I'm so excited. It'd open up all kinds of opportunities I'd never have on my own."

"You're good for the company and with more education I don't see why you couldn't do other work."

Charlotte's eyes shone brightly, then she looked glum. "But I'm a woman and the men would never accept me doing their work."

"Don't think about that now." Deidre raised an eyebrow. "Instead, think about Clarke hiring more women to work in the office with you."

"Soon?"

"Again, I've got to talk with mother. Don't expect

anything right away. It'll probably be months. But it's time for some changes around here."

"Changes?" A deep male voice boomed out.

Deidre jumped in surprise. Looking around she saw one of the Clarke cousins, a Winchell, Wilton, or William. They varied in age but most were of medium height, a little plump, and tended to lose their dark hair early. This one, she realized by the cut of his clothes, must be in charge of something.

"Mr. Clarke." Charlotte stood up. "May I help you?"

By Charlotte's attitude, Deidre decided he might be in charge of everything.

"You young ladies are making far too much noise. You can be heard all over this floor."

Deidre figured the only way that could have happened is if everybody on the floor had been congregated near the door eavesdropping. But she didn't say that. Instead, she smiled pleasantly. "I wouldn't want to interrupt work. In fact, I'm on my way to mother's office now.

Mr. Clarke's face flushed. "Do you need help?"

"Thanks, but no." She started to walk away, then looked back. "Charlotte, I've got an extra ticket for the Woman's Piano Trio tonight. They're playing Clara Schumann and Fanny Mendelssohn. Would you like to go with me?"

Charlotte leaned forward. "Yes. I'd love it."

"Great. Simon and I'll pick you up at seven."

Charlotte's eye widened. "Simon?" She cleared her throat, trying not to look embarrassed. "I wouldn't want to impose. I mean, after all, surely you two want to be alone."

"Just say you'll come with us and all will be well."

"Okay then."

"Great. We'll talk later." Deidre walked around the Clarke cousin with a smile on her lips, humming a popular tune. Until now, she hadn't realized how much she would enjoy shaking up their rigid little world.

Chapter 19

"You're not wearing the pin." Simon took off his spectacles and wiped them with his handkerchief. "You hated it."

"No." Deidre led the way into the parlor, disliking what she was going to have to say and yet feeling excitement at the same time. She wanted to be free of old obligations to go on with her life.

"You're mad at me for last night. I admit I was out of line. I apologize. That's why I sent the pin. I'd never hurt you, Deidre."

She walked over to a rosewood table and picked up the jeweler's box. Turning around, she held it out to him. "I can't accept this because I can't marry you."

Simon put on his glasses and slumped into a chair. "You're furious with me. You think I'm not a true suffragist. You think I'm like all the greedy men who take what they want from women, then go on their way. It's not true. I believe in the suffrage movement."

Deidre held up a hand. "I know you're a suffragist. I know you will do your utmost all your life to help people. You are a good newspaperman. You have a wonderful future. And you'll help many people."

"Then what's wrong?"

She sat down across from him. "I love you, Simon. As a friend. I'll work for woman suffrage until we have the vote and equal rights by law, but I'm no Susan Anthony to devote my entire life to the cause. I want to do other things, too. I plan to attend college, to work at Clarke Shipping, to be with my family, to help women in my own way."

"You can do all those things with me. I'd never try to stop or control you."

"That's what you did last night. That's what you've been trying to do since I returned."

"How can you say that?" His gray eyes were wide in astonishment. "I'd never do that to you."

She smiled sadly. "Think! You are so caught up in what you want to see done in society that no one else quite exists to you as a person."

"That's insulting." He stood up and paced. "I've always supported your goals. And what better base for marriage than friendship?"

"I want more. If I want marriage at all." She walked over to him, clutching the jeweler's box in her fist. "Don't make this difficult for me, Simon. I want us to remain friends. I'm sorry if I've hurt you by not agreeing to marry you, but I have my own life to live."

He stuffed his hands in his pockets. "I still say it's that man. You're not the same. Maybe you're no longer the woman I fell in love with."

"Maybe I never was."

"What does that mean?"

"It means that perhaps you tried to create *your* perfect woman in me."

He turned away.

"And something else. Do you think I couldn't change on my own? Do you think only another man could have made me see life differently?" She took a deep breath. "If that's what you believe, then you're not the suffragist either of us thought you were."

Whirling around, his gray eyes were stormy. "You must think because I support the rights of all people and put their needs before my own that I'm a weak man who can be walked on by any woman who tries. You're wrong."

"I know you're strong, Simon. But this isn't about you. I'm sorry if I've hurt you. I admire you. I value our friendship. But this is about me and what I want out of life."

"And you don't want me." He frowned and clenched his fists. "Is that supposed to make me feel good?"

"I don't feel good about telling you."

"Then don't." He stepped closer to her. "Forget all you've said. Let's set a wedding date. Anything less won't do."

"I guess I've made a mistake. I thought we could still be friends. I thought you'd understand." She stuffed the jeweler's box into his pocket. "Tonight

I prefer to attend the concert without you." She strode toward the door.

"Deidre!" He went after her, grabbed her arm, and whirled her around. "Let's don't quarrel."

She jerked her arm away. "This is no argument. I am *not* going to marry you. If you ever want to be friends again, let me know." She paused, her green eyes cold. "And I'll think about it."

She stepped into the hall and with relief saw both Sam and Maud. They moved forward to block any ideas Simon might have about following her. Never looking back, she walked at a sedate pace toward the kitchen. When she reached the cheery room, she sat down at the table. And waited, tense. When she heard the front door slam shut, she relaxed.

A moment later, Maud walked into the kitchen. "Sam is waiting at the door to make sure he doesn't turn back. But I don't think we'll have any more trouble from him."

"I thought I knew Simon."

"It's time you learned we can never see completely into the depths of another person. I'm sorry it was painful for you, but you did the right thing."

"Thanks." Deidre squeezed Maud's hand. "I don't much feel like attending the concert, but Charlotte's waiting for me."

"It'll do you good to get out. Sam is going to drive you himself. Now, do you want something to eat before you go?"

Deidre shook her head. "I'm not hungry. What if Simon goes to the concert?"

"He won't. If I don't miss my guess, he'll be drowning his sorrows with whiskey."

"I didn't want to hurt him."

Maud patted her shoulder. "You didn't hurt him. He hurt himself. You can't stop people from bruising themselves on you when they want more than you're willing to give. It's a lesson a woman best learn early or she'll give her life away to keep other people happy."

Deidre tried to smile, but gave up. "Coming of age is a lot more painful than I thought it would be."

Chuckling, Maud shook her head. "You might as well get used to it because you won't completely come of age till they lay you in your coffin."

"Thanks. Just what I wanted to hear." Deidre kissed Maud on her cheek. "I might as well go. If I stay here I'll only worry. Charlotte and the Woman's Piano Trio should cheer me up."

"I'll bake you something special for when you get home."

"Thanks, but—"

"I want to do it. Now, off with you. Sam's bound to have the carriage around front by now."

"What's wrong?" Stepping into the carriage, Charlotte obviously sensed Deidre's despondent mood.

"Simon's not coming with us."

Charlotte sank against the soft leather seat. "Why not?"

"I told him I wouldn't marry him and he got upset. He even tried to force me to change my mind."

"And you're surprised?"

"Of course!" Deidre turned toward Charlotte,

but she could see little in the shadows. "I mean, he's a suffragist. He believes in our independence, equality, the vote."

"But he's a *man*. You represent a great deal to him. With your family's power and wealth behind him and you by his side, what couldn't he have done?"

"What about me?"

"I'm sure he loves you. He'd have tried to make you happy. You're beautiful, intelligent. You've got everything. Why wouldn't he love you?"

"You sound bitter."

"I never told you, but Simon was interested in me at one time."

"Charlotte! It's not my fault, is it?"

"No. I'd never have been enough for him. He's ambitious. In one way that's good. He'll help a lot of people. But he used me and walked away."

"Oh, I'm sorry. I wish you'd told me before." Deidre felt terrible for both of them.

"I thought he might be right for you and you for him. That's why I didn't say anything."

"But you've watched and waited, haven't you?"

"Yes. He's a good man, but not for individual women, I think." Charlotte squeezed Deidre's hand. "I'm glad you aren't going to see him anymore. I won't worry now."

Deidre gripped Charlotte's hand. "How can I be so blind about men?"

"You aren't. Simon loves you, wants you. He'd do almost anything to get you."

Deidre sighed. "But does he love me, the real me?"

"Will you ever know? Does it matter?"

"It matters. If I can't be loved for myself, then I don't want to be loved at all."

"I agree." Charlotte pressed Deidre's fingers, then pointed outside. "Look, we're almost there. I'm looking forward to this concert. Don't let Simon spoil it. He'll make his own way through life, with or without you. And he'll do a lot of good."

"But without us."

"We'll do plenty of good on our own."

Deidre nodded. "Right. And the first step is to hear the Woman's Piano Trio. Without him."

Sam stopped the carriage in front of a Quaker church, then opened the door for them. They stepped down. Deidre glanced over at him. Like his wife, he was short, with iron gray hair and hazel eyes. His body was solidly muscular and he wore a bulldog expression on his usually relaxed face.

"Thanks, Sam." Deidre smiled at him. "You can go on home now. We should be done in about two hours."

"I'm waiting." Sam's jaw jutted forward. "Nobody's going to bother you with me around."

"I'm sure they wouldn't dare, but I know you'd be more comfortable at home."

"I'll walk you to the door, then wait in the carriage. You think Maud would ever let me hear the last of it if I left you two alone tonight?"

Deidre relented. "You've got a point. Thanks. I know we'll feel better with you around." So much for independent young women who could take care of themselves.

As they walked up the steps to the front of the church, a man detached himself from the stone masonry and stepped forward. Lamplight fell on his face, casting it in sharp planes and angles. He wore all black.

Deidre gasped, felt faint, then euphoric, then disbelieving.

"What is it?" Charlotte took Deidre's arm and steadied her up the stairs. "Who is that man? He looks dangerous."

"Hunter." Deidre scarcely said the word.

"Do you know him?" Charlotte's words were hissed under her breath.

The man in black stepped out in front of Deidre, looking at her slowly from head to toe then back again. "I've come to get you, Deidre."

Charlotte's fingers dug into Deidre's arm. Sam moved closer to protect her. Deidre could hardly think, much less react as she looked at Hunter in much the same way he looked at her. Hunger. Deep, bone-grinding hunger.

She didn't think she'd ever wanted anything or anyone as much. Without consciously willing it, she reached out to him. He took her hand and pressed it to his lips. His mouth felt warm, hot, feverish. And he transferred the heat to her. Suddenly she was burning up.

"You know this man?" Sam's voice was gruff.

"Yes." Deidre responded faintly.

"Maud sent me straight over from the house. She thought Deidre'd be glad to see me." Hunter smiled his crooked smile. "Maud fed me, too. She insisted I'd still get here first since you had to make another stop."

"That's Maud." Sam relaxed. "If she says you're okay, then you must be."

"Did you come to hear the concert?" Charlotte

regarded Hunter in puzzlement. "It's the Woman's Piano Trio."

"They're to play Clara Schumann and Fanny Mendelssohn." Deidre tried to sound normal. She'd forgotten how deeply Hunter affected her, or maybe she'd forced herself to forget. No wonder she hadn't been able to stand the thought of marrying Simon, good man though he was or thought he was.

"I'm not here to hear music. I'm here to get Deidre." Hunter's voice was low, rough, almost caressing.

Deidre shivered in response and realized he still held her hand. In embarrassment, she pulled it away and turned to Charlotte.

"Now I understand a lot." Charlotte hugged Deidre. "You should have told me."

"But I left Hunter in the Bahamas."

Hunter stepped forward and held out his hand. "Come on, Deidre, it's time to go."

She didn't hesitate. She placed her hand in his as if it were the most natural thing in the world to do. She turned to Sam. "Would you wait for Charlotte and take her home?" With an affirmative nod from Sam, she turned to Charlotte. "Please forgive me, but I want to talk with Hunter. Enjoy the concert."

"I will and thanks for the ticket." Charlotte winked at Hunter. "I'm Charlotte Aiken. I'm a friend of Deidre's and a suffragist, too."

"Somehow I'm not surprised." Hunter grinned, flashing white teeth. "Pleased to meet you. Now if you'll all excuse us, we'll be on our way."

Hunter led Deidre down the steps and to a enclosed carriage waiting nearby. When he lifted her up, his hands pressed tightly around her waist. He gave the driver instructions, then settled onto the seat beside her. In a moment, they had left the small Quaker church behind.

Now that they were alone, Deidre didn't know what to say. She felt hot, flustered, her heart beat fast. She wanted to run, to sing, to dance, to hold Hunter and kiss him and stroke his body and feel him deep inside her. She was much too glad to see him and knew it. Trying to control herself, she stopped the thoughts. And noticed how quiet they both were.

"I thought you might not see me." Hunter's voice was deep, hesitant.

"You surprised me."

"I thought it best."

"Did you get the money I sent?"

"Yes. I gave it to Old Nate. She added it to what you sent her. She's using it to fix up Smuggler's Den and everybody's complaining. She'll probably stop soon."

Deidre could just imagine the salty sailors hating any kind of change. "I miss her. And Imogene."

"Imogene told me to tell you thanks for the contributions and that she's already ordered more books."

"I didn't want her to be dependent on Hayward."

"Do you want to hear about the Graves?"

She tensed. What if he still worked for them? What if he'd gone back to Lady Caroline's bed? She couldn't stand those thoughts. "I hope the wreckers have been stopped."

"Captain Sully and his crew are out of business."

"Really?" She turned to stare at him.

"Did you think I wouldn't keep my word? It's about all I've got, you know."

"I didn't mean to insult you."

"Old Nate's got more clout than you might think and with me there to back her up we got the job done."

"Then Clarke Shipping has nothing to worry about now?"

"Right. But I'd keep the route varied for a while to make sure. Old Nate could turn up dead."

"What!"

"It could happen, tough as she is. I hated to leave her alone, but she told me . . . well you can guess what she said to me. And she's got other friends to help her."

"If you think there's the slightest chance of her getting hurt . . ."

"There's a chance, sure. But there's a chance we'll turn the next corner and be dead. You can't live trying to outrun your time." Hunter glanced at the driver flicking the reins over the horse's backs. "But that's not what I came here to talk to you about."

"You came to tell me about the wreckers. Thanks." She sat rigidly away from him.

"Yes and no." He glanced at her. "You left a lot of unfinished business behind."

She couldn't look away from his warm brown eyes and she couldn't speak either.

"I brought it with me."

Forcing herself to turn away, she gripped the seat of the carriage with both hands. "I think you'd better take me home. I'm not sure I'm ready for this."

"I'm taking you home. I'm going to take you into

a room and lock the door and I'm not letting you out till we've settled this between us."

Anger rushed through her. "How dare you speak to me that way?" She raised an eyebrow and narrowed her eyes. "This is *my* home we're talking about, *my* life and *my* world. Don't you think you're a little out of your depth?"

"No. I've ridden the high road and the low road. I'm not out of my depth anywhere."

"What about at a suffrage meeting?"

He hesitated. "Well, you've got me there. I can't say I know all that much about suffragists, but I could stand being in a room full of women." He chuckled.

"Typical male!"

"I hope so." He nodded at her. "Okay. Let's make a deal. You take me home and talk to me real good and I'll go to a suffrage meeting and listen with all the respect I can muster. What'd you say?"

Actually, she didn't want to talk. She didn't want to go to meetings. She wanted to take him to bed and keep him there until she'd satisfied the hunger gnawing at her. But she didn't tell him that. "You'd go to a suffrage meeting?"

"Deidre, anything that important to you is worth listening to. And I hope you feel the same about me."

She licked her lips. "I—I'm hungry."

Throwing back his head, he laughed. "I'm starved, but I've been that way since you left me."

"Oh!" She felt her face flush in embarrassment. "I meant food."

"You got any Bar J steaks we could cook up at your place or do you want to go to a restaurant? I'll tell you right off I'd rather be alone with you, but if I have to endure people to keep you happy I will."

"I'm suddenly so hungry I could eat the whole Bar J herd."

Hunter laughed again. "Damn but it's good to hear that wicked tongue of yours again."

"It's not wicked. I was merely telling you how hungry I am. Let's go home. Maud promised to leave me something special to eat."

"I think I already ate it."

"Beast!" Without thinking, she hit his shoulder with her fist, then realized she'd touched him too intimately when he looked down at her, a gleam in his eyes. "All right, we can talk. But you must promise to attend a suffrage meeting with me."

"Okay, you've got my promise."

"We eat first."

"Seeing you has slaked some of my thirst, but it's going to take a lot more than that to satisfy me."

She glanced away, unable to stand to see the hunger in his eyes mirror what she felt inside. How could she even talk to him when she wanted to rip off his clothes and throw him to the floor and cover his body with hers? She stifled a groan. Is this what happened to young ladies when they became independent young women? No wonder men were afraid to give women the right to vote. Who knew where it might lead?

Chuckling, she turned to Hunter and smiled, a slow, seductive movement of her lips.

She thought she heard him murmur *wicked* under his breath.

So she leaned closer and smiled a little harder.

Chapter 20

Outside the Clarke mansion, Hunter paid the carriage driver, then escorted Deidre up the front steps. They walked inside and Deidre made sure the door locked behind them. For her, the house suddenly seemed too large, too quiet, too much an accomplice to her private meeting with Hunter. She glanced toward the parlor, remembered her earlier unpleasant experience with Simon, and led Hunter toward the kitchen. She hoped Maud would be there, waiting up to see that she arrived safely home.

But the kitchen was empty. Maud hadn't even put out food. That surprised Deidre, as did the housekeeper's absence. She supposed Maud had already retired to the guesthouse in back where she and Sam lived.

Oddly enough, light glowed in the dining room. Puzzled, Deidre walked in there and stopped in astonishment. At one end of the long Duncan Phyfe mahogany table, a setting for two of linen, crystal, china, and silver had been set out. A candelabrum gleamed in the center, ready to be lit. On the sideboard, a mound of delectible food had been placed on platters, in bowls, and piled onto plates. It was enough to feed a large family.

How had Maud known Deidre would suddenly be famished after having had no appetite for weeks?

She glanced at Hunter. He had charmed her housekeeper, no doubt about it.

A crooked smile touched his lips. "Expecting company?"

"Maud said she'd leave something out for me, but this is an amazing assortment. What did you say to her?"

He shrugged. "We spoke about the beauty of the Bahamas." He picked up a bottle of wine and two long stemmed glasses. "Let's talk."

"What about the food?"

"It'll keep."

"Only if you've already eaten." She picked up a cinnamon roll. It was as if she'd never tasted food before. The roll was wonderful. She groaned in pleasure, then tried a pickled apple slice. When that was gone, she ate a slice of fresh bread, then reached for more.

Hunter stopped her. The touch of his hand against hers made her hunger change. She saw the passion she felt mirrored in his face.

Swallowing hard, she accepted the glass of wine.

He tapped his glass against hers. It rang like a bell. "To understanding."

She nodded and touched the glass to her lips, watching him as she took a sip.

"I want to see your room."

"My bedroom?" She felt hot all over.

"Yes." His eyes darkened to the color of melted chocolate.

"It's not appropriate." She stalled, trying to collect her thoughts. But her rational mind seemed to have deserted her.

"When did we ever care about propriety?"

How true. She shivered, licked her lower lip and watched the hunger in his expression leap another notch. Clutching her wineglass, she turned and led the way back through the house to the staircase. Maud had marked the path with just enough light here and there to see the way. Now she could only think of her housekeeper as an accomplice to her succumbing to Hunter.

As she walked up the stairs, she could feel him close behind her. She reassured herself that they would simply talk. He had a lot of explaining to do. She couldn't take him to the parlor with its bad memories. And her bedroom would be quiet, private. Even as she made excuses for her behavior, she knew she simply rationalized what she wanted to do, where she wanted to be with him.

At the top of the staircase, she paused. She could turn back now. Hunter placed a warm hand against her back. No, the course was set, maybe had been set since Three Rivers. But they *would* talk. Afterward, she would eat dinner until she was too stuffed to move.

She opened the door to her bedroom, stepped inside, noticed even here Maud had left soft lighting. She held open the door. Hunter hesitated on the other side of the threshold as if awaiting her invitation.

She beckoned him inside.

He stepped into the room, shut the door behind him, then locked it. "Thanks." He leaned down and placed a soft, warm kiss on her lips.

Fire burned through her. She felt weak. But she managed to stay in control. She gestured around. "My bedroom."

Hunter took the wineglass from her and walked across the soft carpet. He set the bottle of wine and two glasses on a small table by the wing back chairs. Then he carefully walked around the room, examining the oil paintings on the walls, the view from the windows, the draperies, the bed. He looked at her bed long and hard before turning back to her.

"I thought a lot about where you were sleeping, where you sat and thought, maybe read." Hunter focused completely on her. "I wondered what you wore in your bedroom, if you'd thrown out all the clothes I'd bought you. I wondered if you thought of me when you stretched out on your white sheets that were probably trimmed with fine lace."

He moved over to the nightgown laid across the vanity chair awaiting her. He picked it up and held it to his nose. He sniffed the expensive fragrance that clung to it. His fist crushed the fabric and he looked back at her. "You kept what I gave you?"

She shivered. "Yes."

"And you wore the nightgowns to bed?"

"Yes."

"Did you think of me, dream of me?"

She hesitated.

He tossed the nightgown aside and strode over to her. He put his warm hands on her shoulders. "Tell me the truth, Deidre. I need to know."

She closed her eyes. "Yes."

Pulling her to him, he sighed against her ear. "I can't get you out of my blood, my thoughts, my dreams. What have you done to me? I want you so badly I'm afraid to touch you." He set her back but kept his hands on her shoulders. "Until I saw you outside that church, I thought maybe it was some spell of the Bahamas. But I was wrong."

She bit her lower lip, almost unable to stand the intensity of his words, his feelings, his nearness.

"It's you. You've cast a spell over me. I need you. I want you. I'm humbled before you."

"Oh." She groaned. "Don't say any more, Hunter. I can't stand it."

"Tell me you want me. Tell me some other man hasn't stolen your heart, your desire, your dreams."

"I want you. Oh, how I want you." She twined her hands around his neck. "I burn for you. How could there be another man?"

He smiled, slowly and with deep satisfaction. Then he put his arms around her waist and drew her close until her breasts touched his chest. As if testing himself, he held off until that contact, then his eyes blazed and he crushed her against him. He pressed his lips to hers, then invaded her mouth, pushing into her with burning heat.

Any doubts she had about his importance to her fled as he deepened the kiss, traced the shape of her body with his hands, scorching his imprint into her body. When he finally raised his head, she could think of nothing but passion, pleasure, and her bed.

She stepped back and took his hand. She led him to her canopied bed, where the covers had been turned back to reveal a lace trimmed sheet. Pulling the silk cover further back, she turned to him. "Come to my bed."

His eyes narrowed. "Are you sure?"

Nodding, she tugged him toward the bed. He sat down, never looking away from her. She stepped back, then began unbuttoning her moss green gown, knowing its color matched her eyes, making them sparkle.

When he reached to help her, she pushed away his hands. She'd waited long for this moment and she wanted it to last. If he'd thought he wanted her badly before, she wanted him to burn with such need he could never, ever forget her and what they shared this night.

She slowly stripped for him, one article of clothing after another until she stood in stockings, high-heeled shoes, drawers, and chemise. Sweat beaded his forehead. She smiled in satisfaction and pulled off the chemise, tossing it to the floor. She knew by his expression that her breasts were bathed in soft light and that he ached to touch them. But she was not yet done. She slipped off her shoes, stockings, then her drawers.

Standing nude before him, she raised her arms to slowly, seductively take the pins from her hair. Finally, she shook her head and her hair cascaded down around her in a long, golden mane.

"Damn Deidre!" He stood up and lifted her into his arms. He carried her to the bed and laid her gently down. He touched her, starting with her face as he moved down her body to her feet, leaving no place unnoticed. Then he turned back and cupped her breasts, massaging until the tips hardened and she breathed fast. Nodding with satisfaction, he placed a hot kiss on each nipple, then lowered his hands to her stomach. He stroked the smooth skin, then stopped.

He looked at her face. "Deidre? Are you . . . with child?"

"What?" She sat upright, covering her breasts as if to protect herself. "Why do you ask? What makes you think that?"

"I wondered, worried, after what we did in the islands. I should have been more careful."

It was something she'd thought about, too. "No. I'm not." But now he'd broken the mood and she wished she hadn't.

He eased her back down. "I'll be careful. It's just that my mother died giving birth to my sister and I can never forget that death sits by the bed every time I enter a woman."

"I'm sorry. I didn't know." She could suddenly imagine the motherless boy and felt her heart fill with compassion. "Where is your sister?"

"She died at birth."

"I'm sorry."

"Don't be." He put a fingertip to her lips to still her, then stroked her long golden tresses. "You hair has always looked like gold fire to me. Indians would treasure it."

She covered his hand with hers. "Are you going to join me in bed?" She wanted to heal the loss of his mother and sister although she knew the wound was an old one and that she probably couldn't touch it. For herself, she needed to feel him close.

Hesitating, he looked down her body again. "I told myself I'd stay away from you, that I'd only talk. But I fooled myself, didn't I? I can no more stay away from you than I can stop breathing." He stood up and began taking off his clothes. "I'll be careful."

"Hurry. I need you." She watched him strip, revealing the hard, muscular planes of his body. He was gorgeous and she wanted to touch every bit of him. Nothing else mattered.

When he came to her, she put her hands on his strong shoulders and pulled him toward her. She felt his hardness against her leg as he settled against her. He kissed her lips, the tip of her nose, then moved lower to her breasts. As he sucked her nipples, he stroked her body with his hands, moving lower and lower.

When he reached the triangle between her thighs, he massaged until she moved restlessly against him. He pushed a finger inside, continuing the movement that made her toss her head with need and grasp his shoulders to steady herself. When he moved his head still lower and replaced his finger with his mouth, she cried out. As he increased the tempo, she arched upward against him, moaning until the tension peaked and she fell back against the pillows as waves of pleasure washed over her.

When she could speak again, she touched his face tenderly. "What about you?"

"I said I'd be careful."

"Please. I want to feel you inside me."

He groaned and got up. He walked away and poured them wine. He brought it back and handed her a glass. As he watched her sip hers, he downed his drink in one long swallow. Then he set the glass aside. She handed her glass to him and he finished her wine, too.

He laid down beside her again. "I'll do my best to make us both happy."

Embracing him, she pulled his mouth down to hers and began kissing him with a wild abandon she could not have imagined a few months before. Then she broke the kiss and placed hot, hard kisses over his face, slowly pushing him back so that she leaned over him. She stroked down his broad chest, toying with the thick hair, then moved lower until she captured his erection. He groaned. She stroked him while watching the emotions play across his face.

Finally he reached for her hips and lifted her. He brought her down with her legs straddling his hips. Then he slowly lowered her down his long column. When she gasped with pleasure, he pushed completely into her. And stopped.

Sweat beaded his forehead and his eyes were dark with desire and control. When he began to move her up and down, she quickly caught the rhythm and helped until both of them were panting with growing tension and excitement.

When she could stand no more, her back arched as she called his name. Then she took his mouth, thrusting inside him with her tongue as she felt him thrust deep inside her. Suddenly she shuddered into an ecstatic climax, clinging to his shoulders as the wave washed over her.

Surprising her, he quickly turned her over so that he was on top, then pulled out as he reached his own climax and spilled his seed on her stomach.

Then he rolled to the side, panting, sweating, pleasure lighting his eyes.

But she wasn't quite so happy. "Hunter?"

"I told you I'd protect you, didn't I?" He got up and walked into her bathroom. In a moment he returned with a dampened towel and sponged off her stomach. "That's the best I can do if you want me inside you."

She smiled, realizing what he had sacrificed to protect her. Leaning forward she cupped his face with her hand and placed a soft kiss on his lips. "Thank you. But it's not the same, is it?"

"Not quite. There are lots of ways to slake passion that aren't dangerous for the woman. I guess I've learned them all." He ran a hand through his damp hair.

Suddenly she didn't feel quite so happy anymore. She wished Hunter had used another term for what they'd just done. Slaking passion seemed too casual, too far from love. But what had she expected? A declaration of love? And she didn't want to consider how he had learned his skill with women, especially not with Lady Caroline. She could hardly stand the thought of him sharing passion with someone else.

But she didn't want to think about all that. She felt satisfied, happy, hungry. And still sensual. "Let's take a bath."

"And eat?"

"All the food's downstairs."

"While you get the bath, I'll fill a couple of plates and bring them up here."

305

"Wonderful. But put on some clothes. If Maud saw you like that in the middle of the night, I don't know what she'd think."

"She'd think I left my room to get some food."

"What room?"

"I think it's across the hall from yours. She put my carpetbags in there before I left."

"She did!"

Deidre scrambled out of bed, pulled on a green silk robe, and headed for the door.

Hunter jerked on his trousers and followed her.

She pushed open the door across from hers. Sure enough the bed had been turned down and Hunter's clothes had been laid out. Then she remembered Maud saying she'd better get a room ready for Hunter.

"I'll stay some place else if you don't want me here. Maud insisted so I thought it was okay . . ." Hunter's voice was husky and neutral.

"It's all right. There's plenty of room." She pushed past him. "I guess you've got your own bath."

He closed strong fingers around her arm. "I'll go now if you want. I don't want to impose."

"No. I mean, please get some food. I'll start the bath. We need to talk."

Searching her face, he nodded, then walked past her toward the staircase.

She shut the door, then went back into her room. She felt chilled, feverish, and worried. As she turned on the bath water, she poured bubble bath into it, then stopped, remembering Hunter was supposed to join her. She laughed at the idea of him surrounded by sweet smelling bubbles, then tossed her head. Just let him complain. And what did she care if he stayed here or someplace else? She'd just been surprised. Anyway, he'd probably be moving on soon. He was that kind of man.

Gathering the wine and glasses, she went back into the bathroom. She pinned up her hair, dropped the robe, then poured herself a glass of wine and sank down into the water. It felt good, soft, warm, soothing, but she was more hungry than ever.

She sipped the wine and tried to get her mind in order. Before Hunter returned she had better try to make sense out of her emotions or she was going to find it difficult to deal with him. Make sense? Nothing about the way she reacted to him made sense. Unless she were in love with him. But how could that be? And what would it mean if she were?

Should she be pleased he didn't want her to have his child or glad he was protecting her from having an illegitimate child? Half of her was glad. It was something she should have given more thought to instead of being carried away by the heat of the moment. But the other half of her could imagine what beautiful, intelligent, clever children they could have together.

But that was ridiculous. She had plans. College. Business. Suffrage. Could she add a husband and children to what she already planned to do with her life? And was Hunter the husband for her? As if he were the marrying type.

She set down the wine and hugged her arms across her breasts in a form of self protection. How could she trust herself to know about Hunter? She'd made a mistake with Simon. And what of

Lady Caroline? And Hunter's past, or his goals and plans for the future? When she thought about it, she realized she knew little about him.

"Deidre?"

Jerking her head up, she saw Hunter standing in the doorway. He held two plates piled high with food. "Was I gone that long? That's quite a frown."

She forced herself to smile, then concentrated on the food. "Bring that over her before I faint from hunger." She held out her hands for the plates.

He handed her the plates, then stopped. He warily eyed the bubble bath. "You did that on purpose, didn't you?"

"Come on in. The water's fine."

"You want me to smell like a fancy French—" He cut himself off, glared at her, then dropped his trousers. "You'd better make room."

She pulled her knees to her chin and waited while he stepped into the water, still watching it as he might a rattlesnake about to strike. When he sat down, bubbles floated around him, catching in his chest hair. He gave her a baleful stare.

She couldn't keep from laughing as she handed him a plate of food. "Eat up. You look right smart."

"Thanks. If you ever tell anybody about this, you'll be in serious trouble."

Her laughter subsided as she turned her attention to the food. Eating as fast as possible, she hardly tasted the food as she tried to fill the whole in her middle. She felt as if she hadn't eaten in months. What did Hunter do to her? She only lost interest in the food when he began drawing sensual patterns on her thighs with his toes.

She stopped eating long enough to glare at him. "Stop that. Can't you see I'm concentrating?"

"Revenge."

Cocking her head to one side, she smiled mischievously. "Need me to feed you, big boy?"

He set aside his plate. "I'm hungry, but you're all I want."

She set down her almost empty plate. Licking her lower lip, she reached under the water until she found what she wanted. When she began to stroke his erection, he groaned. She chuckled, feeling excitement build in her at the power she had over him. But oh, how she wanted him. The power worked both ways.

Leaning forward, he placed hands on her shoulders and pulled her toward him. "I'll show you what I do to women who tease."

She splashed bubbles on his face.

He growled, knocked them off, then lifted her up to settle her slowly down the length of his erection.

When he moved inside her, she moaned and clutched his shoulders. Soon she matched his rhythm, toying with his chest, feeling him deep inside her.

"You're not laughing now, are you?"

"No." She shivered.

"Do you still want to tease?"

"I want only you."

He moved harder and faster. "You're never going to hear the last of it when Maud sees this bathroom."

She cried out as ecstasy began to take her, knowing if the whole mansion flooded she wouldn't care.

309

Chapter 21

"You know." Deidre looked mischievous. "If we weren't in the garden where someone could see us, I think I'd just lean over and unbutton your shirt. I'd spread it wide, then I'd use my tongue to—"

"Deidre! Pour me some more lemonade." Hunter glared at her.

She smiled in satisfaction at the sudden moisture beading his forehead. Dutifully, she poured him another glass and watched as he gulped down the cool liquid.

Quite content, she glanced upward. Clouds were gathering and a breeze cooled the late summer morning. Sitting on a white painted iron chair at a matching table behind her home, she sipped lemonade. The scent of flowers filled the air and bees buzzed lazily from flower to flower. Maud and Sam were nowhere in sight, but she knew Maud was busily preparing a feast for the evening meal to prove again how much she liked Hunter.

Deidre liked him, too. A lot. She felt happy, lazy, and utterly content. Rolling the cool glass between her palms, she glanced at Hunter. A frowned marred his forehead. Surprised, she wanted to question his thoughts but hesitated to invade his privacy. They had been together for four wonderful days and three ecstatic nights. Why was he frowning?

Last night they had attended a National Woman Suffrage meeting in the parlor of a member's home. Perhaps he was thinking of all he'd learned there. Charlotte had attended, happy to see them both. Simon had stayed away and she was glad.

The day before Simon had sent back the heart pin, with a note asking to be friends. Hunter had seen the gift and she'd had to explain about Simon Gainesville. She still wasn't quite sure how Hunter had taken the news, for he kept so much of himself hidden that sometimes she wasn't sure how he felt about much of life. But as far as Simon, she had decided to let him cool his heels awhile.

One thing she knew for sure. Hunter wanted her and she wanted him just as desperately in return. What would happen in their future she didn't know. Perhaps she could persuade him to stay in New York. Surely he could find work here and certainly at Clarke Shipping. But she didn't want to push. He probably had his own plans for life just as she did. So for now she simply wanted to be with him and let everything else in life wait its turn. The future could keep.

From under hooded eyes, Hunter watched Deidre. He was thinking of the future, couldn't keep from it. His desire for her made him want all the good things in life. And it reminded him of the bad in his past. Suddenly he was afraid the old would cancel out the new if he didn't do something about it.

New York City with all its businesses, carriages, horses, crowds rushing everywhere was a world apart from what he'd known as a child. He remembered Arizona and its wide open spaces, the cattle, the wild animals, the sedate pace of life. And his father.

It's been a long time since he'd been back. Six or seven years. He wasn't sure anymore. Now he had a hankering to return. He wanted to see his father and his father's family. And he wanted them to see him. He had the money. That wasn't a problem any longer. And he was tough enough to take anything they threw at him.

But money didn't seem to be enough anymore. Seeing Deidre with her parents, seeing their love and friendship, their family closeness made him want something he'd had only with his mother a long time ago.

Suddenly he wanted more in life, but he wasn't sure what. On the other hand, maybe he was sure and didn't want to admit it. If he confronted his past, maybe he would feel free to go on with his future.

He turned to look at the woman sitting beside him, her face raised to the sky, her eyes shut. Deidre was happy, satisfied. And why shouldn't she be? Over the last several days he'd proved himself more of a man in bed than he'd ever thought he was.

And he'd always thought he was pretty damn good. But Deidre brought out the animal in him. And she knew it.

"So, what did you think of the suffrage meeting?" Deidre felt him watching her and opened her eyes.

"As a man, I almost hate to admit it, but the women made sense."

"Why wouldn't a man want women to vote?"

He slanted a glance at her. "I shouldn't tell you. It'll only go to your head. But a woman has so much power over a man, from motherhood on, that I guess he feels he's got to make up for it in other ways."

"That's silly."

"No, it's not. I wouldn't be in New York if I hadn't followed you. And if I could've stayed away I would have. That's power."

"You know it works both ways." She blew him a kiss.

"I'm serious. If a man's open to it, women have a way of making him see too much reality, too much need in the world, too much of the other person, too much of a reason for those equal rights you're talking about."

"What's wrong with that?"

"It makes life a lot harder. It makes taking what you want, anytime, anywhere, from anybody, hard to do. It makes keeping your distance almost impossible."

"That's because it's wrong."

"Right or wrong, it's life. People hurt other people, sometimes on purpose, sometimes carelessly, sometimes because they can't help it. Men have a habit of looking the other way if it benefits them.

They don't want to know about how rough women have it or how children are being hurt in sweat-shops."

"Especially men who are making themselves millionaires that way."

"Right. But men aren't the only villains here." Hunter looked out over the garden, working his mind in a way he wasn't used to doing.

"I know. Women and men have formed groups to try and stop us from getting the right to vote. They tried to stop the abolitionists, too. But slaves are free. Now it's time to free women."

"You've got an uphill battle on your hands, Deidre, I don't mind telling you that. I wouldn't have been sure it was worth it, no matter the fancy words and fine logic of those who spoke last night, if I hadn't learned how the National is financed."

"Oh?" She set down her glass, fascinated by his viewpoint.

"I could hardly believe that most of the money to win woman suffrage comes from those who have the least. Poor seamstresses and washerwomen are making two dollar pledges to the cause. And they pay it off in twenty-five cent installments, meaning they've got to make eight trips on foot because they can't afford a stamp. And that's after working all day.

"When they told the story of the poor clerk who said she made a piece of fancy work in the evenings after twelve hours at a regular job so she could donate a dollar, I understood how much these women want equal rights. That's when I made my donation."

Deidre leaned forward and squeezed his hand.

"Are you questioning the rightness of what you did? A number of men support suffrage."

"No. I feel halfway between a fool and martyr, but I'm proud of helping, too. If women are that desperate and their lives are that hard and they're willing to give part of the little they have, then something is going on here."

"It has been going on for forty years. And more."

"I'll tell you something. If my sister had lived, I'd have liked for her to have had the chance to vote, or teach, or whatever she wanted to do. What I wouldn't have wanted for her was the life my mother lived. And if woman suffrage had been passed years ago, my mother might still be alive. She'd have had the chance at education so she could work and eat right and not be insulted and humiliated with every breath she took."

Deidre felt saddened at the picture he painted, but it was not an unusual life for a woman. And her children.

"I must have lived with male privilege all my life and not known it. But my life's been hard, too. Men work hard and I guess they want a woman to ease life for them. Before now I've had little thought for the plight of women. I think I've been too busy running, trying to prove myself, and make enough money so I'd never again see the look my mother had on her face when she died."

"You don't have to prove yourself anymore."

He focused on her. "Yes, I do. For myself. For my mother." He inhaled sharply. "I might as well tell you. I *have* to tell you because I want to ask you something."

Her heart beat faster. What was he talking about?

315

Was he finally going to commit himself to her and if he did, what would she do?

"I'm not good enough for the likes of you, Deidre. I know it and you know it. I'm not a man a woman like you would ever want to marry."

"But—"

"Wait. Let me finish. I learned that lesson real well growing up on Raimundo Rancho, my father's ranch in Arizona. I also learned there's supposed to be two kinds of women. Good and bad, madonna and whore. But for the life of me I couldn't make sense of it. My mother was called a whore but she loved only one man all her life. Many of the Spanish aristocratic madonnas married, then initiated every local boy who came of age right in their own beds."

Deidre bit her lower lip, hating the story she was hearing but glad he was sharing it with her. She wanted desperately to heal his wounds, to help his mother, his sister. Two members of his family were beyond help, but he wasn't.

"I was named a bastard simply because by church and family law my father couldn't marry the woman he loved, my mother. Instead, he lived with his wife, a woman picked for him by his family. And the stories I heard about her I never let get back to him.

"Madonna and whore." He shook his head. "My mother was half Apache and half Irish. What chance did she have? A half-breed woman. She was kicked by everybody, except my father now and then. But she fought for her life and mine. It weakened her and in the end she gave her life for love of her Spanish grandee. And he let her." Hunter's voice was bitter.

Deidre stood up and put her arms around him

from behind. She held on to him, wanting to ease the pain. "I'm sorry." She kissed his cheek.

"Don't be. Help me get revenge."

"What do you mean?"

"I helped you stop the Graves. We avenged your family. Now it's my turn."

Confused, she sat back down and pulled her chair close to him. "What can I do?"

He looked into her eyes. "I want you to go to Raimundo Rancho with me. And pretend to be my wife."

She inhaled sharply, feeling as if he'd plunged a knife into her chest. How could he ask this of her? How could he make a travesty of all they'd shared? Tears threatened to spill from her eyes. She glanced away, controlling herself with difficulty. Did he think her a whore or a madonna who played at being a whore when no one watched? Either way, he didn't think enough of her to ask her to marry him. And even if he did, after all she'd learned about life, she didn't know if she would.

"My father's family, his wife, my half brother and sister, uncles, aunts, cousins, all treated my mother like dirt and me not much better. I had some education, but not enough. When my father finally offered me college, my mother was dead and I'd had enough. I turned my back on it all and left to make my own way without the power or money or prestige of my father's family."

She began to understand how much this meant to him. Ruthlessly, she pushed her own feelings aside. He needed help. She must concentrate on his problems, not her own concerns.

"Will you do it?"

His offer was bittersweet. She wanted to be with him as long as possible, but she didn't want to be like his mother and countless other women and give her life for love. She didn't want that kind of pain or martyrdom. Still, she wanted to help him as he had helped her in the Bahamas.

"I've got enough money now to take us back in style. With you at my side, they would have to accept their bastard relative as an equal. And I'd like to see my father again. He may be old or sick or needy. And I want to hear him apologize for the way he treated my mother. Will you help?"

She hesitated, focusing her thoughts for her answer. "You know I have my own plans for life. I'm going to attend college and hopefully work at Clarke Shipping."

"And work for woman suffrage. Your life's full, isn't it?" He stood up. "It's all right. I can do it on my own. I ought to get on with my life anyway. Will you tell your parents I'm sorry for any trouble I caused them?"

She stood up and walked over to him. "Why don't you tell them yourself?"

He looked at her in confusion.

"We could go see your father. I've never been to Arizona. After you're finished there, we could go on to the Bar J and talk with my parents."

For a moment he simply stood still, obviously stunned. "You'd do it? You'd go with me? You'd pretend to be my woman, my wife?"

She nodded, pushing past her own reservations about the decision. "You pretended to be my *man* in the Bahamas, so now it's my turn." She tried for a light, natural tone, but her heart was beating fast.

"Remember, I'm an independent young woman. I go where I want, do what I want. I'm not just fighting for the vote, I'm fighting to live my life on my own terms. You helped me, now I'll help you." By the time she finished her speech, she believed it.

Grinning, he lifted her into the air, then spun her around. "Deidre!"

She laughed and hugged him tight. Another adventure. Another right to wrong with Hunter at her side. What could be better? She tenderly touched his face. "You helped me when you didn't have to. If you hadn't turned on Lady Caroline, Hayward, and Captain Sully, I'd be dead now and my parents and brother in danger. You have a good heart. When you learned what the wreckers were doing, you changed to the side of right."

He set her back down, but kept his arms around her. "I'd rather think of myself as hard-hearted."

"Oh, you can be that all right and hard-headed, too."

He laughed.

"You're tough, Hunter. I value that. But I believe you and I live by the same rule. Do as you would be done by. Anything else causes only pain and heartache."

He nodded. "Do you think I'm foolish for wanting to go back and show them my mother raised a smart, worthy, valuable son who got it from her. And that he was good enough to win the most beautiful, desirable, intelligent woman in the world?"

"You could win any woman you wanted." She smiled. "I don't think you're foolish. I think what you plan to do is a wonderful tribute to your mother's courage. And it's about time she had it."

She leaned against him, wanting to feel his strength. "And I want to learn more about her and this family of yours."

"Not all families are like yours." He put his arms around her and held her close. "But I wish they were."

She hesitated, putting herself on the line. "I'm not going simply to help. I want to be with you, Hunter. I have other goals in my life, other plans, my family, but you're very important to me, too."

He set her back to search her green eyes for the truth of her words. For a long moment he didn't say anything. "I'm glad. We make good partners." Then he looked around, clearing his throat. "Come on, I want to do this up right. You'll need some new clothes."

"More?"

"I want their eyes to fall out when they see us. You can find some clothes for me, too."

"Oh, Hunter." Laughing, she hugged him, feeling his strength, his sensuality, his need. Tears stung her eyes as she listened to the beat of his heart. How could she ever give up this man? She looked at him. Chocolate brown eyes melted her heart.

He tilted her chin up and pressed warm lips to her mouth. "Before all that shopping, maybe we ought to go up to your room."

"And take a bath?"

"No. Maud'd never let us in the house again." He nuzzled her neck. "I had another activity in mind."

She reached up and pulled his head downward. "I don't think I can ever get enough of you." Then she kissed him as if she meant it to last forever.

Part Four
Flowers in the Desert

Chapter 22

Hunter drove the wagon he'd bought in Tucson south. Two horses pulled it. Two saddle horses were tied behind. In back, he'd stacked trunks of clothes, blankets, baskets of food, and plenty of water. He'd also brought two rifles, two pistols, two knives, and plenty of ammunition.

He wore black trousers, a black shirt, and the black leather vest he'd kept after the Bahamas for luck. On his head he wore a black John B. Stetson and he'd pulled on a pair of sturdy black cowboy boots. Around his waist he'd buckled on a black leather belt with a silver and turquoise belt buckle. Most important of all, now that he was back in the West, he'd strapped on his gunbelt with the .45 ready to use. He knew he was as prepared as he could be for southern Arizona.

Beside him, Deidre silently watched the surrounding vista of dusty plains and distant purple mountains. He hoped she'd like the trip. He'd packed plenty to see them through without owing anything to anybody at Raimundo Rancho. He hadn't told his father they were coming and he hadn't told Deidre he was taking her to his mother's old place instead of to the hacienda. It'd be crude after what she was used to, but he didn't want to stay at the ranch. He wanted a place of his own. And he wanted to visit his mother's grave.

Now that he was back, the past swept over him. When he'd left, Victoro and his band of Apaches and Mexicans were still raiding cattle from across the Mexican border where Victoro had fled to survive. Geronimo controlled the Dragoon Mountains and the high passes of the Huachucas. But the Apache had been making their last stand. He'd wanted to join them. His mother had begged him on her deathbed not to throw his lot in with the Apache for they were destined to be defeated.

And they had been. In 1886. Hunter had been far away, but not far enough to not feel the pain at the passing of power of a great civilization. Red Devils. Redskins. Readers of newspapers and magazines couldn't get their fill of the glory of the destruction of a proud, strong people. Too many wanted what belonged to the natives. And now they had it all. But it had taken a genocide of white man's diseases and white man's liquor and white man's bullets and white man's greed to get it.

What was left of the Apache had been confined to a reservation. Hunter figured most of his old friends among the Apache were probably dead. And if they weren't, he wasn't sure he wanted to see what they had been forced to become. Or what firewater and starvation had done to them.

But the Apache had strength. They would endure. And he felt a sudden need to help them if he could. Maybe it was being around Deidre and her awareness of the needs of people, of the will to change what didn't have to be. He'd always straddled two worlds, rich and poor, white and red. There might be some way he could be a bridge to help both.

But when had he wanted to help others? He glanced across at the woman who rode beside him. Straight-backed on the hard wooden seat, she continued her study of southern Arizona. Partly brought up on a ranch, she knew what to wear and had chosen a cool cotton dark green split skirt and a long sleeved green and white striped blouse. She wore cowboy boots, as well as a wide brimmed hat and cotton gloves. She understood the fierce sun of the south.

He felt proud of her. And he realized they were more alike than he'd thought. She straddled worlds just as he did, from a Texas ranch to a New York office, from the South to the North, Deidre cut her own swath through them all. And he remembered what she'd told him in Three Rivers about wanting to build a place for herself, a place of her own where she could live free. He wanted the same thing. And he wanted it bad. He only wished he could build it with her.

As Deidre rode, she thought of what lay ahead of her. Deception. She hoped she'd made the right choice. Was being with Hunter, helping him avenge his mother worth the price she was sure to pay?

When they parted ways, it would be all the harder after knowing so much more about him, having seen him with his family. But if he'd wanted to marry her, he'd have asked before they made this long trip. Or would he? Perhaps his pride wouldn't allow him. Or perhaps he feared her rejection. Either way, she had made her decision and there was no turning back now.

But she couldn't help thinking of Mary Wollstonecraft. Before she had written *Vindication of the Rights of Woman*, she had born a child out of wedlock to a man she had desperately loved but who had abandoned her. She had later married a man who shared her philosophy of life, but at thirty-eight she had died from giving birth to their child. Just as Hunter's mother had died giving birth to his sister.

Deidre shivered at the similarity. Death always stood by a woman when she gave birth. But Mary Wollstonecraft's daughter, Mary Wollstonecraft Godwin Shelley, had turned out to be a writer, too. Deidre had read her novel, *Frankenstein*, and been impressed with its power and statement about the creation of another living being. She wondered if the publication of *Frankenstein* in 1818 was a tribute to the mother who had died to give Mary Shelley birth.

Glancing at Hunter, she watched the strong profile, the narrowed eyes, the determined jut of his chin. She was drawn to him as a moth to a flame. To ever be separated from him seemed an unbearable pain. She feared and at the same time rejoiced that she might love him. They came from different worlds. She had so many plans. She knew so little about him. And rather than marry her, he had asked her to pretend to be his wife. But would marriage be wise anyway?

Mary Wollstonecraft's literary career and long struggle for liberation had been cut short when she died. Susan Anthony had never married. Elizabeth Caddy Stanton had married and raised children while working for woman suffrage. Hunter's mother had died giving birth, leaving her son with a fear of causing a woman's death through childbirth.

Deidre decided there were no easy answers for women. Hunter was careful so she wouldn't get pregnant. But what if there came a time when she wanted to have their child? Would he want her not to do so for fear of losing her? Should she even consider risking her own life for that of a child? And what of marriage? Independence? What of her future with Hunter? Would they still be together after Arizona and the trip to Texas?

She shook her head. As usual, she was thinking too much, worrying too much. For now, she should enjoy the present with Hunter, pushing the past and future away. He had helped her in the Bahamas, even saved her life. Now she helped him. It was only right.

Pleasure. She should enjoy their passion for each other while she had the chance. After all, it might never come again. Smiling, she put a hand over Hunter's and pressed. Leather and cotton separated their skin, but it didn't stop the sudden heat from leaping between them.

He transferred the reins to his right hand and took her hand with the other. "What do you think of Arizona?"

"It's beautiful. But I had expected it to be more like southern Texas."

"You don't have the mountains there."

"No. How tall are those in the distance? They look purple and hazy and the peaks are so sharp."

"Maybe eight or ten thousand feet. They're not as desolate as they look from here. The Apache can live in them. They know where to find water, what cactus to eat, what to hunt."

"This land is majestic."

"I hadn't realized how much I'd missed it."

She squeezed his hand. "I can understand why."

"The Apache are mostly gone now. U.S. soldiers killed them. The ones who are left have been sent up to northeastern Arizona on a reservation. That's beautiful country, too."

"Do you know any of them?"

"Yes. Or I did. Now I don't know. Mother was half Apache, half Irish. She was called Flora McCuskar. Her mother died young and her father couldn't or wouldn't take care of her. He left her at a Catholic mission. The fathers and local women raised her. She worked hard, got a little education, and by sixteen was a beauty. That's when my father noticed her."

"How did he meet her?"

"He's Spanish Catholic and supports the mission. One day he stopped by and saw her. From what she said, it was love at first sight on both their parts. I don't know. She was so young."

"But she'd probably seen a lot of life."

Hunter nodded. "Anyway, with my father's power and money and a promise to look after her, the priests let her go to Raimundo Rancho. She was supposed to work as a servant. But that didn't last long. He set her up in a place on the banks of the Santa Cruz River in the shade of cottonwood trees."

"Was she happy?"

"I suppose. She was happiest when he was there. But he was gone a lot, work on the ranch, down to Mexico, his own family. But she always waited. I know she wanted more. But she had no kin, nowhere to go. She didn't want me growing up Apache, although I made friends with them. I learned a lot that way. And they made sure we were safe from reprisal attacks against whites."

"It sounds lonely."

"I guess it was, but for a young boy growing up there was plenty to explore and do. And I think she was used to being alone from her time at the mission." Hunter took off his hat and ran a hand through his hair, then put it back on. "Anyway, she's buried near the mission. I'd like to stop by there and see her grave."

"I'd like to see it, too."

He slanted a glance at her. "You're sure?"

"Yes." She squeezed his hand, then pointed in the distance. "Is that the mission ahead?"

"Right. And we've been following the Santa Cruz since Tucson. The river is the western border of Raimundo Rancho so having my mother living near it was convenient for my father."

"Then she wasn't so far from the mission and her friends?"

Hunter cleared his throat. "No. But she was living in sin. I couldn't bury her in consecrated ground."

"What!"

"She is on the other side of the fence. I had a big fancy headstone put up for her." He smiled. "It shocked everybody in the area and I was glad. She was a good woman."

"And she raised a good son. Children shouldn't be judged and labeled by the condition of their mother's marital status. It's wrong. A child is a child is a child."

"Thanks." Hunter turned narrowed eyes on her. "But if the baby doesn't have the father's name and approval in marriage, it makes for a hell of hard way to grow up."

"I know. It's one of the rights I'm fighting for. Equality for all, no matter what."

"I sure could have used it as a child. And my mother most of all." He shrugged. "But I'm not complaining. For myself, I've done all right."

"Your mother would be proud of you." She hesitated, as she watched the white-washed abode and wood building get closer. "What did your mother name you?"

He grinned. "It's a mouthful. Mind you, she was concerned about preserving my heritage as Apache, Irish, and Spanish."

"Tell me." Suddenly Deidre wanted to know all about him, every single last detail.

"Cazador McCuskar de Raimundo."

"It's lovely. But what does it mean? And why are you called Hunter?"

"That's the Apache part. Champion Hunter. McCuskar means Champion in Irish. Cazador means Hunter in Spanish. Raimundo is my father's maternal name."

"Hunter." She smiled. "Very appropriate."

330

He laughed. "I'd track you down anywhere."

"Then you don't carry your father's full name?"

"No! His family would never have accepted that. Do you want to hear *his* full name?"

"Yes."

"Alberto Cazador Raimundo de Santiago. He's called Alberto."

"That's nice, too. I like your names. You know, I think your mother gave you all the love and dignity any human needs. If law and society wouldn't grant you as much, then they should be changed."

"You've got an answer for everything, don't you?"

"No, but I'm trying. And I mean what I said."

"I know. Thanks." He clicked to the horses and they picked up their pace toward the mission.

Deidre stayed quiet, thinking of everything he had told her, of all the poor bastard children over the country. Their mothers gave them birthright when they put their lives on the line to bring new life into the world. No other birthright should ever be necessary. And she vowed to work harder for that in the future.

Hunter stopped the wagon under a cottonwood tree near the cemetery by the mission. He got down, then walked around to lower Deidre to the ground. Holding her closely a moment, he glanced around the area, then led her toward the small plot of graves, overgrown and uncared for outside the stone and wood fence of the consecrated cemetery. Only one grave had an elaborate marble headstone.

He led her to that stone. It was an intricately carved statue of a winged woman protectively cradling a small child. The marble hadn't weathered at all. A yellow flower bloomed from a cactus nestled against the base of the headstone.

Deidre felt tears in her eyes as she read, "Beloved Mother. Flora McCuskar."

"She did her best." Hunter knelt and pulled out several tall grass strands, brushed away dead leaves, stroked the smooth stone, then stood up. He looked out toward the river, silent a moment, then turned back.

"It's a beautiful headstone."

"I think she'd have liked it." Suddenly Hunter looked up, his eyes narrowed.

A small, plump, bald-headed man in a long black robe hurried toward them. "What are you doing?" A large Christian cross hung from his neck and swayed as he made his way through the main cemetery.

Hunter waited, his fists clenched.

Deidre felt herself stiffen, thinking of what had happened here. Children named bastards. Mothers shut out of consecrated ground. All was far from right in the world.

The elderly priest stopped on the other side of the fence and looked from the headstone to Hunter to Deidre then back to the stone. "You're Hunter all grown up?"

Hunter nodded, then took a deep breath. "Father Sabastian, I'd like you to meet—"

"Your lovely wife." Father Sabastian smiled.

Deidre was glad Hunter had been saved from lying about their relationship.

"Please come up to the mission. We can talk about old times. Are you going to see your . . . are you going to Raimundo Rancho?"

Nodding again, Hunter pointed at his mother's grave. "I'd like for her to be moved to consecrated ground."

The priest stepped back. "You want her moved?"

"Yes." Hunter's eyes narrowed.

Father Sabastian shook his head. "I'm sorry, son. The past cannot be changed."

Deidre took Hunter's hand and held on hard. "It doesn't matter." She lifted her chin. "My family can have her buried in the most important cemetery in the United States if we want." She threw a disdainful glance around the poor mission. "This really isn't good enough anyway."

"Please." Father Sabastian looked concerned. "Don't blame us. We loved the girl like our own. If only she hadn't . . . well, you know . . . the grandee and his family. They will be buried here and church regulations."

Tugging at Hunter's hand, Deidre tried to pull him away. She couldn't stand to see him hurt this way.

But Hunter didn't move. He looked down at his mother's headstone, then back at the priest. "I don't blame you. You follow orders. But, in the name of my mother, a good woman, I vow to see that other mothers aren't treated the way she was treated, even by those who said they loved her."

Father Sabastian looked unhappy but resolute. "I am here for you, my son, any time you feel a need of unburdening your sorrows." He turned and walked back toward the mission.

Deidre tugged on Hunter's hand again. "Come on. You can't do any more here."

He hesitated again. "Then let her always stay outside the circle of her father's religion. Her mother's Apache religion will stand by her. I realize I should have taken her back to her people for burial."

"No, Hunter, you did the right thing. You left her here in view of the river she lived her life by. And near the man she loved. But I swear to you we will raise a flag in her honor." Tears filled her eyes. "We can found the Flora McCuskar Institute for unwed mothers and abandoned children. Her name will become a symbol of hope for all mothers and children."

"Deidre." He took her in his arms and held her tight. "You take my breath away. That's a wonderful idea." He put a finger under her chin and tilted her head back to press a gentle kiss to her lips. "My mother would have loved you."

"I love her now as if I had known her."

"And the institute will take all children, no matter their race or sex."

"Yes. And when the institute is built, you could move her to a special memorial place on its grounds."

Hunter looked down at his mother's grave. "Or perhaps we'll leave her here to remind us that women must be the bravest of us all to endure the special hardships thrust on them by our society."

She hugged him a long moment, looking at his mother's grave, then she tugged on his hand. This time he came with her. When they reached the wagon, he lifted her up, then stopped to stare at her. "I want to pay for the institute with my own money and I want it to be built here in Arizona Territory."

She nodded in agreement. "And perhaps it could be combined with an educational system of some type. I know a lot of fine women who are qualified to work at the Flora McCuskar Institute."

"Good." Hunter walked around the wagon to join her on the seat. A moment later, he turned the horses back toward the road. "I'm going to make a donation to this mission. It helped my mother when she was young and it helps a lot of other people."

Deidre leaned against him, feeling a deep happiness run through her. Without a doubt, she knew Flora McCuskar would be proud of her son.

They rode on in silence, heading south but staying near the Santa Cruz River. After awhile, when the sun was setting in the west, Hunter turned off the main road and drove the horses down an overgrown, rutted road through a stand of cottonwood trees. Cactus, small and large, dotted the ground and tumbleweeds rolled in the breeze.

On the banks of the river, a small adobe house with a flat roof and round wooden poles jutting outward near the roof had been abandoned. Sand colored like the ground around it, the house had no windows and the front door sagged open. A few cactus grew near the door.

Hunter stopped the wagon and stepped down. "Wait here."

He walked to the front door, hesitated, then stepped through the open doorway. Inside, it was cool and dark. None of the former furniture remained. He walked around, realizing he had remembered the house he had shared with his mother as being bigger, better. Looking back, he wished with all his heart that she was still alive so he could buy her the kind of house she should have had all along. Why hadn't his father done more?

Bitterness ran through him, but he forced it down. That was a question he would have answered and soon. For now, how could he ask Deidre to stay here? But how could he take her to the hacienda either?

He took off his hat and ran fingers through his damp hair. It was late. They were hot, tired, and dusty. And it wouldn't be long before Raimundo cowboys knew strangers were camping on the rancho's land. But he doubted if they'd be found before morning. For now, he had to decide what to do about the night.

When he walked back out, Deidre had gotten down and was examining the outside of the building. She smiled at him. "Did you notice how well this is constructed? They make similar houses in south Texas. Adobe is so good for the climate. Part of the Bar J hacienda is adobe. And I love these ancient cottonwoods. The river is wonderful."

"Thanks." He put an arm around her shoulders and led her down to the Santa Cruz. "I suppose you guessed this is where I grew up."

"Yes. It's small but lovely."

"I remembered it as bigger and better. I can't believe we lived here for so long."

"Families larger than yours live in houses this size or smaller for generations. You're just used to more now."

He nodded, squinting into the setting sun.

She pointed across the sparkling water. "I've never seen such beautiful sunsets as over the desert.

It must have been nice growing up here in one place."

He was surprised to hear the longing in her voice, then remembered her lack of a permanent home. He hugged her close. "Would you mind spending the night here? We could go to the ranch tomorrow."

"I think it's a good idea. We have plenty of food, blankets." She smiled up at him. "It's been awhile since we've had a maroon. Why not have one on Raimundo Rancho?"

"I can't think of a better idea."

Chapter 23

"Always check the inside of your boots before you put them on." Hunter turned one cowboy boot upside down and shook it, then the other.

Deidre followed his example, then raised an eyebrow. "And what's supposed to have crawled into them during the night?"

"Scorpions. You don't want to take any chances with those little critters."

She wrinkled her nose. "Bad bite?"

"Sting. Or a rattler could have crawled in for a cozy place to rest."

"Sounds like it might be better if I never take off my boots while I'm in Arizona."

He chuckled. "Check your boots even if you're inside. Okay?"

"All right." She glanced around. "What about clothes, food, water?"

He shook out his shirt. "It pays to be careful when you're living like this." He gestured toward the adobe house. Early morning sunlight streaked it with a golden hue, hiding its blemishes.

She knew with a little work and care the adobe house could be a solid home again. But not for them. She also had come to realize that the caution Hunter had shown everywhere they'd been had been born here. He must have grown up watching his back, for animals, insects, Indians, Mexicans, Spaniards, and Americans. Whom had he trusted? His mother.

More and more she began to understand him. And appreciate him. She also understood why he'd taken the type of work he had. He had nothing to lose and everything to gain. Lady Caroline should never have crossed him. Or Old Nate either. But that was in the past. She wanted to think of now and the future.

They had spent a wonderful night by the river, listening to its gurgle, to the night animals and birds hunting through the brush under the cottonwoods and along the banks of the Santa Cruz. They had snuggled on the blankets he had made into a bed and they'd kept a small fire going. They'd eaten from the picnic baskets, shared stories from their youth, and laughed together. But they had not shared their bodies.

Passion simmered beneath everything they said and did. They touched each other tenderly, but the deep dark vein of desire that drew them together had been kept at bay. She wasn't sure why unless it was the memories the place invoked or the coming confrontation with his family. Whatever the reason,

339

they had both felt a need for tenderness and comfort, rather than the wildness of passion.

She pushed her long hair back from her face as she thought. Oddly enough, she felt as close, perhaps closer to Hunter after the previous night as after their first night together in New York City. That realization brought a new fear to her. If their desire for each other were more than the satisfying of hungry bodies, then how much harder the separation, how much more lonely the denial of the need for another.

But she didn't want to think that far into the future. She wouldn't. They had shared a mystical, magical night by the Santa Cruz. And she believed it had helped to heal some of Hunter's wounds. Today they would ride across the Raimundo Rancho and surprise his family. She hoped it went well. Rather, she was determined it would be to Hunter's satisfaction. Anything less was unacceptable.

And after that they would go to the Bar J. She had sent her mother a telegram, explaining that she was going with Hunter to Raimundo Rancho to settle a family problem before coming to see them. Her mother had replied with her usual advice to be careful and explained that Jake had returned from a successful trip to Louisiana. Relieved to learn that, Deidre decided that Lady Caroline and Hayward had finally been stopped.

"I didn't let you get much sleep, did I?" Hunter pulled on a gray and black striped shirt, then slipped the leather vest over it. Other than the shirt, he was dressed the same as the day before.

"Later there'll be plenty of time to sleep. I loved

the night. It's surprising how cool it gets so fast out here."

He nodded. "You'll get used to it."

"If we're going to ride the horses to the ranch, I don't see how I can wear anything but what I've put on. Will this rose-colored split skirt and the matching silk blouse do? I'll wear my beige hat and boots and gloves with it. It's not fancy."

"You look beautiful no matter what you wear."

"But I brought all those gorgeous gowns from New York. And what about your suits?"

Hunter stood up and held out a hand to lift her to her feet. "Now that I'm back I don't much care. Clothes are not what's important here."

She kissed him on the cheek. "True. But what are we going to do with all this stuff?"

"I carried the trunks into the house. We can leave the blankets and extra food in there while we're gone. I don't know what kind of reception we'll get at the ranch so I'd rather leave our things here."

"I agree. But will they be safe?"

He grinned. "I'm going to get that door shut, then I'll carve an Apache sign and a Raimundo sign on it. Nobody'll open that door on a bet."

"Really?"

"It'll mark the property as mine and promise dire consequences if disturbed."

"I'm glad to know that'll work out here, but I doubt if it'd do much good in New York City. And I don't much think it'll stop any little critters who want the food."

"They'll get some of it, I bet. But the other is sealed good enough. Besides, that house is built

341

tight." He looked around the area, his eyes narrowed. "Why don't we get some breakfast and get on the way?"

She hesitated, searched his brown eyes for worry or fear, found none, then hugged him tight. "If they want to plan a grand ball for your homecoming, we'll return here to dress." She laughed. "We'll be a sight, stepping from our modest adobe home in New York finery."

Chuckling, he held her close. "We can do whatever we want and to hell with everybody else."

"Together, yes."

He lifted a strand of her golden blond hair, stroked it with his fingers a moment, then let the breeze catch it. "I wish you could wear your hair down. It looks like spun gold."

"Too hot." She smiled and placed a quick kiss on his lips. "Wait until tonight."

He nodded, then walked away and began hobbling the wagon horses.

She watched him a moment, then folded up several blankets, checked the food, decided they'd eat the most perishable, then sat down to wait. She felt nervous. Foreign territory. They were walking into the lair of a powerful family. But they were doing it together, just as they had in the Bahamas. As partners nothing could defeat them. They had protected each other's back before and they would do it again.

The sun still graced the eastern sky as they rode southeast away from the Santa Cruz. Deidre found distance hard to judge because of the flat land. Today a few mountains seemed closer, concealed in morning fog or haze, but still purple and jutting into the sky with jagged peaks.

As they continued, Hunter pointed out ancient saguaro cactus, as tall as small trees, barrel cactus that could be cut open for water, and the buffalo grass that kept cattle herds alive. Here and there juniper trees offered shade and a place for birds to perch. The land teemd with a wide variety of life and she soon fell under its spell.

What they didn't see were people, miles and miles and miles of land without people. But she understood the wide open spaces because she had grown up with them in Texas. Yet here it seemed more open. Perhaps fewer people had yet to move in because until two years ago the Apache had still protected the land from intruders, continuing their job as caretakers as they had for generations.

After awhile, Hunter stopped. He pointed ahead. A juniper tree shaded three white cattle skulls that had been nailed onto its trunk.

"What does that mean?"

"We've been on Raimundo land for some time, but that shows we're getting close to the hacienda, the barns, and the corrals. It's a warning of sorts. My father lived at peace with the Apache and the Pima because his family had lived on this land for a long time. And because they always made sure the Indians were not punished if they took Raimundo cattle."

"What about the law?"

"My father's family was the law here for generations. And the Indians had their own law. Now it's changed. If you know how to live with the land

and its people, then you make sure nobody starves. Cattle taken by the Indians was always considered a fair trade for the use of the land."

"So Raimundo Rancho didn't get rustled."

"And the people living on it didn't get hurt." Hunter got off his horse and walked over to the skulls. He took out his knife, cut the tip of one finger, then spread blood on each skull. He stood quietly for a moment, then put the knife back in his boot, and returned to his horse.

"Should I ask what that meant?"

He turned his horse and they started moving again. "It's an old custom. Hard to explain. But basically it's thanking the cattle for keeping us alive and thanking the land for keeping the cattle alive. It's also sort of a welcome home custom."

"I think I have a lot to learn."

Guiding his horse close, he put his hand on top of hers on the saddle horn. "You know plenty. And the Apache ways are dying, killed out." He looked ahead and pointed. "You should be able to see the roof of the hacienda from here. It's built on a rise over a natural spring. Best damn water I've ever tasted and it's never run dry."

Deidre looked where he pointed and sunlight glinted off a red tile roof. Soon she could see the white of a large house with black wrought iron grill work on the windows. A white fence enclosed the encampment. A chill ran through her. The time had come. No turning back now.

As they rode closer, she thought the place looked dangerous and fortified. It was not the easy-going, welcoming Bar J Ranch of Texas. Raimundo Rancho seemed shrouded in secrets, power, and antiquity. What kind of a reception would they receive?

A closed black wrought iron gate with the name of the ranch worked into the iron was barred against them. Hunter stopped his horse and she stopped beside him. The gate was a work of art as well as a way to keep out intruders. She looked around. What was there to be afraid of out here?

Hunter noticed. "It hasn't always been so peaceful. And the family protects its own."

In a moment, a cloud of dust moved at a fast pace toward them from the hacienda.

Deidre urged her horse closer to Hunter.

"It's all right. We're getting an escort."

When the cloud of dust reached them, it revealed five cowboys. They were Mexicans with huge sombreros, crossed ammunition belts across their chests, and rifles in their arms. One of them called out. *"Que pasa?"*

Hunter replied in Spanish and the gate was opened for them. He smiled at Deidre in encouragement, then gestured for her to precede him.

She raised her chin and rode slowly through the group of cowboys. She hadn't felt this uneasy since the Bahamas. This ranch was not like the Bar J. She also realized she'd never heard Hunter speak Spanish before. She supposed he also spoke Apache. Having spent time in South Texas, she knew some Spanish but she realized it wasn't enough to carry on a conversation.

Feeling more troubled all the time, she rode beside Hunter as four of the Mexicans escorted them at a sedate pace while the other raced ahead with news of the visitors' identity. At this point she wouldn't have been at all surprised to be greeted at the door with drawn pistols or sabers. But she didn't want to think that way. This area had recently been war torn by U.S. soldiers and Apache braves. Both sides would have had little time to respect private property. Protection would probably have been needed. But now?

Again, she thrust aside her thoughts. She glanced over at Hunter. He rode his horse easily, seeming not to notice their escort. But she'd been with him enough to recognize the alertness in his eyes, the way his right hand hovered near the .45 on his hip.

She concentrated on looking relaxed herself while she watched the hacienda. It glared white against the sand and sage of the land. The black wrought iron grill work, although decorative, also looked defensive. Built in two-stories, the outer walls were smooth except for an iron-grilled window here and there. For the most part, the hacienda seemed to look inward, showing the outside world little of the beauty she guessed must be inside.

They stopped before an arched entry. The Mexican who had ridden ahead opened the wrought iron gates to the house. Hunter dismounted and helped her down. He put a warm hand at the back of her waist and followed her across the brightly painted tile of the entryway. At the large, carved wooden front door, she took off her hat and patted the moisture off her face.

The door opened.

A young Mexican woman wearing a white blouse and black skirt stepped back to allow them entrance. They followed her down a tiled hall, then to an inner courtyard. It was tiled in a rainbow of colors and intricate designs. A fountain bubbled in the center and a black wrought iron table with chairs and benches occupied one corner near a cottonwood tree. The area was cool and beautiful.

The servant disappeared to be replaced by another young woman of a similar age and appearance. She carried a silver tray with crystal glasses. She stopped by the fountain and filled three glasses before setting the tray on the table. She gestured toward the drinks, then quickly left the courtyard.

Hunter stepped forward, picked up a glass, handed it to Deidre, then lifted the other. He held out his glass in tribute to her, and took a drink.

She sipped the water cautiously, then smiled in pleasure.

"Am I right?" Hunter grinned.

"Yes. It's delicious. So cool and sweet. It's the best water I've ever tasted."

"I'm glad you appreciate the Raimundo Spring." A husky voice spoke from behind them.

Hunter didn't react so Deidre stilled her impulse to whirl around.

A short, plump woman with fading blond hair and pale blue eyes stepped in front of them. She looked Hunter up and down, then turned her gaze on Deidre.

Resisting the impulse to straighten her shoulders, Deidre stared back. The woman was perhaps sixty, well dressed in a blue silk afternoon dress with matching kid leather shoes. She wore a large gold pin on the bodice of her gown and a gold and emerald wedding ring.

The woman looked back at Hunter and spoke in Spanish.

He shook his head. "Please speak English."

She raised an eyebrow, threw Deidre a sharp glance, then focused on Hunter again. "Why have you returned? Did you think your presence would give us pleasure?"

Deidre inhaled sharply at the cutting remark, but remained silent.

"I came to see my *father*. I want him to meet my wife." Hunter took Deidre's hand and pulled it through the crook of his arm.

"Are we not to be introduced?" The woman's tone was icy.

"Deidre, this is my father's wife, Señora Ana Carlota."

"I'm pleased to meet you." Deidre said the words but didn't mean them.

"And this is my wife, Deidre Eleanor. She is of the Clarke-Jarmon family of Texas, Lousiana, and New York."

Ana Carlota inclined her head, then looked at Deidre a little more closely. "Would that be of the Bar J Ranch in Texas?"

"Yes. My father is Jake Clarke-Jarmon."

Ana Carlota smiled, then glanced at Hunter. "I see you have done well." Her gaze went back to Deidre. "You and your parents do know of the unfortunate conditions of his birth."

"But of course." Deidre smiled in return, although her green eyes remained chilly. "His mother was a *McCuskar* and his father is a Raimundo. Such an excellent combination." She held the woman's gaze, knowing she had said McCuskar as if it were a renowned family name and as far as she was concerned it was.

Ana Carlota colored slightly, then nodded. "I understand Americans have a different set of standards."

"Perhaps." Deidre raised an eyebrow. "I only know about my family. We revere all people as equal."

Lifting one shoulder, Ana Carlota glanced at Hunter. "So American. Perhaps in time your young wife will learn that *no* one is equal."

Deidre felt her temper rise. She hated being talked about as if she weren't even there. If she put her boot on this woman's neck, they'd see who was equal or not. But Hunter covered her hand with his and squeezed hard. She bit her lower lip to keep from putting this arrogant, insensitive woman in her place. Perhaps it had been difficult to live with a man who loved another. But it wasn't Hunter's fault.

"The señora is right, Deidre. And that is why it's necessary for those with more equality to help those with less."

"Such as Indians, unwed mothers, homeless children, and women."

Ana Carlota stepped back. "If you are going to be rude, please leave my home."

"Rude?" Deidre tried to move forward, but Hunter held her back.

"We'd like to see my father. Now." Hunter's voice was decisive.

"He's unable to receive visitors."

"What's wrong?" Hunter's voice held concern.

Ana Carlota shrugged. "If you must know, he fell

349

from a horse and he simply seems to have no will to get back on his feet again."

"The doctor?"

Ana Carlota waved a dismissing hand. "He comes from Tucson once a week but can do little. Alberto gets weaker. I suppose it is his age."

Hunter frowned. "I want to see him now."

"He is taking his nap. He is not to be disturbed. If that is all, you may leave now." Ana Carlota picked up a small bell and started to ring it.

Hunter jerked it out of her hand and set it back on the table.

She gasped and put her hand to her mouth dramatically. "Birth tells."

"It's going to tell a lot more if you don't take me to my father at once."

"What's going on in here?" A man strode into the courtyard, throwing aside a hat. He appeared to be in his mid-thirties. He was of medium height, slim, dressed in a gray suit, and had blond hair and blue eyes. When he saw Hunter, he froze.

"Deidre, I'd like you to meet my half-brother, Felipe. This is my wife, Deidre Eleanor."

"She's off the Bar J in Texas." Ana Carlota held out a hand to her son.

Felipe clasped it, then glared at Deidre. "What do the two of you want here? If it is Raimundo stock, forget it."

"The Bar J runs its own cattle and imports breeding animals from England. My father doesn't need your stock." Deidre narrowed her eyes and raised an eyebrow. She could hardly believe what she was seeing and hearing. She understood Hunter even better now and she wouldn't have missed standing at his side for anything.

"I've heard of the Bar J cattle and its family." Felipe raised a shoulder. "Breeding tells."

"It certainly does." Hunter stepped forward.

But Deidre held him back. There was no point in getting into a fight. They'd come to see his father, not these vicious people.

"Americans." Felipe tossed the word at them with disgust.

"Last time I looked, you're on this side of the border." Hunter looked his half-brother up and down.

"The land is Raimundo territory. The Americans can buy whatever they want, this land will still be ours when their country destroys itself in another civil war." Felipe kissed the back of his mother's hand. "What do we care?"

"I came to see my father." Hunter narrowed his eyes. "If you think all this talk is going to stop me, you're wrong. I've come a long way."

"Why don't you leave him alone?" Ana Carlota clutched her son's hand. "My husband is a sick man. He needs peace and quiet. You will simply disturb him. The doctor does not want him upset."

"That is right." Felipe was quick to agree with his mother. "Take your American wife and go away. You aren't needed on Raimundo Rancho and never will be. Why don't you get out of Arizona Territory altogether?" Felipe's upper lip curled. "Why don't you play rancher on the Bar J? Isn't that why you married her?"

Again Deidre had to hold Hunter back.

"If you're trying to goad me into getting off Raimundo, it's not going to work, Felipe. I've come to see my father and I'm going to do it. If you insist on playing games, I'll leave and come back with enough power to take on any of your threats or any of your hired guns."

Felipe's face darkened.

"I came back so my wife could my meet father." Hunter stared hard at Felipe. "And so she could meet my half brother and sister."

Ana Carlota inhaled sharply. "How dare you call them brother and sister?"

"It's a fact, no matter how much you may want to ignore it." Hunter calmly drank the crystal glass of water, then he smiled. "Best water I've ever had."

Deidre followed his movements precisely.

They set their glasses down on the table, then turned back and waited.

Ana Carlota exhaled sharply, gave her son a questioning glance, then stepped back.

Felipe frowned. "All right. But you can't stay long and I'm not leaving the room."

Chapter 24

Ana Carlota led the way across the courtyard to a door that was shaded by the colonnades supporting the second floor balcony overhanging the inner court. They stopped in the cool shade of the balcony. Deidre looked back at the serene beauty of the courtyard, listened to the gurgling of the fountain, and wondered how such a lovely home could have become so cold.

Felipe put his hand on the doorknob. "Remember, you can't stay long. I'll be watching."

"Let me go in first and prepare him." Ana Carlota placed a hand on her son's shoulder. "I don't want Alberto overcome with shock."

"I can't imagine my father overcome with shock about anything." Hunter glared at the closed door.

Ana Carlota gave Hunter a cold stare. "He is sick and not himself."

Felipe opened the door. Ana Carlota stepped inside. Felipe quickly shut the door and stood in front of it.

"Do you really think you could stop me if I wanted to get by you?" Hunter narrowed his eyes in scorn. He was taller, broader, and wore a .45 on his hip.

Felipe ignored Hunter's words because suddenly from the other side of the door a man's voice called out loudly and Ana Carlota's voice rose in response.

Hunter shouldered Felipe aside, jerked open the door, then hesitated for Deidre to enter before him.

"*Hijo!* Son." Alberto sat on a dark leather couch with an Indian blanket over his knees. He struggled to rise, but Ana Carlota restrained him. He pushed her hands away and got to his feet. "Hunter?" Taking faltering steps, he reached his son and looked at him long and hard. "You *are* real." He reached out and touched Hunter's arm, then nodded in satisfaction.

"Are you all right?" Hunter felt shock at the sight of his strong, arrogant father in this weakened condition. What had happened?

Deidre stood quietly beside Hunter, seeing a similarity between the two men, although Alberto had thick white hair and mustache, dark blue eyes, and paler skin. The older man's face was lined but firm. He wore black trousers and a gray shirt. But both looked too big for him, as if he had suddenly lost weight.

Alberto coughed hard and turned to Ana Carlota. "Open the drapes, open the windows, let in some light and air. My son is used to the wide open spaces. And I want to get a better look at him."

"It is not good for you." Ana Carlota didn't move an inch.

Deidre agreed with Alberto. The room was hot and stuffy and smelled of stale air. Glancing around, she realized the room must be the ranch's office and library. It had been turned into a sick room. Alberto had obviously been sleeping on the couch in front of the massive stone fireplace. A crossed bow and arrow, perhaps Apache, adorned the front of the fireplace. She didn't think the room was conducive to rest. Alberto should have been in the comfort of a bedroom. But perhaps this was his choice.

Hunter took Deidre's hand. "Alberto, I'd like you to meet my wife, Deidre Eleanor of the Bar J Ranch in Texas. Deidre, this is my father."

Alberto gave a slight bow to Deidre. And smiled. "Welcome to the family. The Bar J is a good outfit."

She returned his smile, feeling the first thaw in the house. "I'm pleased to meet you, sir."

Alberto looked back at Ana Carlota, then at Felipe who stood in the doorway. "Open those windows or get a servant to do it."

"No need to stand on my account, sir." Deidre was worried about Alberto's health, especially with the stressful atmosphere. "Why don't you sit back down? I'll open the windows. It is a bit close in here."

Alberto gave her a measuringly look, then nodded in approval. "You may call me Alberto. No need to stand on formality in the family." He moved back to the couch and sat down, his face pale and drawn.

Hunter pulled a chair close to the couch and

seated Deidre, then walked over to a window, jerked open the heavy velvet draperies, threw up the window, then went to the next. When light and air filled the room, he turned back.

Ana Carlota's lips had thinned. "I will send immediately for the doctor. He will see that you leave my husband alone."

"Get out of here." Alberto scowled at Ana Carlota and Felipe. "Keep that damn quack away. I've got the best medicine right here." He patted the couch beside himself and looked at Hunter.

Hunter walked over to the door, held it open, and indicated that he wanted to be alone with his father.

Felipe moved quickly across the room to stand in front of Alberto. "You're not going to let that *bastard* walk in here after all these years and have his way, are you?"

Alberto gazed tiredly at his son. "I have *two* sons and I want to talk with this one. Alone." He looked at Ana Carlota. "Ready a room for them if you haven't already."

She straightened her back. "You don't expect me to have them under our roof?"

"I may be old and weak, but I'm still the grandee of this rancho. I'll be dead soon enough, then you can do what you want. But for now everyone in this hacienda will obey my orders." He took a deep breath, then coughed. "Now see to the room."

Ana Carlota turned on her heel and left the room. Felipe gave Hunter a vicious look, then followed her.

Hunter quietly shut the door, then returned to his father and sat beside him on the couch.

Alberto leaned back and closed his eyes. "I thought never to see you again. I know you blamed me for your mother's death."

There was a lot Hunter wanted to say, but after seeing his father so changed from the powerful, virile man he'd known, he hadn't the heart to wound him now.

"I loved her." Alberto inhaled sharply. "My heart broke when she died." He opened his dark blue eyes and gazed at Hunter. "And her son broke my heart, too." He smiled sadly. "You thought never to hear me say a thing like that, didn't you? Oh, I was a proud and arrogant man. But life and love have broken that pride."

Deidre clenched her fists, wishing she wasn't witness to this scene. She shouldn't be here. She should be far away. Hunter had said he needed her. Yet so far nothing at Raimundo Rancho was what she had expected and she didn't know how she could help.

"Why did you come back?" Alberto raised his head to better see his son.

"I wanted you to meet Deidre. I wanted you to know I was well. And I wanted to see how you were doing."

Alberto nodded. "We all get old if we live long enough. But I never thought it would happen to me."

"You aren't old." Hunter's dark eyes narrowed. "You're sick. There's a big difference."

"You're so like your mother." Alberto lifted a hand as if to touch Hunter's face, then thought better of it and dropped his hand. "Dark hair. Dark eyes. Apache. But you're built like my father's fam-

357

ily, big and tall and strong. Felipe takes after his mother."

"In more ways than one." Hunter's voice held bitterness.

Alberto shook his head, then coughed. "I talked like that once, too. But not for a long time."

Unable to watch the sensitive moment any longer, Deidre stood up and walked over to see what type of books lined the floor to ceiling bookcases. She was impressed that someone in the family liked to read.

"Do you read, my dear?" Alberto watched Deidre.

"Don't get her started." Hunter's voice held admiration. "You'll have to hear the plot to *Frankenstein* and any number of domestic novels."

"Hunter!" She whirled around and glared at him. "You're more afraid I'll insist on discussing Mary Wollstonecraft's *Vindication of the Rights of Woman*."

Alberto looked from one to the other, then laughed. "Blood! Damn it's good to see a feisty woman. You'll have strong children with her, Hunter. I'm proud of your choice."

Deidre frowned, raised an eyebrow, and descended on Alberto. "For your information, I am not a brood mare. I am a suffragist. If and when I have children is my concern."

Slapping his knee, Alberto laughed, coughed, then shook his head. "It took a strong man to get you, didn't it?"

She threw Hunter a disgusted look and sat down. "Sir, I think what you need more than anything is a copy of the *Vindication of the Rights of Woman*. I usually carry several with me and I'll be happy to give you one."

Alberto looked delighted. "Will you read to me? My eyes aren't what they used to be and I miss my books."

"I'll be happy to read to you, but it'll be my choice."

Rubbing his hands together, Alberto glanced up at his shelves of books, then slanted a glance at her from under shaggy white eyebrows. "How about a bargain? First you read from your choice, then you read from my choice."

She cocked her head to one side as if considering his suggestion. "Good horse trader, are you?"

"Damn good." Alberto leaned forward, color returning to his face. He smiled.

"I'll agree if you agree that we read outside under a tree. I like fresh air."

"Done!" Alberto looked at Hunter with respect. "I always said if you marry a weak woman you get weak children. It's like cattle or horses. If you breed your bull or stallion to the weakest cow or mare, what do you expect to get? A strong woman makes a strong man and a strong family."

Deidre narrowed her eyes. "I don't mind being compared to a cow or mare, but nobody's breeding me. However, it seems to me you might be a suffragist yourself, sir."

Alberto shook his head. "I don't know about that, but I'll be happy to listen to you tell me all about it."

Looking pleased, Deidre smiled at Hunter.

Although Hunter was glad Alberto and Deidre

were getting along so well he couldn't let himself forget why he'd come. He wanted to talk about his mother, he wanted his father to apologize, and he couldn't forget the pain of the past.

Alberto turned to Hunter. "You'll stay awhile, won't you, son? Like I said, I've always been a proud man. I've never asked anybody for help. I was content to join your mother till you came back." He glanced at Deidre. "Now I find I'm not so ready to go. You two are going to do things and I'd like to stay around and see them."

"We're going to do things all right." Deidre raised her chin. "And the first thing is to establish the Flora McCuskar Institute for unwed mothers and abandoned children." In the silence that fell over the room, she covered her mouth with her hand and looked guiltily at Hunter. "I'm sorry. It was your news, Hunter. I didn't mean to spoil it."

Alberto stood up and walked shakily over to his desk. He sat down behind it and began pushing through papers. When he found what he wanted, he glanced up. Tears filled his eyes. "Not a day has gone by when I didn't think of Flora. Son, I know you didn't think I did right by her and I didn't. But I was filled with pride and arrogance. I was afraid she'd leave me for another man if she lived any better or in a town. I couldn't marry her. I had responsibilities. I was selfish.

"And she paid for it. You paid for it." Alberto got up and moved slowly back across the room to sit down beside Hunter. "But I loved her." He thrust a piece of paper into Hunter's hands. "I went so far as to buy her a fancy house in Tucson right after you were born. But I never told her. I couldn't tolerate the idea of having her so far away."

Hunter looked at the deed, then at his father, then back again. He stood up, crumpled the piece of paper in his hands, and threw it on the floor. "It's too late. Don't you understand? A house like that in Tucson could have made all the difference in her life, in her self-respect. She'd never have left you. She loved you." Hunter paced back and forth.

"I'm sorry." Alberto bent forward and placed his face in hands. His body shook as he sobbed quietly.

Deidre wanted to sink through the floor. She did not want to witness this type of raw, painful emotion. But how could she leave?

Hunter whirled around again. "If my mother had had a chance at education, she'd have taken it. She was smart, beautiful, but she was a half-breed and a rich man's plaything."

"No!" Alberto stood up, suddenly looking strong and fierce. "She was never my plaything. I honored her, worshiped her . . . so much so that I was terrified to lose her and couldn't admit that to myself or her."

"You know how she was treated."

"I know. I made it as good as I could for her." Alberto walked over and put his hand on Hunter's arm. "Please forgive me. You're all I have left of her. You're my true son, more like me than my other children. Don't shut me out of your life to avenge your mother. I made her happy when I could."

Hunter shook off Alberto's hand and stared at him. "She deserved more! You could have protected her from your family, the church, the local people. But you didn't."

Alberto shook his head and walked over to a window. He looked out over Raimundo Rancho. "I helped more than you realize. People wanted to stone her, run her off, take you away from her. You were too young to know about that. I offered once to send her away. She refused. And I never had the heart or strength to offer that again."

"It was worse than I realized?" Hunter's voice was low and rough.

"Yes. When you were younger. But I should have been stronger. I should have done what was best for the two of you, but I—I didn't think I could live without either of you. And in the end I lost you both." Alberto turned from the window and walked over to Hunter. He hesitated, then put out his hand again and placed it on his son's shoulder.

Hunter didn't move for a long moment, then he covered his father's hand with his. They stood that way until Hunter dropped his hand and stepped back.

"I'm glad you told me." Hunter cleared his throat. "I didn't understand."

"Can you forgive me?"

Hunter hesitated. "I don't know. But you're my father. I don't want to lose you, too."

Alberto lifted his head. "I'll do my best not to disappoint you again. But I'm a man like any other and I'm far from perfect."

Hunter nodded.

Alberto picked up the crumpled deed and walked back to the couch. He sat down and leaned back, as if his strength had suddenly left him.

Hunter moved over to Deidre. He placed a hand on her shoulder and squeezed.

She knew that for a moment they had forgotten her, but she didn't care. The important thing was that Hunter and Alberto still had a chance to be a family.

Alberto focused on Deidre. "You are part of my family now. You have a right to know the past. And the future." He smoothed out the deed to Flora's house, then held it out to Hunter. "I would like to give this to house the Flora McCuskar Institute. It would please me to see her memory live on in a way that helps women like her."

Hunter hesitated, then took the deed. "Thank you. It's a good idea since I'd like to set up the Institute in Arizona Territory. I believe she would be proud."

Tears appeared in Alberto's eyes. "And here a short while ago I thought I had no reason left to live. Felipe wants the rancho. Ana Carlota wants to move back to Mexico City to make herself a social power. And Elena wants the quarterhorses for her husband."

"Elena is my half-sister." Hunter quickly explained to Deidre.

She nodded, feeling terrible that a family could be so split, so troubled, and so selfish. But she knew, too, that it was not unusual.

"You don't have to give up anything." Hunter stood up and walked around the room, remembering it from his youth. Power had been wielded here and perhaps that was why Alberto had made it his sick room. Or maybe he had stayed here to protect what he had from his family.

"My father will be working for years to come." Deidre decided to encourage Alberto.

Alberto looked around the room. "But my family has no more use for me. And they have some cause to hate me."

"Oh, no!" Deidre felt shocked.

"After I fell in love with Flora and she had Hunter, they knew who was first in my heart. I can't blame them for their jealousy or their hurt. But I loved them, too. I had room for all of you in my heart, in my life." Alberto shook his head. "I'm not saying what I did was right. But what's done is done. My children are grown. They will stand on their own two feet or fall. I've done all I can do."

"It's time for yourself now, isn't it?" Deidre's voice was soft but sure.

Alberto nodded, then looked around. "I love this ranch. It's in my blood. But it's not all I love or can do." He straightened his shoulders, color came back in his face, and strength showed in the way he moved his body. "Would you two allow me to share in building the Flora McCuskar Institute?"

"What will your family say?" Hunter leaned back against the massive wooden desk in the center of the room.

Alberto shrugged. "At my age, after what I have been through, I no longer care. I only wish I had felt this way thirty years ago. But age gives us wisdom. My family has their own goals and I'm happy for them to pursue them. Now I'd like to do something to honor the woman I loved. And, believe me, I can help."

"I don't doubt it. A man with your political connections, power, money, and purpose could give it a solid foundation." Hunter glanced at Deidre. "What do you think?"

"I think it's a wonderful idea. You two could work together in Flora's memory. But what about your health, sir?"

Alberto stood up, walked around the room, then turned back and grinned. "Give me a little time and I think I'll recover completely. In fact, I'm hungrier than I've been in years." He rubbed his hands together. "Have you seen the ranch yet, the horses, the cattle?"

Deidre shook her head.

"Of course, you're not even moved in. How long can you stay?"

"We're planning to visit Deidre's folks on the Bar J, too." Hunter wasn't sure about his father's health or his change in heart. Everything was happening too quickly and although he wanted to believe it, he'd been skeptical till he met Deidre. She made all things seem possible and maybe this was, too. At least he'd give it a chance.

"There's plenty of time for you to visit her folks." Alberto stopped pacing and sat down. "I guess I'm not as strong as I thought." He looked over at Deidre.

She chuckled and shook her finger at him. "Oh no! You're not going to pull that on us. We just saw how much energy you have." She smiled warmly. "But we want to stay awhile so I can see the place and Hunter can get reacquainted with his family."

"Good. We'll move you into the red suite on the second floor. You'll have anything you want. Where are your trunks?"

"We left everything at mother's place." Hunter

hoped he wasn't making a mistake. Could he really trust his father? Could old hurts so easily be put aside?

Alberto became thoughtful. "It was always so peaceful there and she was so beautiful and you were always getting into some kind of trouble. I have good memories of that time. I hope you can some day, too."

"I do." Hunter rolled the deed up and tapped it against his palm. "And I intend to store up a lot more in the future."

Alberto met his eyes. "It's settled then. I'll send some men over to collect your trunks and we'll have a feast tonight to celebrate your return."

"Please, don't go to a lot of trouble." Deidre realized she had been thinking of herself as Hunter's wife, as part of his family. She felt embarrassed at the lie they had told this man. How would they explain it later? Perhaps it wasn't her concern. She might never see any of them again. That thought made her sad.

Alberto leaned forward. No trouble at all. I want everybody to know I have two sons. And they're both with me now. Also, I want everyone to meet my beautiful, intelligent daughter-in-law. Then I'm going to announce the Flora McCuskar Institute."

"Perhaps you should wait." Hunter looked concerned. "Your family isn't going to be happy about this."

"To hell with them. It's about time they made me happy. And it's about time I got on with my life." Alberto rubbed his hands together in satisfaction. "Now let's get your trunks moved in here." He started for the door.

366

Deidre walked over to him. "And then it's time for you to take a rest."

"Rest! I don't have time to rest. Life's out there waiting for me. Flora's waiting for me to make her memory last forever." He threw back his head and laughed. "I'll rest when I'm in my grave."

He turned toward the door, but it suddenly flew open. A small woman with blond hair and blue eyes, dressed in a black riding habit stood in the hall with her feet planted apart. She snapped a riding quirt against her thigh as she looked around the room. Then she focused on Alberto.

"Father, what is going on here? Why are you up? And what is Hunter doing back here?" Her dark blue eyes, so much like her father's, were filled with anger.

"Elena, please come in and meet Hunter's wife, Deidre Eleanor of the Bar J Ranch in Texas."

Elena stomped her booted foot. "I don't want to meet her. And I don't want them disturbing you. How can you get well if you don't rest? And why *is* Hunter back here anyway?"

"Why don't you ask him yourself?" Alberto narrowed his eyes. "And where are your manners?"

Elena tossed her head, glared at Hunter, then Deidre. "My brother's name is Felipe. His wife's name is Josefa. My husband's name is Luis Arturo. And my children are at boarding school. My family is accounted for. I don't know who these people are and they have no business being here in our home."

"I want to hear no more talk like that." Alberto's eyes glinted dangerously. "Hunter is your half-brother. He and his wife will be staying here for as long as they like. There is plenty of room as you well know. Please go now and ask your mother to ready the red suite and send men to collect their belongings at the adobe house on the Santa Cruz."

Elena's face reddened. "You'd do this to your family, your *real* family?" She stomped her foot again. "Well, I can tell you right now that my husband and I will not stay under the same roof with your *bastard*. We'll go home today. And I won't be the one to give mother your beastly orders."

Alberto stepped close to Elena. "Your behavior is deplorable. I *never* want to hear you speak about Hunter that way again. Do you hear me? *Never*. And you and Luis Arturo will stay under this roof. We will have a feast tonight in honor of my son returning home. And we will have announcements to make."

Elena whirled around and hit the wall with her quirt, then whirled back again. "How can you—"

"I am still head of this family. I will not be disobeyed. Tell your mother what I want done."

Elena looked past him at Hunter and Deidre with pure hatred, then she thinned her lips in a parody of a smile. "All right, father. I'll do as you say. But I'm sure Luis Arturo will want to discuss the quarterhorses with you tonight. Or do you plan to give those to Hunter?"

"I plan to care for my entire family as I always have, Elena. I love all of you. But I will not be thwarted in this."

She bowed her head a moment, then looked back up at him with tears in her eyes. "You know we are only concerned about your health. And too much excitement right now might hurt you."

"I feel better than I have in a long time. Now go and do as I've asked."

Elena nodded, then turned around and stalked down the hall.

Alberto looked back. "Do not be concerned. She will get over it. In the meantime, let me take you to your rooms. Maybe we should all rest before dinner."

Chapter 25

That evening Deidre dressed with care. She also dressed as a lady, a rich sophisticated young lady. Hunter looked the part of a respectable, powerful gentleman. A grandee. Although their clothes weren't a pretense, she knew they covered much richer, deeper experiences and personalities than a simple lady and gentleman going to dinner.

Tonight was a social occasion she very much wanted to fit into, one that would enhance Hunter's standing in the family. If that were possible. Naturally only the best of fashionable clothing would do. After shopping in New Orleans and New York City, they were definitely prepared. She only hoped it would be enough.

She smiled at herself in the full-length mirror, pleased with what she saw. She had decided on a gold satin gown trimmed with green velvet the color of her eyes. Elegant in its simplicity, the gown had a fitted bodice, a skirt pleated in front, a small bustle in back, with bands of green velvet at the waist, hem, bustle, and at the bottom of the long sleeves. Pale gold lace spilled from the edge of the sleeves and around the hem. High-necked, a green velvet stand-up collar encircled her throat.

She patted the small hat of gold satin and green feathers on top of her head, a perfect complement to the simple chignon of her hair. She wore matching green leather slippers. But no jewelry. Satisfied her clothing proclaimed her a lady, she turned to look at Hunter.

For a moment her heart beat fast. Even after all they had been through together, he still never failed to excite her. Tonight he looked particularly handsome in a light gray tweed suit with black braid edging. He wore a simple white shirt with it and a black and burgandy striped tie. He also wore plain black boots.

A gentleman and a lady. She laughed out loud and held out her arms to him. He hugged her carefully, then set her back to look at her more closely.

"If we don't impress them, Hunter, I don't know what will."

"Frankly, I'm not sure I give a damn."

"Hunter!"

"You saw the way they treated us, as well as my father. Can you imagine how much worse it was for my mother?"

She nodded and placed a soft kiss on his lips. "But that's in the past."

"Is it? I wonder." He tucked a strand of blond

hair back under her hat. "I'm beginning to think they'll never let it die."

Shivering, she turned away and caught sight of them together in the mirror. "What matters to you matters to me. But I know your father is glad to see you. And, truly, I think you may have saved his life. Do you mind him working with you on the Institute?"

"No. It's a good idea. It'll give us something in common. Besides, he owes it to my mother's memory and I think he wants to do it. But you're part of this, too."

She smiled, silently wondering if that would ever be possible. If she and Hunter separated, she didn't think she could stand to be with him but not linked to him through passion. Yet she could recommend some talented and dedicated women to help them put the Institute together and run it.

"You aren't backing out, are you?"

"No. It's just that I like your father. I only wish he knew the truth."

"What truth?" Hunter looked puzzled.

"You know! We're *not* married."

"Oh that." He turned away and walked across the room. "I forgot. I guess it was because being married seems so right between us. Doesn't it?"

"Perhaps that comes from being together so much." A sudden formal coolness had sprung up between them. "But what are we going to tell him?"

"Nothing. He's happy believing we're married. I don't know what the truth would do to him. First off, it'd remind him of my mother and their bastard. I don't want that." He took several steps toward her, then stopped. "Don't think your coming here was a mistake. I want you here. I need you." He hesitated. "Can you take my family a little longer?"

"Oh, Hunter." She quickly crossed the room to him and took his hands. "I like your father. The others are so eaten up with jealousy and hatred they're ruining their own lives. If they come to terms with your existence, then I think they can be happy and enjoy you."

"I hope they'll give it a chance." Intensity filled his dark eyes.

"We'll make it a dinner to remember. Yes?"

"Right." He softly kissed her lips, then stepped back.

"Is it time to go downstairs?" She could feel the coolness still lingering between them. She hoped it was due to his distraction at meeting with his family again. But what if it weren't? What if the end had already begun? Hunter had what he wanted now. His father wanted to work with him, plan Flora's institute. What if Hunter no longer needed her?

She tried to stop the sudden ache in her heart. No. It was not all over yet, at least not on Raimundo Rancho. He had helped her. Now she must help him. She would stay until everything had been settled here. Or until he sent her away.

She glanced around the room. She wanted to remember every detail in case memories were later all she had of him. Perhaps she was being foolish, but he had come to mean much more to her than she ever could have imagined and right now she couldn't tolerate the idea of being parted from him.

The suite of bedroom, sitting room, and bath proclaimed the house's Spanish-Moorish heritage.

A massive bed dominated the room. The red suite was obviously named for its decor of dark heavy woods and burgandy drapes, bed covering, carpet, and upholstery. The rich color made the suite feel warm and strong and inviting. A few dark oil paintings of Spanish or Mexican scenes hung on the walls. And the scent of lavender filled the air.

"It's beautiful here, Hunter." Yes, she could always remember this room with happiness.

"It can't compare to you." His eyes were as warm and smooth as melted chocolate.

She felt her fear drain away. It was all simply tension. After this evening all would be well. Whatever came to pass in the future would be right. She must believe in herself and in Hunter. She mustn't let her thoughts weaken her before she went downstairs to confront his hostile family. She took a deep breath and put her hand in his.

He opened the door and they stepped onto the balcony overlooking the courtyard. Bright stars filled the dark night sky. A soft breeze carried the scent of juniper. Lanterns cast soft light in the court below. And silence seemed to make them the only two people in the world.

Deidre sighed with contentment as she absorbed the beauty around them. She wished Hunter's family didn't await them in the house below. If it were just the two of them, they could spend the night in the big red bed making love with the drapes pulled back so starlight shone in on them.

Suddenly she desperately longed for another maroon on Hog Island. She wanted to be with Hunter with no one else around. But that was wishful thinking and she knew it. They had returned on a mission, not to indulge in passion, and it must be completed.

Hunter led her downstairs, through the courtyard and into a softly lighted parlor. She liked the idea that most or all of the rooms of the house could be reached from the center courtyard. She glanced around. Like the red suite, this room was furnished in a Spanish-Moorish decor of dark woods and richly colored fabrics. A huge tapestry of obvious antiquity dominated one wall. But before she could look more closely at her surroundings, Alberto stepped forward.

Behind him, seated and standing, was the family that refused to acknowledge Hunter. And they once more ignored him by failing to look up or stop their whispered conversations when Alberto walked over to Deidre and Hunter.

She felt amazed at the difference in Alberto. Although still thin, he had dressed elegantly as a grandee in a black suit with white trim, fancy black boots with silver trim. He had more color in his face and walked with assurance. She could hardly believe he was the same person they'd met earlier that day. Hunter's return had given the grandee new life.

And his family should be pleased. But as she glanced around at the elegantly attired group, she saw nothing of happiness or pleasure. Instead, she saw resentment, simmering anger, and determination. She decided it was not going to be an easy evening.

"Deidre, you look lovely tonight." Alberto lifted her hand and kissed it.

She smiled with genuine warmth. "I'm impressed with you. I'd like to get Hunter a suit like yours."

Pleased, Alberto nodded. "It will be done if you don't think it is hopelessly out of date."

"Not at all. This grandee style is all its own and I like it."

Alberto focused on Hunter. "By your clothes, I can only assume you've done well, son."

Hunter nodded. "I did what I had to do to get what I wanted."

"But don't ask him what." Deidre's green eyes twinkled mischievously.

"Oh, but I will." Alberto put a hand on Hunter's shoulder. "Later we will have time to share the years we were apart."

"I'd like that." Hunter looked past his father toward the assembled group. He pushed down his anger at the antagonism he felt from them. So far nothing had changed, except with his father. But could he trust that?

Alberto followed Hunter's gaze and turned. "Come. I will introduce Deidre to the rest of the family."

They followed him across the room.

The men stood, but the women remained seated.

Alberto gave a slight bow. "It is my great honor to present my son's wife, Deidre Eleanor of the Bar J Ranch in Texas."

Stony silence and cold eyes were the only response.

Undaunted, Alberto looked around the group, daring them to say anything he didn't want to hear. "Deidre has already met my wife Ana Carlota and my children Elena and Felipe." He extended his hand. "This is Luis Arturo, the husband of Elena. Josefa is Felipe's wife. Elena's three children are at boarding school in Mexico. Josefa has yet—"

"I have yet to be blessed with an heir to Raimundo Rancho. And what could be more important?" Josefa stood up, cast Felipe an angry look, then walked over to a table which held crystal glasses and decanters. She poured herself a brandy.

"I'm sure it is only a matter of time." Alberto smiled at Josefa, then turned back to the group. "Deidre and Hunter have agreed to spend some time with us before going on to visit her parents at the Bar J."

Again silence dominated the room.

Alberto stopped smiling. "I expect each of you to make their stay as comfortable and as happy as possible. Hunter is my son. He and Deidre are members of my family the same as each of you."

Still silence.

"I think you should all know that I am giving Hunter my full last name to entitle him to complete rights as a member of this family."

"What!" Felipe took several steps forward. He pointed at Hunter. "A *bastard*! How can you think of corrupting the family this way? We'll be the laughingstock of the grandee families on both sides of the border. Our bloodline will be polluted. Our children will not be able to find suitable mates. This is not acceptable!"

"That's enough." Alberto frowned, his shaggy white brows meeting across his nose. "Deidre and Hunter will enhance our bloodline. No one would

377

dare laugh at our family. We will be the stronger for this addition. Remember, my blood flows in his veins the same as yours."

"But what about the blood of his mother?" Elena stood and walked over to her brother. "She was nothing but a dirty, conniving halfbreed. Apache! Irish! She was lower than a snake."

"Elena!" Alberto stepped forward and raised his hand, but Deidre grasped his arm and stopped him. His family wanted to push him to violence. She couldn't let it happen, although she wanted desperately to do violence herself. She was glad she had left her derringer and knife in her room.

Hunter faced his sister and brother. "You may think what you wish about my mother. I can't stop that. But don't ever speak of her that way in my presence again, or I will make you sorry you were born. My mother was an honorable, loving woman. She never hurt anyone. I can't say the same for any of you." He turned and looked at his father. "Deidre and I won't sit at the same table with people who slander my mother. We'd rather eat in the kitchen or leave."

"No!" Alberto put out a hand. "I also will not break bread with my family until they accept what I say. I am the head of this family and I will remain so until I die." He took a deep breath and glanced around at the angry faces. "I had thought to give each of you what you most wanted tonight. Felipe control of the ranch. Ana Carlota her social life in Mexico City. Elena and Luis Arturo the quarterback horses."

Elena put a hand to her mouth in dismay.

Felipe scowled.

Ana Carlota got to her feet and joined her children to confront her husband. "And now you would punish us further for *your* sin? Perhaps the woman you kept in the adobe hut by the Santa Cruz was innocent of everything except loving wrongly. She was young and innocent when you took her. But you, my husband, knew better. Do you expect us to welcome Hunter and his bride and their children into our family with open arms after the pain you've caused us?"

Alberto faltered. Deidre and Hunter moved to each side of him for support.

Raising her voice, Ana Carlota's face took on the aspect of a righteous martyr. "We are the innocents here. You are the sinner, Alberto. And we will never elevate your sin to glory. Never!" She turned hard blue eyes on Hunter. "You were born a bastard and you will die a bastard. And you will never be welcomed into our family."

Deidre was horrified at the viciousness of the attack. True, Alberto had violated his vows of marriage, but it was not an uncommon act for a man in their society. And why punish an innocent child for his entire life? And why sully the memory of a woman who had done the best she could in a world hostile to her?

Hunter put a hand on his father's shoulder. "I don't mind being a bastard." Hunter's voice was low and calm.

Glancing up at him, Deidre had never seen such an expression on his face before. He'd been pushed too far. She had never wanted to be the one to do that. But now these people had. What would he do? She shivered and noticed Alberto looking at his son with an expression similar to her own.

"My mother did not have the sanctity of church or government, but she had the sanctity of love." Hunter focused on Ana Carlota. "Señora, you sought love in many men, but you never found it, did you?"

Elena and Felipe gasped. Luis Arturo and Josefa moved closer to their spouses, horrified expressions on their faces.

Ana Carlota drew in a sharp breath. "Watch your tongue, young man."

Hunter smiled, a feral movement of his lips. "Señora, why do you call me a bastard and yet call your own son legitimate? Isn't it common knowledge that his father is not your husband?"

Ana Carlota's eyes grew wide, then she swooned into her son's arms.

Felipe looked up and growled. "I'll kill you for this insult."

"For calling you what you've called me all my life?" Hunter's eyes narrowed. "You're a bastard the same as me, Felipe, only I never rubbed your nose in it every day of your life the way you did me."

"I'm not a bastard!" Felipe looked wildly around the room, then turned to Luis Arturo. "Take mother to her room. Send for the doctor."

Josefa raised her glass of brandy in a toast. "To my husband, the bastard."

"Silence!" Felipe slapped her. "Take mother up with you while I kill this arrogant bastard."

Horrified, Deidre reached out to Josefa and pulled her close. "How dare you hit her?"

"I'll hit you, too, or more than that after I've killed your bastard of a husband." Felipe leered at her.

Josefa pulled away and went to pour herself another drink, obviously not unused to being hit by her husband.

"None of you are leaving this room." Alberto took control, although he looked pale. He walked over and pulled a bell cord. When a servant appeared, he spoke in a low voice, then turned back to the group. "I've sent for armed guards. They will not let any of you leave this room and they will protect me."

"Father, we would never hurt you!" Elena held a container of smelling salts under her mother's nose. "How can you think—"

"No more!" Alberto walked across the room and poured himself a whiskey. He threw it back, then looked around. "Everyone take a seat. Dinner will be delayed."

"Please. Mother is sick. She needs to lie down." Elena had tears in her eyes.

Ana Carlota put a hand to her chest and leaned heavily against her son.

"Sit down." Alberto pulled the servant's bell again. When a young Mexican woman arrived, he took her to one side. "Tell the kitchen that dinner is delayed. And send in Tomas to pour us drinks." As the young woman hurried out, Alberto opened the door to the courtyard.

Deidre held on to Hunter's hand in dismay as she saw Mexican cowboys with ammunition belts across their chests move into place to guard each door and window from outside.

"This is unnecessary and insulting." Felipe threw up his hands. "We need to take mother to her room."

"Sit down." Alberto frowned. "I won't tell you again."

Hunter squeezed Deidre's hand, but when he looked down at her his eyes were as hard and black as the obsidian called Apache Tears. He led her to a wing back chair, seated her, then poured them both a whiskey. He returned to hand her the drink, then stood at her side.

Felipe made sure his mother was comfortable on the couch, then sat down beside her. Elena sat on Ana Carlota's other side and patted her mother's wrist, murmuring comforting words. Josefa and Luis Arturo sat down in chairs near the couch.

Satisfied with the security and that his family had followed his instructions, Alberto turned to Hunter. "Sit down, son. And explain yourself."

Hunter pulled up a brocade covered footstool and sat at Deidre's feet. "My word alone is not enough. Ask Tomas when he gets here. You know he's almost a hundred years old and knows everything that ever happened on Raimundo Rancho."

"That old man!" Ana Carlota pulled a lace trimmed handkerchief from her sleeve and held it to one eye then the other. "How can you even think of listening to that dirty, lying Mexican. He's Indian!"

Alberto shook his head. "I know you have always prided yourself on your family's Castilian blood, Ana Carlota. My family does, too. But that doesn't mean we are the best people in the world."

"Of course it does." She turned to her son. "Do something! Make him stop this inquisition."

Felipe stood up.

"Sit down, Felipe." Alberto glanced at the armed guards looking in the windows. "I don't want you harmed, but I'm going to learn the truth tonight."

Felipe slowly sat down. Ana Carlota moaned. Elena patted her mother's hand.

Tomas walked slowly into the room, looked around, then focused on Alberto. Small, stooped, with little hair on his head, Tomas had a full white mustache and beard. His dark eyes were alert.

Alberto walked over to him. "Tomas, you have been with my family all your life."

Tomas nodded.

"Some allegations have been made tonight about Ana Carlota and Felipe." Alberto hesitated, glanced at each person in the room, then turned back to Tomas. "Upon your honor, will you tell me if I am . . . the father of Felipe."

Tomas paled and stepped back.

Alberto shut his eyes tightly and clenched his fists. When he focused on Tomas again, his face was lined with pain. "As you know, Hunter has returned. He has married Deidre Eleanor of the Bar J Ranch in Texas. I plan to make him legally part of my family."

Tomas nodded.

"But I need to know about Felipe now."

"Nobody wanted to hurt you, sir." Tomas looked at the floor.

Alberto swayed unsteadily.

"Stop that fool." Felipe jumped up and started for Tomas.

Hunter stood up and towered over him. "Come on, Felipe. I'd like to give you what's been coming to you all your life. Come on, just give me a reason to pound you senseless."

Felipe hesitated, looked up at Hunter, then seemed to shrink in on himself. He sat back down. "I will not bring violence into his room." He turned to his mother and patted her hand. "I will protect you no matter what slander these fools say about us."

"Who is Felipe's father?" Alberto pushed, no matter that he looked pale and weak.

Tomas hunched his shoulders. "On my honor, it is hard to say."

"What!" Alberto's voice broke.

Ana Carlota cried out and collapsed against her daughter.

Tomas lowered his voice. "She always liked the young bucks."

"Good god!" Alberto whirled to look at his wife. "And you called me vile. You dared to dishonor my family?"

Ana Carlota stood up. "So! It is all right for the grandee to initiate all the young girls on the rancho into sensual pleasures, but the wife must lie in her bed alone except when the husband wants to make a baby. That is not fair."

Alberto looked wildly around the room. "But you broke the sanctity of your marriage vows." He looked at Elena in sudden horror. "Who's child is she?"

"Yours." Tomas nodded sagely. "Remember, she came early in your marriage."

"Thank you, Tomas. You may leave." Alberto poured himself another whiskey.

Tomas walked over to Ana Carlota. "I am sorry to hurt you, señora. But the children are yours. For you, the father does not matter, does he?"

"Get out!" Tears streamed down Ana Carlota's face. "Of course I love both my children no matter who fathered them." She pointed at her husband. "The father's name matters only to the husband and the church and the law. My children might end up with nothing if they weren't from his loins."

Tomas hung his head and slowly left the room.

But Ana Carlota was not done. She glared at her husband. "After all the love and work I've put into this rancho, I and the children of my body could end up with nothing because of him." She pointed at Hunter. "It's not fair. Nobody gave me a ranch. Nobody gave me an education. A wife and mother were all the choice I had. And I haven't complained because I love my children and I want the best for them. But it's not fair that we have nothing."

Alberto's face darkened and he tossed back his drink.

Clearing her throat, Deidre glanced around the room. "She's right, you know."

Everyone stared in shock at her.

"It's *not* fair. But it is not Hunter's fault either." Deidre hated to defend the woman who had hurt Hunter, but right was right.

Silence followed her words.

Deidre took a deep breath. "If Ana Carlota had inherited her father's ranch or business the same as her brothers probably did, then her children would have inherited after her. There would have been no question about paternity. A woman's child is a woman's child. But a man?" She glanced around the room. "Men have to make sure it's their child and that's why they insist on marriage and fidelity. And that's why so many men feel no need to be as honorable in return."

Alberto threw his glass against a wall. It shattered. "Don't try to turn our lives into philosophy. After my youth, I was faithful to two women in my life. I did not touch the female servants as I know many men do." He glared at Felipe. "As my son has done. But it has always been a man's right to have many women since he does not bear the burden of carrying future generations. And it has always been a man's right to inherit since he will protect the family and provide for them. But now . . ."

Deidre stood up and went to him. She put her arms around Alberto. He allowed her to hold him and she could feel him shaking with emotion. She wanted to help him, help them all, but she didn't know quite how. She straightened her shoulders and stepped back.

"I know change is not easy. But change has come. Women will not accept what went before. Life must be fair to all. You know what Flora endured. You know what Hunter endured. Please don't make the rest of your family suffer for the inequities of our society."

Ana Carlota stood up and walked over to Deidre. She wore a puzzled frown. "I don't understand. Why should you try to help us? No one could possibly doubt that Hunter is Alberto's son, or I would suggest that. As it is, your husband could inherit all of Raimundo Rancho. How could you possibly give that up? What kind of woman are you?"

Deidre smiled sadly. "I don't believe any of you are wrong of anything except hurting each other. You have believed in inequity all your life. I believe in equality. I believe in woman suffrage. That's the kind of woman I am. If everyone has an equal chance at life and happiness, then I believe we will hurt each other much less."

Felipe clapped his hand. "A fine speech. A noble sentiment. But you stand to lose nothing, little rich girl. My life has been destroyed and I know who did it." He gave Hunter a venomous look. "And I won't ever forget or forgive."

Alberto raised his hands for silence. "We have all been shocked tonight. I had happy announcements to make. Instead, I am left adrift. I don't know what to think." He looked at his wife and shook his head.

"What's good for the gander is good for the goose." She raised her chin, refusing to back down.

"I am too old for this." Alberto walked toward the courtyard door. "I'm going to my office. I must think. Alone. Later I will tell you what I decide." He opened the door, then looked back. "In the meantime, try not to kill each other when I call off the guards."

Chapter 26

"Let's get the hell out of here!"

Hunter's words kept ringing in Deidre's ears as they rode across the desert too fast for the darkness of the night. But nothing could slow Hunter as he put distance between himself and the hacienda.

She kept up, although she could feel the heat of the horse rubbing against her bare legs because she still wore the gold satin gown. Hunter had left the house with her in tow, grabbed food from the kitchen, then saddled their horses. Neither of them were appropriately dressed for riding or the desert, but she hadn't protested. She understood his determination to get away. And she didn't think she could have stood another moment there either.

Their New York finery wouldn't survive the ride, but what did she care about clothes in comparison to Hunter's pain or the pain of his family? She only wished she were wearing a split riding skirt for comfort's sake.

As she clung to the reins, she realized she could still hardly believe the turn the evening had taken or the raw emotions that had swept across them all. She didn't know for whom to feel the most sorry. What a tangled web!

They had finally pushed Hunter too far, made him mad enough to play the ace he had held all his life. Would his mother be pleased to know of the turmoil within her grandee's family? Deidre doubted it. This type of emotional pain wasn't good or desirable for anyone. But after a lifetime of accumulated anger, what else could have happened? She wished she could have found a way for them to have avoided it, but that hadn't been possible. At least she had done what she could to ease the tensions.

She understood now they had made Hunter the scapegoat of the family, pushing all their anger, frustrations, and disappointments onto his shoulders. No wonder he had left after the death of his mother. Amazingly, after the years he had been away, they had started the process again when he returned. Or perhaps they had never stopped trying to blame him for all their weaknesses and misdeeds.

But he wouldn't take it anymore. He'd finally had enough. He'd sent their duplicity back on them, in spades. And she couldn't blame him.

Now what would happen? She glanced over at Hunter, wondering what he felt, where he was taking them, what he would say when they finally stopped? She knew one thing for sure. Whatever happened at Raimundo Rancho mattered much more to Ana Carlota, Elena, and Felipe that it ever would to Hunter. He knew how to survive on nothing, no love, no family, no home. They knew only comfort. Whatever the outcome, Hunter would be all right. She didn't know about the rest of them. And she didn't care too much either, not after the pain they had caused him.

As they continued their journey, she grew more tired, her body ached from the emotional stress of the day and the physical exertion of the ride. Her thoughts drifted until she gave up trying to think or reason. She let herself respond simply to the rhythm of the horse, the pattern of the land, and the shifting shadows of the night.

After riding across flat land for she knew not how long, they started up the incline of a mountain that loomed dark and dangerous. Her horse followed Hunter's mount, moving higher and higher, carefully picking their way around cactus, juniper trees, boulders, slipping on rocks, but always moving upwards, with only starlight and a sliver of moonlight to guide their way.

Hunter seemed to be able to see in the dark. He never faltered or stopped. Perhaps he had been there before with the Apache. But tonight they must be the only two humans on the mountainside. They moved higher and higher. The horses were wet with lather, even though the night felt cool.

Where was Hunter taking them? When would they stop? She feared she would have blisters on the insides of her thighs by the time they reached their destination. Feeling tired, hungry, thirsty, with pain throbbing through the muscles of her legs, she realized only too well that she hadn't ridden enough recently for this type of strenuous horseback trip.

She glanced ahead at Hunter. Nothing seemed to touch him, for he rode as straight in the saddle as he had when they had left the hacienda.

And still they rode on, higher and higher until finally Hunter reached a pass and turned his horse into it. He glanced back, made sure she followed, then continued. She went on, feeling an eeriness as if they were watched or as if something had taken place here in the pass that had left a lingering echo through time. She shook her head at her fancy and concentrated on following Hunter through the pass to the other side.

Abruptly he turned his horse to the right to follow an almost invisible trail. They climbed upward again. Finally he rounded a wind-twisted juniper tree and disappeared on the other side. Surprised, she felt a little nervous as she followed. Then understood. The concealed entrance had hidden a box canyon.

Hunter moved downward, zigziging toward the bottom of the ravine. Again she followed, hoping this was their destination because she didn't know how much more she could endure on horseback.

He rounded an outcropping of rock and she followed in his path. On the other side, she caught her breath in amazement. A narrow waterfall cascaded down into a deep pool surrounded by lush vegetation. The water sparkled in the soft light of the night, making music as it fell.

Enchanted, she wanted to share the moment with Hunter, but he quickly dismounted, helped her down, then began removing the saddles and bridles from the horses. His movements were stiff and jerky as if done in anger. For the first time since she'd met him, he seemed unapproachable.

She reached up to help him with the horses, but he shook his head and pointed at the water. She tried not to feel rejected. He'd had a rough time of it, but so had she. She supposed he wanted her to get a drink. She didn't say anything, for somehow the night seemed to press silence on them, as if it would be sacrilegious to speak. Or perhaps she was simply too tired to pursue anything except rest.

Turning her back on him, she walked over to the pool. She knelt, then cupped her hands and drank greedily from the cool water. She splashed water on her face. Feeling better, she pushed her hair back and discovered she'd lost her hat somewhere during the long ride. She shrugged and looked down at her gold satin gown.

She felt caught between dismay and horror. The dressmaker would never have recognized her creation as the dirty, torn, wrinkled article of clothing that clung to Deidre's body. She wouldn't have either if she hadn't been wearing it. Suddenly she wanted nothing so much as to be free of the tight corset, torn stockings, and ravaged dress. She began undressing as quickly as possible.

As she removed one article of clothing after another, feeling her spirits lift as the weight of her clothes left her, she watched Hunter. He let the horses drink from the pool, then rubbed them down with dry grass. After he'd hobbled them nearby, he picked up a canteen from one of the saddles and drank. Wiping his mouth with the back of his hand, he looked at her.

Eyes like Apache Tears. She shivered. This wasn't a man she knew.

Still watching her, he jerked off his clothes and as he tossed them aside he seemed to throw away the trappings of a gentleman. When he stood naked, his body like a sculpture of stone, he was much more akin to his Apache warrior ancestors than his Spanish grandee father. He walked to the water's edge and dove in deep.

Again she shivered, but this time with a primitive longing of passion. But she turned her mind back to business and slipped off her chemise, petticoat, and drawers. At least these garments had made it through the trip intact if dirty. She pushed her hair back into a neat chignon, then stepped to the water's edge.

Hunter surfaced near her, a hungry look in his eyes. True, they had missed dinner, but she didn't think that was the type of hunger motivating him now. Again she felt a flash of primitive need, but she pushed it aside to sit down on the bank and slide into the water.

Hunter didn't move, but he didn't stop watching her either. She washed the dust of the journey from her, then leaned back to float. It felt delightful, soothing to her tired, aching body. At the moment she didn't care if she ever saw civilization again, especially if it were at Raimundo Rancho.

As she looked up into the star bright night, she again felt an eerie sensation wash over her. She frowned and sank down into the water so that she could brace herself on the sides of the bank and look around. But she could see nothing to explain her sudden feeling of unease, even dread.

"It's an old Apache watering hole." Hunter broke the silence as he moved close to her.

"Beautiful." She turned to look at him.

"Bloody."

She shivered. "What do you mean?"

"Out in the canyon, the U.S. cavalry massacred fifty warriors, then came in here and finished off the women, children, and old people."

"I'm sorry." So that is what she had felt. Did Apache spirits still linger here and in the canyon?

"Don't be. It's all over now. The whites have what they want."

"But couldn't there have been a better way, a way to share?"

"Sure." His eyes glinted. "But most people don't want to share."

"Hunter?" She reached out and touched his face. He seemed so far away, so tense. How did she bring back *her* Hunter? "I know it was bad."

"Senseless death always is."

"I meant your family."

He looked savage. "You hate what I did, don't you?"

"What?"

"You'd never have told Alberto about Felipe and Ana Carlota, would you? You're too noble, too fine, too determined to help, not hurt." He took a deep breath. "I couldn't let them say those things about my mother anymore, not knowing what I did. My mother did what they all did. Her only crime was

394

being a half-breed woman. It wasn't fair then and isn't now."

Tears filled Deidre's eyes and she tenderly touched Hunter's cheek. "I'm proud of you. You did the right thing. You defended your mother and yourself."

Surprised, his eyes narrowed.

"Yes, I want to help others. Yes, I want to right wrongs. Yes, I want to vote so I can make a difference in this country. But, Hunter, do you really think I wouldn't fight to save myself or my family or you?"

He reached out to her, almost touched her, then dropped his hand. "But I deliberately hurt them."

"Yes. But only after they had pushed you, and your father, to the wall. You *had* to defend your own. And you know it."

"Damn, Deidre!" This time he reached out, snagged the back of her neck, and pulled her against him.

He was hot and hard and ready.

Pressing his mouth to hers, he thrust his tongue into her mouth, kissing her so intensely that she moaned and threw her arms around his neck to find stability in her suddenly shifting world. He jerked her hair free, letting it tumble into the water. Suddenly he stopped the kiss, looked at her with passionate determination, then lifted her to the banks of the pond.

Kneeling over her, he ran his hands up and down over her body possessively, then pushed her legs apart to thrust fingers inside her. She gasped at the sudden invasion, then moaned with the heat he coaxed from her. He touched her breasts with one hand, teasing her nipples to taut peaks, all the while watching her with eyes that had become all Apache. Her gentleman had disappeared to be replaced by a warrior.

"You're mine, Deidre." He raised her hips with strong hands and positioned his erection to enter her. Then he looked at her face. Silver light made his face all planes and angles.

She shivered, for a moment not knowing this man and a little afraid him. She bit her lower lip and reached out to touch his hard, bare shoulders, reminding herself that she *did* know him. "Hunter. *My* Champion Hunter."

"That's right." He thrust into her. And stopped.

She felt impaled by him, connected to him by more than flesh . . . by time, space, and beyond.

"*My* woman." He put his hands on her breasts. "Never would I allow to happen to us what happened to my father. Never!"

"Oh, Hunter."

"Never!" He pushed into her, then began moving in and out, building passion between them as he watched her face. "You're mine, Deidre, and don't you ever forget it." He moved hard, faster.

Her breath caught. She thrust her hands into his hair, feeling all the tension, all the emotions they had endured at the hacienda center in the vortex of passion he was building between them. She moaned and heard an answering groan from him. Then he stopped and she wimpered in protest, clutching at his shoulders, moving her hips against him, trying to draw him deeper inside her.

"Tell me!" His face was savage in the starlight.

"What?" She dug her fingers into his hair and tried to pull his face down for a kiss.

He resisted. "Tell me you're mine."

"Oh!" She felt fevered, sweaty, in desperate need of release. But a small part of her heard those words and refused to compromise. "Please, Hunter, don't do this to me. I need you." She groaned and lifted herself to meet his face. "Kiss me."

"No. Tell me." He moved inside her until she moaned again and dug her nails into his shoulders. He stopped. Sweat beaded his face and body.

"I'm yours for now."

"Damn!"

He plunged into her, hard and hot and with so much fierce emotion that she could do little but clutch his shoulders and ride the wave of passion that swept over her, binding her to him with fevered ecstasy.

"You're mine and you'll admit it some day."

When he climaxed inside of her, she rode the current with him, treasuring their closeness, their oneness as wave after wave of bliss swept through her.

Only in the aftermath of desire did she realize that their ecstasy together had contained danger for her. Why hadn't he protected her this time from conceiving his child?

She sat up. Looking down at him, she couldn't stop the questions in her mind. Did he only want to possess her, brand her, own her? Was she simply the same as a horse or hacienda to him? His words of ownership rang in her ears. She slipped into the water to wash away her thoughts, her worries, and him from her body, inside and out.

A moment later, she heard him enter the water behind her.

He put strong arms around her and when she tried to twist away he held on. "I'm sorry." He took a deep breath. "I tried to take what wasn't mine. And I tried to do it by getting you with child." He let her go and got out of the water. He stood with his back to her and looked up at the sky, his fists clenched by his sides.

Watching him, she felt a deep fear. Was it already over between them? What if she even now carried their child? What would she do? Would she tell him? Would she marry him? Or would it be best to avoid the entanglements of family and walk away from him?

She left the pool. "Hunter?"

He turned around and lifted a strand of her long, golden hair to his lips. "You're driving me crazy. You know I'm in love with you, don't you? And now when I finally have a chance to be good enough for you, I treat you like—"

Putting a fingertip to his lips, she smiled in relief. No, not over yet. "You've always been good enough for me, Hunter. I'm not your family."

"Family!" He face changed. "With that kind of a past, what do I have to offer? Are you terrified you'd end up in years to come with that kind of situation on your hands?"

"No." She took his hand and entwined her fingers with his. "Didn't you tell me your father's marriage was arranged for the good of their families?"

"Yes."

"Then can you blame them for seeking love and fulfillment where they could find it?"

He shook his head. "I'll tell you straight out, I'd kill any man who touched you."

"You really are half-savage, aren't you?" She put his hand on her breast. "Make love to me, Hunter. Let's put this sorrow behind us."

"It can't be halfway between us, Deidre. You're in my blood, my soul. I want to marry you, to own you, to keep every other person in the world away from you. I'm not sure I even want a child with you because it might come between us or because it would endanger your life."

She pressed a kiss to his lips as she pressed her body against him, feeling his erection grow.

"Don't tease me." His voice was gruff.

"I'm not."

"You don't seem to understand. I'm not always a gentleman. I can't be. I don't want to be. And I won't always be kind. I'm selfish when it comes to what's mine. And I'll fight to protect what's mine. I won't always agree with you. Damn it, I'm a man and you're a woman. We're not alike. We want different things in life."

She smiled, enjoying his passion, his pride, his determination, even his jealousy for her. But it wasn't a mental reaction to his words. It was a purely emotional and physical response. She gloried in his desire and love for her. Stroking his chest, she felt his nipples harden under her fingertips. Yes, she even enjoyed her power over him.

"You're not listening. You can do better than me. Take that Simon Gainesville, for instance."

Shaking her head, she picked up a strand of her long hair and tickled his chest.

Finally, he threw back his head and shouted, perhaps as his Apache ancestors had before him. "You're the damnedest woman I've ever known. Nothing scares you, does it?"

"What I feel for you scares me. Sometimes." Her green eyes shimmered with emotion.

"What do you feel for me?" His voice was low and raspy and he put a finger under her chin to lift her face so he could see into her eyes.

"I think I love you, too."

"Think?"

"Well, it's hard to know for sure. I've never felt this way before."

He looked disgusted.

"And it might go away."

"Go away!" He lifted her in his arms and spun her around. "What do I have to do, get thousands of names on a petition and take it to Congress and get them to pass a law that says Deidre Eleanor Clarke-Jarmon can love Hunter?"

"Perhaps that's a little public."

He set her down. "This isn't funny."

"I know." She reached up and stroked his face. "I want to be with you every moment of my life. I want you touching me, inside of me all the time. I dream of you. I want to help you, make you happy. But, Hunter, what of my other dreams, what of college, what of Clarke Shipping, my family, your plans with your father for Flora's Institute?" She took a deep breath. "Can we have it all?"

"If I have to pistol whip every damn man in the U.S. Congress you'll have your right to vote, Deidre. And you'll have your college and your business and whatever else damn thing you decide to do.

But I must have you. First. And you must take me and keep me and never let me go."

Tears blurred her vision. She shut her eyes before she felt his feverish lips press against hers. She felt his hands roam over her body, as if to reclaim her, to make her his once more. And when he laid her down on the ground again, she opened herself to him, knowing that somehow, someway they would have love and life and happiness.

Together.

But as he pushed inside of her and she cried out with passion, she thought she could hear the cries of women and children dying, crying out to each other, trying to reach each other for one last embrace before soldiers destroyed their love and life and happiness.

Forever.

She embraced Hunter as if he would suddenly be wrenched from her. As he drove over and over into her, her passion rose until she writhed beneath him, pressing hot kisses to his face, holding him as fiercely as he held her.

When bliss finally claimed her, she felt him pull out of her to spill his seed on her stomach. Tears ran from her eyes. She felt happy and sad and lost and afraid.

How could she ensure a life of happiness when all about them was chaos?

Chapter 27

Hunter stood at an open window inside his father's office in the hacienda. He watched Deidre and Alberto in the courtyard. She'd had pillows and blankets piled in the shade to make a comfortable place for them. She read and Alberto listened. Hunter figured she was reading from the *Vindication of the Rights of Woman* because every few pages she would stop and they'd discuss what she read.

He could tell they were having a good time together. It should have made him glad, but it didn't. He turned his back and walked across the room, noticing how much the same and yet how different it looked now than in his youth. It reminded him of how much he had changed and yet how much he'd stayed the same.

But his mind was really on Deidre. He walked back to the window and looked out again. He tried not to show it or feel it, but he knew he was jealous of her relationship with Alberto. Three days had passed since they'd returned from Apache Pass. He hadn't touched her in all that time.

It wasn't for lack of wanting her. But he'd lost control up there in the canyon and he didn't want to do it again. He needed to take charge of his feelings for her, but nothing seemed to help. He was jealous of every laugh she had for someone else. And he was jealous of the easy friendship she'd developed with his father. Something he might never have himself.

Yet if Deidre and Alberto hadn't gotten along well, he wouldn't have liked that either. He shook his head, then paced the room. He knew he would have to get used to sharing a certain part of Deidre with other people or he'd lose her. She wasn't a woman to be walled up in an ivory tower and, in truth, he didn't want her there. He loved her adventurous spirit as much as every other part of her.

Love. He'd never thought to feel this way. It scared him and he didn't scare easy. He'd run from his feelings for her as long as he could, but up at Apache Pass after the confrontation with his family he'd finally known exactly what he wanted. Deidre. And he'd do anything to have and keep her, except hurt her or interfere with her dreams.

Maybe it'd be best if he stepped aside. Maybe he'd send her on to the Bar J alone. He'd done what he'd set out to do here in Arizona. He could stay and build a life, build the Flora McCuskar Institute with his father. He'd explain Deidre's absence some way. Blame himself.

But did he have the strength to send her away, even if it was for her own good?

"Hunter?"

He whirled around.

Deidre beckoned him from the window.

She wore a green and white striped dress of cool cotton. She'd pulled her hair back in front but left the back long. With all that wild hair spilling around her, she looked like a Golden Goddess. The Ice Princess was gone. Forever, he hoped. He felt the familiar ache of wanting her. It wasn't something that could easily be pushed aside. But he tried.

"Come on out. Alberto wants to talk with us." She pouted. "Besides, I'm lonely for you."

"I'll be there in a moment." He felt the muscles in his chest tighten as he watched her walk away.

There had been no more discussion about the family, or what Alberto had decided. For three days his family had done its best to avoid each other while living in the hacienda together. Nobody had changed their position one bit. That was damned obvious. They simply waited for Alberto to release them so they could go their own ways again. If they ever could.

He realized now he'd expected too much. He guessed people changed little. After he'd turned the tables on Felipe, there was no hope of going back. He'd never been friends with Felipe and Elena. He'd thought it was because he was a bastard. Now he understood it was much more basic, much more mercenary than that.

They had realized in a way he hadn't that Alberto loved and cherished Flora and her son. They had feared Hunter would grow up and receive the position and wealth they wanted for themselves. They had hated and feared him for that reason. It was ironic that the very thing they had tried so desperately to prevent stood a good chance of coming to pass anyway.

What was the price of love and friendship and family? As far as he was concerned, Ana Carlota, Elena, and Felipe had put too low a value on what really counted and too high a value on what could be bought and sold. Money ruled their lives and he pitied them for it. They had lost a special part of Alberto in their determination to have all he owned.

And they'd lost Hunter, too. Not that they'd ever wanted him except to kick around. But now he'd given up any illusions of being family to them. Of course, he wasn't even kin to Ana Carlota and Felipe, but Elena had made her choice. Power and position over friendship with her half brother. Fear of losing Alberto's money and property had dominated their lives. He'd never had anything to lose except his mother.

And now Deidre.

He watched her and Alberto from the window. Suddenly he had a lot to lose. He felt fear, but he wouldn't let it rule him. He would set them both free before he would compromise any of them. He knew a tough life had given him enough strength to continue on his own after knowing love again. But he didn't want to go on alone. He wanted Deidre.

He saw her beckon to him. Heat ran through him. He grimaced. To be with her and not touch her required almost more strength than he had. He would have to make a decision soon.

Fixing a smile on his face, he walked into the

courtyard. The serenity and beauty were in direct contrast to the seething emotions that filled the hacienda.

"Hunter, sit by me." Deidre reached up to take his hand and pull him down to the pallet.

He sat close to her, although it made him much too hot. Alberto looked more himself, but he was still too thin. Hopefully, time would take care of that.

Alberto smiled at his son. "I've done a lot of thinking the past three days and I've come to some decisions." He glanced at Deidre. "Without realizing it, your lovely wife has helped me reach them."

Deidre squeezed Hunter's hand.

"I can't undo the past, but I can change the future." Alberto cleared his throat. "I wish to hell somebody had told me about Felipe before now. It would have hurt a lot less."

"Who would you have believed?"

Alberto furrowed his brow. "You're right, but I know now. I've loved and raised Felipe as my son. Nothing changes that. As far as I'm concerned, there is plenty for everyone."

Hesitating, Alberto glanced around the courtyard then focused on Hunter again. "I'm going to let Felipe run the ranch. He's trained all his life for that. I've had enough of it and I have other goals in my life now. I'm giving Elena the quarterhorses to breed, but they will be *hers* and the bloodlines go to her children.

"Ana Carlota has been a good wife. In most ways. I'm going to give her a generous allotment to allow her to live in high society in Mexico City.

"Hunter, you are the only son of my flesh. That carries a heavy responsibility if you are willing to accept it. I know you haven't been trained to carry on the Raimundo line. You should have had college."

"He still can." Deidre held tightly to Hunter's hand. "Why can't he go to Harvard?" She turned intense green eyes on Hunter. "I could go to Radcliffe at the same time."

Hunter simply regarded them in stunned silence. Heir to Raimundo? Harvard with Deidre nearby at Radcliffe? Were all his worries for nothing?

"Good!" Alberto leaned forward. "I'd be glad to see you go to Harvard and I'd pay all your expenses. As long as I'm alive, the family responsibilities won't fall too heavily on your shoulders." He smiled at Deidre. "And we can still make plans for Flora's Institute together, then I would carry them out. A few years away and you'd both be back in Arizona Territory."

"What do you think, Hunter?" Deidre squeezed his hand again.

"I don't know." But his mind had been racing ahead of their plans, focusing on something that had been growing in his mind since New York City. Everything he had seen and heard since returning to Arizona had simply reinforced his thoughts. His only concern had been Deidre.

Alberto's white brows came together. "Son, I should have explained myself better. Felipe will take care of the ranch, but his children will never inherit it. He doesn't carry Raimundo blood. You do. You are the next grandee and your children will inherit the ranch. And I know you and Deidre will care for it as I have."

Hunter started to speak, but Alberto held up his hand. "You would have stood a good chance of inheriting anyway. Felipe has never been my first choice. He needs guidance and direction. And he has no children yet. You and Deidre will have strong, healthy children to carry on the Raimundo line. That's what I want."

Deidre couldn't stand the deception any longer. "But we're not—"

"Felipe and Elena will never accept me." Hunter interrupted her.

"They will accept you or they will get nothing." Alberto's voice was cold. "Believe me, it will change their lives little. They will do and accept anything to keep their position in the grandee families."

Nodding, Hunter could believe that.

Deidre bit her lower lip to keep from shouting out that they weren't married. But this was Hunter's concern, not hers. Yet she had come to hate the deception.

"Will you accept what I'm offering you, Hunter?" Alberto looked anxiously at his son.

Hunter cleared his throat. "I wasn't raised a grandee. I've lived a life that has made me different, made me see through eyes that judge and value on quality rather than quantity. Deidre has opened my eyes even farther. It's not the responsibility that I mind or even dealing with your family. But I wonder if I'm the best choice. Elena has children who could inherit."

"No." Alberto frowned. "You and Deidre. You

are my choice. Believe me, I know best. And you are more than my son. You are Flora's child, too."

Hunter glanced at Deidre and saw the concern in her eyes. He knew what she was thinking. Marriage. He looked back at Alberto.

She caught her breath.

"Would you still want me to become the grandee of Raimundo Rancho if I wasn't married to Deidre?"

Alberto's face drained of color, then he focused on Deidre.

She blushed. "Hunter helped me with a problem for my family. That's when I met him. We even saved each other's lives. It drew us close."

Alberto shut his eyes and shook his head. Finally, he looked back at Hunter. "I don't understand. You two are very much in love. Any fool can see that. Are you telling me that you *aren't* married?"

"Yes." Hunter's voice was low. "I didn't know what I'd find here, but I wanted to impress the family that had looked down on me all my life. And I wanted to avenge my mother's memory. I asked Deidre to pose as my wife. I knew she would impress even Ana Carlota." He hesitated. "I never thought it would go so far."

Alberto sat still for a long moment, then he shook his head and slowly began to chuckle. Finally, he laughed out loud.

Shocked, Deidre and Hunter simply stared.

Wiping tears from his eyes, Alberto grinned at them. "What can I expect from my own wild son? Apache. Grandee. Irish. And you, Deidre. Right off the Bar J, one of the toughest outfits in the

West. Could I expect you two to do anything but what you damned well please." He pointed a finger at Hunter. "Yes, I want you to be the next grandee. And I want her to be the mother of my grandchildren. Marry her before she gets away. There won't be another like her."

"I'm not so easy to marry." Deidre raised an eyebrow. "I have goals. The Raimundo Rancho won't be my life." She glanced up. Had she heard a rider came in fast, then shouting outside the hacienda? For some reason, she felt a sudden chill run up her spine. But it was hard to tell what was going on beyond the secluded courtyard. And right now she didn't much care.

Alberto threw up his hands. "Modern women! But I didn't do so well myself. Maybe you two know what you're doing. But I'll tell you this. You won't be tied to the ranch. Felipe will run it." He looked from Hunter to Deidre, then back again. "Now what do you say?"

"I'll be the next grandee." Hunter's words sounded like a solemn promise.

Tears misted Alberto's eyes. "Thank you, son. You won't regret it."

"Deidre has plans to work with her mother at Clarke Shipping in New York City. And I have some plans of my own." Hunter hesitated. "I'm planning to run for Congress."

Deidre gasped.

Alberto sat up straight.

"You're what?" Deidre turned to face Hunter.

"I've been thinking about it since attending that woman suffrage meeting in New York. There is a lot of work that needs to be done to help women,

410

children, Indians, and other poor and needy. From where I stand, I think I can do a lot to help."

Deidre threw her arms around Hunter's neck. "What a wonderful idea."

"Don't rejoice just yet. It'll take awhile. I'll need to go to college, then I'll need to work in Arizona Territory. But eventually I want to be in Washington, D.C., getting you and all women the right to vote."

"Oh, Hunter." Deidre pressed a passionate kiss to his lips, then sat back to look at him in wonder.

"You want me to help, don't you? You need a partner, don't you?" Hunter held his breath as he watched Deidre's eyes.

"Harvard?"

He nodded.

"Radcliffe for me."

He nodded.

"New York City isn't so far from Washington, D.C., is it?"

"No, it's not." He grinned.

"I suppose you'll want to have the wedding on the Bar J." Alberto grumbled, tugging at his mustache. "And it looks like I'll have to put Flora's Institute together myself. But don't worry yourselves, I can handle it." He noticed they weren't listening to him. Eyes only for each other. "Anyway, I always wanted to meet the Bar J crew and go back East. I only wish Flora were alive to share this."

"What do you say, Deidre?" Hunter gently wiped away the tears from under her eyes.

"Oh, Hunter, I—"

"Señor Alberto!" A young Mexican woman hurried across the courtyard holding out an envelope.

"A rider brought this telegram for Señora Deidre. He said she must get it right away."

Deidre felt chilled again. She pulled away from Hunter and stood up. "Here, hurry!" She took the envelope. As the servant left the courtyard, Deidre stood still, hating to read the telegram. But she was being foolish. It could be good news.

"What is it?" Hunter moved to her side.

She ripped open the envelope, scanned the message, then buried her face against his chest.

"Deidre, what has happened?" Alberto got to his feet and joined them.

She took a deep breath, then read, "Your mother is very ill. Hurry to the Bar J. She needs you. Jake Jarmon."

"Oh no. I'm so sorry." Alberto patted Deidre's arm.

"We'll leave at once." Hunter held Deidre tightly against him. "Don't worry. She'll be all right."

Deidre raised her head. "But what if we don't get there in time? She's always been so healthy. I don't understand. What could have happened?"

"She lives on a ranch." Alberto's voice was matter of fact. "A lot of things can happen, but it doesn't have to be fatal. You know that. Look at me. A horse fall, but I'm well now."

"Let's get packed and get on the road." Hunter took control.

"I'll go with you to Tucson." Alberto stroked Deidre's hair.

"No." Hunter locked eyes with his father. "You've got a lot to take care of here. The family. The ranch. If you'd send two drivers and a change of horses for the carriage, we'd make good time.

Once in Tucson, we'll take the train to San Antonio."

Alberto nodded in agreement. "Take Deidre inside and get her a glass of brandy. I'll order the servants to pack your things and make ready for the trip."

"She has to be all right, doesn't she?" Deidre looked from Hunter to Alberto, then in the direction of Texas. If only she could fly.

Her thoughts churned, then turned into a chant. Mother. Wait for me. I'll be there as soon as I can. Mother. Wait. For me.

But the Bar J was so far away.

Part Five
Wish Upon a Star

Chapter 28

Deidre held on tightly to her emotions as the stage-coach pulled into Three Rivers, Texas. Although their accommodations on the Tucson to San Antonio train trip had been the best, she'd been unable to sleep and eat except fitfully. She had tried to tell herself that Alberto was right. A lot of things could happen on a ranch. It didn't have to be the worst. But her mother sick?

The chill that had invaded her at Raimundo Rancho when she'd received the telegram had refused to leave her. Not on the train. Not on the stage. Not even here in Three Rivers. She felt as if something terrible had happened or was going to happen at the Bar J. She felt as if only she could stop it. She and Hunter.

As passengers began to debark, she glanced at Hunter. He gave her a reassuring smile. But it didn't reassure her. The only thing that would help would be to get to the ranch and see that her mother and father were all right. She supposed Thor would be there, too. If they had sent for her in Arizona, they would have sent for him at college. And they would have done that only if her mother were seriously ill.

She had sent a telegram from Tucson to the Bar J, so she expected a cowboy and wagon to be awaiting them or pulling in any moment now. At one time she wouldn't have questioned that assumption. She certainly hadn't the last time when Hunter had picked her up at the stage office. But now after the Bahamas, New York City, Raimundo Rancho, and the telegram from her father, she didn't much count on anything.

If a telegram or a cowboy from the ranch weren't awaiting them, she'd rent a wagon and start out herself. She leaned against Hunter, thankful to have him with her. He'd been a rock of support during this time, comforting her, making sure everything went smoothly. She was so distracted she had needed help and he hadn't failed her.

She felt his comforting strength against her cheek. At one time she'd probably not have allowed anyone to do anything for her, but that was when she had been so determined to prove herself. Well, as far as she was concerned, she'd proved herself strong enough to be able to stand on her own two feet but to lean on someone else once in awhile. It was a wonderful revelation. Not that it made her any less a suffragist or any less determined to get the right to vote. But it did mean she could share her life, good times as well as bad times.

And the telegram she held in her fist was definitely a bad time.

Hunter leaned over and pushed the stage door open, then got down. He held out his arms to her. She tucked the telegram into her reticule next to her derringer, then pulled the drawstrings closed. She let him help her down. He held her against him for a moment, then set her down on Texas soil. It felt good to be this close to home. She glanced around.

Three Rivers hadn't changed. It was still a small, dusty Western town. Hunter had been waiting here for her before, but she hadn't let him help her down from the stage that time. He'd simply been an irritating stranger. She glanced up at him and slipped her hand through the crook of his arm. She couldn't have imagined then how much he would come to mean to her, how much they would share, and how many plans they would have for the future.

Or they'd had.

Until she reached the Bar J, all their plans were pushed aside. As she stood there with the late afternoon sun hot on her, she felt a shiver run through her. Danger. Every part in her body screamed that word. But she could see nothing wrong here. It had to be her mother. She felt a wild need to get moving again.

They walked into the shade of the depot office and watched as their trunks were unloaded. She glanced up and down the street, looking for a Bar J cowboy. But no one came to them. Finally, when their carpetbags and trunks were stacked near their feet, she turned to Hunter.

"I think we'd better check to see if there's a telegram waiting for us from the Bar J."

Hunter nodded, searching the street. "Somebody ought to be here."

"Maybe he's down at a saloon."

"Should be meeting every stage."

She nodded in agreement, looking up and down the street.

"I don't know what's going on, but I've got a bad feel." Hunter's face was grim.

She put a hand against her chest. "You mean you think mother . . . that it's too late."

"No!" He gripped her hand. "Something else. I can almost smell it. Familiar, too."

She couldn't keep the shiver from running through her. "I don't care if the Bar J sent anybody or not. Let's rent a wagon and get on out there."

Hunter glanced up at the sky. "It'll be dark soon."

"I don't care."

"I do."

"We can't wait." She turned to face him. "I won't."

"I mean I'd like to get there after dusk in case there's some kind of trouble."

"What trouble?"

"I don't know. Like I said, I've got a bad feel about this. We'd better be careful." He looked down at her, his eyes hard as Apache Tears. "Tell you what. I'll take you over to the hotel and get a room."

"Hunter, I *can't* wait."

"You're tired. You've got to eat. It's a long, rough ride out to the ranch. I'll get some food sent up. You wash up, rest, eat. While you're doing that I'll go down to the telegraph office. If there's no telegram waiting for us, I'll rent a wagon and have

420

our trunks loaded. Then I'll come back, eat, and we'll get on our way."

"I'll go with you."

"Deidre." He shook his head. "There's no point in us both wearing ourselves out. This is rough on you. I know it. You know it. But Alexandra is strong. She's waiting for you. I know it."

"Do you really think so?"

"Yes. And it won't do her any good to see you looking half sick yourself."

She put a hand to her hair. She knew she was dusty, stained, thin, and hardly her usual self. Hunter was right. She smiled, a wan movement of her lips. "We can't wait long."

"We won't." He squeezed her hand. "Just a minute." He walked away, talked with the stage driver, then came back. "They'll hold the trunks for us till I get a wagon." He picked up two carpetbags.

They started down the boardwalk.

"If nothing else, you can read that book of yours."

"*Frankenstein* would appeal to me most now."

Hunter chuckled. "That's the attitude. Don't let this get you down. You've got to be strong for your mother."

Shocked, she glanced up at him. "Am I acting weak?"

"No. You're fine. Just remember Alexandra needs you and she needs you in good health."

She nodded, still watching the street for a Bar J wagon or cowboy. Nothing and nobody looked familiar. She grew more worried than ever. "Hunter, if there's a telegram waiting, come straight back to the hotel."

"Sure. I won't keep you waiting."

They stepped into the Three Rivers Hotel. Deidre hurried over to the desk. "Do you have a telegram or a message for Deidre Clarke-Jarmon?"

"Or Hunter?" He stopped beside her.

The clerk shook his head.

She tried not to feel disappointed. If her mother were this sick, all attention would be on her.

"I want a room for the lady for a few hours. And send a couple of dinners up. We'll eat in the room."

The clerk snickered. "We don't rent rooms by the hour." He gave Deidre a calculating glance.

Hunter leaned over, grabbed the man's collar, and jerked him halfway across the desk. "This *lady* is daughter of the Bar J. I'm here to get her home safely and quickly." He shoved the man back. "Now, get me a key and get those dinners up there fast or you'll be sleeping on Boot Hill."

The clerk seemed to sink upon himself. "Sorry. No harm meant. You got to pay for a night." He flinched. "I mean, that's the rules."

Hunter threw down money, then jerked a key out of one of the slots. "Get the food."

Nodding, the clerk backed as far away from Hunter as he could get.

Picking up the carpetbags, Hunter indicated for Deidre to precede him up the staircase. She threw the clerk a withering look, then hurried away. They walked up the stairs to the hall above. Hunter had picked a room close to the staircase and they quickly stepped inside.

She glanced around and felt relief. At least this had stayed the same. Homey, the room was very much like the one she had stayed in before.

He set the carpetbags down on the quilt covering the double bed. "I'm sorry."

"Don't be. It doesn't matter. Just hurry."

He opened a carpetbag, pulled out his gunbelt and strapped it on. He loaded his .45, then slipped it into the holster. Finally, he put the room key in his pocket. He turned to her, took her by the shoulders, and pulled her close. "Don't worry. Whatever happens we can handle it." He pressed a hard kiss to her lips, then walked over to the door. "Lock it behind me."

As he stepped out of the room, she shut the door behind him and locked it. But the action didn't make her feel safe or secure. Until she reached the Bar J nothing could do that.

She walked over to the window and pulled back a sheer lace curtain. The sun was lowering in the west as Hunter walked down the street. Wearing all black, he looked tall and menacing. Hurry, she thought. Again, she searched the street, but could find nothing that resembled a Bar J wagon. Why had no one met them?

But she still had no answer. She forced herself to turn away from the window. Waiting and watching would do no good. She needed to do something useful to keep her mind off her mother and father. Glancing down, she noticed the dust clinging to her clothes. She brushed at it until she could do no more good.

She might as well clean up some more. She walked over to the washstand and poured water from the pitcher into its matching white bowl. She splashed water on her face, patted her hair back into place and adjusted the chignon, then washed her hands. She dried them on a hand towel, then hung it back in place.

How long had Hunter been gone? She walked back to the window and looked out again. He wasn't anywhere in sight. Sighing, she turned back again. She stopped in front of the mirror over the washstand. She looked pale and thin. Her green eyes seemed too big for her face. And her blond hair looked dull.

She glanced down at her clothes again. She'd dressed comfortably in a burgundy cotton skirt and a white cotton blouse. She'd worn as few underclothes as possible, even foregoing a corset for comfort. But she'd carried the beautiful, colorful shawl Hunter had bought her in the Bahamas. She picked it up and draped it around her shoulders. It had brought her comfort all through the long trip, reminding her of the good times with Hunter and of what they had survived together.

Moving back to the window, she looked out again. Lady Caroline. Hayward. Captain Sully. She was glad Old Nate and Hunter had put an end to their wickedness. Yet she suddenly couldn't help wondering if so long as Lady Caroline were out there, would any member of her family be safe? She shook her head. She was letting worry and fear make her imagine the worst. The wreckers were over and done with and she knew it.

She must simply concentrate on remaining strong for her mother. When the food arrived, she would eat as much as she could and start getting her strength back.

But where was Hunter?

As if in answer to her question, a knock came at the door. Relieved, she knew it was either Hunter or the food. Both would be welcome. She hurried over, unlocked the door, and pulled it open. She froze.

"Don't make a sound." Lady Caroline held a pistol pointed straight at Deidre's chest.

"Back up into the room." Hayward also held a pistol pointed at her.

Deidre could hardly believe her eyes.

"Do as we say. Now!" Lady Caroline's voice was hard and sharp.

Deidre glanced wildly around the hall, hoping someone would see what was being done to her. But the hall was empty. Where was Hunter? Had he seen the Graves? Or was he in as much danger as she?

"I'm not going to tell you again." Lady Caroline cocked the hammer of the pistol.

"You're not going to shoot. It'd make too much noise." Deidre stalled, thinking about her own derringer in her reticule and hoping Hunter would suddenly appear.

Hayward leaned forward and shooved her back into the room. Lady Caroline followed him, closing and locking the door behind them.

Deidre backed away, resisting the impulse to rub at the sore place Hayward had left on her chest. She had almost fallen back into the room. She moved closer to the bed where she'd tossed her reticule. If possible, she'd get her derringer, but her chances for that didn't look good. She tried to think logically, but her emotions threatened to overwhelm her. She must be cool. She musn't panic. Hunter would return for her.

"Surprised to see us?" Lady Caroline looked smug.

"Yes." Deidre's mind raced as she took in the details of her captors, hoping some bit of information would help her escape. Lady Caroline looked every bit a rancher in a dark blue split skirt and light blue blouse. She also wore brown cowboy boots and leather gloves. She fit into Texas just fine, as did Hayward, who had dressed more like a gambler or lawman than a rancher. No one would have looked at them twice.

Hayward put his .45 in the holster on his hip and stepped toward Deidre. "Seems I couldn't get you out of my mind." He reached out and stroked her cheek.

She slapped his hand away. "Keep your filthy hands off me."

"Still haughty, are you?" Hayward's lips curled in a smirk. "You thought you were smart getting our wrecking business stopped. You weren't. Now you're going to pay a heavy price and I'm going to enjoy every minute of it."

"Tie her hands behind her." Lady Caroline produced a coiled length of rawhide from a pocket and handed it to Hayward. She never looked away from Deidre.

Hayward moved toward Deidre again.

"Get away from me." She backed toward the window, hoping to alert Hunter or someone.

"Stand still!" Lady Caroline frowned. "If you

want your precious Hunter to stay well and healthy, you'd better do exactly as we say."

Deidre stilled. "You've got Hunter?" Her heart beat fast. "Is he all right?"

"We don't have him yet. But he'll be coming back here. We don't need him for our plans. We'd just as soon kill him when he gets here." Lady Caroline raised an eyebrow. "If you're a good little girl, we might keep him alive."

"When Hunter gets here, he'll—"

"He'll be expecting nobody but you." Hayward stepped close to Deidre. "It'd be easy to knock him out when he steps through the door, then knife him through the heart." He held out the rawhide. "What's it to be? Life or death for Hunter?"

Deidre held out her hands, exposing her wrists. But her mind was racing in all directions, trying to think of some way to overpower them.

"No. Turn around. Put your hands behind you."

Deidre did as he commanded, desperate to save Hunter, desperate to get away, and more desperate than ever to get to the Bar J. Her mother needed her and she couldn't even get to her. She could still hardly believe what was being done to her. But when Hayward bound her wrists, she knew it was all too real. Although she tightened her muscles like she had in the cave in the Bahamas, she didn't have much hope of escaping without water to loosen the rawhide.

When Hayward was done, he put his hands on Deidre's shoulders and turned her around. "Your beauty rivals your mother's. I've wanted you both more than I've wanted any woman. But you both rejected me for lesser men." He stroked his hands up and down her arms. "You deserve to be punished, but I'm going to give you pleasure instead. You and Alexandra both."

Deidre frowned. "Alexandra?" She jerked her shoulders out of his grasp and glanced at Lady Caroline. "What does he mean?"

"You can't turn away from me now." Hayward pulled the pins from her hair until it cascaded down her back. He ran his hands through it, smiling. "So beautiful."

"Take your hands off me." She shook her head and stepped back.

"Stop!" Hayward's eyes darkened with anger. "Every move you make to reject me will be taken out on Hunter when he gets here."

Deidre inhaled sharply and stood still.

Hayward looked pleased, then took out his pince-nez and clipped them on the bridge of his nose. "Let me get a better look at you, my dear." He stroked her face, felt of her lips, then moved lower to begin unbuttoning her blouse.

Lady Caroline laughed. "Hayward will show you and that bitch Alexandra what it feels like to have a man you don't want use you. I think it's only justice since the men I wanted would not be used by me. A mistake on their part, trust me."

"What are you talking about? What about my mother?" Deidre flinched as Hayward squeezed her breasts through the fabric of her blouse. She bit her lower lip to keep from reacting to his touch.

"You aren't wearing a corset." Sweat beaded Hayward's forehead. "Caroline, I want her now."

"Fool!" Lady Caroline sat down on the bed, rest-ing the .45 on her crossed knee. "You know we haven't time. You're getting yourself excited for nothing."

Hayward unbuttoned Deidre's blouse to the waist, then thrust a hand underneath her chemise to grasp her naked breast. He squeezed it hard as he watched her face.

She shut her eyes against the pain and invasion. No matter what he did, she'd never give him the pleasure of hearing her beg or plead to stop. Nausea cramped her stomach, but she stood still.

"You like this, don't you?" Hayward breathed hard as he kneaded her other breast. "I'll make you forget Hunter."

At the mention of Hunter, Deidre could be quiet no longer. "You're disgusting! As if any man could compare to Hunter." Deidre threw a quelling glance at Lady Caroline. "Ask your sister."

Hayward pinched her hard, then pulled her against him to press fevered lips to hers.

"I told you we didn't have time for that, Hayward." Lady Caroline stood up and moved toward her brother, then stopped and jerked her head toward the door.

A key turned in the lock.

Hayward pushed Deidre back as he pulled his pistol from its holster. He put the end of the barrel against Deidre's temple.

Lady Caroline moved near the door so that when it opened she would be out of sight. She gave Deidre a warning glance, then lifted her pistol.

They all watched the doorknob as it turned, then the door opened. Hunter stepped inside, carrying a tray of food. He saw Deidre, dropped the tray, spun around as the door slammed shut behind them, then abruptly stopped when he saw Lady Caroline's pistol leveled at his chest.

She smiled. "Welcome back, my dear. I'll just relieve you of that." She took his .45 from its holster and set it on the washstand, all the while keeping her pistol trained on him.

"What the hell's going on?" Hunter stood still, his hands clenched in fists at his sides at the sight of Deidre's disheveled appearance. "Get away from her, Hayward."

"Now that you're here, Hunter dear." Lady Caroline patted her hair. "The party can begin."

Chapter 29

"Better tie up Hunter." Hayward gripped the pistol he held at Deidre's temple.

"No need to do it. You've got Deidre under control." Lady Caroline kept her focus on Hunter. "You're not going to give us any trouble, are you?"

"What the hell do you think you're doing?" Hunter stepped around the spilled food toward Deidre.

"Don't move." Lady Caroline frowned. "You spoiled our fun in the Bahamas. Did you really think we'd stand still for that?"

"I stopped your wreckers. That's all." Hunter glanced back at Lady Caroline and ran a hand through his hair. "You couldn't leave well enough alone, could you?"

"You also stopped my fun with *you*, Hunter." Lady Caroline gripped her pistol. "Jake Jarmon did the same thing. I'm tired of men hurting me, ruining my life. Now it's my turn. Isn't it, Hayward?"

"Right."

"Let Hunter go. It's me you want, isn't it?" Deidre's gaze met Hunter's dark eyes. She knew neither of them would do anything to endanger the other. It made them vulnerable to the Graves.

"Actually, the two of you are simply a means to an end." Lady Caroline motioned toward a chair with her pistol. "Sit down, Hunter."

He followed her instructions, but it was obvious he simply awaited a chance to jump her.

Lady Caroline walked over to the window, pulled back the curtain, and looked outside. Smiling, she turned back. "All right. We're going to take a little trip now."

"Where?" Hunter sat rigidly in the chair.

"You'll know soon enough." Lady Caroline glanced at Deidre. "That shawl is excellent. Hayward, it'll conceal your pistol when we walk out."

He nodded and lowered his gun to Deidre's side, hiding it beneath her shawl. At the same time he put an arm around her waist and pulled her against him. Satisfied, he looked over at Hunter and smirked.

Hunter clenched his fists. "You hurt her, Hayward, and you're a dead man."

Lady Caroline chuckled. "You escaped us once, but not again. Now, Hunter, you're going to pick up the carpetbags and walk out of here with me. If you speak to anyone or try to escape, Hayward will shoot Deidre."

"You can't get away with it." Hunter looked

432

around, trying to think of something he could do to help them.

"Of course we can. We have a boat waiting for us on the coast. It's not that far away and nobody knows us around here. We can and will do whatever we want." She aimed her pistol carefully at Hunter's chest.

"You'll get caught again." Hunter tried to reason with her.

Lady Caroline shrugged. "This must look natural." She walked over to the bed, set her gun down, and picked up Deidre's reticule. She opened it, then pulled out the telegram. She waved it at Deidre. "Nice touch, don't you think?"

"What do you mean?" Deidre didn't dare move, although the hard muzzle of the gun hurt her ribs and Hayward's embrace made her sick to her stomach. But most of all, she was terrified Lady Caroline would notice the derringer in her reticule.

Lady Caroline pushed the telegram back into the reticule, then pulled the drawstrings closed. She walked over to Deidre. She slipped a knife from her boot and cut through the rawhide thong tying Deidre's hands together. "Button your blouse." She pushed the reticule into Deidre's hand. "Carry this as you normally do."

"What did you mean about the telegram?" Deidre could hardly believe her good luck. She let the reticule dangle from her wrist as she quickly buttoned her blouse. If they didn't retie her hands, she should be able to use the derringer or Hunter might be able to get to it. He knew she carried it with her. Now they had a chance, one the Graves didn't know about.

Lady Caroline tucked the knife back in her boot and slipped the leather thong into the pocket of her skirt. She picked up her gun again and smiled at Hunter. "I'm glad you were a good boy. It'd have been a shame to cut Deidre with my sharp knife, wouldn't it?" She glanced at Deidre. "We'll discuss the telegram later."

Hayward pulled off his pince-nez and stuffed it in a pocket. "Maybe I'll use a knife on you later, Deidre. I could carve my initials on you."

"I might like to watch that." Lady Caroline turned toward Hunter. "Take off your gunbelt and put it in a carpetbag. I'm taking no chances with you carrying a pistol."

"I won't look normal." Hunter stalled, trying to think of some way to ruin their plans. So long as Deidre was held at gunpoint he couldn't chance her life. But if he got the opportunity, he'd use her derringer on them. One thing for sure, he'd never scoff at her choice of weapons again. The small gun might save their lives.

"You'll look normal enough."

Hunter did as she bid, then watched Lady Caroline stuff his .45 in the other carpetbag.

"All right, Hayward, you and Deidre go ahead. We'll be right behind you. Hunter, pick up the carpetbags." She concealed her pistol in the folds of her skirt, then opened the door.

Deidre and Hayward walked outside.

Lady Caroline hesitated, then looked at Hunter. "It needn't have been this way."

He stood and picked up the carpetbags. "You can't force somebody to love you, Caroline."

She shrugged. "I'm soon going to be in a position

to buy all the love I want. Then I'll forget about you and Jake Jarmon. Now, come along."

Hunter left the room and heard Lady Caroline shut the door behind them.

"Follow them." She put a hand on his back. "Remember, any move I don't like and Deidre dies."

Hunter walked down the stairs, watching Hayward and Deidre. If Hayward wavered for an instant, he'd be on him. But Hayward held Deidre close. Frustrated, Hunter followed. As they crossed the lobby, he glanced over at the desk. But the clerk he had intimidated earlier sank back against the wall and pretended not to see them at all. Cursing to himself, he knew he'd scared the clerk out of doing anything even if he noticed something wrong.

Hunter stepped outside onto the boardwalk and glanced around. Later, when he didn't pick up the wagon loaded with their trunks, somebody would come looking for him. But by then it'd probably be way too late.

He focused on Deidre again. How the hell had he let this happen? He'd known something was wrong, but he'd been concentrated on the Bar J. He'd never expected this kind of trouble. Caroline and Hayward had slipped right over the edge to do this. It was up to him to stop them. Once more.

A wagon pulled up near the boardwalk. Hunter was surprised, then realized he shouldn't have been, to see Captain Sully. Dressed as a cowboy, Sully held the reins, a hat pulled down low over his eyes. What the hell were they planning to get out of this? It seemed an awful lot of trouble for revenge.

Lady Caroline gripped Hunter's arm. "Get in the back after Hayward and Deidre."

Hunter followed her instructions again. He sat as close to Deidre as he could, then watched Lady Caroline get onto the seat beside Sully. The wagon moved forward. As they rolled out of town, he kept alert, watching for anybody who might be of help. But he didn't see a single familiar face.

Once they were out of town, the wagon picked up speed as dusk rapidly descended.

Deidre glanced around, then gripped the edge of the wagon in shock. "We're heading toward the Bar J." She started to rise, but Hayward pulled her down again.

"Be still." His fingers dug into her waist.

Lady Caroline turned around. "That's right, Deidre. We're going to the Bar J. No one will stop you and your friends from going right inside your parents' home, if anyone is watching this time of night."

Deidre gasped. "But my mother is sick! You can't bother her now."

Chuckling, Lady Caroline aimed her pistol toward the back. "Sick?"

"No, she's not." Hunter eyes were black with anger. Apache Tears. "Nobody on the Bar J sent that telegram, did they?"

"You're quick." Lady Caroline looked smug.

"What!" Deidre tried to get at Lady Caroline, but Hayward pulled her back and jammed the barrel of the pistol into her side.

"I suppose you got the telegram we sent to Three Rivers." Hunter's eyes narrowed.

"Good guess." Lady Caroline stroked her gun. "It was easy to find out where you'd gone from the main office at Clarke Shipping. They were so happy to help your friends from the Bahamas. And the merchants of Three Rivers couldn't have been more gracious to friends of the Bar J."

"Then my mother's just fine?" Deidre felt a rush of happiness combined with fury at the worry and pain she had been caused. Her mother had been in perfect health all along. Until now. She gripped her reticule. She had to do something soon.

"Not for long she's not." Lady Caroline smirked and turned back to watch the road.

Deidre glanced at Hunter. He nodded in encouragement, but she felt a hollowness in the pit of her stomach. "What are you planning to do with us?"

"Don't spoil the surprise." Lady Caroline glared at Hayward. "Keep her quiet. Sound carries out here."

Hayward put a hand over Deidre's breast and squeezed.

Hunter jerked toward them.

"Go ahead." Hayward smiled pleasantly. "If you want her dead."

Hunter clenched his fists, but said nothing.

The wagon lumbered onward, drawing closer and closer to the Bar J. Soon night darkened the landscape. The only sound came from the wagon, the horse, and nocturnal predators roaming the land. Finally, the wagon rolled under the archway announcing the Bar J Ranch. A house, barn, and outbuildings could be seen up ahead.

At the sight, Deidre closed her eyes, drawing all

her energy together. She would have to fight to keep her family alive. She was the pawn in this game. Hayward held the pistol on her. If she let him kill her, the others could probably get free. But she didn't want to die. She had so much to live for now. She looked at Hunter. His expression was grim. They had escaped together before. She must give them that chance again.

Lady Caroline glanced in the back. "When we get to the house, I want Deidre to call out. Get your parents to come outside. And, remember, the moment your parents step out, I'll have my pistol aimed at them. Don't warn them. I'm an excellent shot."

Deidre believed her. But she also knew the sound of the wagon would bring her father outside anyway.

Hayward touched his mouth to her ear. "Later we're going to your bedroom. You're going to beg me to take your lovely body in your own bed."

She bit her lower lip, but didn't respond.

Soon the wagon rolled to a stop in front of the house. Captain Sully pushed his hat back from his face and looked at Lady Caroline.

She nodded, then glanced at Deidre.

Deidre hesitated.

"Now!" Lady Caroline's voice came out in a hiss.

"Mother!" Deidre's voice was faint.

Hayward took the pistol from her side and aimed it at Hunter. "Will this make you try harder?"

Hunter shook his head. "They can't win, Deidre."

She turned toward the house and called again, but people were already moving inside, alerted by the sound of the wagon just as she'd expected.

Jake Jarmon stepped outside, holding a lantern in one hand and a .45 in the other. Alexandra was right behind him.

"Stay back!" Deidre struggled to stand, but Hayward jerked her back down. He put the gun to her head.

Lady Caroline stepped down, holding her pistol on Jake and Alexandra. "Drop the gun, Jake. We've got your daughter and Hunter. If you don't want them hurt, you'll do as I say."

"Deidre? Are you all right?" Jake didn't move.

"Yes." Deidre realized how good it was to see her parents, but felt horrible at having brought this trouble to them.

Jake threw his .45 aside, then put his arm around Alexandra and pulled her close.

"Sully, help Hayward get them all inside, then stand guard out here."

Captain Sully wrapped the reins in place, then jumped down.

As he went behind the wagon, Lady Caroline stepped into the light of Jake's lantern. "Remember me, Jake honey?"

"Caroline!" Jake cursed.

"What are you doing here?" Alexandra moved forward. "And what are you doing with Deidre?"

"You'll know soon enough. Get back in the house." When they didn't move, Lady Caroline raised her pistol. "You want to leave your daughter an orphan?"

Jake and Alexandra waited until they saw Deidre and Hunter get safely down from the back of the wagon, then turned and went inside the house.

Lady Caroline followed them into the main room. "Sit down. In separate chairs."

They obeyed her, but gasped in shock at the sight of Deidre. Hayward held her to him, his pistol against her side.

"Hunter, take that chair." Lady Caroline pointed. "Hayward take Deidre to the couch." When everyone was arranged to her satisfaction, she took a quick glance around the room. "Where are the servants?"

"They're gone. None of them sleep here." A worried frown on her face, Alexandra studied her daughter. "Are you truly all right, Deidre?"

"Yes." Deidre gave her parents an encouraging smile.

Lady Caroline walked around the room. "This place isn't much. I'd have expected more." She turned back. "You should see our mansion on New Graves Plantation now. It's a work of art."

"And how did you pay for it?" Hunter's voice held scorn.

"Shut up!" Lady Caroline paced. "This is wonderful. I've thought about being here for a long time." She looked at Jake. "Age becomes you. I'd still like to have you in my bed, but I'm afraid that won't be possible."

"Remember your promise, Caroline." Hayward caressed Deidre's arm. "I get Alexandra and Deidre both."

"You can have them, dear. Dead or alive?"

Hayward laughed.

"What do you want?" Jake glanced from Lady Caroline to Hayward. "Name your price."

Lady Caroline shook a finger at him. "Naughty

440

boy. *You*, all of you are the price. You and Hunter both used me, then abandoned me. Your precious little daughter ruined my wrecking business. Did you think I'd do nothing?"

She paced again, then stopped and looked around. "You owe me. All of you owe me. If Jake had married me, I'd be part of his wealth, here and in Louisiana. I'd have children to inherit." She frowned. "But no, you left me with nothing. And you did the same to Hayward. Alexandra and Deidre rejected Hayward's love. He's going to punish you."

Deidre decided to try reason on this woman who seemed to be existing in her own dreamworld. "Lady Caroline, this is not the way to get justice. Punishing other women for having what you don't will not help. Instead, work with them to change the law so we all have justice."

Lady Caroline whirled around. "You silly suffragist. Do you really think men are going to give you anything, much less equal rights? No! And why shouldn't I punish you? You took Hunter just like Alexandra took Jake." She glanced slyly around the room. "But I'll have Thor and this ranch and the plantation and the shipping firm."

"What?" Alexandra leaned forward, her hands gripping the arms of the chair. "Thor has nothing to do with any of this. Leave my son alone."

"Thor." Lady Caroline licked her lips. "Like father like son. Is that right, Jake? Thor will get nothing unless he pleases me, in bed and out."

Alexandra gasped and turned to Jake.

"Don't say a word." Lady Caroline took aim at Alexandra. "I'm not through."

"If you want money, you'll get it." Jake spoke in clipped tones. "But there is no need to hurt any of us."

"Fool! I've just told you the many reasons you'll be hurt. But first, you and Alexandra are going to sign over all your property to your good friends, Caroline and Hayward."

Shocked, Jake shook his head. "Why would we do that?"

"It will keep Thor alive. And Deidre and Alexandra for as long as Hayward wants them."

"We're not that stupid." Jake clenched his fists.

Lady Caroline smiled at him. "Do you want your loved ones to live?"

Jake nodded.

"Then you'll do exactly as I say." She walked over to him. She caressed his cheek, then slapped him hard.

He didn't move.

"You always were the toughest sailor in the Caribbean. Remember the Blockade Runners' Ball?"

Jake nodded.

"I doubt if any of us will ever celebrate anything so grand or exciting as that. I'll be sure your son gets a demonstration of what we did afterward." She glanced at Alexandra. "Maybe your wife will watch."

Jake growled, but didn't move.

Deidre took a deep breath. While Hayward had been focused on Lady Caroline's speech and undercover of her shawl, she had managed to slip her derringer out of her reticule. But she didn't know how she could use it. She glanced at Hunter and tried to send him a message.

442

Hunter nodded, then suddenly jumped up and let out a bloodcurdling Apache yell.

Lady Caroline whirled around, startled out of her complacency.

Shocked, Hayward loosened his grip long enough for Deidre to twist aside. Hunter lunged for Hayward as Deidre tried to get free. Hayward brought up his pistol and aimed at Hunter.

Deidre had no choice. She pointed the derringer at Hayward and shot him in the stomach. As he slumped, Hunter jerked the gun away from him.

Lady Caroline turned her pistol toward Hunter. Jake noticed and leaped from his chair to stop her. She whirled around and shot him. He crumpled to the floor.

Hunter aimed his .45 at Lady Caroline. "Drop the gun."

Heedless of his warning, Lady Caroline spun around and started to pull the trigger. Hunter shot. She collapsed, holding her chest.

Alexandra cried out and fell to her knees beside Jake. He lay still. Blood stained his shirt where he clutched his side. She moaned as she pulled his hand away to check the wound.

Jake raised himself up on an elbow. "It's not as bad as it must look. I've had worse." He kissed Alexandra. "You're not getting rid of me yet."

Smiling, she gently touched his face. "You'd better be around for a long time."

Relieved her father was all right, Deidre slumped against Hunter. He hugged her hard. Then she looked down at Lady Caroline. Kneeling, Deidre decided to try one last time to reach her before she died.

"It didn't have to be this way. We're both women. We should have helped each other."

Blood trickled from Lady Caroline's mouth. "Maybe I've won after all." She inhaled sharply. "You'll waste your whole life trying to get the right to vote. But you'll never get it." Her head fell to the side and her eyes glazed over.

Hunter lifted Deidre to her feet and pulled her against his chest.

She raised her head. "Is Hayward dead?"

"Yes. It's all over."

Epilogue

Deidre and Hunter stood on a windy hill, the summer sun warming them as they looked across the Bar J Ranch.

A coolness had sprung up between them since the night before when they'd finally dealt with Lady Caroline and Hayward. They needed to talk and Deidre had brought Hunter here to be alone with him.

After the shootout, Captain Sully had fled in the wagon, not doubt running as fast as he could back to the Bahamas. If they wanted him, they knew where to find him. But Deidre realized Old Nate would take care of him when word reached her of what had happened. They were sending the Graves back to the Bahamas to be buried on their plantation. Greed and revenge had ruined their lives. But after all they'd done, she couldn't feel sorry for them.

Her father was already better, but her mother looked worried anyway. They had praised her courage, but they also figured if she hadn't gone to the Bahamas she'd have stayed safe. Sighing, she watched the cattle herd grazing in the distance. She'd begun to realize that she'd always be their little girl no matter how old she got. And maybe that wasn't so bad as long as she knew she had come of age.

This morning she had told her parents over breakfast that she was going to college in the fall. They hadn't protested. Then she had explained that she eventually wanted to help her mother run Clarke Shipping. She'd been surprised and pleased when Alexandra had told her she'd been thinking along the same lines. She felt encouraged. Maybe mother and daughter would yet manage the shipping firm. Of Hunter, she hadn't said a word, but she guessed it was fairly obvious how they felt about each other.

She glanced up at Hunter. He'd been reserved since the night before, taking care of business and saying little. She felt concerned. "Hunter?"

He turned. "I guess I'd better be getting back to Arizona. You don't need me anymore."

Shocked, she shook her head. "Leave?" She touched his arm. "I'm sorry about Lady Caroline and Hayward. People don't have to live their lives that way. That's why I want to make difference. And I know you do, too."

Hunter nodded. "You know what I want, Deidre." He hesitated. "I'll always want you, but I've got family and plans of my own now, too."

She lifted a hand to touch his face. Didn't he understand? They were family. "I love you, Hunter. I need you. I want to spend my life with you."

Picking her up, he whirled her around.

She threw back her head to look up at the wide blue sky of Texas. "I'm so happy to be alive. The only thing that could make my life better is getting the right to vote."

Pressing a hot kiss to her lips, Hunter looked into her green eyes. "Together we'll get it for you. Partners?"

"Yes!" She threw her arms around his neck and kissed him with all the fervor of a suffragist.

Author's Afterword

The Anthony Amendment, the woman suffrage measure pertaining to the right to vote, was introduced in the United States Congress in 1878. Forty-two years later it became law.

Sixty-eight women and thirty-two men signed the Declaration of Principles at the first woman suffrage convention in Seneca Falls, New York in 1848. Charlotte Woodward alone lived to vote for the President of the United States in 1920. For this right, she fought seventy-two years.

Two hundred years after the 1792 publication of Mary Wollstonecraft's *Vindication of the Rights of Woman*, female citizens of the United States of America, a nation founded on the principle of equality, do not have equal rights under the law.

Woman suffrage continues.